i

FOUND ON
16TH AVENUE

FOUND ON 16TH AVENUE

KAREN ROTH

THE
WATERCRESS
PRESS
2006

Scripture quotations are taken from the King James Version of the Bible. Song lyrics are from "Puttin' On the Ritz" by Irving Berlin, "Stormy Weather" by Harold Arlen, "Love Lifted Me" by James Rowe and Howard E. Smith, and "Precious Lord" by Thomas Dorsey.

Cover design by Blair Gauntt
Photo by Lauren Oujiri
Typography by Fishead Design Studio & Microgallery

A Watercress Press book from
Geron & Associates
San Antonio, Texas

Readers are welcome to contact the author
at www.karenrothbooks.com

ISBN 13: 978-0-934955-67-6
10: 0-934955-67-0
Library of Congress Control Number 2006929001

This book is dedicated to

my father

Alvin F. Oujiri

ACKNOWLEDGEMENTS

To the staff and volunteers
of the National Czech and Slovak Museum and Library, Cedar Rapids, Iowa,
and to Harald Becker from Guaranty Bank, Cedar Rapids, Iowa:
thank you for so generously sharing your marvelous resources.
May our common heritage and memories of life "on the Avenue" live forever.

To my first readers
Susan, Rosa, Carole and Janet from church;
Daw, Chigger, and Tathar from SoA;
and Bernie, Michelle, Julia, Sherry and Joan from the far corners of the world:
thank you for your inspiring enthusiasm and faith for this story.

To my two families, the Roths and the original Oujiri clan from 16th Avenue:
thank you for all the shared holidays, parties, lunches, suppers, adventures
and constant good cheer through the good times and the bad.
I am humbled and blessed to share your lives.

To my son Steve, who always believed that I could write a book,
and to my husband Larry, for his incredible support:
thank you from the bottom of my heart.
You are the darlings of my life and the wind beneath my wings.

And last but also first:
My Lord God,
my Savior Jesus Christ,
and the mysterious but always-dependable Holy Spirit:
thank you for loving me so much, in spite of everything.

CONTENTS

One: November / *The Arrival*

Cedar Rapids, Iowa
November, 1933

Joe Vesely heard his mother die on a cold gray November afternoon, while he lay in the front seat of the abandoned car where they both lived. He lay there in despair and listened as her breaths slipped away, each one shorter and quieter, from where she sprawled in her drunken stupor in the back seat behind him. At the end, she choked out one last strangled cough, and then did not take another breath.

The car was cramped and dirty. The worn-out rubber tires had been sold long ago to the junk man. Metal springs poked out of the frayed fabric seats and filmy layers of dirt coated the windows. But at least it was private. No one could see them, or bother them, or tell them to get up and go somewhere else. When they first found the car, his mother had taken the back seat to sleep in, which was bigger and more comfortable than the front, saying that she was tired and that Joe was smaller anyway and would fit on the front seat better. He had not tried to remind her that he was fourteen now and taller than she was. His mother hadn't seemed to hear him anymore when he talked.

The car sat in a field near the railroad tracks on the northeast side of the city, where the city's homeless people drifted into a tangle of shacks and tents. At first Joe and his mother had found ways to spend nights with other families, or with the men who hung around the shanties at night, but Joe was not welcome when his mother spent a night with a man, and he had finally found the abandoned car on the edge of the shantytown. They lived in the car after that.

Joe closed his eyes and turned over, restlessly searching for a comfortable position on the worn car seat. He blew on his cold-reddened fingers and stuffed his hands into his jacket pockets to keep warm. The first storm of winter had blown in and he could see snowflakes falling. His stomach growled. Soon he would have to go out in the cold and hunt for something to eat. His mother had picked up a little cash from her last man friend, and she had bought some bread and lunchmeat, but she had bought liquor as well. Joe couldn't remember for sure how many days ago that had been. The food and the liquor were both gone now anyway.

He tried to go to sleep and not think about his mother. If he didn't think about what had just happened in the back seat, perhaps it wouldn't be true. No matter how bad life was with his mother, the thought of life without her was horribly worse. If he didn't admit to himself that she had died, then maybe she wouldn't really be gone. He would just go to sleep in the front seat. Later on, perhaps somehow she would come back and call his name, and be his mother again.

Sleep would not come, though. He opened his eyes to watch the snowflakes swirl and start to build up on the windshield. As the dark evening came on, a man bundled in a coat and hat came into view at the window, looking at him and saying something on the other side of the glass, but Joe closed his eyes and turned away, and when he looked out again the man was gone. Good. He didn't want anyone looking at him. It hurt too much. People mostly ignored him, but if they did take the time to look at him, they usually frowned at what they saw.

He turned over on the car seat again and thought of the family that lived in the nearest shanty, only fifty feet away. There was a mother and a father there, and food that came from different places so that the boy and girl could eat every day. Joe stared and stared into the raging white-gray whorl of the storm, wishing for a mother and father, until he closed his eyes again and started to cry.

Two days later on the southwest side of the city, where the Czech shops and taverns clustered along 16th Avenue, the Reverend John Mark Starosta, Joe's uncle, said prayers with his two sons and tucked them into bed. He had just sat down in his front room to relax for the evening when footsteps thumped up the porch stairs and a furious pounding shook the door. John Mark and his wife Kate looked at each other.

"Who on earth would come over now?" Kate asked. Emergency visitors were part of their life, but a heavy snow was falling outside, and most men in their Czech-immigrant neighborhood worked long hours in the factories during the day and went to bed early at night.

The visitor turned out to be a policeman, a cop John Mark knew, standing on the porch kicking snow off his overshoes and brushing it off his coat.

"What is it?" he asked as the policeman took off his cap and stepped inside. The man did not answer right away, but shot him a warning look instead.

"Sorry to have to come over so late," he began, and then looked at Kate and stopped.

"Who is it?" she asked. Kate's white-haired mother, Josefina Vesely, came hobbling out of her bedroom, clutching her robe about her. John could hear boys' footsteps running above them, hurrying across the attic floorboards and down the stairs.

"Mrs. Starosta," the policeman began, "and Mrs. Vesely," he said next, with a polite nod to Kate's mother, "I'm so sorry to have to tell you this." He stopped and looked down, then looked back at John Mark and went on. "I got some bad news for you." He stopped again.

"Go on," John Mark said. He had an idea of what was coming next.

"It's Marie," the man said, and John Mark let out the breath he had been holding. Marie was Kate's younger sister, Josefina's other daughter, and he had been expecting bad news about Marie for a long time. "I'm so sorry, Mrs. Vesely," the policeman went on. "Some people found her . . . I'm so sorry, but they found her and she had passed away. They found her in an abandoned car yesterday."

Kate closed her eyes. Old Josefina's mouth twisted. The policeman turned back to John. "I would have waited until tomorrow to come over, except they found her son with her. The boy said his grandmother's name was Josefina Vesely, and everybody's been trying to figure out who she is. When I came on tonight and heard about it, I told them she lives here with you, so they told me to bring the boy over here. He's in the car outside."

John Mark's sons peeked around the corner into the room. "Oh, wow!" John Mark heard the older one say. "Oh, my," Kate whispered next. Josefina began to weep and stumbled from the room. Kate went after her mother and the two women swept past the boys and into Josefina's bedroom beyond. The door slammed shut behind them.

The two men looked at each other. John Mark sat down in the big wooden rocker and ran his hands over his face.

"Well, let's get him in here," he said. The cop put his hat back on and headed out the door into a shower of snowflakes.

"Dad?" His twelve-year-old son Johnny slipped over to his side. "Joe's coming here? To stay?" Johnny's face was alight with curiosity. Little Stephen followed behind him, his sleepy face framed by tousled blond hair. John Mark pulled Stephen into his arms and absently gave him a hug as he thought about Joe.

He was not surprised to hear that Marie was dead. Marie had disappeared from their lives when she became pregnant without marriage at seventeen. Her parents had thrown her out, and she had not come back except for a few visits over the years. Her last visit had been a disaster. She and her blond-haired son had come to the house one Sunday afternoon, both smelling of liquor and smoke, and looking far too thin to be healthy. Josefina began the visit by criticizing Marie viciously for shaming her family by the life she led, and the two of them bickered all afternoon. Then, during supper, Josefina told Marie that she was not a fit mother for any child and that she should leave Joe with them so that he could receive a proper upbringing and not turn out to be a failure as she herself had done. Marie put up with the lecture until the meal was finished, and then she pulled Joe away from the table and walked out the front door, head down and lips trembling. Kate ran after her sister, but Marie only shouted and cursed at her through her tears, and headed on down the street, dragging Joe behind her. Kate was so shocked that she stopped and let her sister go. And now that would be the last visit from Marie, ever.

"Dad?" Johnny asked again, draping himself over the rocker's broad arm. "What are we going to do?"

"Let me think a minute," John Mark replied, absently raising a hand to stroke his older son's brown hair. There would have to be a funeral, and if Marie had been dead for a while, it would have to be soon.

He pulled Johnny around and looked at him. Johnny looked back, waiting. "Go get the extra quilt from the closet and put it by the furnace. Then go light the water heater in the bathroom and get some water warm so Joe can take a bath." He thought for a moment. Joe was two years older than Johnny and probably would not fit into any of his son's spare clothes. "Get him a clean towel and my pajama bottoms for him to sleep in." He looked into his older son's eyes, which were a changeable shade of hazel, just like his own. He gave him a little smile. "Okay?"

Johnny nodded, and then asked, "Where's he going to sleep tonight, Dad?"

"Upstairs with you and Stephen, I guess," he replied. "We'll just have to figure something out. We'll have to have a funeral," he said, more to himself than to his son. "Even if it's small." He paused, thinking about all the work of arranging a funeral. Then he thought about what kind of condition Marie's son might be in.

"And light the kitchen stove and heat some water," he went on. "We can make some oatmeal for Joe."

———   ———

Johnny fetched the extra blanket, the towel, and his dad's old pajamas, then went into the chilly kitchen and turned on the light. Stephen followed him. "I'll light the stove," Stephen offered, and Johnny gave him a long wooden kitchen match and took another one for himself. Stephen was allowed to light the kitchen stove, now that he was six. It only needed to have the ashes cleaned out and a new fire started in the grate. The bathroom water heater was trickier to light, because it had to be filled with kerosene first, so Stephen was not allowed to start it by himself yet. Johnny worked on the kerosene heater and filled up the vat with water for the bath, then came back to the kitchen and brought out the oatmeal bin from the pantry shelf. He peeked into the breadbox to see if there were any leftover slices of bread to snack on, but the new loaf was still untouched and his mother would know if he took any of it. He closed the breadbox cover with a sigh.

"Is Joe going to live with us now?" Stephen asked.

"I guess so," Johnny replied.

"What's he like?"

Johnny considered the question. "Well, he looks more like Mom and you, not much like Dad or me." Like most Czechs, Kate and Stephen had blond hair and blue eyes, not brown hair like Johnny and his father. "He's thin. He's taller than me. And he smokes and drinks and cusses."

That day when Marie visited, Johnny and Joe had gone into the back yard in order to get away from the arguments inside, and as soon as they left the house Joe had pulled out a pack of Wings cigarettes and smoked one behind the old shed. Out of earshot of the adults, Joe had talked more freely, bragging about the wild life he lived and introducing Johnny to a whole new string of bad words. Johnny had not been sure about what to say in reply. He knew that his parents would not approve of Joe doing those things and talking that way, but Joe was older, and the stories were interesting, so he had said nothing, and listened.

Sitting in the kitchen now, thinking about Joe's visit, Johnny and Stephen shared a look. Cussing was absolutely forbidden in their families, and smoking cigarettes was considered somewhat wrong-headed — something that was tolerated in elderly men, who usually rolled their own, but never to be taken up by the young. Most fathers that Johnny knew had told their sons not to start.

"I remember him," Stephen said as he stood barefoot in his rumpled pajamas, warming himself by the stove. "Mrs. Vesely said he looks like my brother." Josefina intimidated all of them so much that they called her "Mrs. Vesely," not the familiar *Babi* or *Matko* as other families in their neighborhood called their grandmothers and mothers-in-law. "She wanted Joe to come live here. Is he going to sleep upstairs with us? Whose bed is he going to sleep in?"

Johnny frowned. That problem was bothering him too. He had spent years sharing a bed with his little brother, putting up with all the bumps from Stephen's knees and elbows during the night, but this year his parents had acquired a second bed from another family and given it to him for his birthday. It was small, but all his own, and he relished the freedom of sleeping just as he wanted to without Stephen's hot breath and clingy arms around him. If Joe slept upstairs in the attic with them tonight, then one person would sleep in one bed and two people would have to share the other. That meant Stephen would be sleeping with him again.

Johnny felt a little guilty as he considered the problem. Poor Joe had just lost his mother and had no father either. That was a lot worse than having to share a bed with Stephen. But still, he loved sleeping alone so much, and now it looked like that luxury was gone, maybe for a long time, because free beds were hard to come by.

Oh, Lord God, Johnny said to himself, remembering how his mother and father would sometimes pray during the day. *Can't you find a way for me to keep my bed? I love it so much, please God . . . And please help Joe too,*" he added hastily to his prayer, feeling selfish again.

"I'm glad Joe's coming to live here," Stephen announced, and then yawned. "Dad will help him."

"Yeah," Johnny said out loud. *I wonder*, he added in his heart.

——— ———

Joe sat waiting in the police car, looking out at the small wooden house with a light on in the window. The snow was still falling and the drive through the drifted streets had been slow.

He wished with all his heart that he could have just stayed at the police station. The men had sat him down in a chair in a corner by a heat register and given him sandwiches and coffee and cigarettes while they tried to find his grandmother. Women came over and patted his back and clucked sympathetically at him, which was not as comforting as the cigarettes but which was still not bad, as long as they didn't actually try to make him talk. There was a restroom, and someone gave him an old coat to use as a blanket. Joe had been comfortable and hoped that the police wouldn't find his grandmother after all and that he could just live there in the station for a while. He had dozed pleasantly with a full stomach and the warm nest of coat around him, listening to the hum of voices that filled the room.

But they had found his grandmother. The question he kept hearing the policemen ask, "*Do you know anything about a Josefina Vesely? With two daughters, named Kate and Marie?*" had finally been answered. "*Yeah, yeah, I know them, that's John Starosta's family over on 14th Avenue. His wife is Kate and his mother-in-law lives with him, Mrs. Vesely.*" Joe had been bundled straight off into the police car. He felt terribly disappointed, but at least they let him keep the coat.

The policeman had told him that he was going to his uncle's house on the southwest side of town, and now he could smell the same awful smell that he had smelled when he came here before. He remembered it very well. His mother had told him that the stink came from the corn syrup factory by his uncle's house.

The policeman finally came back from the little house. Joe was pulled out of the car and marched up the steps to the door. Someone opened it right away and he was pushed firmly inside. A lot of people stood there looking at him.

"Hello, Joe," someone said, but he did not look at who said it, because he suddenly saw his grandmother coming toward him. Josefina had the same yellow-white hair in a bun as he remembered, the same blue eyes and stooped back. She held out her arms and all of a sudden he was hugging her and crying. He felt a little ashamed, because some part of his mind said that he should not be crying in front of all these strangers. But now his grandmother was crying too, and when he heard her cry he felt better, because he was not so alone anymore.

The other people were talking now, but his grandmother took his arm and led him out of the room to a kitchen, where it was quieter. She pushed him down in a chair and told him to sit there, and then brought him a bowl of hot oatmeal and a spoon. Joe looked around to see if anyone else was eating.

Two boys stood there looking at him. Joe remembered them, especially the little blond boy who stood at his elbow. He looked back down at the oatmeal, his appetite gone. He wished they would stop looking at him. He had no idea what to do next.

"Do you want some milk?" the little blond boy asked.

"I think we're out of milk," the other boy said. "Go down to the cellar and take a look."

"Okay," the little boy said, and disappeared.

"The bath water's ready for you, if you want to take a bath," someone else said. "There's a towel and pajamas in there for you."

Joe stared at the oatmeal. He did not want eat with all these people looking at him or take a bath in this strange house. He wanted to be left alone.

The little boy returned with a glass milk bottle. An inch of milk was left in the bottom. "Here you are," he said, and put the bottle on the table. Then he sat down across the table from him and waited.

After a silence, during which Joe kept his eyes on the oatmeal and didn't move, his grandmother slapped the table. "Out. All you, get out," she said in her strong old-world accent. "The poor boy needs to eat. Stop staring at him. Leave him alone."

Everyone disappeared. Joe's grandmother closed the kitchen door behind them and then bustled over to the stove, took a china sugar bowl down from a shelf, and set it on the table. "There, there, eat, *Pepik*," she said to him, using the nickname from the old language. "Go ahead, have sugar." She shuffled back to the stove and left him alone.

Joe sat still for a moment, then stole a quick glance around. The kitchen had a wood floor, with the table and chairs in the middle of the room. A sink and a wood-burning cooking stove stood along one wall, and a large dish cabinet along another. His grandmother was busy at the stove and did not look at him. After a minute, he pulled the sugar bowl closer and spooned some of it into the oatmeal. The inch of milk followed next. His grandmother came and sat down at the table with him, but she did not look at him because she was carrying a cup of tea. Joe quickly ate the oatmeal.

"Good, good. You're a good eater. Wonderful," Josefina said to him. "It's good you're here. I always wanted you to come. Go take your bath. Clean up before you sleep. We put a towel and pajamas for you." She paused. "I'll cut your hair after the bath. Wash the hair and behind the ears. You look like you have no bath for a year."

Joe looked at her, then looked away. He heard his grandmother sigh, and then she got up and came around the table and took him by the arm. "Go now, *Pepik*," she said a little more gently. "Go wash. You're filthy dirty. You can't sleep like that. Brush your teeth too." Joe could not think of any argument that would stop her, so he got up and let Josefina point him into the bathroom.

John Mark stood in the front room and talked with the policeman after Josefina ordered everyone out of the kitchen. He had expected Joe to look poorly, but even so, he was dismayed by the boy's ragged appearance and blank expression. His clothes were filthy, and his hair was long and so dirty that it looked dark, not light. Dirt was crusted around his face and neck.

"So how did you find them?" he asked.

The policeman shifted and looked uncomfortably at Kate, as if he wished that she would leave the room. Kate was red-eyed and still weeping a bit into her handkerchief, but she looked back at the officer and didn't move. "Well, people in the shanties knew that they were staying in the car," he began, and then stopped when Kate exclaimed sharply and turned her head away. She took a breath and looked back at him. "Then, when it started to snow, one of the men got worried about them and walked over to see if they were still there. He's the one who saw her in the back seat. He tried to get the boy to come out, but he wouldn't unlock the door, and the fellow was afraid to break the window and try to make him come out, so he told the cops about it. We finally got him out by holding up some sandwiches and a bottle of pop where he could see them."

The policeman lowered his voice. "I'm sorry to be the one to tell you this, ma'am," he said to Kate, "but she was a mess. Empty liquor bottles all over the car. Not a scrap of food or a bit of water. Just terrible." During the past few years, policemen had become used to seeing families live in cars, which was similar to seeing them live in tents, but not in the middle of winter. And usually it was the men, not the women, who drank themselves to death.

"We'll make sure she gets a decent funeral. Where do we . . ." John Mark began, and then stopped when Johnny and Stephen came hustling back into the room. He had been going to say " . . . claim the body," but he didn't want to discuss that detail in front of the boys. "What's the matter?"

"Mrs. Vesely told us to get out. She's taking care of Joe," Johnny explained.

"I can stay up late, right, because tomorrow isn't school?" asked Stephen.

"Yes, you can," Johnny said.

"I'll be the judge of that," said John Mark. His words came out sounding a little sharper than he intended, and Johnny turned around, startled, to look at him. John Mark winked to show that he was speaking in fun and not scolding him. "Tomorrow's going to be a busy day."

The policeman cleared his throat and looked at his watch. John Mark brought his attention back to the subject at hand.

"Kate, let's go outside to talk about this . . ." He nodded at the policeman, and the adults moved outside and stood in a tight little group in the shelter of the front porch, discussing the details of Marie's death and what still needed to be done.

After the policeman left, Kate went into the kitchen and John Mark sat down in the rocker again to think about what he needed to do next. His older brother, Vincent, lived two blocks away and owned a car and a telephone. He could walk over to Vincent's house in the morning and telephone the news of the death around the neighborhood. Marie's body had already been buried, but they could still hold a memorial service for her at the church. Afterwards people would expect to come to the house for a meal, so Kate planned to send Johnny to the meat market for short bologna. They already had potatoes and sauerkraut to go with it.

From where he sat in the front room, John Mark could hear Kate telling Josefina about the plans for the next day and then patiently listen to her mother's tales of woe. He stayed there for a while in the rocker, listening to the women's quiet voices and waiting for Joe to come out from the bath. Stephen had fallen asleep on the couch. Johnny sat by the window in the other wooden rocker, wrapped in a blanket to keep warm. He watched John Mark expectantly, waiting for him to start talking.

"So, Mrs. Vesely wanted to take care of Joe, huh?" John Mark asked Johnny. He exchanged a puzzled glance with his son, wondering why the usually scornful, sharp-tongued Josefina would suddenly want to take care of a dirty teenager.

Johnny shrugged. "She wanted him to come live here, ever since that day with Aunt Marie," he said. "She always wanted him to live here. Like he's special to her. How come she likes him so much, Dad?" Johnny looked a little put out by Josefina's sudden partiality. Mrs. Vesely usually did not like to have children around, including her own grandchildren, even though both Johnny and Stephen had tried hard to be nice to her since she moved in with them.

John Mark considered his words before he spoke. Johnny would not be satisfied with a trite answer, and he would rather tell him the truth anyway, as much as he could to someone so young. "Well, she always felt bad about the way Marie was living. She always wanted to help Marie and Joe, and she . . . couldn't. Not until Mr. Vesely died and she moved in with us."

Johnny frowned at his answer. "Why not?"

"They just didn't get along very well, son. Mr. Vesely wouldn't let Marie come back to the house."

"Why not?" Johnny persisted.

John Mark sighed. "It's a long story, and someday I'll tell you the whole thing, but not tonight." He looked out the window at the falling snow and thought about Josefina's husband, his father-in-law, now dead. The name Vesely meant "cheerful" in the old Czech language, but that bitter old man, and most of his family after him, had been far from cheerful. Old Mr. Vesely had made his wife and daughters miserable almost every day of their lives. And now here was another Vesely come to live in his house, a younger one this time, but just as hurting and needy. He glanced over at the kitchen and decided that it was time to go in and find out how his nephew was doing. As he expected, Johnny's head came up when he rose to his feet.

"I'll come, too, Dad," he said.

"No, *Jan*, stay here," John Mark said, giving Johnny's name the old-language pronunciation. "Joe looks like he had a pretty hard time of it. Probably better if we don't all try to talk to him at once." He paused for a moment. "I think that we'll have him sleep here on the couch, close to us and Mrs. Vesely, for tonight anyway," he added, and wondered why Johnny suddenly ducked his head to hide a smile.

When John Mark entered the kitchen, Joe was out of the bath, dressed in pajamas and sitting at the table, and Josefina was cutting his hair. Kate was sitting with them. Joe glanced toward him, then looked down without meeting his eyes. Josefina gave John Mark a warning stare, like an angry old goose guarding her gosling, but he ignored her, sat down at the table, and spoke to Joe.

"Well, Joe, we're glad you're here," he began. Joe's eyes flickered toward him again, then looked back down to the table. John Mark glanced at Kate, who nodded slightly, and went on. "We're so sorry about your mom, and we'll do our best to help you. I hope you'll be happy here, after you get used to us." Still no response. "Did you get something to eat?" Josefina held back the hair clippers for a moment as Joe nodded.

John Mark kept quiet after that and watched Josefina work. With one hand she ran a comb through the boy's straight hair, and with the other hand she trimmed off inches of damp blond locks. Joe had closed his eyes and was sitting very still. For a while, the only sound in the kitchen was the snipping of the clippers and the soft crunch of hair being cut.

While the boy had his eyes closed, John Mark looked him over. His face was shaped like Marie's, with high cheekbones and a straight nose. A trace of an old scar ran down one cheek from his ear to his jaw, and the skin along the inside of his right thumb and first finger was oddly puckered, as if it had been burned. He was good-looking, except for being so thin that his cheeks were hollow and the line of his collarbone stood out sharply under his skin at the open neck of the pajama top. John Mark wondered what his life had been like. From the rumors he had heard about Marie, it could not have been good. He knew that after she left home she had lived with different men, some of them wealthy bootleggers, but he wasn't sure how she had lived after the Crash when all the money dried up.

Finally Josefina parted Joe's hair neatly on the side with her comb, ran her fingers through it one last time, and shaped it into place. Joe opened his eyes, gave a hurried glance around, and then looked away from John Mark.

Clean and trimmed up, the boy looked better, but he still wore that same blank expression that had so bothered John Mark when he first walked in the door.

"Well, Joe, you look just fine." Joe looked at him, and then away again. "I think we'll have you sleep down here with us tonight, on the couch. We'll get some clothes for you in the morning. Tomorrow's going to be a busy day, so let's all go to bed and get some rest." He rose, and waited for Joe to stand up. "Come on, son," he prompted, and Josefina gave Joe a tap on the arm. He stood up then, and they filed out into the chilly front room. Kate woke Stephen, and John Mark sent the boys upstairs to their beds.

"Goodnight, Joe," Johnny said, and patted him a little awkwardly on the arm as he left.

" 'Night," Stephen yawned, and hugged him. A flicker of surprise crossed Joe's face.

"Well, here you go," John Mark said, and handed Joe the blanket. "I'm going to stoke up the furnace so it'll be warm in here tonight." Josefina patted Joe on the back, said *"Dobrou noc,* good night," and went to her room. Kate gave Joe a kiss and a hug, and murmured, "Good night, honey. I love you. You'll be all right, Joe, you'll see, so sleep tight and don't worry," before she went into the front bedroom and closed the door.

The boy sat gingerly on the couch, holding the blanket and looking around. Besides the old couch, there were two wooden rocking chairs and a side table with a lamp and a radio. An oval rag rug covered the wood floor, a framed photo hung on one wall, and a cast-iron furnace sat in one corner. John Mark squatted down in front of the furnace, clearing out the ashes and adding a little more coal than he usually did at night. When he was done, he turned back around, still half-sitting on the floor, and reached out a hand to touch Joe's knee. The boy jumped at his touch and then sat still, watching him.

"We're glad you're here, Joe," he said again, trying to look him in the eye and speaking very softly. "I hope you feel at home soon." No answer. "You can tell me if you need anything. Are you all right?" Joe looked at him then, and nodded before he looked away. "Well, that's good," John Mark said. "I'll be up early in the morning to get the heat going again. Good night." He stood up and turned off the lamp, and then opened his own bedroom door, leaving it open for warmth now that Kate was in bed and the light was off. He heard the blanket rustle and the couch creak, and knew that Joe had lain down.

John Mark usually sat in the front room for a while before going to bed, reading his Bible and praying a bit before turning in for the night. Tonight, in order to let Joe sleep, he took a seat in his bedroom chair and looked out the window instead. The sky had finally cleared of clouds, and moonlight made the blue-white drifts of snow glisten in the dark. The trees were traced with white along each branch. The world was incredibly quiet. He could hear Kate's soft breathing close beside him.

He sighed and leaned his head against the windowsill. He was worried about Marie's son coming to live in his house. The poor boy was so worn out with grief and trouble. Given some love and care he would probably get better, but . . . John Mark hadn't wanted to say it in front of Kate, but the hard truth was that Joe might be a liar and a thief, and maybe a drinker and a bully as well. John Mark would have to keep an eye on him and figure him out. A boy like Joe might cause a lot of trouble.

Just that morning John Mark had read Matthew 25, and dwelled for a long time on the words:

. . . For I was an hungered, and ye gave me meat; I was thirsty, and ye gave me drink; I was a stranger, and ye took me in; Naked, and you clothed me; I was sick, and ye visited me; I was in prison, and ye came unto me . . .

. . . Verily I say unto you, Inasmuch as ye have done it unto one of the least of these my brethren, ye have done it unto me . . .

Lord, John Mark had prayed that morning, *You are so amazing, saying that You know what it feels like to be poor, or sick, or in prison . . . and that You care about people who are having hard times and even consider Yourself as one of them.*

Full of faith at the moment, sitting there with his morning reading, he had promised, *I'll be that person who will give to those who need it . . . I'll help when I see people hurting . . .*

John Mark had thought of his congregation at the time, and had prayed for those whom he knew had heavy needs. Now, tonight, he looked back at his innocent morning prayer with a suddenly gloomy heart.

Lord, I know that You are sovereign over all, and therefore Joe coming here must be Your will, but . . . another boy to feed! I can barely keep everyone fed now! And a kid who will probably steal us blind! Why are You doing this to me? This is not what I meant when I prayed that prayer this morning. I already have more work than I can do. Why do I always end up doing everything?

He felt somewhat ashamed of himself then, and added, *I'm sorry. I know You'll provide. You always have. We haven't ever gone without a meal, and that's only because of You. Lots of people, good as us or better, go without meals these days. If you sent Joe to us, I'm sure You'll send us whatever else we need too. Including food.* He sighed, thinking about how the Lord had promised to meet his every need. *And time. And strength.*

He looked out the window again at the sparkling snow. A little design of frozen crystals had built up around the edges of the window, framing the outdoor winter scene with lacy ice. *The snow is so beautiful, even though it makes things harder for us. Oh, Lord, please help the poor boy get over this terrible death. Help him get well again. Give him a better life than he's had so far. Give me wisdom . . . show me what to do . . . help me be a good husband and father.*

Still gazing out the window, he thought of Psalm 68. *What was that verse? Something about how God is a father to the orphans . . . it says that He puts the lonely in families . . .* God had put this lonely boy here, in his family. Perhaps He had a plan. John Mark grinned in the dark. Of course He did.

A sudden rustle of clothing and squeak of floorboards interrupted his thoughts. Joe had gotten up from the couch and was walking back towards the kitchen. *Maybe he needs to use the toilet,* John Mark thought, and waited, listening. He heard the distinctive sound of the breadbox cover rolling back, and then, a moment later, the clink of the sugar bowl lid. *Josefina must've left the sugar bowl out.* Joe was probably dipping bread in the sugar and eating it in the dark.

John Mark considered what he should do, but in the end he did nothing. He already knew that Joe smoked, and he had an idea of what other things the boy might know about, living the life that Marie had led. He had probably seen a lot of things he should not have seen, and done whatever he needed to do to in order to stay alive. If John Mark were to catch his own boys sneaking bread and sugar in the middle of the night, he would not hesitate to go in and give a lesson on the subject of saving food for family meals, but in this case . . . *let the boy eat what he wants tonight,* he thought. There would be other times to talk to him about saving food for family meals. And there would probably be worse things to deal with, in the days that lay ahead.

"Johnny!"

Kate listened intently from where she stood in the kitchen at the bottom of the attic stairs, hoping to hear an answering voice, or, better yet, hear feet hit the floorboards above her. Pale morning light flooded the kitchen. It was early, but she needed to get Johnny up.

"John Carl!" she called up the stairs again.

Kate Starosta was usually the first one up, lighting the stove and warming the kitchen before the rest of her family came in for breakfast. This morning she had already started the bath heater and put extra water to warm on the stove. Usually they all took their baths on Saturday night, but because of the funeral today she intended to have her family bathe this morning instead. She already had finished her own bath, put on the black dress that she always wore to funerals, and put her curling iron to heat on the stove. It was seven o'clock and she wanted to send Johnny to the meat market now so that he would be back in time to clean up.

She took a deep breath. "John Carl!" They had given their first son the name "John" when he was born, but now, with two people in the house sharing the same first name, it was helpful to use the middle names also and call out *John Mark* or *John Carl* when she needed to make her meaning clear. Even John's men friends called him John Mark now, after hearing her say it so often. Kate actually preferred calling her son John Carl anyway, because the name had a bit more of a crackle to it than the plain name Johnny, and she liked the way it rang out when she called it up the attic stairs.

But so far there was no answer. Kate paused, listening again for sounds from the attic above her. It was cold up there. Johnny was probably cuddled into his quilts and struggling with the idea of getting up so early on a Saturday morning. She couldn't blame him, but she needed him to go to the market now.

"John Carl," she called up the stairs again, "I want you to go to the meat market for me right away."

She turned away and began to measure out coffee for the morning's pot. Floorboards creaked above her. She smiled to herself. Johnny loved to shop at the meat market. The butcher always gave him a free wiener, and Johnny was always hungry. It was worth a five-block walk in the snow.

After a few minutes and more shuffling noises from the room above, Johnny came down the stairs and sat at the table. Kate put a bowl of oatmeal in front of him and dropped a morning kiss on his hair, still ruffled from sleep. "Good morning, honey. There's a little more milk down in the cellar for you, if you want to go get it." They did not have an icebox, and the cellar was the coolest place in the house.

Johnny yawned. "No, there isn't, Mom. We let Joe have it last night." Puzzled, Kate looked around for the empty bottle. Her mother must have rinsed it and put it out with the other empties. The milkman would not come again until Monday, so she took out a can of condensed milk and pierced two holes in the top. "Here, use this," she said. "What's the sugar bowl doing out?"

"I think Mrs.Vesely let Joe have some," Johnny said, and yawned again. "What do you want me to get at the market?"

Kate counted out some coins from her purse. "Well, I guess you can have a little sugar today. I want you to buy as many short bolognas as you can get for this." She set the money on the table. "We'll have them for the meal after the funeral. Walk in the street and not in the deep snow so you don't get your shoes soaked through. Hurry because I want you to take a bath as soon as you get home. I'm going to iron the good shirts while you're gone."

Johnny pulled over the sugar bowl and lifted the lid, then got up from the table and fetched the sugar canister in order to refill the bowl. Kate watched him thoughtfully as she laid out the white shirts that John and the boys would wear to the funeral, dampening them down for ironing. She could remember the level of the sugar in the bowl yesterday. The boy must have used quite a bit for that snack last night.

Johnny stirred sugar into his oatmeal and rubbed his eyes. "Is anyone else up?"

"Not yet," she said. "I'll wake them up after you leave." John Mark would be busy most of the day with Marie's memorial service, and then he was scheduled to work the night shift at the oat factory. Right after he came home from work, he would give the sermon on Sunday morning. The weekends were hard on her husband. He had been off last night, fortunately, but he would have to go in and work tonight, so she intended to let him sleep as late as possible.

"Do you want some toast?" she asked, smiling at her son, who was being so good about going out early to do the shopping.

Johnny brightened. "Sure."

Kate opened the breadbox and caught her breath. More than half of the new loaf from last night was gone. She blew out a little huff of air. "John Carl, half the bread is gone. Did you boys eat it last night?"

"No," he said. "We just made oatmeal. I figured you were saving it." He caught her look and shrugged a little, pointing with his chin towards the front room where Joe still lay on the couch, hidden beneath the blanket. Kate thought about the possibility that Joe might have eaten the bread during the night, and sighed. The poor child was going to have to bury his mother today, and if half a loaf of bread helped him through it, then she wasn't going to scold him about it. They would deal with that kind of behavior another day. She'd have John Mark talk to him about food when they were past some of this grief.

"Well, we won't worry about that right now," she said to her son, and laid out a slice of the bread to toast over the fire. "But don't you go getting any ideas," she added with a frown. "Here." She drew another coin out of her purse and laid it on the table with the others. "Pick up a loaf of Vienna bread at the bakery, when you go to buy the meat." After a moment, she laid down yet another coin. "And get yourself a *kolache* to eat, too."

Johnny grinned at the thought of the sweet, fruit-filled pastry, and turned back to his oatmeal. Kate finished toasting the bread and set it out for him along with a generous spoonful of homemade grape jelly. She put the clothes iron on the stovetop to warm, and then stepped into the bathroom to curl her hair, letting Johnny eat his breakfast and wake up a little more before she sent him out into the cold.

Her hair was thick and straight, blonde like her mother's, and it would never hold a curl well, so she ended up twisting it into a French roll in back and just curling her bangs in front. She patted the stray ends into place with a little pomade and checked the bathroom heater to make sure that water was warming for the baths. Satisfied with the progress she had made so far, Kate went back into the kitchen where the coffee was perking and filling the room with its heavenly scent. She pulled out her old Bible from the shelf where she kept it and sat down to read. It was going to be a difficult day. She needed to pray and get ready for it.

Later that morning, Joe stood on a chair in his grandmother's bedroom while Josefina hemmed up his new pants. The rest of the house buzzed with activity. Adults were talking and boys were running back and forth getting dressed. Josefina had put a belt and suspenders on him to hold the pants up around his waist, but the legs were too long and she made him stand on the chair so that she could hem them up quickly. After the haircut last night and the fuss she was making over him now, Joe was beginning to feel more comfortable around his grandmother.

He looked over at the small pile of folded clothes on the bed. Earlier that morning, two people had walked in the front door without knocking. Uncle John had introduced the new arrivals.

"Vincent, this is Joe," John Mark had said. "Joe, this is my brother, your Uncle Vincent." Vincent had graying hair and wore a sad expression along with a black coat over his white shirt and tie. He said, "So sorry about your mother, Joe. Good to have you here," and held out his hand. Joe was surprised, but managed a shake.

"And this is your cousin Anton," John Mark went on. Vincent's son Anton was dark-haired and looked only a little bit older than Joe. Anton gave him a small stack of folded clothes.

"Hi," he said. "We brought you some clothes. I hope these fit you all right." Then he added, "I'm sorry about your mother. My mother died, too, last year."

Joe wanted to say something to him, so he finally said, "Thanks," but his voice came out sounding a little strange, probably because he hadn't talked much for a while. Then his grandmother had hustled him into her room to see if the pants fit, and now she was hemming them up. Joe stole glances at himself in her bedroom mirror while she sewed. He thought that he looked very sharp.

As soon as the pants were finished they bundled into Vincent's car and started for the church. John Mark, Johnny, and Anton had left earlier, walking, so that the rest of the family could ride. Vincent drove slowly through the snow, with Kate sitting up front beside him and Josefina, Joe, and Stephen squeezed together in the back. When they reached the church, Johnny and Anton were already standing on the front steps, looking down the street and watching for them. Stephen wriggled quickly out of the car and ran to meet them, but Joe hung back and walked behind Josefina as they all went inside together.

In later years, Joe could not remember much about his mother's memorial service. The little group of people at the church sang some songs. He remembered sitting between his grandmother and Aunt Kate, and he remembered very clearly that his grandmother wore black gloves made of some thin leather. Josefina had cried, but Joe felt no tears. He felt as if he were in a kind of dream world, and that his mother was still alive but had gone somewhere else and left him. Joe could not think about whether or not he missed her, or if it was bad or good that she was gone. Afterwards he stood in the back of the church with his grandmother. Women hugged him and men patted him on the back, and everyone said things like *How terrible* and *I'm so sorry* and *We'll have to see what we can do to help out here.*

They piled into the car again and drove back home. Joe looked out the car window at the little wooden houses and grocery stores and taverns flickering past. When they finally reached the house, Josefina headed straight to the kitchen and sat at the table, still dabbing at her eyes with her handkerchief. Kate swept off her coat and hat and hung them on a stand by the door. She turned to Joe and briskly unbuttoned his coat, sliding it off his shoulders and hanging it up next to her own.

"Vincent, if you don't mind, I'd like you to stay in the front room and take people's coats," Aunt Kate said. "Stephen, leave your coat on. I want you to take out the kitchen ashes for me before you sit down. Joe," and here she paused, looking at him for a moment, "just go in with your grandmother for now.

Joe sat with his grandmother while people came through the front door, handed their coats to Vincent, and brought platters of food and bakery into the kitchen before going back out to talk. Kate boiled dumplings and heated sauerkraut. The kitchen table and sideboard began to fill up with bowls of sausage and potatoes, plates of *kolaches* and loaves of braided Czech bread. Joe drew a little closer to Josefina as people filled the house and the noise grew louder. His grandmother was speaking in Czech to the other women gathered at the table, but Joe could tell that she had not forgotten about him, because she selected little samplings from all the food and put them on a plate for him so that he could eat while the people talked.

"Oh, Kate, I'm so sorry. What a dreadful year. First Vincent's wife, and now this," Joe heard someone say. "Do you need clothes for him? How old is he?"

"Fourteen," he heard his Aunt Kate reply. "Yes, everything will help . . ."

"How sad for the boy. What happened to Marie?" came another voice.

"Well, let's not talk about it just now . . ."

"Joe, want to come out and play?" Stephen was standing at his elbow. Joe shook his head no. He had never been sick to his stomach before, but he was beginning to feel that way now.

John Mark came into the kitchen and said a prayer, and then people came and went for a long time, filling plates and eating. Someone brought a plate of food for him so that he did not have to get up. Joe could not eat anymore, though, and after a while his grandmother looked at him and spoke to him in English.

"Go to my bedroom, *Pepik*. Take a nap. Go on."

Joe got up and made his way through the crowd of men's suits and women's dresses. He went into his grandmother's bedroom and closed the door. The sudden quiet in the room and the sheer bliss of privacy filled him with relief. He pulled the tight suspenders off his shoulders, unbuckled the heavy belt around his waist, and stretched out on his grandmother's bed. It felt wonderful to lie down on a real bed. Her pillow smelled like old flowers. He closed his eyes and sank into a deep well of sleep.

Johnny sat on the front porch after the meal, listening to the men play accordion and sing. Four of them were in a band that was going to play at a dance that night, and they joked that they might as well rehearse, since they had an audience. The sun was shining, the day was warming up a little, and Johnny was eating his second slice of prune cake after a very satisfying plate of pork ribs with dumplings and sauerkraut. Anton lounged beside him against the railing, singing the famous beer barrel polka, *Skoda Lasky*, along with the band.

The front door banged open and a stream of little boys came out, winding their way through the men as they headed for the front yard. Johnny suspected that his mother had shooed them out of the house in order to let the women visit in peace. Stephen led the little pack around to the back, to play in the more interesting garden and alleyway section of the yard.

Kate leaned out the front door and looked around the crowded porch until she spotted Johnny. "Keep an eye on them," she called. Johnny nodded, but didn't move from his spot on the porch railing. The men brought out a clarinet and got ready to play a new round of tunes.

His father was teasing someone about going to the dance. "All those good-looking women out there trying to get married and you're staying home? You like listening to the radio by yourself at night? You better get out there and get a move on." The man grinned and blushed at the same time, shaking his head and telling John Mark to shut up and mind his own business.

The band started up again, playing *Koline, Koline*, and Johnny wished that he and his family could go out to the dance. He knew they would stay home instead because of the funeral and Joe. But there would be plenty of food, and a night spent listening to the radio and snacking on leftover bits of *jiternice* sausage and sweet *babovka* poppyseed cake was not bad either. He perched himself up on the porch rail and wrapped his legs around the rungs.

About the time the band started playing *You're An Old Smoothie*, Johnny heard the thin wail of a little boy crying. He ignored it for a while, hoping it would stop. But it didn't, and he finally sighed and climbed over the porch rail and jumped down to the yard below, picking through the slushy snow around to the back to see what the fuss was about.

Stephen turned out to be the one who was crying. He was standing in the middle of a circle of nervous boys, all of whom looked relieved to see his older brother approach.

"What's the matter?" Johnny asked, not too concerned, because if Stephen could stand there and cry that loudly, he couldn't possibly be hurt very much. Stephen looked around at the sound of his voice and Johnny groaned. His little brother's jacket was unbuttoned and hanging open, and his face and the front of his good white shirt were covered with wet black ash.

"Oh, Stephen. Are you ever in trouble now," was the only thing he could think of to say.

His brother started wailing again. The other boys, looking solemn, started to back away.

"What on earth were you doing? Playing on the ash pile? In your good clothes? Are you nuts?" Stephen was completely filthy, all up and down his front, as if he had fallen right into the ash pile that accumulated all winter long in the back of the shed by the alley. Even his face was smudged with ash. He sobbed even harder at Johnny's words, then wiped his nose and got ash all over his jacket sleeve.

"The . . . the snow covered up all the ash and I . . . I didn't *see* it, and I . . . I . . . *tripped*," Stephen gasped between sobs. He looked up at Johnny with despair, his lashes stuck together around his wet blue eyes and his face streaked with sooty tears. Johnny just shook his head, and Stephen started crying again.

"Don't you have any sense? Come here," Johnny ordered. He started trying to clean up his brother as much as possible before they took the sad trip into the kitchen. "Here. Wipe off your hands with some snow." He scrubbed at the ash on Stephen's palms and was relieved to see it start to come off. He looked at his little brother and had another idea. "Take off your jacket so it doesn't get any dirtier" — it was already unbuttoned — "and I'll wash your face." Stephen slipped off his jacket and raised his face, still sniffling. Johnny scrubbed at his cheeks with handfuls of snow.

"Oh, Stevie. What on earth did you do?" a voice said behind him, and Johnny turned around to see Anton. The other boys had all left the yard.

"Fell in the ash pile, like an idiot," Johnny said. "Now the shirt's ruined and his jacket's all messed up. And I'll probably get in trouble too."

Anton hunkered down in front of Stephen and pulled out a handkerchief. "He's going to catch his death out here without a jacket and you rubbing snow all over him," he pointed out, and started mopping at Stephen's face, which was bright red now under the film of sooty ash. He wiped Stephen's nose and frowned at the shirt. "Maybe it'll come out in the wash."

Johnny snorted. Anton might be sixteen, but he knew absolutely nothing about laundry. "That shirt's a goner. So's your handkerchief."

Stephen started sobbing again at the loss of his best shirt. Anton went back to cleaning off his cheeks, and said, "Well, you've almost grown out of the shirt anyway. I don't think it's a big deal. You'll live, Stevie. Don't worry. Let's go inside." He picked up the smudgy jacket and set it back around the little boy's shoulders. "Come on."

Johnny hung back as the three of them made their way into the kitchen. By unspoken agreement among the three boys, Anton presented Stephen to his mother and explained what had happened. Kate looked so tired and disappointed that Johnny almost wished that she would go ahead and be upset instead of looking so sad. The other women just shook their heads and joked about raising boys.

Josefina, still sitting at the table, scowled at Johnny.

"You should know better. You're supposed to watch him. That's a good shirt all ruined now," she said.

Johnny's heart hurt at the truth of the statement. "Yes, Mrs. Vesely," he said, because it would be rude not to reply, and that would land him in even deeper trouble. He turned back to fuss over Stephen, pulling off his coat and shirt.

"Johnny, take that dirty shirt and coat to the cellar and don't let them touch anything," his mother commanded. "Then wash his face and hands and get him into a new shirt. I'll go down later to see what I can do about it."

"I can put on my own shirt," Stephen grumbled.

"Fine," Johnny sighed. He headed down the cellar stairs, giving Josefina a wide berth. The band had stopped playing outside. The women were washing the dishes and getting ready to leave. The house would quiet down soon. He laid the clothes on the side of the laundry tub and looked at the ashy shirt with regret. But then he thought of the plate of *kolaches* he had seen left for his family on the kitchen sideboard, and cheered up again. It would probably still be a good night.

———— ⌁ ————

John Mark sat at his kitchen table after supper, working on the next day's sermon while the rest of the family listened to dance music on the radio in the front room. From where he sat he could see Kate and Josefina in the two wooden rockers, wrapped in robes and shawls, worn out from the day. Johnny was on the floor, his head pillowed on a folded blanket, feet keeping time to the music. Joe and Stephen were sitting on the couch. The song lyrics drifted back to him in the kitchen:

> *A man makes a pie, I say my oh my,*
> *He makes mistakes, I say that's the breaks,*
> *Is he short or tall, I don't care at all,*
> *If he's got money, he's for me!*

John Mark watched Joe for a while, wondering how the boy was doing. Josefina had made him get up for their little evening meal, and after he had been up for a while and had some water to drink and a bite to eat, he had begun to look better. He still hadn't said much, but he had listened to Stephen's prattle during supper and watched the little boy with more expression in his eyes than he had yesterday. He still seemed unable to meet John Mark's eyes, though, or even Johnny's or Kate's.

Stephen jumped off the couch and trotted into the kitchen. He headed straight for the sideboard and uncovered first one plate, then another, until he found a platter of date cookies left over from the dinner. Carefully selecting three, he covered the platter again, grinned at John Mark, and ran back out to the front room. He handed one cookie to Johnny, then scrambled back onto the couch and gave one to Joe. The older boy took it and watched Stephen as they ate and listened to the radio. Stephen was telling Joe the long list of all his favorite cookies, and Joe was listening to him and saying something in return.

Cheered by the sight of Joe talking, John Mark went back to his work. Ah, here he was. Matthew 5:3. *Blessed are the poor in spirit: for theirs is the kingdom of heaven.*

Joe sat on the couch in his uncle's house listening to the radio and to Stephen chattering away at his side. He was warm, full, and feeling better, but then he began to feel guilty for enjoying himself when his mother was not there to enjoy herself too. Somehow it didn't seem right to feel better when she had just died. He still felt as if she was alive somewhere, and that he could find her again if he only went out and looked hard enough. He wondered if people blamed him for letting her die, and if he could have done something to save her. Why hadn't he gone to get help? How could he have let that happen and not done anything?

He sat and thought, sometimes listening to the music and sometimes listening to Stephen. At times he stared out the front window and didn't listen to anything at all. The room, the food, and the little boy all seemed unreal, like a dream that would go away soon. He felt more lost in this house than he ever had felt before, as if he had walked into a place where he did not belong and would be told to leave at any minute. But then Stephen would ask him a question, and pat him on the arm to get his attention if he didn't say something in return. Then Joe would pull his thoughts back to where he was, sitting on a couch with a little boy who was his cousin. Most of the time he hadn't heard what Stephen had said. But that was all right, because the boy didn't seem to need an answer. If Joe didn't say anything, he would just go right on talking.

After the music program ended, his grandmother got up from her rocking chair. "*Dobrou noc*," she said, and walked stiffly toward her bedroom door. Kate yawned and looked into the kitchen where his uncle was sitting.

"John Mark? Are you ready for work?" she called out, a little more quietly than he remembered her talking during the day.

After a moment, he heard his uncle say "All right," and then the chair scraped back from the table and his uncle came into the room. "Time for bed, boys," he said, and he smiled in a way that made his eyes crinkle. "Go get ready and I'll be upstairs in a minute."

"Can we stay up for one more program?" Johnny asked.

"Not this time," his uncle answered. "It's been a long day. Go on now."

Johnny got up slowly from the floor. Stephen gave a great yawn and slid off the couch. His aunt got up and went into the kitchen. Joe sat still. His uncle was looking at him. He seemed incredibly tall, and his dark brown hair made him look even taller in the front room's golden lamplight.

"Joe, do you want to sleep upstairs with the boys tonight, or do you want to sleep down here again?" he asked in the mild voice he always used when he said something to Joe.

Joe could not bring himself to look up, but he licked his lips and said, "Down here." Then, because his words sounded a little rude after he said them, and he did not want to seem like a troublemaker, he added, "If it's all right."

"That's fine," his uncle said. "You can wash up after Johnny and Stephen are done. Kate, I'll get the furnace before I leave," he called back to his wife in the kitchen.

His aunt came in and put a worn metal lunch box on the side table by the couch. "Thank you, honey. Here's your lunch. Goodnight, boys. Give me a kiss." His cousins hugged her and said good night, and headed for the bathroom.

"Good night, Joe," Aunt Kate said, and came over to hug him too. He took it awkwardly, still sitting on the couch, not sure if he was supposed to hug back. She patted him firmly on both arms.

"You were very brave today," she told him, and he saw her eyes suddenly fill with tears. Then his eyes began to fill with tears too, and he hastily looked away, but she sat down on the couch beside him and hugged him again. She held him for a long time, and he thought that it should make him feel better, but it did not make the misery deep inside him go away.

Kate finally went to bed and John Mark came down from the attic. He started working on the furnace, and then looked over at Joe.

"Go on and wash up now," he said. "By the time you're done it'll be nice and warm in here. Remember where your pajamas are?" Joe looked at him blankly. "Come on. I'll show you." Joe followed his uncle to the bathroom and watched as he got out the towel and showed him where his pajamas were. Joe felt no need to wash, especially since he had had a bath just last night, but his uncle put the towel firmly into his hands and said to come back out when he was through.

When he came back to the front room, the pillow was on the couch and the quilt was spread across it. His uncle was stoking the furnace, adjusting the grate and piling coal into a heap in the center. John Mark glanced around and nodded at him.

"I work nights at the factory, so I'm going to leave in a few minutes, and I'll be back in the morning," he said in that special quiet voice. "Your Aunt Kate will be right here in case you need anything. This furnace should last all night now. Do you think you'll be warm enough?" He looked around again, and Joe nodded. He felt quite warm already.

"Well, that's good then. Sleep tight now." He looked at Joe again, and Joe looked down at the floor. "You did good today, son," his uncle said. He rose and came over to the couch. Joe flinched in surprise when his uncle put out a hand to touch his hair. "You may not feel like it right now, but tomorrow will be better, and then next week will be better too. You just sleep for now and don't worry about anything. We'll take care of you."

Joe could not speak because his throat felt tight and hot. He nodded, though, and that seemed to satisfy his uncle, because he sat down and pulled on his black rubber overshoes. Then he put on his coat and hat and picked up the lunch box. "See you in the morning!" he said, and turned off the light and went out. Joe heard him lock the door from the outside.

After his uncle's footsteps faded away and the house grew quiet, Joe thought about the covered platters on the sideboard. He pushed back his blanket, tiptoed into the dark kitchen and helped himself to an apricot-filled *kolache*. He sat at the table and munched it, looking out the window at the back yard where the moonlight sparkled on the snow. After he finished the first *kolache* he took a second, and then a third, but after that he felt full and decided he didn't need to eat any more just then. He tiptoed back out to the front room and snuggled in under his blanket. The room was warm, and the rest of the *kolaches* would still be there tomorrow. Although he could not see ahead to a day when he would be happy, perhaps his uncle was right. Tomorrow he would still be in a warm house and have food to eat. As far as anything else, he would have to wait and see.

Two: December / *Christmas*

Joe frowned and tried to burrow back under his blanket when a hand shook his shoulder and a voice said, "Come on, Joe. Rise and shine." Then he recognized the voice and knew that he had to get up. It was Uncle John.

Johnny had already called him once for breakfast, and then Stephen had come in and tried to wake him up, but Joe had stubbornly stayed on the couch under his quilt. He had lived with the Starostas for three weeks now, but he still felt awkward and uncomfortable around them. They smiled too much, and it made him nervous. He wondered sometimes if they were all hiding a secret from him, and if they would all turn against him one day and suddenly throw him out of the house if he did something wrong. Especially in the morning, after a long night of broken sleep and bad dreams, he was irritable and in no mood to get along with people who acted so strangely. When his cousins tried to wake him up, he ignored them. But when Uncle John himself came in to the front room and shook his arm, he knew he had to get up and go into the kitchen.

He sat by his grandmother at the table, feeling safe next to her as she scowled into her coffee. Johnny was uncapping a fresh bottle of milk and Stephen was busy spreading grape jelly over his piece of toast. Both boys were dressed in their school clothes. John Mark said that Joe didn't have to go to school yet, but that he still had to get up in the morning. He was not used to waking up early and he didn't like it at all. He was trying to let people know how much he disliked getting up by not talking during breakfast, but since he didn't talk much anyway, the plan wasn't working very well.

Everyone ate in silence for a while, except Stephen, who sang an aimless tune as he ate his toast. Kate kept an eye on him to make sure that he didn't get jelly on his shirt. She wore a blue dress with a white lace collar, which meant that she was going out that day. John Mark was still in his work clothes from the night before and looked tired. After he finished eating, he reached across the table for Kate's Bible and said, "All right, boys, let's have prayers. We're going to read the beginning of Luke today because it's getting close to Christmas."

Joe kept his head down. Bible readings and prayers made him uneasy and he always stared down at his plate until they were over. He had lived in some strange places, such as corners of different men's apartments or abandoned cars, but never in a place where people got up early in the morning, ate breakfast together at a table, and said prayers. He knew, without anyone exactly saying so, that his uncle and aunt did not approve of the way his mother had lived, and he suspected that they did not approve of him, either.

"Dad, are we having Christmas here this year, or are we going to Uncle Vincent's?" Johnny asked when prayers were over.

"Let's go to Anton and Uncle Vincent's," Stephen said. "I like their house. Besides, we had Christmas Day here last year."

"We'll see," John Mark said with a yawn. "I have to ask Vincent first."

"I'll buy a little sugar today when I'm done at the Havliceks,'" Kate said. "Tonight I'll make fudge and divinity. Tomorrow I'll make cookies. And then," she looked at Stephen, arching one eyebrow, "pretty soon we'll eat them, because it'll be Christmas!" Stephen bounced in his chair with joy and almost lost his grip on his toast.

"Are you going to make that special bread with the cherries and nuts and frosting on top?" Johnny asked.

"I think I will," Kate said. "That would be a nice change from *kolaches* for Christmas morning."

"What?" asked John Mark.

Almost at the same time, Johnny said, "You're still going to make *kolaches*, aren't you?"

Kate gave them the same arch look that she had given to Stephen a minute before. "As much trouble as you give me, you better be extra nice this week if you want *kolaches* and cherry *vanocka* both for Christmas morning." Everyone grinned except for Josefina and Joe.

John Mark pushed back his chair. "You boys be good at school. Joe, your Aunt Kate is going out today, so help Mrs. Vesely with the chores." He paused for a huge yawn. "I'm going to bed. Wake me up if you need anything."

After the boys left, Kate gave Joe instructions for the day. "Shave up a good bunch of soap chips and soak them in this bowl for the laundry. Pull the wringer washer out of the bathroom into the kitchen. Your grandmother's too old to be doing that herself anymore. Keep the water hot on the stove for the wash. It's windy enough today to dry some things outside. Remember to bring in the clothespins." She paused and looked at Joe. "Mother will tell you what to hang outside and what to keep in here." When he didn't respond, she said, "Joe?"

"Yes, Aunt Kate."

She looked at him and sighed. "Honey, I have to go to work now. I'll be back after lunch. Take care of the house for me, all right?" He could feel her looking at him and smiling, but he kept his head down and refused to smile back, even when she gave him a quick hug before she left. He didn't want anyone to think that he was happy. He wasn't. No matter how many times his aunt, or uncle, or cousins smiled at him, he could not imagine ever being happy like they were. He wanted them to know that.

Although Joe wanted people to know that he was not happy, he privately liked the days when Aunt Kate went out to work. Right after breakfast he and his grandmother both went back to sleep. Midmorning, Josefina made a second breakfast for Joe. He liked this breakfast much better than the first one, because it was just him and his grandmother.

After that came chores. He carried out the ashes and swept and mopped while she washed the dishes and baked bread and rolls. On days when snow fell Joe shoveled the walk in front and around the side to the back door, so that the milkman could get to the milk box on the back steps. Monday was laundry day, and he carried the pots of hot water from the stove to the washer and hung up the wet clothes to dry, either in the cellar or outdoors, whichever direction his grandmother pointed him toward. On Tuesdays they ironed, and he did the easy things, like dish towels and sheets, and his grandmother did the shirts and trousers.

His grandmother found other chores for him to do on days when they didn't do laundry. One time she made him scrub all the dusty ash off the baseboards around the floors of the house. Some days she pulled out old paper shirt patterns and sewed shirts for him and his cousins out of the piles of fabric she kept stacked in a corner of her room. Joe liked those days, because she would make him stand in front of her while she fitted the fabric to him as she worked, and the calm, undemanding touch of her hands felt good on his arms and back. She let him sew the shirts' long seams on the sewing machine and then she did the elaborate work on the buttons and collars. He cleaned and oiled the sewing machine and treadle stand for her, and even whittled a new wooden bobbin for her thread when he had nothing else to do.

Josefina sent him to the 16th Avenue Market one day to buy soap and vinegar. Joe felt timid at first as he walked down the street alone, because he was worried that he might get lost. He finally reached the main street that everyone called the Avenue, and then he became even more anxious because all the people he passed on the sidewalks were speaking Czech and he couldn't understand them. Most of the signs on the stores were in Czech, too, and he couldn't read them, so he had to walk up and down the street looking in the shop windows to find the grocery store.

The shop windows turned out to be interesting. He passed a bank, a lawyer's office, two bakeries, two butcher shops, four taverns, a dress store, a music store, and a feed store before he finally found the grocery. He took his place in the line of customers at the register and wondered if people would stare at him in disapproval, as they had when he lived in the shanties, or refuse to talk to him because he couldn't speak Czech. But when he came up to the counter he saw a sign taped to the ornate cash register that read, "I Complained Because I Had No Shoes, Until I Met A Man Who Had No Feet," and he began to feel a little better.

When his turn came to order, the grocer said "*Mohu vám pomoci?*" just as he had said to everyone else, and Joe said in English as quietly as he could, "Uh, soap and vinegar, please." The man smiled, fetched the order, and rang it up.

"Here you are, young man, soap and vinegar," he said as he wrapped the soap in brown paper. Suddenly everyone started speaking in English.

The man in line behind Joe called out, "Well, Ed, got any shoes yet?"

The clerk looked up. "Shoes and feet both. Can't complain." The people in line all laughed, and the clerk handed Joe's soap and vinegar to him with another smile.

Joe felt encouraged after that, and tried to bum a few cigarettes from the men standing in front of the store. One of the women who had been behind him in line came out, looked right at him, and scolded him in English for smoking. That made him nervous again, but after she left one of the men gave him a sympathetic wink and slipped him a few smokes. Joe thanked him and tucked them away in the worn paper cigarette pack that the policemen had given him. He was trying to make his cigarettes last, smoking just a few puffs at a time when he could sneak out into the back alley behind the shed at home. He could tell that his aunt and uncle disapproved of smoking.

After lunch, Joe and his grandmother finished up their chores and then took another nap. Joe had trouble sleeping at night, but his daytime naps were peaceful in a way that his nighttime sleep was not. Almost every night he woke up, soaked in sweat, shivering in horror from some bad dream where he had seen his mother's corpse again, with its open, blinded eyes and gaping mouth, and he had to get up for a drink of water and something to eat before he could calm himself enough to go back and lie down and feel sleepy again. But during the day, with his grandmother close by and the nightmares kept away by the afternoon light, he could stretch out on the couch and slide into a deep, dreamless sleep.

At some point during the day his uncle would wake up, read his Bible for a while, and then go out to his other work at the church. That didn't bother Joe. But later in the afternoon his aunt would come back from work, and Johnny and Stephen would come home from school. The boys would change out of their good clothes into overalls and Aunt Kate would start assigning chores. Stephen would come over to the couch where Joe was pretending to still be asleep, and do things like blow on his hair or pat his arm in order to get him up.

Joe looked forward to the afternoon radio programs like *Tom Mix* and *Jack Armstrong* that came on after school was out, but Johnny and Stephen had to do their homework before they were allowed to listen to the radio, and sometimes the lessons took a long time. If people came to visit, the boys had to turn off the radio and go into the kitchen or up to the attic bedroom in order to give the adults privacy. Joe felt uncomfortable in the attic bedroom, because there was nothing in it except two beds and a small chest for clothes. There was no light, either, except from the window, and only a rough wood floor. But if he went back downstairs, people looked at him and talked, and expected him to say something in return.

All the expectations trapped him into an agonized awkwardness. The strange smiling faces pressed on him, suffocating him with words. When the torment became unbearable he would slip out of the house, his pockets stuffed with scraps of food pilfered from the kitchen during the day, and roam the alleys looking for the friendly ragged men who lived the way he used to, and who would trade a smoke or a swallow of liquor for food.

Then he would gaze down the street that led to the grocery store and taverns, and think about how good it would feel to just keep walking. But when his stomach growled, he always turned around and headed back to the little house where the smell of supper filled the air. Then he would stop thinking about walking away, and instead wonder why he would ever want to leave a nice warm house with food.

On this night they had beef heart with prune dumplings for supper, along with a jar of green beans from the shelf of canned goods in the cellar. Stephen told a long story about walking home from school and making snow-balls, and Johnny interrupted from time to time to tell his side. Joe kept his head down and ate. John Mark served out the beef and dumplings, but the bread plate passed around the table often, and Joe took two slices every time it came around.

"So, what about Christmas, Dad? Did you talk to Uncle Vincent and Anton yet?" Johnny asked.

John Mark and Kate exchanged a look. "No, but I think I'll go over there after supper," John Mark said.

"Can I come too?" Stephen wanted to know.

"No, Stevie, stay home and help your Mom," John Mark said. When Stephen began to protest, he followed with, "Mom's making candy tonight, so that's a good deal for you, right?" He made a funny face at Stephen, who temporarily forgot his argument and giggled. "Keep Joe company. I bet he'll enjoy that," he said next, and winked at Joe, surprising him enough to make him grin.

John Mark grinned back at him. "All right, then. Joe, clear the table. Johnny, get the dishes started. Kate . . ." Joe watched cautiously as his aunt and uncle went out to the front room and talked, their heads close together and their voices low. After a while, he saw Uncle John pull his aunt close and kiss her, so he got up and carried the plates to the sink so they wouldn't think he was spying on them. His aunt and uncle had an easy way of talking to each other, and most days Joe felt reassured when he heard their voices as they moved around the house. But now he suddenly wondered what they were talking about, especially if they were talking about him, and what they might be saying.

"See you later, boys," he heard his uncle call after a few minutes. "No radio till the dishes are done." Joe looked at the kitchen clock. It was 5:30. He started hurrying with the dishes. *Captain Midnight* came on at 5:45.

Kate put Stephen to bed right after the candy-making was finished, and then washed the pots and pans. She yawned and thought about making a cup of tea, because she wanted to stay up until John Mark got home. They'd had hardly any time together today, and she missed her husband.

When he returned, Josefina and the two older boys were in the front room, wrapped in quilts and listening to the radio. John Mark came in and sat down at the table with her in the darkened kitchen. She had kept out a plate of fudge for him.

"Did everything go all right tonight? With Joe?" John asked.

"Oh, it was fine," Kate said, studying the plate of fudge and picking out a small piece to sample. "Joe helped a lot. The handle on my eggbeater broke and he fixed it for me."

"Huh." John Mark thought about that as he picked out his own piece of candy. "How'd he do that?"

"He chopped up a piece of wood and whittled it down to fit in between the handle bars, and then he tied it with some string for me to use tonight. He said he'd fix it for good tomorrow."

"Hmmf," John said through a mouthful of fudge. "He actually talked to you?" He gave Kate a grin.

She sniffed at him. "Yes, he actually did. He's coming along. We just have to be patient." She sighed and leaned her head on her hand. "I think we should just treat him like a normal kid. I don't think you need to be so extra careful with him. Send him to school, and that'll stop all this wandering around the house that he does at night. I talk to him every day exactly like I do the boys, and someday he's going to start talking back."

John finished his fudge. "I don't know," he said. "That might work for you, but I don't think it'll work for me. He never looks me in the eye. He jumps every time I go near him. He's edgy, like he's feeling guilty all the time." He picked out another piece of fudge and chewed for a while before he spoke again.

"He seems to be a good boy, hon, and I don't mean to talk bad about him, but we got to face the fact that he was raised hard and we don't really know what he's thinking, because he hardly ever talks. I can't figure him out. He works fine around the house but then he'll take off for hours at a time and won't say where he's been. He could just steal us blind some day and never come back, or only come back once in a while when he wants a meal and a new pair of shoes."

"I don't think that's fair. He's been through a lot and I don't think he'd do anything like that," Kate said after a while. "He talks to me, a little. Maybe he feels safer around me because I'm a woman."

John Mark was quiet, thinking about that idea. "He doesn't say much to Johnny, either," he finally said. "He'll talk to Stephen, if I'm not around. But hardly ever to Johnny." He threw a glance at Kate. "And don't think Johnny hasn't noticed. I have to talk to him every day about remembering that Joe's been through a hard time and we need to be patient with him."

It was Kate's turn to be quiet. She finally said, "I wish so much that I had made Marie stay with us that day. I think we could have saved her."

John Mark reached for her hand. "We tried. More than once. She wouldn't stay. Even if she had stayed overnight that time, I don't know if we could have kept her here for very long. Don't make yourself feel so bad, thinking that way." He pulled up her hand and gave it a little kiss. "You did the best you could. You always do."

They sat for a while, listening to the music playing in the front room, until Kate gave herself a shake and sat up a little straighter. There were some other things that she needed to talk about.

"What did Vincent say about Christmas?" she asked.

"He wants to have Christmas Eve with presents over here with us, and then have the big meal on Christmas Day over there at his place," John Mark said as he reached for a second piece of fudge.

"Do you think it's a good idea?" asked Kate. "It's a lot of work to cook everything, and if we do dinner like Amalia used to do, it'll bring up memories, and if we don't do dinner like she used to then that'll be sad for them too. I think they should just come over here." Vincent's wife Amalia had died just before Christmas last year, but Vincent and Anton had come to their house as usual for dinner on Christmas Day. They had both been quiet and sad, and they left soon after the meal was over instead of staying for carols and games. John Mark had walked them all the way back home that day, not knowing what to say, but wishing he could ease their grief.

"Right. I thought about that," John Mark agreed. "But he wants us to come over. He said he already has a goose ordered and he wants to buy some special *kolaches* and *vanocka* bread at Sykora's bakery. He has it all planned out. He said to tell you to just bring some side dishes." He paused for a minute. "It's been a year since she died."

Kate frowned. "Holidays are hard on people who just lost someone, even if it's been a year. I don't think he knows what he's in for." She stopped talking and thought for a moment. "I've still got some pickled beets from last summer we can take. And I'll make potatoes and sauerkraut. We have canned corn too. And we'll have the candy and cookies." She watched John Mark eat yet another piece of fudge. "Are you sure it's a good idea?"

"Oh, don't worry." John Mark stretched and sighed. "It'll be fine, and they're probably going to be a little sad and a little happy no matter where we eat. At least we'll all be together. We'll have a good time." He grinned at her. "How much do you want to bet that one of the boys gets in trouble before the day's over? It'll just be Christmas as usual." He leaned over and stroked a stray strand of hair back from her face. "Your fudge is great. Can I put the rest in my lunch for tonight?" He leaned over a little further and gave her a long hug and kiss in the dark.

***

Two blocks away from John Mark's house, his sixteen-year-old nephew Anton Starosta woke up early on Christmas morning and decided to make breakfast for his father.

The house was still cold, and the pale light of the late winter morning had barely touched the front room when Anton looked in to see if his father was awake yet. Vincent was sitting in the chair by the piano, his head propped on one hand, gazing out the window at the dim gray yard outside.

Anton retreated to the kitchen and lit the stove. The little rustles and clinks of activity would tell his father that he was up. They would have breakfast, go to church, and then come back and get ready for Christmas dinner.

First thing was to get the coffee started. Next was to set the table for two. Anton hunted through the drawers for the special Christmas napkins embroidered with green holly leaves and red berries, but he couldn't find them and had to settle for the plain daily napkins instead. Well, that was all right. Coffee cups, plates, silverware, and butter and jam from the icebox. He poured a little milk into the cream pitcher and set it next to the sugar bowl, then sliced some bread to toast. There were *kolaches* in the bread keeper and two loaves of sweet *vanocka* bread with red cherries and white icing, but they were saving those for later, when everyone came over to eat.

Anton looked at the table and frowned. It didn't look special enough for Christmas. He poked deeper into the kitchen pantry shelves and pulled out a jar of canned peaches from last summer. Peaches in little glass bowls by each plate would look nice. That was the kind of thing his mother would have done.

Finally the table looked right. Anton slipped back to the bedroom and pulled out his present for his father, a new shirt and tie. They had taken some other presents to Uncle John's house last night for his cousins, but he and his mother and father had always opened their own special presents on Christmas morning. He hadn't been sure what to get, but Uncle John said that his father would appreciate a new shirt for work and helped him pick one out. Anton put the present on the table and went to call his father.

"Dad?" he said tentatively into the gray light of the front room. "Dad, the coffee's ready."

His father didn't stir. Anton studied him for a moment. Vincent was still gazing out at the snowy front yard, one fist pressed to his mouth. "Dad?" Anton called, a little louder. "I made breakfast."

Vincent looked around then and stood up, smiling, although the smile took some effort. "Well, *Veselé vánoce*," he said. "Merry Christmas. Breakfast, eh? Not burning the toast, now, are you?" Anton had a habit of putting bread on to toast and then forgetting about it. He hastily looked around to check, and then moved fast to pull the toast out onto a plate before it got too dark. "Nope, it's perfect," he announced, and sat down to butter it while it was still hot. "Come on, Dad, don't let it get cold."

"You shouldn't drink so much coffee," Vincent chided him as he sat down and saw coffee cups at both places. "It'll stunt your growth."

Anton put a piece of buttered toast on his father's plate. "I'll put lots of milk in it," he said agreeably. "Don't worry, Dad, I don't think it's bad for me. I don't drink it that much." He looked over at the present. His father hadn't said anything about it yet.

"Got a present for you," Anton said.

"Hmm, I see that," Vincent said and smiled again, a real smile now that made his eyes crinkle at the corners. "I'm trying to remember if I got a present for you this year. Let me think a minute. Oh, yes, now I remember. A present. Where'd I put it?" Anton grinned. His father always liked to stretch out the anticipation of opening a present for as long as he possibly could. When Anton was little, he had half believed his father's teasing and spent long moments in exquisite agony over the idea that his father might have forgotten to buy him a present. Even now, when he was grown up, it felt nice to be indulged by the old routine.

The two of them ate in happy silence for a while. Finally Anton cleared away the plates and Vincent went to search for his present, still claiming that he had forgotten where it was. Anton listened carefully and heard a soft thump and rustle of paper as his father paused and set something down just outside the kitchen doorway. But when he came in he had only an envelope in his hand.

"Well, not much this year, I'm afraid. The stock market crash and all, you know," Vincent said with elaborate nonchalance as he sat down and handed the envelope to Anton. "But I hope you like it. Open it, open it," he went on as Anton looked at him and laughed. "We have to be thankful for what we've got, as your uncle says. Go ahead now. I can hardly stand the wait." Anton shook his head at his father's little game and opened the envelope. Inside were two pieces of thick cream-colored paper, elaborately drawn to look like tickets. On each ticket was hand-printed "Admission: One. Orchestra section. *The Marriage of Figaro*. Coe College, February 14, 1934. 7:30 p.m."

Anton nodded. His mother had loved that opera. She had told him the whole convoluted story of *Figaro* and taught him to play the best-known melodies from it on their piano when he was a boy, but he had never seen an actual production of the opera. The college was presenting it and his father must have made special arrangements for them to see it, because he was still close friends with his mother's former music instructor. Going to the opera was a nice idea, although it wasn't really a convincing Christmas present. The real gift was still waiting for him, just outside the kitchen door.

"Thanks, Dad. This is a great Christmas present," he said with a straight face. "I was beginning to think I'd never see *Figaro*. I can't wait to go." He paused and grinned. "Open mine now."

Vincent sniffed a bit, feeling like he had just been humored, but he went ahead and picked up Anton's present, shaking it and making outrageous guesses about its possible contents. He finally opened it and was suitably pleased with the shirt and tie. Anton sat back and sipped his coffee. The morning was going fine.

"You know, I think I remember buying something else for you," Vincent said slowly. "I'm trying to think where the heck I put it." He glanced at Anton and laughed, giving up the pretense. "All right, here it is." He got up and retrieved the present that he had left in the front room earlier. It was long and unwieldy, wrapped in soft paper but not in a box. Anton knew immediately what it was.

He ripped off the paper. It was a tennis racquet, the wood perfectly polished and painted, newly strung and gripped just the way he liked. He hefted it, feeling the balance in his hand, and let out a long breath. He knew he should say thanks, but the word by itself wasn't enough.

All last year, Vincent had been more determined than ever that Anton continue piano lessons, even though his mother was no longer there to oversee them. But Anton was bored with piano, and the more his father pushed him to practice, the less he wanted to play. He played tennis instead during his free time. The two of them had finally gotten into a fight over it, and Anton had quit talking to his father about either tennis or music. He had not played the piano at home since then.

Anton got up and walked over to stand behind his father's chair and give him an awkward hug. He unexpectedly felt tears start in his eyes. He blinked hard and managed to say "Thanks, Dad," without letting his voice shake. "Must have been tough to find one of these, what with the stock market and all, like you said," he added lightly, trying to make a little joke.

His father reached up and patted his hand. "Well, yes, I had to do a little fancy footwork." Like Anton, he was trying to get past the moment without choking up. He cleared his throat. "And I have some more news for you. I set you up for lessons with the tennis coach at the college. He said for you to come see him right after the Christmas break. You can start as soon as the weather warms up."

Anton was blinking back tears in earnest now. He stayed standing behind his father so Vincent wouldn't see, and gave him another hug, longer this time. His father was blinking hard too. Both of them took deep breaths and avoided looking at each other for a moment. Finally Anton said, "Did Uncle John have something to do with all this?"

Vincent laughed. "Probably." Anton laughed, too, and went to refill their coffee cups. "Do you want me to make another pot?" he asked.

"No," Vincent said. "How can you be a champion tennis player if you drink coffee all day?" Anton smiled at his father's new joke. "We'll make another pot after the meal today. Let's just clean up and get ready for Ruzina.

She said she'd be early to start the goose."

Ruzina and Karel Prazsky lived in the old building at the back of Vincent's lot. It had originally been a stable, but the Prazskys had remodeled it into a house when they came over from Bohemia in 1914. Vincent's family and Karel's family had been neighbors back in Prague before Vincent's parents emigrated to the United States, and the two men had been friends when they were boys. They were almost the same age, and had married at almost the same time, although on different continents. Vincent had been delighted when Karel wrote to him with the news that he was coming to Cedar Rapids with his new bride. Vincent had made Karel an offer: live in the old building as long as he wanted while he got settled in the new country, and take care of the garden and laundry in exchange. Since Karel was a carpenter and Ruzina was an industrious young woman, the Prazskys jumped at the chance to get ahead right away. Almost twenty years later, they still lived there, the old stable now turned into a small but respectable home. Their three children had grown up with the Starosta boys, and the work of the garden and laundry were still exchanged for rent. The Prazskys always joined the Starostas for the holidays. This year, Ruzina had promised to come over early and bake the goose.

"All right, I'll do the dishes," Anton said, and moved over to the sink. "Where's the box where Mom put all the Christmas things? I need to get the tree done before everyone comes over." His father had unexpectedly brought home a Christmas tree yesterday, and they hadn't had time to decorate it yet.

"I think it's in the attic." Vincent looked at his son critically. "You go ahead and shave while I get it down, and then I'll get ready while you do the tree. There's plenty of time. May as well enjoy the peace and quiet before Stephen and Johnny get here." He threw a dish towel over his son's shoulder and headed up the attic stairs.

———

Later that day, Kate brought her husband and three boys, each carrying a bowl of hot food, into Vincent's kitchen. She followed them in just as Ruzina finished giving John Mark a hug and kiss.

"*Veselé vánoce!*" they greeted each other, and then Ruzina turned to hug Johnny. Kate set down her heaping platter of candy and cookies and pulled

Ruzina's eleven-year-old daughter Rose into a hug of her own.

"Rosie! *Veselé vánoce!* It's been forever! Just look at you! Adorable!" Kate finished off the hug with a kiss and then looked Rose up and down. Ruzina moved on to hug Stephen and then Joe, who still only tolerated hugs. John Mark and all three boys, relieved at having delivered their bowls with no spills or other problems, left the kitchen for the front room, where Anton was trying to drape strands of lights on the Christmas tree.

Kate smoothed Rose's red dress and white lace collar. "This is beautiful, Rose. Did you sew it yourself? You look lovely in it." Rose's blonde hair was braided and tied with red and white ribbons, which made her blue eyes look even brighter than usual. Kate sighed. "Ruzina, she's as tall as I am."

"Mom helped me. We had to buy new shoes because my feet grew a whole size," Rose said. "Do you like them?"

"I love them," Kate said promptly. "Honey, turn around and let me see the back of your dress. Beautiful!" She hugged Rose again as the girl turned back to face her. "I miss you so much!"

Ruzina laughed and patted with her apron at the sweat on her forehead. She also wore a red dress trimmed with lace, but hers was elaborately decorated with brilliant colored ribbons and embroidered flowers. Her plain round face was flushed with heat from the stove. "The way you carry on, you act like you didn't see her for a year."

"It feels like a year," Kate said as she slipped out of her coat and into an apron. "I hardly ever see you now." When their children were smaller, Kate and Ruzina had been in and out of each other's houses constantly. Now, with all the children in school and Kate working, they saw each other only once or twice a month, usually at a dance or the market. "How's the goose?"

"It's coming along. Another half hour, I think," Ruzina replied. "Rose, did you iron those tablecloths?"

"Come and look, Mom." Rose headed into the dining room and turned to her mother and aunt, anticipating their reaction. Anton had found the special embroidered Christmas tablecloths and napkins in the box with the decorations, and Rose had pushed two tables together and set places for thirteen with china and wine glasses. She had arranged red and green ribbons up and down the length of the tables, and cut some sprigs of evergreen from the back of the Christmas tree to use for extra decoration on the ribbons. The chairs didn't all match, but that wasn't important.

Kate and Ruzina were impressed.

"Very good," nodded her mother.

"Yes, very nice, Rosie," Kate echoed. "You really did all that yourself?"

"That's how Aunt Amalia did it two years ago," Rose said. "The ribbons were in the Christmas box. I remembered how pretty it looked."

"You are a very smart girl," Kate said wonderingly. "You couldn't have been more than nine."

"Oh, she's smart all right," Ruzina said. "She's going to be the sharpest one of the bunch, I tell you. Smarter than the boys already."

Rose smiled down at her shoes, and Kate saw her cast a quick glance into the front room to see if any of the boys had heard the comment. They were all busy with the Christmas tree lights and acted as if they hadn't heard.

Kate smiled and tapped Rose on the shoulder. "Come on, put on an apron to keep that lovely dress clean so you can help me. Where's the big saucepan, honey?" Rose went to pull out the pan, and Kate looked around Vincent's kitchen with a little stir of envy in her heart. Vincent had an icebox, an electric toaster, and an assortment of other gleaming appliances that Kate herself would love to own. Amalia had brought her family's money with her to her marriage, and Vincent, who worked at a bank, had invested it during the booming years of the 1920s. As a result, they had furnished their home beautifully over the past decade, while Kate and John Mark had been newly-weds struggling to live on an assistant pastor's salary.

Kate gave herself a little private talking-to as she set out food and checked the goose. *Someday*, she told herself firmly. *Someday I'll probably have these things too. Until then, I'll just enjoy Vincent's things while I'm here, and be grateful that I still have all my family with me. I wouldn't want to change places with him for all the world.*

Rose found the saucepan. "Aunt Kate?" she said as she held it up. "What do you want me to do?"

"Start opening the jars, Rosie, and let's get that corn going," Kate said briskly. "And I need to keep these potatoes warm too. Ruzina, where can I put them?" And they all began the familiar work of bringing a meal to the table.

———— ⁓ ————

Joe finally sighed, put down his fork, and pushed back his plate. He could not remember being so full in his entire life. He had taken third helpings of everything, including the crescent rolls, except for the pickled beets.

Stephen had dropped a forkful of purple beets on his new Christmas shirt, and Josefina had immediately scolded him for staining it. Joe figured that eating beets wasn't worth the risk of spoiling his shirt. Christmas was too good to ruin for the sake of a pickled vegetable.

Three weeks before, on December 6, they had celebrated *Svaty Mikulas* by draping their socks over the couch at night before bed and then waking up the next day to find them filled with the oranges, walnuts, and hard candy that St. Nicholas brought during the night. A week later they had decorated the Christmas tree with delicate hand-painted ornaments. Last night, Vincent and Anton had come over right after dinner, and they had all eaten Aunt Kate's candy while they opened presents. Stephen's presents were a wind-up car and a Parcheesi set. Johnny had received two books, *Dick Tracy* and *Terry and the Pirates*, and a baseball glove. All three boys had been given heavy socks to wear to school during the winter.

Joe put his hand into the pocket of his new pants. His presents were new shoes and a jacket. But what made Christmas so good was that his grandmother had given him a whittling knife, with a handle made of black wood and steel, and with its own brown leather sheath that snapped over the handle to hold it safely in place. It was beautiful. Only grown-up men had special whittling knives like this one. Joe had hardly slept at all last night for the sheer joy of holding such a thing in his hand.

Now that he was finished eating, he looked around the table at the other people. This house had a dining room, and two tables had been pushed together in order to seat thirteen people – Vincent and Anton, the six from John Mark's house, and five blond-haired, blue-eyed people that he didn't know. They had been introduced to him as the Prazskys, but Joe couldn't remember all their first names. There was a round-faced mother who was busy talking to Kate, two tall boys who ate as much as Joe did, and a father who was taller than the boys and very big in the shoulders. A beautiful girl wearing a red dress sat next to the father, and Joe had stolen fascinated glances at her when he wasn't busy eating. John Mark sat next to Mr. Prazsky and Vincent, and the three men had laughed through the whole meal, mainly at the boys' appetites.

"*Ano*, yes, your father and I used to have eating contests back when he was young," Mr. Prazsky was telling Johnny. "He was a lot skinnier then but he could eat more. We used to put whole *kolaches* into our mouths and see who could swallow first."

Johnny was listening in awe. The girl in the red dress looked skeptical. The big man sipped his coffee and kept talking. "And then Ruzina would come out and get mad at us for eating all the food the same day she made it." He waved his coffee cup toward the boys grouped at the other end of the tables. "Now don't you go try that today!" he boomed. "It's bad for you! Terrible! No eating *kolaches* without permission!"

"It's real bad," Uncle John laughed. "Never start a *kolache* eating contest, boys. It'll kill you. Not the *kolaches*. Karel will when he finds out they're all gone."

"We could handle those eating contests when it was just the three of us," Uncle Vincent said. "With Joe here now we've got five of these eating machines. They'll eat us right out of the house if they ever get going."

Joe kept looking around while the others laughed and the men went on telling stories. Lace curtains hung at the windows, and a polished wood cabinet with glass doors gleamed with plates and crystal glasses inside. A patterned carpet covered the floor. White tablecloths decorated with red berries and green leaves were on the tables, and all the plates matched. Small straight wine glasses with dark purple homemade wine sat beside every plate, except Stephen's. Joe's own wine glass was still full.

"You don't want your wine?" Anton asked, as the men traded jokes and roared with laughter at the other end of the table.

Joe shook his head and pushed the glass toward him. Anton poured the wine from Joe's glass into his own. "Thanks." Joe could feel Anton looking at him, so he kept his eyes down and looked at his empty glass instead. A pattern of grapes and leaves was etched around the crystal rim.

"My grandma brought those over on the ship from Moravia," Anton offered, trying to talk to him. "Her family made wine back there. My mom always said that it was a miracle they didn't all break on the trip." He paused, as if waiting for Joe to say something now.

Joe tried to come up with something to say. "So, you're rich?" he asked after a moment.

Anton looked surprised, then recovered himself. "No," he said. "My dad lost his job at the bank after the Crash. He waits tables at the Harmony Café now."

Joe had no idea of what he could possibly say after that. His try at conversation had not gone very well. He kept his face expressionless, said "Huh," and looked back at his empty wine glass.

Joe had looked at the wine greedily when they first sat down to eat. He had picked up his glass right away, seeking the feeling of relief he remembered from the times when he pilfered drinks of wine from his mother and her friends. But when the wisp of the wine's scent met his nose at the rim of the glass, his stomach had turned over, and he had suddenly seen the interior of the old rusted-out car again and smelled the stench of liquor and bile that had filled it like a fog the day his mother died. He had seen the inside of that car and smelled that smell, clear as day. He had finally blinked away the sight of the car to see Johnny looking at him curiously and trying to hand him a bowl of corn. Joe had given Johnny a cold stare in order to stop his curious gaze, and had grabbed the bowl roughly from his hands. But then he had felt dizzy, and his hands shook as he ladled corn onto his dish. He kept his head down and willed himself to sit quietly until he felt calmer. He left the wine alone after that, for fear that the horrible vision might rise in front of him again.

The girl in the red dress was telling a story. " . . . and after Johnny left the kitchen I went and counted the dumplings, and there were only three left in the soup!" Everyone was laughing, except for Johnny, who turned red and said, "Hey, I don't think you counted right. There were more than three left," which made the rest of them laugh even more.

All of a sudden everyone was pushing back chairs and getting up to go into the front room. "*Jingle Bells! Jingle Bells!*" Stephen shouted.

"Quiet down, Stephen," Aunt Kate said. "Anton can decide what to sing first."

Joe snuck one last bite of goose from the platter before he followed them out of the dining room. His grandmother sat on the sofa with Aunt Kate and Mrs. Prazsky. Stephen sat on the middle of the piano bench and Anton pushed him to the side so he could sit down too. Johnny sat on the arm of the couch, while the tall blond boys crowded around the piano, looking through stacks of music books.

"Here it is," said one of the tall boys. "*I Got Rhythm*. Can you play that?"

"Carols first, Rudy," Mrs. Prazsky said. "You boys can fool around afterwards and play for us while we do dishes."

"*Jingle Bells* first," Anton said. "Then Aunt Ruzina gets to pick. Yes, I can play that." He opened the cover to the keyboard, blew off some dust from the keys, and began to play.

⬥

Vincent watched his son run through a quick scale in C to warm up, pounding out a few extra chords at the end and making a ferocious face at Stephen for fun. Anton moved up to D and began another scale, but stopped in the middle of it and started playing his father's favorite melody from *Figaro* instead. He finished off the tune with a little flourish of his own making, then effortlessly transposed the melody up to the next higher key and played it again as if for a music lesson, throwing a glance at Vincent and laughing.

He loves to play, Vincent thought. *Why won't he just apply himself? He's so set on throwing his talent away, after all these years of lessons.* He frowned to himself in frustration, while all around him the others began to sing the happy words of *Jingle Bells.* John Mark elbowed him in the ribs, and he was jolted out of his thoughts and began to sing along. Amalia had always said that his mission in life was to sing the bass melody.

He watched Karel sing along with his daughter Rose, standing at the side of the piano. Karel was keeping an eye on his sons, Wenceslaus and Rudolf, to make sure they did not slip out to the kitchen for an advance taste of dessert. Wence and Rudy sprawled on the floor and shoved at each other, missing some of the words in the verses but belting out the chorus each time it came around. Ruzina and Kate carried the tune with their clear soprano voices. Josefina Vesely was frowning, because she did not like *Jingle Bells,* but Vincent knew she would sing the old Bohemian carols like *Narodil se Kristus Pán* and *Good King Wenceslaus* when someone asked Anton to play them.

Vincent's favorite photo of Amalia sat on the piano. The photographer had caught a certain incandescent look in her eyes, while she was just barely smiling and holding three-year-old Anton on her lap. The photo was tinted, showcasing the identical blue of their eyes and the dark brown curls of their hair. Amalia had always played the carols on Christmas. Vincent thought of her now, how her hands had moved so magically over the keys, turning a simple family sing-along into a concert. Anton was not doing too badly, he thought appraisingly, although he could tell that his son was more interested in making Rose and Stephen laugh than in the quality of his playing. Amalia had loved the Christmas season and played the carols with as much passion as other pianists poured into Bach and Rachmaninoff. Vincent had to stop singing and press his fist against his mouth for a moment. John Mark left him alone this time.

Eventually they went through all their favorite carols, and Anton began to play *I Got Rhythm*, with Stephen still sitting beside him. Rudy and Wence sang along and clowned as they sang, taking up almost all the space in the room with their big shoulders and long arms and legs. The women got up and went into the kitchen. Karel and Johnny set up a game of pinochle on the dining room table, and John Mark went to join them.

Vincent stayed in his chair, listening to Anton play, and saw Joe move out from the corner where he had been lingering and lean against the piano. The boy had lost his usual blank expression and actually began to look happy as the family sang carols and the boys horsed around.

Good to see him smile, Vincent thought. *Poor kid.* Joe was altogether looking much better than he had last November. He had put on some weight. His face had filled out a bit, and Vincent could see that he had inherited all of his mother's good looks. Dressed in his Sunday clothes, the boy seemed healthy and handsome. But John Mark said that he still wasn't talking hardly at all, and that he had bad dreams almost every night. John and Kate had planned to start him in school in January, but now they were having second thoughts about it. They weren't sure how well Joe could read.

Vincent felt his mouth start to tremble again. *So much grief, so much pain, everywhere you look.* He abruptly got up and went outside for some deep breaths of cold winter air, and blinked hard to hold back sudden tears.

The front door banged shut as someone else came out. "Here," John Mark said, holding out his coat.

"Hmmf, I won't be out here that long," Vincent grumbled.

"You dumb Bohemie," John Mark said, throwing the coat at him. Vincent put it on.

"That worked out pretty good, huh?" John Mark asked.

"Anton playing again? I guess so." Vincent frowned with exasperation. "John, I wish he would practice. He just won't apply himself. If he just would get serious about his life, he could do so well. At everything. I don't know what's got into him lately. He needs to straighten out before it's too late."

John Mark laughed at him. "You're complaining about Anton? The angel child? You're blessed with that one, Vince." He draped an arm around his brother's shoulder. "I'll tell you what. We'll trade. You take Stephen, Johnny, and Joe for a week, and I'll take Anton. In fact," and he pushed at his brother a little bit to tease him, "I'll go even better. Take one of them for a week and let me have Anton. That'll teach you. You'll take him back with open arms and let him do whatever he wants for the rest of his life. You don't know how much worse it can be."

Vincent smiled a bit in spite of himself. "They aren't such bad kids," he said.

"Want to find out?" John asked. Vincent laughed.

They could hear *I Got Rhythm* come to an end and *Puttin' on the Ritz* begin. Anton was hamming it up, pounding away on the bass notes, and the boys were singing so loudly that Vincent and John Mark could hear them outside.

If you're blue and you don't know where to go to
Why don't you go where fashion sits
Puttin' on the ritz . . .

Stephen's and Rose's high voices joined in now.

Dressed up like a million dollar trooper,
Trying hard to look like Gary Cooper,
Super duper . . .

"Well, it's nice to hear him play something again. Even this stuff," Vincent finally admitted.

Have you seen the well-to-do, up and down Park Avenue,
On that famous thoroughfare, with their noses in the air?
High hats, Arrow collars, white spats and lots of dollars,
Spending every dime for a wonderful time?

"How's Joe doing?" Vincent asked, changing the subject.

John Mark shook his head. "Kate seems to think he's coming along fine. She says to just be patient and he'll start . . . acting more normal, I guess. Maybe he will. But I can't ever tell what he's up to. I don't trust him any further than I could throw him."

"What's the matter with him?" Vincent asked.

John Mark shrugged. "I don't know. He barely talks. He won't even look at me, or Johnny either. He jumps if I move too fast around him, like he thinks I'm going to hit him or something. He sleeps during the day and walks around the house at night. I don't think he can read very well." He looked over at Vincent. "What do you think is the matter with him?"

"Hard to say, the way Marie lived," Vincent said. "A different guy every couple of months, is what I heard."

"We're still thinking about starting him in school after New Year's," John Mark said. "Maybe getting out and being back with other kids will help."

"Might make it worse," Vincent offered after a moment.

John Mark looked around. "What do you mean?"

"Sometimes it just takes longer than you think," Vincent said, staring down the street at nothing in particular.

Puttin' on the Ritz came to an enthusiastic end, and after some noisy discussion inside, *Stompin' at the Savoy* began. The two men heard Kate's voice rise above the music, demanding that the boys stop and choose a different song to sing on Christmas. Vincent and John Mark exchanged a glance and laughed, then turned to go inside.

———— ～ ————

Joe was disappointed when Anton stopped playing. He followed everyone into the dining room for cherry pie and poppyseed cake, and ate dessert without attracting attention to himself. All the talk and laughter made him lonely and miserable, and he wanted desperately to go smoke a few puffs by himself out in the alley.

But everyone else was still having fun, and Joe could tell they were not planning to go home any time soon. Aunt Kate, Mrs. Prazsky, and his grandmother were sitting in the kitchen, talking in Czech and eating Kate's candy. Uncle John and Karel Prazsky were playing chess. Vincent was explaining a new card game to the older boys, who were not really paying attention, while the girl in the red dress sat next to him and tried to help explain the game. Joe sat at the table, watching Vincent and the girl, and Stephen sat beside him, chin resting on his folded arms. He looked like he was going to fall asleep.

Then Wence, who was playing with a yo-yo at the side of the table, accidentally spun it out too far and hit the window sill behind him. The sharp *clack* made Karel jump and spill his coffee. Vincent looked around. Joe froze where he sat, waiting for a fight to start.

"What was that?" Karel demanded.

"I'm sorry," Wence stammered.

Vincent was on his feet now, looking at the place on the window sill where the yo-yo hit. "No harm done, Karel," he said.

But Karel was not finished with Wence. "You brought that toy in here? What did I say about that? Take that back to the house right now."

Wence flushed red and took a deep breath. Joe looked away, not wanting to make him feel worse. Wence looked more like a grown-up than a boy, and Joe felt embarrassed for him, hearing his father speak to him so harshly in front of everyone. He risked a quick glance to see what was happening, and saw Wence staring back at his father with a glare of his own. Joe's stomach clenched up as he waited for the fight to start.

But no fight started. Wence seemed to reconsider and said, "Okay, Dad. Sorry, Uncle Vincent."

"*Rádo se stalo*," Vincent said. "No problem. Do you still want to play this game?"

"I think you boys should go outside," Karel Prazsky said, with a tone in his voice that let them know to get up and go. "Go out and run around for a while."

Joe tried his best to sit unnoticed as Wence and Rudy rose and left the room. It would be better to sit inside and be warm and miserable than to go outside and be cold and miserable.

Aunt Kate had come into the dining room when she heard the raised voices. "Joe and Johnny, you go too. Run off some of that steam. Come back when it's dark and we'll have sandwiches," she called so that Wence and Rudy would hear her.

Anton had already left the dining room. Johnny was slowly getting up. Joe stayed put in his chair, trying to be invisible.

"Joe, go ahead like your aunt says," Uncle John said in that special quiet voice. Joe frowned as he got up, but suddenly he felt better. If he was going outside, then he could smoke.

The boys went out the kitchen door into the back yard. The sun shone weak and low, throwing faint blue shadows on the snow. Wence and Rudy headed to their little house to get their coats. Anton and Johnny followed, lagging a bit behind, and Joe came last, buttoning his jacket against the icy winter air. A black dog suddenly raced toward them, barking furiously, until it came up sharply against a chain that tethered it to the side of the Prazsky's house. Joe jumped at the noise. The dog stood snarling and growling, chained just far enough from the door so that Wence and Rudy could slip past and get into the house. Joe came to a stop behind Anton and Johnny, keeping them between himself and the growling dog.

"Geez, what a horrid dog," Joe said to no one in particular.

"Yeah," Anton agreed without looking at him. "That's Skippy. Karel's watchdog. We're all just waiting for him to die." They watched the dog run back to the door when the boys came out.

Wence and Rudy burst out of the house with coats on and wooden sleds in their arms. Rudy pushed Wence into Skippy's territory, and Wence yelled and jumped as the dog dove at him. They ran out through the yard and toward the alley, where they flung the sleds down onto the hard-packed snow and jumped on them, gliding down the slight hill to the street. Joe and the others ran after them, and Anton threw a snowball as he ran and hit Wence on the back of his head. Johnny whooped and threw his own snowball, but missed Rudy and hit a tree instead.

"Riverside Park," Wence called. The boys ambled down the street, kicking the sleds along the icy road and throwing snowballs at street signs. Joe threw his own share of snowballs and hit every sign he aimed at. Rudy looked at him.

"Hey, you play baseball?" he asked.

Joe shrugged. "Sometimes," he said.

"Are you going to play leagues this spring?" Rudy asked.

Joe kept his face expressionless to hide the fact that he had never played in the city baseball leagues, although he had watched other boys play. "I dunno," he said, but he felt a bit of pride stirring inside. He knew he was a good player. In the sandlot ball games where he had played, he was always picked first for teams.

"You want to be on our team?" Rudy went on.

Joe stiffened. He didn't know if he could do that. "Maybe."

He felt Rudy looking at him, so he dropped back in order not to talk any more. He glanced around to make sure that he was out of sight of Vincent's house, and then pulled out a cigarette. He lit it up and watched the other boys react.

"Where'd you get those?" Johnny demanded. Joe ignored him.

"You'll ruin your wind, idiot," Rudy said.

Joe blew smoke coolly into the winter air, relishing the idea of breaking a rule and making someone upset about it. Especially Johnny, who acted so smart all the time and probably had never known a problem in his life. He felt a rush of superiority as he took another drag. At least he had this one thing that they didn't. He blew another plume of smoke and glanced over at Johnny, to make sure that he saw.

They reached a little park between the corn syrup factory and the river. Wence kicked his sled over to the crest of a hill that sloped down toward the river below. Anton tackled him from behind so that they both fell on the sled and skimmed down the hill together. Johnny tried to pounce on the other sled but Rudy beat him to it and went down the hill alone. The snow had softened during the day and then had frozen again in the late afternoon, and now the hill was so icy that Johnny slid down on his feet, crouching low to keep his balance, although he lost his footing at the bottom and pitched over into the snow. Joe finished his cigarette and flipped away the butt with casual style as he had seen gangsters do in the movies, but no one was watching anymore, so when the boys climbed back up the slope and went down again on the sleds, he joined them.

The shadows in the park grew long and finally disappeared altogether in the gray December dusk. The snow along the hill became even icier as they went down the runs, until the slope was slick and fast.

When the first stars came out, Wence reminded them about the sandwiches.

"Ready to go?" he yelled as they pulled the sleds up the hill again. Their mittens and collars were coated with droplets of ice, and the cold wind was sharper now that the sun was gone.

"Let's do one more," Johnny said.

"Let's all go one more time to see who can go farthest, then go home," Anton proposed. "I went farther than ever last time."

Wence and Rudy went first. They zipped down the icy hill but ground to a halt soon after hitting the softer snow in the field below. Johnny and Anton went next, going farther across the snow field because of their lighter weights on the sleds. Johnny went a little farther than Anton, marked the end of his run with a snowball, and then the two of them dragged the sleds back up the hill. Joe got ready for his run.

He had already noticed that one sled was lighter and faster than the other, and he studied the slope and field in the moonlight, planning to take the iciest track down the hill and across the snow in order to go as far as he could. He had waited in line until last, in order to have his pick of sleds and to get as much advantage as possible. When his turn came up, he picked up the lighter sled, took a fast starting run, and flung himself down the hill.

He kept his head low. The glittering slope rushed just a few inches under his nose as he flew down the hill. He stole quick glances ahead in order to steer onto the iciest track across the field, feeling the sled's runners clatter beneath him. He could not see Johnny's snowball marker, but he felt sure he had passed it. He dimly saw the shadowed trees and shrubs that lined the side of the river — and then suddenly the sled was in the middle of the undergrowth, bumping over roots and banging into stiff snow-covered bushes. Joe felt stings on his face and dragged his feet as hard as he could in order to slow the sled. Then he felt a sharp blow to his shoulder as he ran into a tree trunk and flew off the sled and into a snowdrift. He sat up slowly, rubbing his shoulder and shaking snow out of his eyelashes.

The sled rested behind him at an awkward angle, half buried in soft snowdrifts under a tangle of branches. Joe was lying right on the bank of the river, barely an arm's length from where it dropped off to the thin ice below. He caught his breath when he saw how close he had come to falling into the water, which was frozen along the bank but still running openly in the middle of the channel. Then he caught his breath again, because there on the ice, about ten feet out from the bank, was his new knife, the snap on its leather sheath glinting softly in the moonlight.

No, he thought as he looked at the beloved Christmas gift beyond his reach on the thin ice. *No.* This could not be happening. He had just been getting ready to claim the victory of the longest run, and now this disaster had happened instead.

Joe gave himself a shake. Perhaps this was a nightmare, like his other bad dreams that disappeared when he woke up. If he blinked, surely it would go away. He blinked hard, but nothing changed. He could hear the other boys' voices now, calling him, and he knew deep in the pit of his stomach that this was no dream. It was real, and he was an idiot again, because he had let his beautiful, expensive knife fall out of his pocket at the end of his winning run. He didn't know which was worse, the thought of losing his knife, or the thought of being so stupid as to lose it this way.

He could hear the voices growing closer now. The rest of the boys were coming to find him. Joe was torn between wanting to enjoy his victory and wanting to get his knife back before they arrived and saw what had happened.

Anton was the first to reach him, and gave him a hand up out of the snow. "You okay?" Anton asked, dusting snow off his coat. Wence came next and pulled the sled out of the snow.

"Gee, look how close to the bank you went," Johnny marveled, arriving on the scene with Rudy.

Joe could not reply to that. "Look," was the only word that would come out of his mouth. He pointed to where his knife lay gleaming on the ice.

The boys gathered up to the bank and looked at it. "Oh, man," Joe heard someone say. He started down the bank, intending to inch out across the thin layer of frozen water and retrieve the knife by himself. He kept going even when the others called out, warning him to stop. He put a shoe onto the ice, felt it shift and heard it creak beneath him, and then a hand grabbed the collar of his coat and pulled him back up onto the bank. He whipped around, ready to fight off whoever it was, but he lost his balance instead and fell against Wence, who was standing behind him, still holding onto his collar.

"Wait, you *pitomec*," Wence said, using his father's word for *idiot*. "Geez, Joe, you're going to kill yourself. We'll get it. Find a stick that'll reach it." The boys fanned out through the snow-covered shrubs, looking for a suitable branch, and Wence finally broke one off a tree. They took turns poking it out over the ice, trying to hook the knife with it and pull it back to shore.

But the ice was rutted and bumpy, and the knife was too slick for the branch to get enough grip to pull it over the ruts to the shore. After making painful progress by inches over the bumps, the knife came to rest against an icy ridge of dirty snow, and then refused to budge again. It was still far enough away from the bank that no one could reach it.

"I can make it now," Joe said suddenly. He had watched glumly as Rudy and Wence, who had longer arms, strained to move the knife out of the hollow. He had pulled the branch out of their hands and tried to move the knife himself. He was in agony as he watched the others working to fix the problem that he had caused by his own stupidity, and he was miserable at the thought of returning home without the knife. It looked tantalizingly close.

"I can make it," he said again. "If I fall in, it's not that deep. I don't care if I get wet."

"Forget it. That ice won't hold you, and then you'll lose the knife anyway when it breaks," Anton said. Johnny stood beside him, hugging his arms to his chest and trying to keep his teeth from chattering.

"Hey, if Wence holds my hand, I think I can swing out far enough from the bank to pull it in," Johnny said suddenly. "Or maybe he can hold my arm and you guys can hold my legs, or something like that. I'm the lightest."

Joe, torn between pride and misery, looked at Johnny to see if he was serious. Johnny was only looking at the knife, not at him, and his teeth had stopped chattering. Wence and Rudy eyed the distance from shore that Johnny would have to stretch across.

"I think he could do it," Anton said. "If you guys think you can hold him."

"I'll hold his arm, and you guys hold my other arm," said Wence. "Someone hold his legs."

In a minute, Johnny was angled in midair over the ice, one bared hand straining for the hollow of dirty snow. He was still a few inches short.

"Pull in," Wence ordered. Rudy helped him pull Johnny upright. "If we get six inches closer, he'll get it," Wence said, and repositioned his right foot on the thickest part of the ice by the bank. "Come on."

Johnny leaned out over the ice for the knife again. All the boys strained to let him stretch one more inch. His fingers reached the snowy ridge and scrabbled on the ice.

"I got it!" he yelled. Rudy and Wence leaned back to haul him up, but then the ice under Wence's foot cracked and with a splash he slid knee-deep into the water at the shore. Johnny's feet slid into the same hole of black water that Wence was now standing in, and he instinctively put out his free hand with the knife towards the ice below him, trying to keep his balance. His hand punched through to the water, and the ghostly sound of crackling filled the air as the thin shell of ice began to shatter. Rudy and Anton hauled on Wence's other arm, trying to keep the boys from falling in any farther, and

Joe jumped down into the water, caught Johnny's dry arm, and helped Wence pull him out.

At last they all stood on the bank, panting and catching their breath. Johnny opened his hand and the leather-sheathed knife glistened damply in the pale winter night.

Anton gave a whoop and pounded Joe on the back. Wence gave Johnny a bear hug that lifted him off the ground. When he was back on his feet, Johnny turned to Joe and grinned.

"Here you go," he said, holding out the knife. Joe took it, and looked at Johnny awkwardly through the dusk.

"Thanks," he said, and looked away. Rudy punched him on the arm. The boys began to walk back home, feeling the cold now that the excitement was over. Joe fell behind a little, unnerved by the sudden rush of relief and the uncomfortable feeling of knowing that Johnny had helped him out, right after he had smirked at the younger boy about the cigarette. He was shaking in the cold, even inside his jacket, and he tucked his chin down into his collar against the freezing wind. Little icy daggers prickled his wet feet with every step he took. Anton was in front of him, checking Johnny's coat for wetness. Wence broke into a jog, calling over his shoulder for them to hurry. Joe started to run, hoping that would warm up his feet. He pulled alongside Johnny.

"Hey," he panted. Johnny looked over at him and sneezed.

"Really, thanks," Joe huffed out as he trotted along. Johnny gave another tremendous sneeze, and grinned as they all struggled home.

Three: January / *School*

Joe wanted to die, or at least disappear. The English teacher was talking to him. "This is the third time this week that you haven't turned in homework. I know that you're *behind*, but you still have to try. You have to turn in something. Otherwise you'll make an F and have to stay behind next year."

Joe wished that the floor would open up and swallow him. Finally he dredged up the words "Yes, ma'am."

"Today's Friday. You have the weekend to catch up," the teacher continued. As she talked, Joe stared at her hair. It was blonde, and done up like his mother used to do her hair. Every time he looked at the English teacher's blonde hair, he thought about his mother. He remembered her voice, and the way she laughed when she had a good day.

"Do you hear me?"

Joe came back from his daydream. "Yes, ma'am," he said again.

The teacher looked at him. "What did I just say?" she asked.

"For me to do my homework over the weekend," Joe muttered.

"You should ask your cousin Anton to help you," the teacher said after a pause. "Or your cousin Johnny. Just because you're working at home doesn't mean you can't get help. If you bring your assignments in on Monday, nice and neat like I said, you'll be caught up." The teacher gave him a smile that Joe thought looked hideous, like a pig's grin.

Back in his seat, he opened the top cover of his wooden school desk and tried to disappear behind it.

He knew that the girl who sat to his left had heard. The whole classroom must have heard. So now they all thought he was stupid, plus they probably knew by now that his mother hadn't been married and he was illegitimate. He stared into the dark insides of his desk for a while, and then out the window at the blue sky and snow-covered branches outside. He wanted to get up and leave. He especially wanted to have a smoke. Joe sighed and pushed his books around the inside of his desk instead. There was no way he was going to walk across the classroom in full view of all those curious students and leave before the bell rang.

When it finally did ring, Joe slipped past the teacher, keeping his head down, and worked his way down the hall and out to the door where Anton and the Prazskys waited for him. He had chosen to go to high school, even though his uncle was concerned that he was too far behind to do well in his proper grade level.

"Joe, you can go to eighth grade at Johnny's school or ninth grade at high school with Anton and the Prazskys," his uncle had said. "I think you'll have an easier time of it if you go to grade school, but it's up to you." The mere thought of being in a classroom, or even a lunchroom, with Johnny and other little kids was enough to make up Joe's mind. Johnny seemed so much smarter at schoolwork than Joe, and the thought of being in the same class as Johnny scared him. Better to look stupid in front of a lot of strangers than to look stupid in front of Johnny, Joe had thought at the time. Now he wasn't so sure.

He found Anton and Rudy outside the big double doors of the ornate brick school building, mixed in with the other teenagers thronging on the walkway. Joe stood by them and tucked his chin down into his scarf and jacket collar as the freezing January wind whipped through the crowd.

"What are we waiting for?" he asked. He would warm up if they started walking.

Anton, his nose and cheeks red from the cold, pointed with his chin toward Wence, who was talking to a girl with smooth brown hair and a light blue coat and hat. They were standing close together, smiling into each other's eyes. Joe watched them, envious of their love. A whole shining future seemed to stretch before them, as if any minute they would turn and walk away down the street arm in arm, eventually ending up in a house of their own and talking in that intimate, confident way that his aunt and uncle had with each other.

He looked away. There was no shining future with a girl like that waiting for him, because of who he was and what his mother had been. He did not fit in here. These girls would not want to be seen with him, a fatherless boy with only his dead mother's last name. Even though he was standing next to Anton and Rudy in the middle of a crowd, Joe felt an intense wave of loneliness surge through him. He looked over at Rudy.

"Does Wence have to talk to her every single day?" he asked. The weather had turned bitter cold, and the walk to and from school had become a torment. His nose froze and his throat hurt when he breathed, even though he kept his wool scarf wrapped around the lower part of his face. It was so cold that his aunt fixed hot boiled potatoes for him to hold in his pockets and warm his hands while he walked to school in the morning. The afternoons were better than the mornings, but still cold, and Joe wanted to start walking as soon as possible.

"This is the only time he gets to talk to her," Rudy said. "Her family doesn't like him."

Joe looked back at Wence. It was hard to believe that anyone wouldn't like him. He was tall and good-looking, with his father's muscular build, and besides having helped Joe rescue his knife, he was always friendly and said hello or some such thing to him, even though Joe hadn't said much to Wence yet.

"Why don't they like him?" he asked.

Rudy snorted. "Because Dad's a Freethinker." When Joe looked at him, not understanding, Rudy added, "We don't go to church."

"That's all?"

"Pretty much. It's a political group from the old country, but the church part is why they don't like us. Hey, let's go. He can catch up. Wence! See ya!" he called, starting across the street. Anton raised his hand in a goodbye wave at Wence and followed. Joe jumped after them, relieved to get away from school.

When they walked home from school they reached Anton's house first, and Anton always pulled Joe in for a snack. Ruzina was usually working in the kitchen, and there would be something for them to eat. Today it was a platter of peanut-butter sandwiches. After wolfing down his share, Joe looked around. Ruzina was ironing while Rose folded clothes and made stacks of clean laundry on the counter. A pot simmered on the stove and the smell of chicken and dumplings filled the air. The kitchen was blissfully warm.

"Where's Wence?" Rose asked.

"He stayed late talking to Rachel Sedlak," Rudy said through a mouthful of sandwich.

Rose looked prim as she folded laundry. "She's going to get in trouble," she said.

"Not unless someone tells," Rudy threw back.

"That's enough," Ruzina said. "Do your homework. Rose? Do you have homework?

"I did it already, Mom."

"Rudy? Do yours now, before you go to work." Rudy worked at a feed store after school, hauling sacks of grain and sweeping floors. He swallowed his sandwich, sighed, glanced at the clock, and pulled out an algebra assignment from his book.

"You too, Anton." Ruzina paused a moment, and then said, "Joe? Don't you have homework? You should do it now so Anton can help you."

Joe looked down. He had been in school only two weeks, but it seemed like everyone knew he was behind.

"What kind of homework do you have?" Rose asked. She came over and stood beside him, and he caught the clean scent of laundry soap from her clothes. "I'll help."

Joe flinched inside at the idea of eleven-year-old Rose helping him with high school homework. Having people know that he needed help was bad enough, but for a pretty girl to help him would be humiliation worse than death. "That's all right," he said. "I'll go on home and do it there."

"I'm going to the front room to do mine. You can come with me," Anton offered.

"No . . . I have to go," Joe said vaguely, and set out for the last part of the walk home.

He walked with his head down and scarf up against the icy wind. He didn't really want to go home. After supper, his uncle would make him sit down with his books at the table, while Johnny and Stephen went into the front room and listened to the radio because their lessons were already done, and he felt ashamed that he needed so much help.

Life was horrible now. Instead of spending quiet days with his grandmother, he had to get up early, dress in good clothes, and sit in school all day, struggling with assignments that he didn't know how to do. He would see his mother's blonde hair at the front of the room and start thinking about her. Sometimes he ached to see his mother again, just one more time, and feel her hug him and know that someone loved him. Sometimes he was relieved that she was finally dead, and that he lived with a regular family now, and didn't need to worry anymore about whether or not she was drinking and if he would have something to eat that day. Other times, he wondered if he had been the cause of her drinking so much, because she hadn't been married when he was born, and so he had ruined her life. It was hard to sort out how he should feel.

He would sit in the classroom, thinking about his mother, and then the teacher would ask him a question and he wouldn't know the answer. He hated school.

As he walked, Joe scuffed at the chunks of ice in the street, kicking loose bits of it down the road in front of him. All day long he looked forward to getting out of school, yet even then he was still miserable. He was no good at anything. He wasn't confident like Wence and Rudy. He wasn't talented like Anton. He wasn't as smart as Johnny or as innocent as little Stephen. He had no mother that he could talk to about how much he hated school. His mother . . . if his mother had been a better mother, maybe he wouldn't have turned out to be such a loser. If she had just been more like other people's mothers . . . he thought of Ruzina, her plain round face smiling at him in the warm kitchen scented with bakery and soap, and he suddenly had to wipe away tears as he walked. It was so cold that if he cried, the tears froze on his face.

And worst of all, he was out of cigarettes. He had hoarded his supply, smoking only a few precious puffs at a time, but finally he smoked them all, and now he was out. He hadn't been sent to the store since he started school, and the cold weather kept him from roaming the alleys in the afternoons. The high school's fierce-looking principal had scared him from asking any other boy about cigarettes, and there was no way that he could ask a girl. It was a cruel joke that right now, when he needed a smoke so desperately, he couldn't get one.

As he turned the last corner before arriving home, he looked longingly down the street that led to the little stores and corner bars, and then on over the river to the railroad tracks. His feet stung from cold and his throat hurt from breathing icy air, so he had no choice but to go inside and get warm. He would not go down that street tonight, but soon, when the cold weather broke, he would leave for freedom.

John Mark sat back in his chair at supper later that night, grinning as he watched his family eat. All three boys had taken mountain-sized helpings of mashed potatoes. Johnny was working his way through second helpings. Stephen was noisily relishing every bite of his meatloaf, even though he was eating a little more slowly than usual because they were letting him cut his own meat now. Joe was almost finished, neatly wiping up the last bits of food from his plate with a piece of bread.

"This meatloaf has too much oatmeal," Josefina said to Kate.

Stephen forked up another heaping mouthful from his own plate. "I love Mom's meatloaf," he announced through a full mouth.

Josefina glowered at him. "Be quiet and eat."

"I love Mom's meatloaf too," John Mark said, looking at Kate and smiling. She smiled back, and the little frown that was starting to show between her eyebrows went away.

Johnny suddenly yelped as Stephen's knife and fork sent meat and potatoes flying through the air. John Mark handed Johnny a napkin to clean up the table. Joe leaned over from Stephen's other side and picked bits of food out of the little boy's hair, then mussed it with his own napkin and said, "There you go, pal," in a voice so low it could barely be heard.

John Mark studied Joe for a while. The boy looked so sad these days. For the first two months that Joe lived with them, he had been irritable and sullen, sometimes answering a question with a smirk or ignoring it altogether. He would slip away from the house at times without telling anyone where he was going, and come back hours later smelling of tobacco and garbage. Johnny, who had hoped that Joe would be like a new brother, had been first puzzled and then offended by Joe's unfriendly manner. John Mark had told Johnny that Joe was still getting over his mother's death and that they all needed to be patient and pray for him, but even he felt insulted by Joe's standoffish ways, and his patience was stretched thin with the constant strain of trying to coax his nephew into the kind of behavior he expected from a fourteen-year-old boy.

These days, Joe only looked numb, with the same blank expression he had worn that first night in November. He had to be told exactly what to do every day, as if he forgot from one day to the next what had happened the day before. John Mark wondered sometimes if Joe found ways to get drunk when he disappeared from the house, or if he was just not right in the head. His teachers said that Joe was quiet in class, but that he didn't turn in his assignments. John Mark wished the boy would show a little more energy, or even a flash of that old sullen smirk. At least that would be a spark of life.

So it was good to see him fuss a bit over Stephen. Joe still avoided Johnny, not meeting his eyes or talking to him. But he helped Stephen comb his hair and fix his suspenders in the morning before school, and he sat next to him on the sofa when the boys listened to the radio at night. The weather was so cold now that all the boys slept together on the floor in the front room next to the coal furnace, and Stephen was always the one in the middle, curled up next to Joe for warmth in the nest of quilts and down featherbeds. John Mark smiled a bit at the thought. Johnny hated to be touched by his little brother while he slept, but Stephen loved to cuddle, especially at night, and it looked like maybe Joe did too.

Kate rose from the table and gave directions to the boys for cleaning up. John Mark went to tend the furnace so the front room would stay warm for the evening.

"Boys, did you do your homework?" he called out to the kitchen.

"Yeah," Johnny and Stephen called back over the clatter of plates and silverware.

Josefina shuffled into the front room, wrapped in a thick woolen shawl against the cold, and turned on the radio before angling herself into her favorite rocker. John Mark looked over his shoulder at her, so hunched and cross as she rocked. *All these Veselys, he thought. Every one of them, so sad. Except for Kate.* He could hear her voice now in the kitchen, still organizing the last of the housework to be done that night, bright and energetic even at the end of the day.

"Mrs. Vesely, would you like a cup of tea?" he asked Josefina.

She glanced at him. Her mouth twisted, almost like a scowl, but he had lived with her long enough to know that she was smiling.

"That's very nice of you. *Mockrát děkuji,*" she said, thanking him.

"*Rádo se stalo,*" he replied. It's no problem. Don't mention it.

He went back to the kitchen. "I told your mother that I'd get her a cup of tea," he said apologetically to Kate. She threw him an aggravated look because she had just finished cleaning up the kitchen. He made a funny face at her and mimed begging forgiveness, until she smiled and shook her head at his antics. The stove was still hot, and she banked up the fire and set the kettle over the warmest spot on the range.

"Joe, time for homework," John Mark said after the boys finished the dishes and headed toward the front room.

Joe turned back from the kitchen door as if he had just received a death sentence.

"We don't need to be long," John Mark said, trying to cheer him up. "Just show me your lessons." Joe pulled out some crumpled pieces of paper from his pocket and John Mark tried to help him make sense of the math and English assignments, but it was hard, because Joe seemed to lose focus from one sentence to the next. After repeating his explanations several times and still not seeing Joe make any progress, John Mark became exasperated in spite of himself.

"Joe, you wanted to go to high school. You're smart enough to figure this stuff out and catch up. But you have to try. I can't do it for you," he finally said, and got up to make the tea. "See if you can just write this essay. I'm taking this tea in to Mrs. Vesely. If you're finished by the time I get back, we'll call it a day. You can do the rest tomorrow, or Sunday."

By the time he came back, Joe had made a credible attempt at his English assignment. The handwriting was messy, but he had put together enough sentences to fill the page. John Mark smiled, praised him, and then told him to copy it over onto a clean sheet of paper. "You'll get a higher mark if it's neat. Just do that much, and you can go. And change this word here. Like this." The kitchen was getting chilly now that the heat from the stove was dying, and Joe bent quickly to his task. John Mark went to the wood bin and placed another log on the grate.

The boy left for the front room and the radio as soon as he finished, but John Mark stayed in the kitchen and turned off the light. After a minute, Kate slipped back into the darkened room and sat at the table with him. He reached out and put his arm around her, scooting his chair over by hers. Friday was his night off, and he could stay home.

They just sat at first without talking, and after a while John Mark heard Kate give the little sigh that meant that she was finally relaxing from the effort of keeping up with the house and family. He stroked her arm through her red wool sweater as he told her about what he had done at church that day, and listened while she talked about the house where she worked. They grew quiet again, and he drew her closer in the dark. Through the open doorway, they could see the boys sprawled over the couch and floor, listening to the radio. Johnny rolled over from his spot on the floor and accidentally rolled onto Joe's foot. Joe twitched away with a grimace.

"Go on, that wasn't anything," Johnny said, with irritation edging his voice. John Mark could hear the hurt underneath the irritation. Johnny was always either hurt or mad because of the way Joe ignored him.

"That poor boy just isn't getting better," Kate whispered

"He's not that bad," John Mark whispered back. "I was worried that he'd be cussing all the time, or stealing things around the house, but he's okay."

"I should think that he'd be talking more than this by now, living here with us. Especially as much time as you spend with him," Kate said. "No wonder Johnny's jealous."

John Mark sat still for a while, watching the boys. "I just can't figure out why he's not coming along," he finally said. "I pray for him, and for me be a good father to him, a good uncle anyway, but he just seems to get worse instead of better." He twisted around a little to look at her. "You know what I mean?"

"Yeah," she said, and sighed again, deeper this time. "It's like he's in a fog and getting deeper. Maybe school wasn't a good idea after all."

John Mark was slow to answer. "He needs to go to school, though. He's smart. It's a shame for him to stay home and do laundry all day. I'd like to see him finish high school." He stopped and thought. "Or at least the school year. If he quits now, he'll feel even worse."

He felt Kate shiver as the chilly night air stole through the kitchen again. He wrapped both arms around her and kissed the side of her neck for a while. She snuggled closer and laid her head on his shoulder.

"You know," Kate said, and then stopped.

"What?" John Mark asked after a moment.

"You should touch him more," Kate said. "That'll help."

John Mark sat up. "What?"

"You know, pats on the back, hugs, stuff like that. You ought to touch him every time you talk to him." Kate looked at his skeptical expression and arched a brow. "I hug him a lot, and he's talking to me. I think that's what he needs."

John Mark shifted in his chair. "Ah, I don't know. He'll wonder what I'm up to."

Kate was not put off. "You do it to Johnny and Stephen all the time, and you don't even know it. Joe needs that too. It's really bothering me, how he still looks so sad all the time." She ran a finger through his hair. "You could hug me more, too."

"All right," John Mark murmured. He pulled her closer and turned up her face to his, then kissed her for a long time there in the shadows of the darkened kitchen.

He finally finished his kiss and settled her head down on his shoulder again. He heard her laugh a little bit, and sigh.

"I'm closing the bedroom door tonight. I don't care how cold it gets," he told her. "Don't those boys have to go to bed now?"

———

Kate went to 16th Avenue the next day with Karel and Ruzina in Vincent's car, to do her Saturday shopping. Usually she walked, with one or more of the boys to help her carry her packages home, but because of the cold weather Karel had offered to drive her instead. Kate, Ruzina, and Karel had made a day of it, walking from store to store to see what was new, and then stopping in at the tavern before going on to the grocery and the meat market. Even in cold weather plenty of people were out shopping on the Avenue, and the day was late by the time they drove back home.

Karel pulled up to the front of the house and helped Kate carry in her groceries. She had purchased veal cutlets and enough sugar to bake a cake for after dinner, and she was looking forward to cooking a fancy meal.

The house was a disaster. Socks, shoes, books, and blankets were strewn about the front room where Stephen lay asleep on the couch. John Mark's empty coffee cup and a plate with crumbs of toast sat on the floor by a chair. The furnace had burned low and the room was chilly. Joe and Josefina were stitching up a shirt on the sewing machine in Josefina's bedroom, and John Mark was working on his sermon at the kitchen table, oblivious to the clutter. Johnny was nowhere in sight.

Karel set down the groceries in the kitchen and Kate went into action as the men talked in Czech, catching up on local gossip and political problems in Europe.

"Joe, go put on more coal," she called out, and waited, listening, for the sounds that meant Joe was doing what she said. It took a moment, but she heard him go into the front room. "And put that room back in order. Wake up Stephen and make him help. Where's John Carl?"

No answer. Kate went into the front room where Joe was on one knee by the furnace. She remembered to pat him on the arm as she asked again, "Where's John Carl?" Joe jumped and threw a questioning glance over his shoulder, then turned back to his work on the furnace.

"Anton's," he said.

"Hmm." Kate looked at the clock. "If he's not home by five o'clock, I want you to run over and get him for supper." She patted his arm again. "All right?" Joe didn't jump this time, but he gave her another curious look, and nodded his head.

Kate moved on to Stephen, shaking him awake and getting him started on picking up the shoes and socks. She took the coffee cup and dirty plate back to the kitchen. Karel was leaving, so she said goodbye and thanked him for the ride, and then began putting away groceries.

"John Mark, are you going to help, or are you going back in the front room to work on your sermon?" she asked crisply.

He looked up and blinked. "What are you going to do?"

"Make supper, you *bouktha*," she said, and then ran her fingers through his hair and down his neck under his shirt. "Just keeping up with the plan," she said, with an arch of her eyebrow. He grinned.

Kate turned back to the groceries. "Here." John Mark obediently put away cans of food and dry goods for a while, then picked up his books and papers and slipped out of the kitchen. Kate tied on her apron, pulled out the heavy meat mallet for tenderizing the cutlets, and started to work on the veal, pounding it thin to make the best *wiener schnitzel* her family had ever tasted.

When Johnny finally came in through the back door, bringing a rush of cold air and a shower of snow with him, Kate had the dumplings ready, the sauerkraut hot and fragrant, and the veal keeping warm in the oven. She had fried up the leftover *schnitzel* coating with a little extra salt and pepper for a crispy side dish, and was just finishing the gravy. Stephen was setting the table.

"Stephen, why did you put out the wine glasses?" Johnny asked.

Kate turned around from the stove. "I didn't . . ." she managed to say before Stephen lost his grip on the bottle of grape juice he was pouring into the little wine glasses. The bottle rolled off the table and crashed to the floor, sloshing purple juice across the tablecloth and around the kitchen. Glass shards flew everywhere.

"Oh, Stephen!"

Stephen stood still for a moment, looking at the mess, and then he started to cry. "I'm sorry . . ."

Kate closed her eyes and drew a deep breath. She had put up the juice from her own grapes last summer, and each bottle was precious to her. She had laid a special cloth on the table for dinner tonight. And the food was just now ready to eat.

Dear Lord, give me patience. Don't let me be horrible and mean like my parents were . . . A broken jar of juice in her own parents' kitchen would have sent her father into a rage and her mother into tears. Kate had decided long ago to not let scenes like that happen in her own home. Still, she had to bite her lips to hold back the words *Will you stop that crying* and *Why do you always break things?* She opened her eyes. Stephen was trying to explain.

"I just wanted to . . . make the table pretty like . . . like Uncle Vincent's," he wailed between sobs. Tears rolled down his cheeks.

Johnny, the soul of common sense, had already grabbed the broom and was sweeping up the broken glass. "Stephen, don't move. Stand right there and don't move. Don't move!" he repeated as Stephen immediately began to take a step. "Mom, why would you even let him near the grape juice?"

"I didn't," Kate groaned. "He did it on his own."

Joe came in, keeping his head down but joining Johnny in cleaning up the mess. He pulled out a cleaning rag from the kitchen rag drawer and began mopping juice off the chairs and table while Johnny gingerly picked slivers of glass out of the cracks in the wood floor. Kate took the stained cloth off the table. Stephen was still standing where Johnny had told him to stay, watching.

"Can I help?" he asked.

"No!" everyone said.

John Mark appeared in the doorway just as Joe and Johnny bumped heads over the mess on the floor. They pulled back and glared at each other.

"Watch where you're going, idiot," Johnny snapped.

"John Carl!" John Mark rapped out.

The boys went back to their work, sullenly avoiding each other. Kate worked silently, laying a new tablecloth and putting the plates back in place. Her happy anticipation of dinner was gone. All of a sudden her back hurt, her shoes pinched her feet, and the constant chilly draft from around the kitchen window made her want to scream.

"Can someone please get the milk from the cellar and pour drinks?" she asked, and her voice came out a little more sharply than she intended in the quiet room. "Not you," she said to Stephen, when the little boy started to move. "You sit down at your place and stay there."

"John Carl, let's go down and get the milk," John Mark said without any of his usual good humor. The two of them disappeared into the cellar and Kate started putting food on the table.

"Thank you, Joe," she said in something closer to her regular voice. She remembered to pat him on the shoulder as she said it. He looked around at her but didn't say anything, only moved to wring out his rag in the sink and then went back to washing the floor.

"You can leave that now," Kate added. "I'll work on the stain after dinner. No sense letting food get cold. Go ahead, sit down," she said, and her heart softened as he looked around at her again, as if he were afraid that she was going to yell at him. *He looks as guilty as if he was the one who broke something. Well, he's not the one in trouble now. The only one, in fact,* she thought, and smiled to herself as she pictured the lecture that John Mark was probably giving to Johnny right now in the cellar.

Johnny and John Mark finally reappeared with the milk. "Sorry about what I said," Johnny said to Joe. Joe did not look at him, but nodded stiffly. Kate went to call her mother, and everyone sat down to eat.

John Mark prayed before dinner, instead of asking one of the boys to pray as he sometimes did, and Kate began to feel better as the platters and bowls were passed around. The *schnitzel* was wonderful and her special gravy was perfect. The boys took enthusiastic second helpings. For a while, everyone was quiet, relishing the meal. *Stephen's idea of the wine glasses and the grape juice would have been a nice touch. Too bad about the spill.*

Suddenly Stephen gave a little jump and there was another crash, this time as his milk glass slipped to the floor and broke. Stephen started crying again and Kate rolled her eyes and shook her head. *I must be dreaming. This couldn't possibly happen twice. It would be funny except that it's a waste of good milk.*

Josefina's voice rose above Stephen's sobs. "*Poslouchejte! Opartrnû!*" she shouted uselessly at him. "*Pitomec!* Why don't you listen, you idiot! Watch out! Now you wasted all that juice and all that milk too!" Stephen cried even harder. Joe and Johnny sat as if frozen in their seats.

"Mrs. Vesely!" John Mark spoke sharply, cutting through the racket. "It was an accident. No need to shout at him like that. *Dodržujte ticho, prosím.* Quiet, please."

Josefina said something under her breath and then stopped talking.

Stephen sobbed. Joe and Johnny stayed perfectly still.

"I don't care about the milk," John Mark said. "Kate, let's eat the cake in the front room tonight. Everybody leave the table. Go on." The older boys hurried out, and Josefina sniffed at him and followed them.

"Stephen," John Mark said, "come here."

Stephen slid off his chair, still crying.

"I'm sor-, sor-, sorry, Dad," he gasped out between sobs as he walked across the milky floor. John Mark picked him up and settled him into his lap. He patted his back and wiped his face with a napkin, talking softly as Stephen's sobs turned into gasping hiccups.

Kate sat back in her chair and watched her husband and her son cuddle and calm each other down, as John Mark talked to Stephen and told him that he wasn't angry. He stroked Stephen's hair and guided his head down against his chest, and then Stephen heaved one last little hitching sigh, and relaxed in his father's arms.

Kate got up and began to clear the table. There were leftovers — something that didn't usually happen when Joe and Johnny ate their fill — but *wiener schnitzel* kept well and would still be good tomorrow. She touched John Mark's shoulder as she passed his chair. Stephen was almost sleeping in his lap, worn out with the strain of crying so much. Broken glass covered the floor and she went to get the broom.

"I'll get it," John Mark said.

"Oh, it's no trouble," Kate heard herself say, and wondered where she found the strength to say it at the end of such a long day. "You just stay there." She sighed sharply, thinking about Josefina's hurtful words. "John, I talk to *Matka* all the time about the way she yells at the boys, and it doesn't seem to do any good."

"I'll talk to her too," John Mark said after a while. "After Stephen goes to bed."

Kate cut slices of cake and carried them out to the little group in the front room. By the time she finished, Stephen was asleep. John Mark carried him to their own bed so he could sleep in a warm room, then came back to the kitchen. He sat down with a sigh and propped his head in his hands. Kate turned around from the sink and watched him. He looked tired, and he still had to go to work at the factory.

"Kate," he said, and then stopped. She waited.

He looked at her. "I hate to leave you here by yourself at night. With the boys, with your mother . . . ." He rubbed his face with both hands. "The factory's laying off more guys every week. There's more people at church who need help than I can ever get around to. And look what's going on in our own family. Your mother . . . even Johnny's giving us trouble now. There must be something I'm not doing right."

"I think you're doing a great job," she said. "We're rich in the things that really count." He shot her a disbelieving look.

"I mean it," she said. "We are. It's just a hard night. Things'll get better." She sat at the table and took his hand. "You're wonderful," she said. "Things aren't that bad. You're just having a . . . a moment. You're too tired, is what's wrong." She paused, watching him. "Maybe the Lord wants you to feel like this for some reason," she said shyly. The one place in her heart where she didn't feel confident was when she tried to advise her husband about his preaching or his relationship with God. She had her own way of thinking about God, but she often felt that John Mark had a special kind of faith, a way of connecting with his Creator, that was different from her own.

Nevertheless, she was going to have her say. "Everybody else is going through these exact same things too. What's your sermon for tomorrow?"

"Faith in God in the face of problems," John Mark said after a moment. "Zechariah four. *Not by might, nor by power, but by my spirit, saith the Lord of hosts.'*"

"Well, there you go," Kate said with a bit of her usual briskness. "See? Eat that cake I made for you."

John Mark absently took a bite. "How come you made a cake?"

"Oh, I just wanted a special treat for everybody tonight," Kate said, and smiled at him. "I didn't think that we'd need it so much." He finally smiled back at her, and she added a kiss to all the other things that she had done that day.

Joe sat in his English class later that week with his eyes fixed on the window, where wet tree branches swayed in the sunlight outside. They were wet with melting snow. His teacher was talking, but he paid no attention. The weather had changed.

A January thaw had blown away the arctic freeze. A clear sunny morning and a soft warm wind from the south had softened the snow and turned the streets into rivers of melted ice. Joe had walked to school that morning with no hat and his coat hanging unbuttoned in the mild air. He felt the need for a smoke again, even more keenly now, because he planned to have one by that night. He was going to walk to the store that afternoon before returning home.

"Joe," the teacher said at his elbow. He jumped and pulled his eyes back from the wet tree branches. "You need to get started." She must have been walking around the classroom, checking on the students.

"Yes, ma'am," he said, picking up his pencil as if to go straight to work. He actually wrote a sentence before his thoughts drifted again. He watched the teacher walk back to her desk and sit down. Her hair was like his mother's . . .

His mother had blonde hair, and he could remember times when she did it up like the teacher's, clean and pretty. Usually it was when she had just met a new man friend. Joe had eventually learned that when his mother was in a good mood, generous with her laugh and smile, it was because she had met a new man. Those were the best days. The new man would take his mother and him out for dinner, or at least bring food and special treats to wherever they were living at the time. Everyone would smile and get along. His mother would make a huge fuss over him, telling her new man friend what a good boy he was. Joe almost always liked the men when they were new. His mother would be sweet and the new man would be attentive. Usually they would move into the new man's place for a while. And there would be lots of food.

Joe snapped back into focus as he realized that the teacher was looking right at him. He hastily picked up his pencil and looked at the sentence he had just written in order to remember what he was doing.

Oh, yes. The days with new men friends. Those were wonderful. New men friends always had food around, and Joe would pilfer snacks like bread and cheese to hide and keep for himself in case he got hungry and no one was around to make a meal. Men friends brought his mother cigarettes too, and Joe would make sure that he got his share when no one was watching. That wasn't hard to do. When his mother met a new man, they would forget that Joe was even there after a while. They would go into the bedroom, or out to the clubs hidden away because of Prohibition. Then he would eat his hidden snacks, and go out himself to see what kind of fun he could find.

"Time to finish up, everyone," the teacher said, and Joe started writing again, hurrying to finish before the bell rang so that he could hand in a paper like everybody else.

Men and cigarettes. Even though his mother was gone forever now, he knew where he could find them. He knew where the train tracks ran through town and where there were men who were like him, or at least like the way he used to be when he lived with his mother. They would probably let him stand around and smoke with them, he thought to himself as he finished his meaningless writing assignment. In fact, they might even let him stay with them. No one there would care if he went to school or not.

He looked out at the wet branches again. Back when he lived with his mother, the good days with a new man friend had never lasted long. Sooner or later, Joe would make some mistake, like breaking something or walking into the bedroom at the wrong time. He would get a whipping and a fight would start. His mother would get drunk and cause problems. Then life would be nothing but fights and misery for a while until they moved out, and his mother found a new man. But if Joe went to live in the shanties by himself this time, he wouldn't get drunk and ruin things like his mother always did. He would just be friendly.

When the bell rang, he laid his paper on the teacher's desk like all the other students. He knew it wasn't good. He didn't care. He didn't plan to be back in class the next day.

Joe walked down the hallway with confidence now. He wasn't like all these other students, but that fact didn't bother him anymore. He was who he was, his own man, and he was going to live like he wanted to live, and they could all just be sorry they hadn't understood him better. Full of new courage, he pushed people out of his way as he went out the door and headed to the street.

"Hey!" Someone grabbed him by the arm and hauled him backwards. Joe looked around into the irate face of a boy he didn't know. "Watch out, pipsqueak," the boy said, before he was suddenly pushed away by a long arm that ended up being Wence Prazsky's.

Joe jerked his arm away and said "Thanks, pal." Wence looked surprised at his self-assured tone. Joe looked around until he saw Rachel Sedlak, grinned at Wence, said "See ya later," and headed out to the street that would take him over the bridge to freedom.

John Mark stood in his shirtsleeves on the back stoop of his house, enjoying the mild evening air. A few days of warm weather seemed to come around just in time every January, giving him a welcome break from the daily battle to keep his house warm. He breathed in the fragrance of wet bark and melting ice, and looked at the golden glow of sunset through the bare tree branches above.

A sudden blast of colder wind caught him by surprise. He turned and looked at the northern sky. A straight line of low-lying, slate-blue clouds stretched like a new roof over the horizon, moving toward him even as he watched. Another ice-cold whisper of wind made him shiver.

Well, no thaw lasted forever in January. John Mark reached for the door knob, then turned and looked out at the street. Joe wasn't home. Usually he stopped at Anton's after school for a snack, but he didn't stay there long.

He went inside to the front room. "Johnny? Do you know where Joe is?" he asked.

"Nope," Johnny said flippantly, but then caught sight of John Mark's expression and grew serious. "Maybe he's at Anton's."

John Mark looked out the window for a moment, gauging the amount of light left in the day, and then went into the kitchen to tell Kate he was going over to Vincent's to look for Joe, and to not wait supper for him.

Dear Lord, he prayed as he walked, *please be with me tonight. Guide me, because I'm not sure what I'm doing. And be with Joe, wherever he is. Please help him get better. I don't know what he needs, but You do. Please help both of us tonight.*

"Is Joe here?" John Mark asked as soon as Anton opened the door.

"No. He didn't walk home with us today," Anton said. "Something wrong?"

"He's not at the house. Is your dad home yet?"

"No," Anton said again, and studied his uncle's face. "Are you worried about Joe? Maybe he just went down to the Avenue, or something like that."

"Yeah, I'm a little worried." John Mark paused. Anton waited for him to go on, looking at him with the quiet attention that always reminded John Mark of Amalia and her special way with people. "Maybe he did just go somewhere after school, because of the thaw. But it's turning cold now. I think I ought to go look for him. Did your dad take the car to work today? Can I use it?"

"He took the streetcar today," Anton said. "That's why he's so late. The keys are in the cupboard. Do you think Joe ran away? Do you want me to come with you?"

John Mark felt a little stir of gratitude at the offer of help. *Thank you, God. Thank you for Anton, and for the car being here. That's a start.* "Yeah, I think he might have run away. Don't you think so?"

"Maybe. But maybe he only went to the store." Anton went to fetch the car keys. "He's so sad all the time. It's like he's never happy. And I've been trying, Uncle John. Every day I try to help him." Anton met his eyes for a moment as he pulled on his jacket. "He doesn't want any help from me, I guess."

"He doesn't seem to want any help from me either, but I'm going to go look for him anyway," John Mark replied. "I better go alone, but help me get the car out of the garage. We'll have to shovel snow."

Joe had walked down the melting streets in the bright mild sunshine after school, hands in pockets, and whistling. The sky was blue and the air was sweet and fresh. He had turned down the Avenue and walked past all the shops, heading for the bridge that stretched over the frozen river. He glanced down at the ice below as he crossed. It had not quite melted through, but there were dark patches in the middle of the river where it had grown thin from the thaw.

The beautiful steeple of St. Wenceslaus's church sparkled above the rooftops clustered on the other bank. Birds were busy in the air overhead, soaring and diving in the sun, and Joe felt his heart rise with them. No longer would he have to face strangely smiling people who expected him to talk to them. No more would he have to get up early and endure a day of embarrassment in school. He suddenly thought of Stephen, and then of his grandmother, but he hastily pushed those thoughts away. They would just have to get along without him. He wouldn't think about them anymore. The thought of Stephen nagged at him again, though. He could picture the little boy in the kitchen, asking Kate where Joe had gone, and how his eyes would get wide and fill with tears when he finally understood that Joe wasn't coming home again.

Joe struggled to explain his thoughts to his mind picture of Stephen as he walked, but he finally abandoned the effort and focused instead on the men gathered in front of the Little Bohemia bar at the other end of the bridge. He got friendly nods from them as he passed, but none of them were smoking, so he did not stop to talk with them. He continued on across the street to the train tracks that led out of town.

He walked south along the tracks for a long time, but he saw no one else standing or walking anywhere along the slushy stretch of railroad. He finally turned around and walked back again, searching for the men who always gathered close to the empty railway cars in the evenings, after the shops closed down. These tracks were in a different part of town from where he and his mother had lived, but surely, if he walked long enough, he would find someone. The sky was darkening. The wind turned cold, and he buttoned up his coat as he walked. He wished he had brought his hat and scarf.

Finally he saw a far-off flicker of fire, sheltered between a line of railroad cars and a thicket of trees. He broke into a trot, stumbling along the railroad ties as he ran, and then slowed down to a wary walk as he drew nearer. He finally stepped into the circle of ragged men standing around the fire.

They looked at him, then looked away. Joe stepped closer, warmed his hands, and waited. He felt suddenly timid.

"What're you doing here?"

It took Joe a moment to realize that someone had spoken to him. "Uh . . . ," he said. Wasn't it obvious? He was going to join them, live like them. After a while, when he didn't say anything else, the men lost interest and looked away.

"Looking for a smoke," he finally said. He remembered other times when he had run away from his mother and taken refuge with the groups of men by the railroad. They had usually been friendly, and shared a little food or whatever else they had.

"Get outta here," someone said. "Go home."

Joe began to tremble, although he couldn't tell if it was from nerves or from the cold. He couldn't go back to his uncle's house. He didn't belong there anymore.

"Go on," the man said again. "You don't belong here, son." The other faces looked at him, then looked away again.

Joe was shocked. He belonged. He had spent his whole life in rail yards, on the fringes of neighborhoods, picking through garbage and sharing what he found. Always, he had shared. He knew the life. These men should know that he was like them. It was how he had grown up. He had come back now.

The wind blew colder and the men shifted their feet as they stood, holding out their hands to the flames for a while and then putting them back in their pockets. A few of them continued muttered conversations, bits and pieces of words in the dark. One of them brought out a bottle, and they passed it around. None of them passed it to Joe. He looked at their faces in despair.

He looked down at his feet for a while, and then he saw the problem. He was wearing his new high-top leather Christmas shoes. In fact, he was wearing his new jacket, too, and he had a fresh haircut from the week before. He glanced at the men around him, at the worn-out shoes and coats, the ragged bits of hair straggling from under stained hats, the stubbles of beard, the dirty hands held out to the fire.

He was not like them anymore. He was like a person with a family and a home to live in. They would not take him in.

After a while, Joe backed out of the firelight. He stood for a long time at the edge of the group, until the freezing wind made him double over from the cold and crouch down for a moment, trying to curl into himself to keep warm. The men had closed up their circle tighter around the fire. Eventually they would break up and go find places to doze inside the railway cars, but Joe knew he could not join them.

He finally straightened up and began the dark walk back to the bridge. He couldn't stay here, but he couldn't see himself going back to his uncle's house either. They would know that he had run away. There was no future anywhere now, no hope of growing up and someday being tall and strong and in love with a special girl. He had failed at everything. He had failed to save his mother, failed to fit in with his new life at his uncle's, and now he had even failed at going back to the life he had known before.

It was too hard. It hurt too much to keep on trying and failing, embarrassing himself every time he failed again. There was not enough good in the world to make this kind of pain worth fighting through. He looked up to see if the bridge was any closer yet. Yes, there it was, street lights strung along it like stars in the night, sparkling through the blur of his tears.

John Mark drove up and down 16th Avenue, and then across the bridge and up and down the streets on the other side, looking for Joe. Groups of men still congregated outside the shops and bars, but they were breaking up as the wind turned cold and the early January night settled over the city. He turned back and drove through the neighborhoods where he lived, but saw no sign of Joe walking home. He paused for a moment at the corner close to his house, wondering if he should just go home and wait to see if Joe would return, but then he headed back to the bridge one more time.

Joe had probably gone looking for cigarettes, or he might actually have decided to run away. Either way, he would have headed for the shops along the main streets, not to the homes in the neighborhoods. He would need to eat and find a place to stay. He'd probably look for the same kind of roving groups of people he had lived with when Marie was alive.

John Mark drove up and down the alleys behind the stores this time, instead of staying on the streets. As the evening darkened, people gathered in the back lots of buildings and poked through restaurant garbage for something to eat. He stopped each time he saw them, asking if they had seen a blond-haired fourteen-year-old boy.

Finally, after an hour of driving, he parked the car close to the bridge and turned off the engine. This had been nothing but a waste of gasoline. Vincent could drive for a week on what he had just used up searching for Joe.

He looked out the window for a while. Clouds hung low over the city sky and reflected the faint yellow glow from the factories up the river. Each street light dotted the bridge with a globe of light, shining into the cavernous dark of the river far below. John Mark could feel the icy night air creeping through the car. Soon it would be ridiculous to sit out here in the cold, waiting for someone who might be far away.

He put his head down on the steering wheel and wondered what to do. *I need to pray. I should have been praying all this time, instead of just driving around.*

John Mark prayed every day. Sometimes, when he was tired, he simply prayed over those things that were closest to his heart — Kate, of course, and the boys, and his church — but usually he poured his heart into his prayers instead of just going over a checklist. Other times, when he prayed aloud with friends or with his congregation, he felt an overwhelming sense of wonder as he thought about the creator of the universe listening to people praying for help. But once in a while John Mark prayed because he was desperate.

Dear God, please, please, hear me tonight, he thought as closed his eyes and begged so hard that his heart hurt. *Help me find Joe. Bring him back to us. It's too cold for him to be out alone looking for a place to stay. Help me find him, God, and then please help him get over this . . . these . . . problems that he has. He's just a kid, God . . .*

he didn't have any choice about his life . . . please God, have mercy on him. Please, God, give him a chance with us. And please, work through me, even if I don't understand what he needs or what You're doing. Help him come around. He's smart, he's healthy, I know he could be happy, if You help him. Please, God. Your Word says that You are full of love and faithfulness to us, especially to orphans like Joe. Please, let him have a time of Your favor, Lord. Give the poor kid a new life.

He raised his head and opened his eyes, looking at the street lights again but not really seeing them. *You are so high above me, so much greater than I. I know that I don't even deserve to talk to You, let alone for You to listen to me. But I'm praying now. I'm asking, like You say to ask. I'm asking for Joe to come back.*

Someone was walking toward him along the sidewalk of the bridge, going slow and looking over the side at the water. John Mark watched absent-mindedly for a moment, still wrapped up in the intensity of his prayer. He blinked. It took another moment to be sure, but then he saw. It was Joe.

He started the engine and drove onto the bridge, made a sharp U-turn and came up alongside Joe. The boy jumped and shied away. John Mark threw the gearshift into neutral and leaned over to open the passenger-side door. Joe looked at him, thunderstruck, and then surprise and relief dawned in his face.

"Well, hop in," John Mark said with a grin. "It's too cold to keep this door open. Let's go get doughnuts."

He drove to a café that stayed open late. They sat in a booth back in a corner, and John Mark ordered hot chocolate for Joe and coffee for himself, because he would go in to work later that night. The man behind the bar brought over a plate of doughnuts, and they each picked out two. For a while, they ate in silence. Joe finished his doughnuts first, so John Mark went over to the glass holder on the bar and picked out two more.

"Joe, you've been looking sad all month. What's the matter?" John Mark finally said.

Joe looked out the window. John Mark could see tears welling in his eyes. He pushed his napkin across the table to the boy.

"Ah, it's all right. Blow your nose," he said.

Joe took the napkin, rubbed his nose and sniffed, then looked down at his plate for a long time.

"Well?" John Mark asked. "We'll be better friends if we both talk instead of just me rattling on here all by myself."

Joe gave a little involuntary smile at that.

"So, tell me what's the matter," John Mark said again.

Joe looked out the window again. Finally he muttered, "It's all my fault."

John Mark held his breath for a moment, resisting the urge to exclaim his disagreement. Finally he said, "What's your fault?"

Joe stared out the window and sniffed back more tears. "My mom dying."

John Mark sat still, trying to be sure that he had heard him right. "How is that your fault?" he finally asked.

"I should have . . . saved her," Joe said unevenly. "I should have done something, got help or something. I think everybody thinks so."

John Mark felt tears in his own eyes. *Oh, Lord, give me words.* He took his time before trying to answer.

"Kate and I tried to save her, too, you know," he finally said. "We asked her to move in . . . But she just didn't want it. She just kept leaving us. We couldn't help her either." John Mark looked out the window himself for a while, thinking about Marie, then gave himself a little shake and went on.

"We feel terrible, too, like maybe we could have tried harder. Like we should have done something more. I don't know . . ." John Mark privately doubted that anything they could have done would have helped Marie. How could they have made her stay with them and sober up, when she didn't want to? He brought his thoughts back to the boy sitting across the table.

"So I don't think that you could have done anything to stop her from . . . living that way," he continued, sounding a little lame to his own ears. "If us two grownups couldn't, then how could you, just a kid?"

Joe stubbornly gazed out into the night, but he was listening.

"But one thing I know for sure is that it wasn't your fault," he went on. "Your mother . . . chose to live like she lived. You didn't ask her to live that way. You had no choice about it. That means it wasn't your fault."

Joe blinked a bit at that, and finally looked over at him.

"Joe," John Mark said, "You couldn't help it. I think it must have been pretty hard on you, staying with her." He could feel a plan growing inside. "Only a strong person, a real hero," he looked firmly at Joe to make his point, "keeps on going when things get that bad. And here you are now, still getting up every day and fighting through all this, trying to get over it and go on."

Joe dropped his eyes and toyed with his last few scraps of doughnut.

"You've been carrying a heavy load that you shouldn't have had to carry in the first place," John Mark went on after a moment. "No kid should have to go through what you did."

Joe looked up at him again.

"Moms and dads are supposed to take care of the kids, not the other way around," John Mark said, heartened by the attention. "It's like one horse trying to pull a cart by itself in a two-horse hitch. It doesn't work and it ends up ruining the horse. You need a little time to just rest and get to feeling better." Joe looked back down and John Mark ducked his head, trying to catch his eye. "And eat more. Want another doughnut?"

"I never thought I'd get sick of doughnuts," Joe said after a moment, "but I guess I am now."

"That's the longest sentence you've ever said to me," John Mark said. "I oughta have another doughnut just to celebrate." Joe gave a breathy little hitch that sounded almost like a laugh.

The man behind the counter came over to refill the coffee. After he left, John Mark said, "What else?"

Joe looked up, startled.

"What else is the matter?" John Mark repeated.

Joe looked out the window for a long time. John Mark wondered if he was going to say anything at all, and what else he might bring up. But after a long pause, he only said, "Oh . . . school."

"Yeah, I figured," John Mark said, and was silent for a while. "I bet you want to quit," he added.

"Yeah," Joe said hopefully.

John Mark sat still for a while. "But you're so smart," he finally said. "Joe, you're smart, you're good looking, you have common sense. I hate to see you stay home and just do laundry all day with your grandma. You ought to improve yourself a little bit, while you can, before you go off and get a job and get married."

Joe snorted.

"It's going to happen," John Mark said. "You're going to grow up, whether or not you go to school. You'll be better off if you go. I don't mind helping you with your lessons. Why don't you just bring them all home and I'll help you? Is that so hard to do?"

Joe blew out his breath. "I hate getting help," he said. "No one else has to get help."

John Mark considered that statement as he sipped more coffee and looked around to check the clock on the wall. He still had a little more time before they would have to head back home.

"Did you ever hear the story about the guy with the Model T that broke down on the side of the road?" he asked.

Joe had heard plenty of his stories by now, but he shook his head.

"A guy was out in his Model T when it broke down on the side of the road out in the country," John Mark started. "He opened up the hood and looked around, because he knew a little bit about cars. Probably about as much as most guys. Know what I mean?" Joe nodded. "He tried one thing and then another. Nothing was working.

"Finally some guy came up and stood looking over his shoulder and said, 'Want some help?'

"'Naw, I think I got it,' the guy with the car said.

"'Are you sure? Don't you want some help?' the other man said.

"'It's all right. I can do it by myself,' the guy said again. 'You go on.'

"The other man stood and watched for a few more minutes while the guy with the car tried to figure out what was causing the problem and which piece connected with what in the engine. Finally he said, 'Young man, if you'll just let me help you, I can fix your car.'

"So the first guy finally moved over to let the other man look at the engine. The man had it fixed in less than two minutes.

"'There you go, young man,' he said to the guy with the car. 'And by the way, let me introduce myself. I'm Henry Ford.'

"And that's a true story," John Mark said, and took another sip of coffee.

Joe was scowling at his plate.

"So," John Mark said, and looked at him when Joe finally raised his head. "Want some help?"

Joe looked back down, still scowling.

"You can make it through school, easy. All you have to do is let me help," John Mark said. "Hey, I went clear through college. Divinity school," he added as Joe looked up at him in disbelief. "I'm not making as much money as Vincent did with his business school degree, but I can help you with anything you run into in high school. You can be smart and get help and do it the easy way, or you can make it hard for yourself and not get help and be miserable." He took another sip of coffee. "Either way, you're in our family now, and in our family the kids go to school. But the dad helps, so it's not so hard."

Joe was quiet, but at least he was no longer scowling.

"Anything else?"

Joe sighed and shook his head.

"Well, there is one more thing," John Mark said. "What about Johnny?"

Joe blinked and then hastily looked away.

"You two have to get along," John Mark told him.

"We get along," Joe protested.

"Hmm?" John Mark looked at him and smiled, and Joe looked away again. "I don't mean just not fighting. I mean really get along. You're in our family now, so that means you have to be friends. You have to look at him and talk to him, like you do to Stephen. Otherwise both of you are going to be running around getting your feelings hurt all the time, and when someone in our family gets their feelings hurt, we need to do something about that."

Joe chewed on his bottom lip and studied the doughnut scraps as if they were fascinating.

"You're in my family now," John Mark went on. "I'm glad you're here. You're a little older, you know a little more. You do things to help out, like when you keep up with the furnace. You know more about fixing things than I do. I couldn't have fixed that eggbeater."

Joe glanced up at him, as if to see if he was joking.

"I'm serious. I couldn't have fixed it," he said again. "You know stuff that none of the rest of us knows."

"I'm not very good at school," Joe said to his plate.

"Then let me help you with your homework," John Mark said. "Besides, nobody's good at everything. Johnny's not good at fixing things. Me either." Joe grinned.

John Mark grinned too, then turned serious again. "Look, you got to do your best at whatever you're doing. I always do my best. That's how it works."

Joe settled back and pulled up one foot to rest on his knee. He looked out the window for a long time, and after a while he gave a slow nod.

John Mark finished the last of his coffee and looked up at the clock again. "Time to go, or I'll be late," he said. They scrambled out of the booth, paid the waiter, and headed for the door.

Once outside, John Mark remembered what Kate had said. He put his hand out to ruffle Joe's straight hair, and somehow ended up hugging him instead. Joe threw his arms around him and clutched him hard, and he could feel the boy's face pressed up against his coat and the ragged breaths tearing through his lanky frame. So he just held him for a while, silently patting his back, and the two of them stood there in the dark, until the sobs finally went away.

Four: February / *John Mark*

J ohn Mark gave his sleepy wife a last goodnight kiss and left the bedroom to get ready for work. To his surprise, the front room furnace was already stoked and set for the night. Joe turned over in the nest of bedding on the floor and looked up at him, to see if he noticed.

"Nice work on the furnace," John Mark said as he gathered his hat and lunchbox.

Joe nodded and pulled a quilt back over his head. The muffled words "See ya," drifted up from beneath the layers of blankets. John Mark grinned and said "Goodnight" to the shapeless bundle of boys sleeping on the floor, then turned off the lamp and headed out for the cold walk to work.

The thought of Joe's little gesture with the coal furnace kept him smiling for a while as he walked. The boy was coming around. He talked more, and sometimes, like tonight, he went ahead and did some little chore without being asked. Kate had been impressed with John Mark's account of finding Joe.

"I found him on 16th Avenue. On the bridge," he whispered to her later that night, sitting in the kitchen for a moment before he left for work. "I think he ran away and then had second thoughts. I took him out for a doughnut and he finally started talking to me. He thought it was his fault that Marie died."

"That poor boy," Kate had whispered back. "I wonder what he'd have done if you hadn't found him."

"I think he would've come back anyway," John Mark had said, although he, too, privately wondered what might have happened. "Kate, it was so amazing. I bet he'll start getting better now. Let's just give him lots of attention these next few days and see what happens."

"Johnny too," Kate reminded him.

So things were looking up. John Mark hummed an old Czech walking song as he headed down First Street toward the oat factory on the other side of the river. He tucked his chin deep into his scarf as he came closer to the river and the wind blasted him over the snow-swept ice. The terrible freeze that had clamped over the city during January was gone now, but even in February the nights were bitter cold. A familiar tingling started up in the tips of his ears. It had bothered him throughout the winter. Kate was afraid it was frostbite, and told him to keep his ears covered.

The winter seemed like the coldest one they'd had for years. They had intended to buy a bed for Joe, but the cold was so intense that they could hardly keep the house warm, and had to purchase extra coal and kerosene instead. Plus, they had to buy so many other things for Joe. Even though Josefina sewed shirts for him out of the piles of old fabric she kept in her room, and cut down some of John Mark's pants for him to wear, he needed things like shoes and underwear, and a coat and hat.

And the boys were always hungry. Kate added two extra bottles of milk to their weekly order from the milkman, but they still mysteriously ran out of milk every weekend. John Mark even considered going down to the court-house to apply for vouchers for food rations from the government, but he worked two jobs, and by most people's standards, they were not really poor. There were others who were far worse off. John Mark finally decided that they had never gone without food, and because of God in heaven they never would, so they didn't need to get the vouchers. And although potatoes and dumplings were sometimes the only food on the table, there had never been a day when there had been no food at all.

He checked his watch and walked faster. He could see other men walk-ing now, all of them moving fast to stay warm and get to work on time. A job at the oat factory was precious, and no worker wanted to be late and risk los-ing his position. Groups of unemployed men waited outside the doors when the shifts began, hoping to be called in to work if someone didn't show up. John Mark was always early for his shift.

The huge factory sat near the railroad bridge on the other side of the river. Even in the black winter night, the golden-orange glow from the red brick buildings cast a bright nimbus of light on the clouds above the factory and the frozen river below. The railways and streets around it were kept clear of snow so that the constant stream of trains and trucks could arrive unhin-dered by any weather. Men worked around the clock every day, hauling grain up into the towering white silos, or tending the clanking lines of machinery that turned raw oats into food and supplies for the rest of the world.

John Mark pushed his way with the other men into the freight elevator that carried them to the upper floors above the heavy machinery. Chains rumbled and wood creaked as they rose slowly up the shaft.

"Hey, Rev," someone said behind him. John Mark recognized the voice.

"Hey," he said over his shoulder. "Where you working tonight?"

"Furfural," the other man said. "I'm in with you guys. Think we'll get a full shift?" Sometimes, if work was slow, men were sent home early.

"I dunno," John Mark said noncommittally. He was a hard worker and had never been sent home before the end of a shift.

Two other men got off with him on the fifth floor, above the furfural vats. Their job was to haul hundred-and-fifty pound bags filled with oat husks to the hopper in the center of the floor and pour the husks into the huge vats below, where they were mixed and boiled into the specialized furfural solution that was eventually used for road pavement. The three men from the afternoon shift, covered with a thick layer of gray oat dust, nodded wearily at the night crew and left. John Mark and the other men stripped off their overcoats and laid them aside in order to start working before the foreman checked on them.

All three men grabbed the first bag of the night and poured husk and chaff down the hopper. A fine cloud of oat dust sifted through the air as they worked, settling in their clothes and hair and making them sneeze. The mixture below them boiled at three hundred and sixty degrees. In the summer the heat was almost unbearable, but in the winter it was only uncomfortably warm.

The work was routine, the same every night. The men pulled bags of husk from a pile stacked against a wall, dumped the contents down the shaft, then flung the empty bags into a bin with the other empties and went to haul the next bag over to the hopper. They hauled bags from the pile until the load was gone. The foreman's job was to make sure that another pile of bags was delivered to them before they were finished with the first. Unless some mechanical problem temporarily stopped the process below, they hauled bags of husk over to the hopper all night long. At thirty cents an hour, it was a very good job. John Mark knew other family men who worked at newspaper routes or shoveled snow for ten cents an hour.

A sudden grinding and clanging of gears, followed by the foreman's shout, signaled a halt in the process. All three men immediately sat down and leaned against the wall, wiping dust from their eyes and mouths.

"Say, Rev," one of them said, "where's your church?" The men who worked with John Mark always found out that he was a minister, because sooner or later they noticed that he didn't curse, and that he wouldn't drink bootleg liquor. Then they would either taunt him or ask questions, and the word would get around. When he first took the job, every day at the factory had been a trial, with men mocking him to his face and behind his back. But over the years the taunts had stopped and a rough respect had taken its place. He had a reputation now as a hard worker, an honest minister who would do a funeral service or a wedding for free, if people were too poor to pay.

John Mark rested on the splintery wood floor with the other two men, wiped oat chaff off his face, and talked about his church. It was not the largest one in town, but he was proud of his congregation. Although the weekly offering was now only one-tenth of what it had been back in the nineteen twenties, the attendance had grown, not diminished. Economic disaster brought in people who had not felt any need of help from God when money was plentiful. Some people even came over the bridge from the east side of town for Sunday service.

"So, you coming out this Sunday and hear me preach?" he asked when he was finished.

The man shifted his feet. "I gotta see what the wife says," he replied. "If you have a church like that, how come you're out here hauling husk?"

John Mark wiped off another thin layer of dust from his face for a moment, wishing he could just rest and not have to go back over the whole sad story of what had happened in 1930. "When the Crash hit, people mostly stopped giving money," he told the other man. "A guy paid off the building mortgage for us in back in twenty-seven, so we had the building, but he didn't pay off the rectory, so we lost that. I got evicted." The man looked at him with disbelief. John Mark nodded and went on. "I moved in with my brother."

"That happened to me too," the man said. "We're in with my wife's mother now."

"So people would show up day and night, kids with them, stuff packed in bags, nothing to eat, nowhere to go," John Mark continued. "We use most of the collection money for food now. But people keep showing up on Sunday, and I still want to be a minister, so I got a night job." He leaned back and stretched "Still here, four years later."

Thank God, too, he added to himself. When the news of the stock market crash had first reached them, no one in town was sure if a commotion like that, far away in New York, would really mean anything to them. But the answer became painfully clear all too soon. First, workers got cuts in pay. Next, hours were cut, from six days a week down to three or four. Businesses went bankrupt or laid off most of their workers. Before the year was out, people who had thought themselves secure were evicted from their homes and living in shanties or cars. John Mark had naïvely assumed that his job as a minister would protect him from trouble, but his salary disappeared along with his parishioners' paychecks, and when the church could no longer afford the monthly payment for the rectory, the landlord threw him out. It was only by God's grace that he had found a job — factories in Cedar Rapids managed to stay open because they processed mostly grains and meats — and that his family lived in a house today.

"Didn't you go to college, though?" This man was awfully energetic, John Mark thought, to be asking all these questions when he had a chance to rest. He looked over at him. All three of them looked like cartoon characters because of the dust and sweat on their faces. "Yeah, I went to college. Me and my brother both. That and a nickel will get you a cup of coffee these days."

His father, a work-hardened illiterate peasant worker from the old country, had been tremendously proud of the fact that his two sons attended college. John Mark remembered Vincent's graduation day. His father had hugged Vincent, pounded him on his back, and hauled him off to the neighborhood bar to celebrate. The first time Vincent dressed up in a suit to go to work at a bank, his father sat at the kitchen table and wept, undone by the realization of how far his family had come since he had left Bohemia in 1897.

His parents had not been as enthusiastic about his own choice of study, John Mark recalled wryly. They had hoped he would follow in Vincent's footsteps and study business or science, subjects which were more suitable for the new world in which they lived.

"What? Study for ministry?" his father had yelled in the old language. "*Jsi trouba!* You idiot!" What good will that do you here? Who do you think you are, Jan Huss? Look what happened to him!" Jan Huss was a Czech minister of medieval times, who preached in the common language instead of Latin and urged the faithful to seek Christ in the scriptures rather than in miraculous signs. He had become rector of the University of Prague and even influenced Martin Luther, but in the end he had been burned at the stake for his beliefs. The story was still common knowledge among the American Czech immigrants.

"Come on, Dad, this is what I really want to do. Nobody gets burned at the stake anymore," John Mark had argued back, trying to explain his idealistic calling to his pragmatic father.

In the end, they were each too stubborn to give in to the other. His father refused to pay for his schooling, although he had paid for Vincent's. Undeterred, John Mark applied for a scholarship from the Czech community's *Matice Vyssiho Vzdelani*, as the Council of Higher Education was called at that time, and paid for his own first year of college. His parents had eventually resigned themselves to his decision and helped pay for the rest of his schooling. They bragged about their sons' educations for the rest of their lives.

John Mark looked back at the dusty man beside him and grinned. "I'll tell you one thing I learned about oats from college," he said, and paused with unconscious comic timing, a habit for him now after so many years of preaching sermons. The two men looked at him, waiting to hear what he would say. "The English put in their dictionary that oats are something eaten by men in Scotland, but only good enough for horses in England. So the Scots came up with a dictionary that says eating oats is what caused England to have such good horses and Scotland to have such good men."

The other two laughed, then settled back into silence, leaving John Mark to his thoughts. Good thing his father hadn't lived to see these days, he reflected. The man had put his two sons through college, and now one of them worked in the furfural room of the oat factory and the other waited tables at the lunch café across the street from the bank where he used to work. A sad end for such a hopeful beginning, he thought, and leaned forward with his face in his hands.

A squeal of gears announced the machines starting up, and the foreman shouted at them to start dumping husk down the hopper again.

"C'mon, Rev, put that brain to work," the young man said, and they hauled husk as fast as they could for a while, until the vat was filled and they could ease off the pace. All three were coughing and spitting globs of dirt now, trying to keep their mouths closed against the dust.

John Mark kept thinking about Vincent as he dumped chaff down the hopper and wiped dust out of his eyes. Vincent had warned him and Karel about the problems with the banks, and all three men had pulled out their savings just before their bank closed in 1932. But Vincent had not foreseen that he would lose his own job. Stunned by the banking world's collapse, he sat in his front room for three months, hardly leaving the house. He pulled himself together and looked for work again only after Amalia threatened to go to work herself as a maid at the downtown hotel.

John Mark laughed at the thought, even all these years later. Amalia, a hotel maid! With her fine airs and manicured hands! He had never been sure if she had really meant to take that job or if she was just forcing Vincent out of his chair and back into life again. Vincent had gone out that same day and called in some favors from his old friends. He found a job at the Harmony Café, right across the street from the closed Cedar Rapids Savings Bank where he had worked before, and he was still working there now.

"What's so funny, Rev?" a voice called through the dust.

"I'm thinking about what I'm going to do with all my money!" John Mark called back. "I think I'll buy spats!"

He heard the other man hawk and spit. "Right," the voice called back. "Sure, you're in the money. I didn't think you preachers lied like that."

John Mark gave him a good-humored whack on the arm as he passed him on the next round, and then went back to his memories. Karel had probably been the least affected of the three of them, he thought. Buildings continued to break down and need repairs even during hard times, and Karel was an excellent carpenter. He was almost as strong as two regular men, and he used his sons as unpaid help on jobs. Because of that he could underbid most other carpenters and keep some work coming in. And, of course, he did not pay monthly rent because of his original agreement with Vincent. The only thing Karel had done differently after the Crash was to buy the fiercest guard dog he could find, because now his own and Vincent's life savings were hidden in cash at their homes.

The long night passed. The three men ate their lunches in shifts so that there were always two still working to keep the vats filled. When the day crew finally showed up, they sat down with relief for a moment to rest, then got up again, dusted off the worst of the chaff, and headed down to the company shower to clean up before going home.

"Hey, Rev," John Mark heard again as he stood, eyes closed, in the steamy shower room with the rest of the men, washing dirt out of his hair and ears and thinking about the long walk home. He ached all over. Furfural was really a young man's job. Perhaps he could get a ride.

"Rev."

"Yeah?" John Mark was getting tired of hearing that word.

"Can you give me a ride home?"

John Mark kept his eyes closed. "I don't have a car. I was going to ask you for a ride." He heard the other man laugh.

Maybe if I pray, someone will drive me home, John Mark thought. It sure worked good the other night. Dear God . . . .

"Well, if I get a ride I'll pick you up too," the other man said.

They finished their showers and left for home, moving slowly in their fatigue. The other men from the furfural crew headed east and north, away from John Mark's direction, and he looked around hopefully for a car going his way. No one came by, though. Most men were walking. A few cars pulled out, but none that he recognized. He stared in disappointment at the departing cars. He was going to have to walk home.

Lord . . . what about that prayer? He sighed in frustration, and finally started walking.

He reasoned with himself as he crossed the street. God didn't always answer every one of his prayers exactly like he wanted. *That would be too easy, huh, God,* he thought as he walked along. *If it was that easy, everyone would be a rip-roaring Christian, and then You wouldn't know for sure who really loved You and who just wanted prayers answered.* Well then, if the Lord wasn't going to answer all of his prayers right away every single time, this wasn't such a bad one to not get answered. There were other things he was praying about that were more important. At least the morning was calm and clear, without the freezing wind from the night before. He raised his head to watch the first rays of sun color the clouds in the morning sky, and started back over the bridge toward home.

The sweet scent of fresh bakery met him as he opened the front door. He hung up his coat and pulled off his overshoes. The boys were already dressed and in the kitchen, and John Mark joined them, finding Kate scrambling eggs at the stove. He gave her a hug and a kiss on the cheek before he sat down at the table. Johnny poured him a cup of coffee.

"How was work?" Kate asked.

"Fine." He yawned. "Sure smells good in here. What's for breakfast?"

"*Babovka,*" Kate said. John Mark looked over at Johnny and grinned. They both loved the sweet poppyseed breakfast loaf. This was going to be a good meal.

The boys milled about the kitchen, impatient for the eggs to finish cooking. Even Josefina was watching from her chair. When Kate finally brought the steaming bowl to the table, John Mark said a short prayer and let the meal begin. He let the boys pass the *babovka* around and take as much as they wanted, but he served out the eggs himself.

For a while, the room was silent as everyone ate. John Mark looked over at Stephen, who was shoveling eggs into his mouth and then crowding *babovka* in behind them. His cheeks were pink and his hair damp from the morning's wash. Joe and Johnny also had clean faces and freshly combed hair. All the boys were dressed in their good flannel shirts and corduroy trousers for school. Everything was set for the day.

"Kate, honey, pass me your Bible," John Mark said. They had finished the Gospel of Luke and the Acts of the Apostles. They were going through Romans now, but slowly, because he liked to stop and ask the boys questions after he read and find out what they were thinking. He read from chapter eight for a while and stopped after verse twenty-eight.

"So, what does it mean that all things work together for good to them that love God?" He sat back, sipped his coffee, and let the question hang in the air for a while. Usually Johnny or Stephen would offer a thought, even if only to win his approval. If the boys couldn't come up with anything, Kate would take pity on him after a while and say something.

"God has a reason for everything," Johnny announced through a mouthful of eggs.

"That's one thing," John Mark agreed.

"Don't talk with your mouth full," Kate said.

"What else?" John Mark said. There was silence for a while. Then Kate and Stephen both started to say something at the same time. Kate stopped and let Stephen talk.

"God loves us," he chirped in his fluty little-boy voice.

"That too," John Mark said. "Put those two together and what do you get?"

Silence reigned. John Mark stole a peek at Joe, wondering if he would ever say anything during these conversations. The boy's eyes were glued to his plate. Evidently not today.

"Even when it looks like bad things are happening, God's working it out to help us somehow?" Johnny offered after a while.

"That's right," John Mark said. "Now, usually you have a problem during the day. When your problem comes up today, remember this verse, and keep on going. God works it all out for your good in the end, even though you might not see it at the beginning." Josefina snorted with contempt at his words, but John Mark ignored her. "Good job, boys. Let's say prayers now."

After prayers, the boys left for school and Josefina cleared the dishes while Kate got ready for work. "John Mark, did you get a chance to talk to Vincent about driving us to the dance tonight?" she asked. "If it snows again, I don't want to walk in my good shoes."

"Yes, he'll drive you and Ruzina and Rose in the car," John Mark said after a moment. He was tired, and Kate's voice had seemed to come from far away. "We'll probably send Stephen with you too. I'll walk with Karel and the boys." On a dance night, whole families went to the community hall on the other side of the 16th Avenue bridge, and the boys were looking forward to going out as much as Kate. John Mark liked going to dances too, but right now all he wanted to do was close his eyes and sleep.

"Alice Svoboda wants to talk to you tonight," Kate was saying. He pulled his eyes back open and frowned.

"Is it about her husband again?" he asked. Kate nodded.

"If you see her coming, don't leave," John Mark said. "Won't she talk to you instead?"

"Oh, no, she only wants to see the Great One," Kate teased. "Only you will do."

"I'm serious, Kate. If you see her coming, don't leave," John Mark said again. "Can she come over to the house instead, maybe tomorrow when we're both home?"

"I'll try." Kate had put on her coat and hat, and was standing at the kitchen door now, pulling on her gloves. She was quiet for a moment, and he knew she was looking at him. "You're going to sleep now, right?"

"Yeah," he said, and yawned. "I'll shave tonight before we go."

"All right then," Kate said, and kissed him goodbye on his scratchy cheek. "See you when I get home."

Someone was shaking his arm. John Mark tried to keep his eyes closed, hoping that it was a bad dream that would go away, but the person kept shaking him. He finally dragged himself out of a deep well of sleep and opened his eyes, squinting against the sunlight that someone had let into the room.

Josefina was leaning over him. John Mark blinked, trying to wake up.

"*Probuž! Probuž!* Get up!" she yelled. "*Záchod přetýká!* The toilet broke and water is all over! Hurry!"

John Mark groaned. He pushed himself up on one elbow and nodded. "*Dobrý, Dobrý, pani Vesely,*" he told her. "All right, all right, Mrs. Vesely. I'm getting up." She left the bedroom and he hauled himself out of bed and pulled on his work pants to go look at the problem.

The toilet was old. He should have replaced it, but he had been so busy . . . He looked in the kitchen and groaned. Water was gushing from the tank, and both the bathroom and kitchen floors were flooded. Josefina was trying to dam up the water with towels in order to keep it from going into the front room.

What to do . . . John Mark stepped gingerly into the bathroom and turned off the water supply valve; at least that was a start. The water stopped running. Josefina brought in the mop and bucket, and for a while they both worked to get the water up off the floor as fast as possible. After they had soaked up the worst of it, Josefina sat down on a kitchen chair and looked at him expectantly.

John Mark frowned and wondered what to do. The toilet was the old kind, with a wooden tank placed up high on the wall, six feet above the toilet bowl itself, and connected to it by a long brass pipe. He really needed a ladder to see what was going on, but a chair would do. He dragged one over and stood on it to see the problem.

The tank was cracked. It would have to be replaced. John Mark climbed down slowly from the chair, and then sat on it while he thought. Maybe the hardware store would have a tank. But the toilet was so old, a replacement might be hard to find. Did they even sell these kinds of tanks anymore? How long could they go without a toilet?

Well, he would have to start work on the problem right now if they were going to have a working toilet again today. Maybe he should remove the tank for a start. It wasn't going to magically fix itself. John Mark went to the cellar for his old canvas tool bag, and when he came back up he found Joe standing in the bathroom doorway, looking at the mess on the floor.

I knew it, John Mark thought. *He's skipping school. Doggone it, I knew this boy would be up to no good.*

"What are you doing home?" he asked. Joe jumped and turned around.

"Uh, I'm sick," he said, with a guilty little glance.

John Mark decided he was too tired to argue about it. "Do you know anything about toilets?" he asked.

"Some," Joe said. "What's wrong?"

"Tank's cracked."

Joe hopped up on the chair. He was not as tall as John Mark but he could see where the crack was and where the fittings connected the valve to the tank. "We have to take this off," he said. "Do you have a candle and some pliers?"

"I have pliers," John Mark said. "What's the candle for?"

"You got to warm up the nuts before you can get them off," Joe told him. "Brass is like that when it's old."

"Oh," John Mark said, and went to find a candle.

Joe worked on the fittings, warming them gently with the candle and then slowly turning them loose. John Mark handed him tools and helped him pull the tank off the wall. Clumps of dank black grime came with it, spreading over their hands and everything they touched as they wrestled the heavy oak tank down to the floor. They sat down, sweating and panting, and looked at the grey spot on the wall where the tank had been for so long.

"What's next?" John Mark asked.

Joe shrugged. "Got to get a new one," he said. "Put it on."

John Mark looked at him. "How come you know so much about plumbing?"

Joe's gaze drifted past him, out to the kitchen beyond. He didn't answer right away. "Oh, one of . . . my mom's friends . . . used to take me with him on jobs," he said after a while. He seemed to be looking at something. John Mark looked out to see what it was, but there was nothing in the kitchen, just the table and chairs, as always.

He glanced back around as Joe suddenly gasped and bent over, one hand covering his mouth. He made for the toilet bowl as if to throw up, but recovered himself halfway there and sat back down, breathing hard. He closed his eyes and doubled over, arms crossed over his stomach.

"Joe?" John Mark moved over to him and put a hand on his back. It was damp with sweat. "You need to throw up?" He felt guilty for doubting the boy earlier.

Joe shook his head. "What's the matter then?" John Mark asked.

"Oh . . . I'm just . . . sick," Joe said. John Mark sat back in puzzlement. What on earth could he say to that?

"Want a glass of water?" Joe shook his head. Something about the way his shoulders moved looked like he was holding back tears.

John Mark sighed and leaned back against the wall, looking at the toilet tank, the grimy floor, and the crying boy. He knew that he should do something about each one of those problems, but for the moment he just leaned his head back and closed his eyes, feeling himself drifting . . . he jerked his head back up and looked around. Joe was sitting up now, eyes red, still looking out into the kitchen as if he could see something there.

"Joe."

The boy started and looked over at him.

"You all right?" He nodded.

"We got to get this tank replaced," John Mark said.

"Be hard to get one like it," Joe told him.

Especially if it's expensive, John Mark thought, but all he said was, "Let's go over to Vincent's. Maybe we can use his car."

Vincent was not home, but John Mark went to the Prazskys' house, ignoring the dog that was barking itself into hysterics, and knocked on the door. Karel came out. The two men talked for a while, and then Karel went to fetch the key to the car, and John Mark called Joe to help shovel out the entrance to the garage.

"Where do you want to go?" Karel asked, once they were on their way.

"Let's go to the Avenue hardware store first," John Mark said after a while. When they got there, the manager told them that he no longer carried that model of tank, and referred them to another store.

They piled back into the car and headed down the road again. Karel was shaking his head as he drove.

"I know, I know," John Mark said with a touch of irritation. "I should buy a new style tank."

"Well, yes," Karel said. John Mark looked out the window in despair. Payday was not until next week.

"Uncle John, remember your Bible verse this morning?" came Joe's voice from the back seat. "God works out problems so things are better than before?"

Karel snorted. "If there is a God, you mean," he said. "If there isn't, looks like I'll have to buy you a toilet today."

John Mark pulled himself up from where he had slumped against the seat. *Be strong now*, he told himself. "This world didn't get here by accident," he said. "There's a God. Let's just see what happens." *Not much of a defense*, he thought miserably, but that seemed to be all he could come up with at the moment.

God, why are You doing this to me? he pleaded silently. *I don't have even a dollar to spend, and here I am, trying to buy a toilet part that nobody carries anymore, and I'm sitting in a borrowed car with a Freethinker and a . . . a boy I can't figure out for the life of me. Have I made You mad or something?* John Mark caught himself before he went too far down that line of thought. No, it was just that the toilet was broken. That was all. The Lord never promised that things wouldn't go wrong once in a while.

"I think God should take better care of you, seeing as how you work for Him and all," Karel pointed out.

"There's lots of things I don't understand, but that doesn't mean there's not a God," John Mark said stubbornly. Thankfully, the second hardware store was in sight. "There's the store." He was grateful to get out of the car and away from the argument. He didn't feel like he was holding up his end very well.

They came back out of the store no better off than before. Only new toilets were for sale, no old models. Karel pulled out his pipe and filled it with elaborate patience, plainly waiting for John Mark to decide what to do.

"I know a place," Joe said.

John Mark looked over at him. "What kind of place?"

"Where they have lots of old parts."

"Where is it?"

Joe frowned. "Over by where I used to live," he finally said.

John Mark looked at him, thinking. The policeman who had brought Joe to the house last November had told him about the shanty camp where he had been found. It was across town, but they had enough gas to get there.

"You want to go?" he asked Karel.

The big man took a long pull on his pipe and grinned. "Sure," he said.

"Here it is," Joe finally said, and Karel stopped in front of a rickety garage on the northeast side of town. The boy jumped out of the car and went in. The two men followed, a little more slowly. The store was dark inside, filled with barrels of greasy machine parts and piles of scrap metal and old rope. Joe had already threaded his way through the junk to the back of the room, and John Mark could hear him talking to someone.

A wrinkled old man dressed in incredibly dirty overalls greeted John Mark and Karel from a chair in the back of the store. Joe was standing just behind him, peering into an even darker room farther back in the building.

"Heh, heh, heh," the old man chuckled, shooting a glance at John Mark as he laughed. "Looking for a washdown tank? Not much call for those these days."

"Yes sir, we are," John Mark said, hoping that the old man was all right in the head.

The man showed no sign of getting up to find a tank. He peered at John Mark in the dim light, looking him up and down. "So this little fella's living with you now," he said after a while. "Feeding him good?"

"We're trying," John Mark replied, warming to the old man a bit. "Hard to keep up with him."

"Well, well. Looks like he's grown, anyway," the old man said, and got up to shuffle into the back room. Joe was already inside, and the two of them clanked and thumped in the dark. John Mark and Karel looked at each other, then looked around. Dirt covered every surface in the store. Loops of oily chain and buckets of rusty hardware hung on the walls. A rat scampered across the filthy floor and disappeared under a table.

The old man came out, shaking his head. He shot another glance at John Mark. "I dunno. I thought I had one. Well, let's look some more," he said, and led them out the shop's back door. A pile of discarded sinks and toilet parts sat there, covered with snow.

"Here's one!" Joe called. He pulled out a snow-covered lump that turned out to be, indeed, a washdown tank. John Mark and Karel hurried over to look at it. John Mark's heart sank when he saw a long crack down the side, almost exactly where his own tank was cracked.

"Hmm, yeah, that's what happens to 'em," the old man said, poking at it with his shoe and pushing it back into the pile. "You don't want that one." John Mark wondered why anybody would bother to keep a worthless toilet tank that would do no one any good.

"Here's another one," said Joe from the other side of the pile where he was rooting around in the junk. John Mark went over and crouched down to see what Joe was pulling out. It was not a washdown tank. It was a brand new china tank, the close-coupled type that most bathrooms had now.

"That's not the kind we're looking for," John Mark said.

"No, no, the boy knows. That'll fit what you've got," the old man said comfortably. "You just need the part that connects 'em. And then you need to change out the water pipe and the washdown valve." He winked at John Mark. "Good amount of brass there when you take it all down. Junk it for a pretty penny when you're done."

John Mark looked at Karel. The big man shrugged and nodded after a moment. "We could do that," he said.

John Mark stood up. He felt very uncomfortable now that he had to ask the price. He had less than a dollar in his wallet, he was still unshaven from the night before, and he was covered with black grime from the toilet. *I guess I fit right in here though,* he thought. *Maybe the guy will go easy on me.*

"My uncle's a minister," Joe said to the old man.

Oh, no, John Mark thought. *No, Joe, not now. This guy's gonna think you're lying. Or else bump up the price.*

"Are you, then," the old man said.

"Um, yes," John Mark said. "Ah, how much for the tank?"

The old man turned around as if to go back inside, then stopped and scratched his head. "Oh, just take it," he finally said. "And if this young fella," he pointed to Joe, "can find the connector, take that too. Nice to do something for a man of the cloth. Don't see them out this way too much." He shuffled back inside the building.

John Mark gaped after him. A free toilet! *Lord, you have done it again. Took care of the problem and taught me a lesson, all at the same time.* He looked over at Karel. They both looked at Joe. The boy nodded, as if to say "See?" and then turned back to root through the pile of parts, looking for the connecting piece.

"Well, let's load up," Karel said after a moment. John Mark helped him put the tank into the back of the car. Joe gave up looking for the connector in the outdoor junk pile and went inside the garage again. John Mark followed him in and found the old man watching Joe as the boy rummaged through buckets of parts.

"Thank you," John Mark said. He pulled fifty cents from his wallet and laid the coins on the counter.

"Naw, naw. Keep your money," the old man said. "Look in that next one, son," he called out to Joe. The boy moved over to the next pile of junk and came up with a part. "There you go." He winked at John Mark. "Now you boys go on. Can't keep the missus without a crapper."

John Mark and Joe burst out laughing. Kate, without a . . . ! They waved at the old man and left, still laughing.

"What's so funny?" Karel asked when they got into the car.

Joe started to explain. "He said . . ." and soon Karel was laughing too.

By the time they were near the bridge and their own part of town again, John Mark had nodded off more than once. He shook himself awake and looked over at Karel.

"Thanks for coming," he said. "Can I buy you a beer?"

"Sure," Karel replied. He pulled up to the Little Bohemia bar and turned off the engine, but John Mark didn't move.

"You gonna sit here in the car all day, or you gonna come in and buy one for yourself too?" Karel finally asked.

"If I drink a beer now, you're going to have to put in that tank by yourself," John Mark yawned, "because I'll go to sleep."

"Ah, well, I have the master plumber here to help me," Karel said with a glance toward Joe. "Let's go in."

John Mark was sleeping . . . he was sleeping . . . someone was sitting on the bed beside him, and it wasn't Kate. He opened his eyes with a start, wondering who it was. Johnny sat there, watching him.

"Hi, Dad," he said. "It's five o'clock."

John Mark closed his eyes again, sinking back into slumber. He felt as if he had just lain down a minute ago.

Johnny shook his shoulder. "Mom says it's time to get up and eat so we can go to the dance."

Eyes still closed, John Mark rolled onto his back and flung his arm across his face. He gave a yawn that turned into a groan. After a minute he put down his arm, opened his eyes, and looked around. Johnny was still there, looking at him.

"Are you tired, Dad?"

Was he tired. Oh . . . could they all just stay home tonight, or could the rest of the family go without him? John Mark grimaced a little as he thought. No, and no. Everybody needed a little fun, and they all wanted to go to the dance. Kate would not go without him. They had been looking forward to it all week.

He heaved another groan and looked up at the ceiling for a moment. *Oh, dear Lord, help me,* he began, and then stopped and laughed at himself. He was going to a dance, not facing some terrible problem. Things could be worse. Taking his wife out for some fun was a lot better than, say, being burned at the stake, like poor old Jan Huss. He would feel better once he got going.

"Johnny . . ." He looked over at his son, still watching him, now with a worried frown. John Mark reached over and patted his leg. "Can you go heat some water for my shave? And make a half a pot of coffee? Then come back and get me when it's ready?"

"All right," Johnny said. John Mark was asleep again before Johnny got off the bed.

In what seemed like only seconds later, Johnny brought him a cup of coffee and a peanut butter sandwich. He sat up and ate and drank for a while, slowly waking up, while Johnny sat companionably beside him on the bed. John Mark shared the last part of the sandwich with his son and then swung his legs to the floor.

"Come on in with me," he invited, and Johnny came into the bathroom and sat on the closed lid of the toilet, a little awkwardly because he wasn't used to the tank being so close to the bowl. John Mark flicked a little spray of water on him to make him smile. "So, how 'bout the new toilet?" he asked.

"It's great. It's like all my friends' toilets now," Johnny said. "What about the wall?" The place where the old high tank had been was now a dirty gray blotch.

John Mark tried to yawn and shave at the same time. He had to stop and finish first one job, then the other, before he could talk again. "Oh, we'll do something," he said vaguely. "Maybe Mom can hang a picture up there."

"My friend's mom put up a cabinet there when they got their new toilet," Johnny told him.

"We could do that," John Mark said agreeably.

"Maybe we can get a telephone next?" Johnny asked.

"I don't think so," John Mark started on his other cheek. "Joe needs a bed first."

"Right," Johnny said quickly, then put his head down.

John Mark glanced over at him. "How's school going?"

"Fine," Johnny said. "I got an A on my math test."

"That's great," John Mark said. "That's the way to go. You're better in math than I was at your age."

"Joe skipped today," Johnny said. John Mark looked down at him again.

"I think he was sick," he said tentatively, and glanced at the door to make sure it was closed all the way. "He came home early and he did seem sick to his stomach."

"I think he just skipped school," Johnny said.

"Johnny, you don't know that," John Mark said.

"If that'd been me, you would've been mad," Johnny went on.

"Not if you were really sick," John Mark pointed out.

"You know what I mean," Johnny persisted.

John Mark sighed and sat down on the edge of the bathtub, drying his face with a towel. "I think that what you think is that I . . . you think he gets away with stuff I wouldn't let you get away with. Is that what you mean?" he asked.

Johnny nodded and looked down. "Well, yeah. Like smoking."

John Mark looked at him for a moment. "I'll tell you, *Jan,* I don't always know what to do about him either. But don't you think he's better now, though, than he was when he first got here?"

Johnny's head hung a little lower. He sighed. "Yeah."

"And don't you think that he's had a lot harder time than us, trying to get over his mom dying and all that?"

Johnny sighed louder. "Yeah."

"So, I want you to be patient with him. I'll talk to him," John Mark raised his hand when Johnny started talking again, "about the smoking. I think we need to not jump all over him about everything right now. Just let him get better for a while. Everything's going to work out for the best."

Johnny heaved a huge sigh. "You always say the same thing."

"It's always true," John Mark told him.

Vincent, dressed in his best suit, walked into the kitchen later that evening just as they finished supper. "The family taxi is ready to take Mrs. Starosta to the dance," he said. "Where's this free toilet everyone's talking about?"

"It's a beaut," John Mark said. He had finished a second cup of coffee and was feeling better. "Joe found it and Karel put it in. *Mockrát děkuji* for letting us use the car, *bratr.*"

"*Rádo se stalo*," Vincent replied, from the bathroom where he was inspecting the new tank. "What'd you do with all the brass?"

"Karel's going to sell it tomorrow," John Mark told him. "I'm giving him half of whatever he gets, for helping."

Anton came into the kitchen and leaned against the doorjamb.

"Annie!" Stephen yelled, and ran to him for a hug.

Anton picked him up, hugged him, and turned him upside down. "Don't you dare call me that at the dance tonight, *chlapecký*, you little troublemaker," he said. Stephen squealed with joy at the attention.

"Anton, he just ate. Put him down," Kate said.

John Mark watched Anton set Stephen on his feet and swat him lightly on the behind. His nephew looked like he had just washed and shaved, and he was wearing a new sweater that made his eyes look very blue. John Mark knew that Karel's two sons insisted on washing and shaving before they went out to a dance, steaming up the whole little house with their demands for hot water. Even eleven-year-old Rose was dressing up on dance nights now. He looked back over at Joe and Johnny, still sitting at the table in their school clothes. It would be a few more years before those two started dressing up for a dance, if he was lucky.

"Well, Kate, are we ready to go?" he asked.

"Let me drive you and the boys over first, then come back for the ladies," Vincent said. The dance was on the other side of the bridge, which was a fairly long walk. "We don't want to take them first and leave them without escorts at the dance." He winked at Kate. "Too many good-looking young guys out there. We can't handle the competition like we used to."

Kate finished pinning her mother's garnet brooch to her best dress, made of burgundy velveteen and trimmed with lace at the neckline and sleeves. She arched an eyebrow at Vincent. "That's right," she told him. "Hurry up, then. I'm ready to go."

A burst of voices and polka music met John Mark and the boys as they walked into the auditorium of the old brick C.S.P.S. Hall, named for the Czech-American benevolence society that had built it in the 1890s. On most nights, men's and women's social groups met in the lodge rooms, or theatrical groups used the stage to rehearse their plays. Tonight the chairs were cleared out of the auditorium and a band was playing. Couples were already circling around the floor.

John Mark led the boys to the dining area by the bar, where they could hold a table for Kate and Ruzina, but Stephen wanted to go and play with the flock of little boys running up and down the balconies on the upper level of the hall. Johnny looked around at all the dancing couples for a moment, and then threw a bashful look at John Mark and headed upstairs as well. Anton and Joe sat down at the table, but got up again when John Mark gave them a quarter and told them to go buy root beers at the pass-through window to the bar. Women and children generally did not go into the barroom, which was a long, smoky space packed with men ordering beer at a fifty-foot-long wooden bar, but there was an open window from the bar to the dining area, and drinks could be ordered there by anyone who could pay. Anton and Joe, at their age, could have worked their way into the bar for their root beers, but they went to the window for now. The night was just beginning.

Karel and his sons joined them, along with some of their neighbors. The men bought beer and pulled tables together for the group. Vincent finally showed up with Kate, Ruzina, and Rose, and as soon as everyone was settled, John Mark pulled Kate out to dance.

The band was played a set of waltzes and polkas. John Mark danced with Kate for a while, then traded off with Vincent and partnered Ruzina for the rest of the set. Unmarried men and women clustered in groups on opposite sides of the room, and pairs or threesomes of bachelors would make the trip across the floor and invite the women to dance. The band finally took a break and everyone sat down to catch their breath and have a drink. When the music started up again, Kate pulled Anton out to dance and Karel took Ruzina's hand, so John Mark invited Rose.

"Rosie, you're almost as tall as Kate," he said as he guided her around the floor. "Who's been teaching you to dance?"

"I practice with Mom at home," she said. "Or Wence, if he lets me."

John Mark led her through a little twirl. "Very nice," he said. "Did you sew this nice dress yourself? Your dad is going to have to fight off the boys with a baseball bat when you grow up." Rose looked almost grown up right now, in her flowered dress and black shoes with ankle straps.

"He already does," Rose giggled. "I'm not allowed to dance with anyone who's not married." John Mark laughed and twirled her again.

The band was playing a set of American tunes now and the music was slow. John Mark caught sight of Wence Prazsky on the dance floor, not far from them.

"Who's Wence dancing with?" he asked Rose.

"Rachel Sedlak," she said. "She's not supposed to be here."

John Mark looked back at Wence. He was smiling down at a young woman with brown eyes and smooth brown hair, softly singing the tender words of the song to her as they danced.

Don't know why, there's no sun up in the sky,
Stormy weather, when my gal and I ain't together,
Keeps raining all the time . . .

"Why isn't she supposed to be here?" he asked Rose. "Aren't her parents with her?"

"She doesn't live with her parents. She lives with her grandparents. They run the Otis Street grocery store by St. Wencelaus's church, and they don't like Freethinkers," Rose said. "They don't even like the C.S.P.S.. Hall, because the Freethinkers meet here."

"What happened to her parents?" John Mark asked after a while. Rose shrugged.

"I don't know. I think her mom left, or something."

John Mark looked at the girl again, then back at Rose.

"How come you know all this stuff?"

"Her sister's in my class," she said with a confidential grin.

John Mark glanced back at Wence just in time to see him pull Rachel deeper into the circle of his arms. He was still singing to her, more quietly now, because their heads were so close together.

Can't go on, everything I had is gone,
Stormy weather, since my girl and I ain't together . . .

John Mark led Rose into a turn that brought him alongside the younger couple. If they kept on dancing that closely, the gossip about Rachel would get back to the Otis Street grocery store before she did.

"Not so close there, you two," he warned, with a grin to take the sting out of his words. "Gotta watch out for this guy," he teased Rachel, with another smile. "Let me know if he gets out of hand."

"Aw, Uncle John, go on," Wence groaned. Rachel smiled shyly at him, and they pulled away from each other, but only a little.

When the song ended, John Mark escorted Rose back to the table and looked around for Kate. She was dancing with Vincent. John Mark sat down and realized how good it felt to be off his feet. All of a sudden the little wooden chair seemed marvelously comfortable. He tipped his head back against the wall and closed his eyes for a moment.

Stephen and Johnny roused him, just as he was drifting off, when they ran down the stairs from the balcony and surrounded him, one on each side. They were flushed and panting. "Can we have some root beer, Dad?" they begged. John Mark dug his other quarter out of his wallet and gave it to them. "Bring me change," he called as they dashed to the pass-through window and lined up with all the other youngsters waiting to buy drinks.

He looked around. Joe was sitting at the table with a smile and a bottle of cream soda in front of him.

"Hey, where'd that come from?" John Mark asked.

Joe nodded at Rose, who sat at the other end of the table, talking with a cluster of schoolgirls.

"Rose bought you a cream soda?" Joe nodded again and grinned.

John Mark almost laughed. What was Rose up to? Talk about young ladies looking for trouble! He didn't need to look any further than his own table tonight.

Joe sat with his soda, watching the dancers and tapping one foot to the music. John Mark shook his head. The boy must have a gift for getting things for free. Like the toilet tank. He wondered foggily how long it had been since they had fixed the toilet. It seemed like a long time ago, but it had been only this afternoon. Was that possible? John Mark blinked hard and came back from his wandering thoughts to the present.

Johnny and Stephen returned with their bottles of root beer and put the change down on the table before heading back up the stairs. Rose glanced over at Joe and smiled. Joe grinned back. The girls all giggled, expecting Joe to invite Rose to dance, but then Joe lost his smile, looked away, and left the table to join the other boys upstairs.

John Mark blinked. Joe's face had looked so much older for a moment . . . old and sad, as if Rose's flirtatious glance had awakened some past grief. What on earth had happened to the boy, to make him look like that? He sat at the table and thought about it for a while, wondering.

Vincent came in from the dance floor and sat down. John Mark looked around for Kate.

"She's over there," Vincent said. John Mark could see her now, talking with a group of people on the other side of the room.

"Come on, let's get a beer," Vincent said, and pulled John Mark into the bar. The smoky room was full of men shouting into each other's ears. The brothers pushed their way through the crowd and ended up in line behind the band's accordion player and cornet player, who were both at the bar buying beer.

"Bernie Drahozal! What are you doing in here?" Vincent yelled at the accordion player. "Aren't you supposed to be playing?"

"Naw! We found some kids to play for us! Gotta take a break!" he shouted back. People would dance past midnight and on into the morning, as long as the accordion played.

"Who you buying all that beer for, Bernie?" John Mark shouted.

"I'm going to dance with Barbara Barta tonight if it's the last thing I do," the accordion player yelled back. He picked up two mugs and headed for the dance floor. "Hey, Starosta! Your boy's playing this set for me!"

Vincent and John Mark both glanced over at the band on the stage. Anton was playing accordion and his friend Robert Stastny was playing cornet. Both boys looked out of place in the group of older men, and the other players were laughing, joking with Anton as he played, because he was not nearly as good on the accordion as Bernie. He kept up with the beat, though, and finished the song with a decent musical flourish and a grin. John Mark smiled and looked over at Vincent.

Vincent was trying to hide his pleasure. He cleared his throat, then frowned and shook his head. "What's he doing up there? He's terrible on the accordion, terrible. And look at his hair. I gave him fifteen cents to get his hair cut today and he went and forgot all about it."

"Right," John Mark agreed. "We better trade right now. It'll take me two or three years but I think I can straighten him out." He smacked Vincent good-humoredly on the side of his head and almost made him spill his beer.

"Hmmf," was all Vincent said, but he smiled.

Men were still arguing all around them in the bar, condemning the devaluation of the dollar and talking about the danger that Germany was becoming to Bohemia. The shouting would get louder as the men drank more, and there would probably be a fight outside before the night was over. John Mark left the bar and looked around for Kate. He finally saw her at a table across the room, chatting with a group of women.

Kate was easily the most beautiful girl at the dance, he thought. He watched her as she smiled and laughed. Her hair was done up in a French twist, but little strands were coming loose around her face, and she was wearing the garnet earrings and necklace that he had given her years ago for a Christmas present.

He drained his mug and set it down. The band wouldn't play forever, and he wanted to dance with his wife. Unlike Wence, he was a married man and did not have to worry about gossip, so he headed straight over to the table and took Kate's hand, ignoring the amused looks from the other women, and led her out to the floor. The band was playing a lovely slow tune from the old country. He drew Kate in close to him and put his head down to her hair, breathing in her special scent. *Rejoice with the wife of thy youth*, the Lord said. He would do that tonight. He pulled Kate even closer, and felt her laughing in his arms.

Five: March / *Kate and Marie*

Kate started every day early. She lit the kitchen stove and put the coffee on, then lit the bathroom water heater before she made the boys' lunches for school. She liked to take her own morning wash before the rest of the household woke up. The coffee was ready by the time she was dressed, and then she had a few minutes to read her Bible and pray. She needed that time with the Lord before her mother came in.

All too soon, she heard Josefina stirring in her bedroom. Her mother shuffled into the kitchen and headed to the bathroom.

"*Dobré jitro, Matko,*" Kate said pleasantly. Good morning, mother.

"*Dobré jitro,*" Josefina replied as she closed the door. Kate put away her Bible and went to wake the boys. Now that March was here and the nights were not so cold, Johnny and Stephen had gone back to sleeping upstairs, but Joe was still sleeping in the front room. That was going to change soon. Joe needed a real bed of his own, just like the other boys, and besides, she was tired of having a teenage boy sleeping six feet from her bedroom door.

Back in the kitchen, Josefina sat at the table, stirring sugar into her coffee. Kate pulled out the oatmeal bin and started making breakfast.

"If that husband of yours had proper work like his brother instead of being a fool-headed minister, he'd be here to light that stove for you," Josefina said in Czech, as she did almost every morning.

"Mother, that job is a blessing from God. John works hard to put food on the table and you should be grateful," Kate replied in the same language. "I don't mind lighting the stove." She refrained from adding that Josefina herself had lit a kitchen stove almost every morning of her life, until she moved in with them after Kate's father died. Josefina was old and didn't take well to smart remarks.

"That's why those boys are so lazy," Josefina continued after a while. "They see their father sleeping all day like a lazy good-for-nothing. They're growing up just like him. When I was their age I was working a full day on the farm, not sitting around the house and getting into trouble."

"That's not true, *Matko,*" Kate said. She had decided long ago to be as firm as possible with Josefina while still being respectful. "John Mark is a good provider and a wonderful father. He works very hard and we all know it. Stop talking bad about him. The boys go to school and do chores. Times are different now."

"Hmmf," her mother sniffed. Kate sliced bread for toast and set out jam and milk as the sky grew light outdoors. Johnny and Stephen came thumping down the stairs.

"*Dobré jitro*, Mrs. Vesely," they said together as they passed her on their way to the bathroom. Josefina ignored them. Kate went into the chilly front room again to shake Joe's shoulder and get him up and about. She glanced out at the sky. John Mark would be home soon, and she liked to have all the boys finished in the bathroom by the time he arrived.

"Mommy?"

Kate looked around. Stephen, still in pajamas, had followed her into the front room.

"Go back and wash your face," Kate told him.

"Mommy, there's no soap."

"Stephen, you know right where the soap is. Go get it and wash your face, now, before your father comes home." Kate bent down to clean out last night's ashes from the furnace and stir up a bit of warmth from the fire before it went out for the day.

Stephen started to cry. "Mommy, there's a big spider in there."

Kate shook her head absently, trying to push the leftover coal into just the right kind of pile to make it burn a little longer. "I can't come right now. Ask Johnny to get it."

Joe swung his legs off the couch and stood up. "Come on, Stevie, I'll get it for you," he said, and headed off to the bathroom.

Kate was still intent on the coal, but she remembered to say, "Thank you, Joe," before he left the room.

Breakfast was ready and the boys were dressed when John Mark came through the front door. They ate in silence, except for Stephen, who liked to sing bits of songs and talk to himself at breakfast. Josefina frowned at him and opened her mouth as if to tell him to be quiet, but she settled back without speaking when she caught Kate's warning glance.

"Mom, are you going to the Havliceks' today?" Johnny asked. Kate cleaned house for an elderly couple three days a week.

"Yes, and then I'm stopping on the Avenue before I come home. I'm going to look for a bed," Kate said. "Stephen, eat your toast."

John Mark looked up from his oatmeal and grinned. "Tired of waiting for me to find one?" he asked.

"I'm just going to look around. The hardware store might have something. I have to go to the meat market anyway, for dinner tonight." She had already planned her day and had the money for her purchases tucked into her handbag. The freezing weather stopped her from going out much during the winter, but now that the ice was melting and spring was in the air, she had the urge to go shopping for more than just meat and cheese.

"I'll talk to Karel," John Mark said, and yawned. "Maybe he'll help me build a frame, and then we can just buy the mattress."

"Umm-humm," Kate agreed. She took a sip of coffee to hide her smile. He had said that every week for two months. "Well, there's no harm in looking."

John Mark had seen her smiling in spite of the coffee cup. "Kate, I promise. I'll do it this week."

"All right," she said, and smiled some more. He was already yawning again.

She sent the boys off to school after prayers and closed the bedroom door after John Mark went to bed. "I'm going to buy a chicken tonight, Mother," she said as she gathered up her hat and gloves. "I'll be home a little late. Will you peel potatoes for dinner, please?"

"Yes, yes, I will," Josefina muttered, shaking her head and scowling. "You shouldn't have to go out and work like this, daughter. It's a shame. Your husband . . ." she began, and then stopped when Kate looked over at her.

"It's all right, *Matko*," Kate said. "Don't tire yourself out today. Wait for the boys to come home so they can do the heavy chores." Sometimes her mother still hauled buckets of water for the washing or carried ash out to the pile behind the garage. "*S Panem bohem*, go with God. I'll be home as soon as I can." She gave Josefina a kiss on the cheek and left the house.

Kate relaxed as she sat in the streetcar and watched the houses go by. She earned a dollar a day with the Havliceks, and now that John Mark was working and they had money coming in, she spent a nickel for the fare instead of walking. After years of traveling to the same house three days a week, the conductor knew where she got off, and he would stop there and let her out even if she forgot to pull the bell to remind him.

She thought about how much she was willing to spend for a bed. She wanted to get an icebox, a telephone, and a bed. The bed seemed most important. She couldn't justify the luxury of an icebox or a telephone if she had a fourteen-year-old boy in her home who didn't have a bed to sleep on. And she wanted to move him upstairs with the other boys so she could have some privacy at night. But they needed an icebox, too. She didn't want to go through another hot summer without one. Then they could get a telephone after that.

Although . . . she frowned as she remembered that Johnny was growing out of his shoes. The boy was sprouting up faster than she had thought possible. Probably Joe was growing out of his shoes too, although he might not have said anything about it. Both boys would need new shoes soon. That set her plans back a bit. Kate mentally reworked the figures and decided to buy the bed first and set aside money for the shoes next. After that, she would start saving for the icebox.

After a while, her thoughts turned back to Josefina. Sometimes her mother seemed like a mean old hen who just wanted to pick on others for no good reason. Josefina complained about John Mark and Johnny behind their backs, and she was harsh with Stephen, who was still little enough for her to bully. She was nasty to everyone except Joe. For some reason she had made Joe her pet, sewing extra clothes for him and saving special snacks for him to eat, to the point that Kate herself felt a little envious, wishing that her mother would show some of that attention to the rest of them.

Kate tried hard to help her mother be happy. When Josefina had moved in with them four years ago, after Kate's father died, Kate thought that perhaps her mother would eventually smile and enjoy life more, now that she was free from that cruel old man. If Josefina felt happier now, though, it was hard to tell. She was as difficult to get along with as ever.

But her mother had lived a life of disappointments. Kate would never know for sure, but she always wondered if perhaps she herself would be a bitter old woman, too, if she had lived Josefina's story.

In 1890, Josefina Dvořák was the middle child of five children born to a poor tenant family living in the heart of Bohemia. Her father was a serf, a farmer bound to the land by ages of tradition and heavy taxes. He brought up all his children to work in the fields along with him, but Josefina was blonde and pretty and had hopes of a better future than working her father's fields. She sewed beautiful clothes for herself and embroidered them with brilliant designs in the tradition of her village. Her family went into town on feast days, and Josefina wore her finery to church in the morning and to the dances in the town square later in the day. She married the first man who proposed to her.

Josefina's joy at becoming a married woman was short-lived. Her new husband, Martin Vesely, lived with his parents and did not move when he married. He spent his days idling at home or visiting nearby farmers, looking for work. Most days he came back drunk on homemade beer and frustrated by the lack of opportunity. Martin wanted something to do, and Josefina wanted a home of her own, but there seemed little chance of either wish coming true.

An uncle of Martin's had emigrated to America and wrote a letter to his family back home, describing the abundance of work and the amazing freedom available across the Atlantic. He offered to send tickets for the passage to any other man who wanted to come over and live there with him, and finally Martin decided to go.

Josefina wasn't sure that she wanted to move so far away from her family, but she didn't want to continue living with her husband's parents either, so when the day came to decide, she packed her suitcase and walked with Martin to the train station. Once on the train, there was no turning back. They traveled to Hamburg, took a ship to Liverpool, and finally boarded the ocean liner that would transport them across the Atlantic.

The passage was a nightmare. She was sick to her stomach, and Martin lost money playing cards with the other men. They each slept on a narrow bunk in a foul-smelling room with twenty other travelers. The food was bad and the cots were filthy with sweat stains and grime from previous voyages. When she finally saw the city of New York and its watchful statue looking out across the harbor, she was so grateful that she wept.

"Stop it! Stop crying, you stupid woman! You're embarrassing me!" Martin shouted at her as they stood in line waiting to be questioned and examined before they could walk out into the fine new world. "What's the matter with you? Maybe you should have stayed behind! It's a little late now, don't you think? If you didn't want to come here then you should have said so in the first place!" The other people heard him yelling and looked at her with curiosity and pity, a weeping woman with a suitcase and a disagreeable husband, as she moved forward with the great mass of people from the ship.

Martin's uncle had provided them with train tickets to Cedar Rapids, and once they arrived in that city they settled into a community almost completely populated by Bohemians. Everyone in their neighborhood spoke Czech. The churches held services in it. A local newspaper was printed in that language and offered more freedom of speech to the immigrants than they had ever known back in Bohemia. The men organized fraternal associations and the women formed social clubs. Josefina unpacked her embroidered dresses, and hoped to be happy.

Newcomers blended easily into the city, because huge grain factories and meat-packing plants sat along the river that ran through town, and they employed thousands of work-hungry eastern European men. Established American families with elegant homes hired diligent young Czech women to clean house and do laundry. The industries expanded, the immigrants made money, and the city boomed with growth.

Martin's uncle helped him get hired at the meat-packing plant, and eventually he and Josefina moved into a little apartment of their own. Every day Martin walked to work, and every evening he stopped by the corner bar to enjoy life a little before he came home. Josefina missed her family, but life was better now that Martin was working and they had their own home. Eventually they had a daughter that Josefina named Kateřina.

Martin was disappointed that the child was not a boy, and he blamed Josefina. When she bore him a second girl a year later, he blamed her again. When Josefina became pregnant a third time, her labor was especially hard, and her midwife had the neighbors bringing in extra linens and hot water for a whole day and night before the baby finally arrived. It was a boy, but again Josefina's joy was short-lived, because the child turned blue and died before it even cried out once for breath.

Kate remembered the following year as a kind of confusing bad dream in which her mother sat in a chair all day, forgetting to shop or cook, and her father came home at night and shouted at all of them until Josefina wept and the two girls hid in their bedroom closet. That was the year Kate learned to cut bread and cheese for sandwiches, even though her head was no higher than the kitchen table. Her father brought home groceries and flung them down in the kitchen before he went back out again after work, but Josefina usually just sat and stared out the window and did not get up to make a meal.

Someone had to feed little Marie when she cried, and so Kate learned how. She learned how to make toast that year, too, and how to put out the empty milk bottles so the milkman would bring new ones.

Eventually Josefina's women friends persuaded her to come out of her stupor and go back to the routines of housewife and mother. Kate was happy when her mother started sewing and cooking, dressing up and talking again. But Martin spent less and less time at home. He had turned out to be a mean, small-minded man. He became even more abusive as he grew older, raging at his family and handing out slaps and insults at any provocation. He spent money freely at the bars but kept Josefina and his daughters in a cramped apartment in the corner of a rooming house. At first, Josefina grieved from loneliness and from the bitterness of seeing her hope of happiness go sour, but eventually she became hardened to her husband's tyrannical ways. She argued back when Martin cursed her, risking the occasional drunken slap and hardly caring if it came. She tried to ignore him as much as possible and poured her life into her daughters instead, sewing and embroidering beautiful dresses with matching hats and coats for them to wear to church. Martin did not go to church, and so Sunday became the best day of the week for Josefina and her daughters.

Kate came back from her memories when the streetcar stopped and the conductor called her name. "*Na shledanou, pani Starostová!*" See you later, Mrs. Starosta! he said as she stepped off.

"*Ano, mockrát děkuji, pana Kovar.*" Yes, thank you very much, Mr. Kovar, she replied, and walked down the block to the Havliceks' home.

Ben and Betty Havlicek lived in a small brick house shaded by elm trees and surrounded with lilacs and roses. Today there was only melting snow and wet patches of muddy grass on the lawn, but the sun was shining and the buds would burst out soon. Little purple crocus flowers would pop up out of the snowdrifts first, and then tender violets would follow as the days grew warmer. When the roses bloomed they would have fresh flowers for the house every day until the first frost of autumn.

Kate came through the back door into the kitchen where Ben and Betty were finishing breakfast. They had been old when she first met them fourteen years ago, and now they were stooped and frail with age. They looked up and smiled when she came in.

"*Dobrý jitro, Kateřina,*" they said together.

"*Dobrý jitro*," Kate replied. "*Jak se máte?*" How are you?

"*Dobrý, děkuji. A vy?*"

"Fine, thank you too." Kate poured herself a cup of tea and sat down. The Havliceks did not drink coffee anymore, saying that it upset their stomachs. Ben was listening to the news on the radio and Betty was looking at the newspaper.

"Oh, my," Betty said, her mouth trembling and her wrinkled hands shaking as she held the newspaper. "Kate, dear, do you see this news? There's people rioting and smashing grocery store windows in order to go in and take food! The government soldiers are coming out to make them stop!"

"What? *Pani Havlicková*, what are you talking about?" Kate asked her. "There's no government soldiers coming out around here."

"That's far away, dear," Ben said. Betty looked at him blankly. "That's far away, dear!" he said, louder, so she could hear him. "That's out East. New York or someplace like that. Nowhere near us," he shouted, looking at his wife to make sure that she understood him.

"Things are just getting worse and worse all the time," Betty Havlicek fretted, not comforted by Ben's remark. "Look at this poor woman in this picture. All these people wandering around with no home and no food. Just terrible. Ben, I don't know what the world's coming to anymore." She shook her head, and her fingers trembled as she looked back down at the paper.

"I'll tell you, we've been protected here where we live," Ben said, wagging a finger at Kate to emphasize what he was saying. "We've been protected here!" he shouted when Betty indicated that she couldn't hear what he was saying. "People always have to eat, and as long as we keep on producing the food for them, there'll be money in this town. It's those Communists we have to worry about. They're trying to get into the White House," he said, nodding his head and tapping his finger vigorously on the table. "And then we'll all be in trouble because they'll want to take over our factories and they'll just run them into the ground. Mark my words!" He stopped for breath, clutching his cup and saucer as he frowned over the possibility of such a thing happening.

"Now, *pana* Havlicek, don't work yourself up into such a state," Kate soothed. She had heard this speech many times. "We're doing fine. I don't think there's any need to worry. Did you tell me that you want to shine shoes today? Let me take care of these breakfast dishes and I'll get out the polish and rags. Let's turn off the radio for a while."

Kate had known the Havliceks even before she met John Mark, and taking care of them was a bit like taking care of family. They had come to her wedding and brought her a gift. They had encouraged John Mark to continue in the ministry, for his congregation's sake, when the church ran out of money and he was ready to quit in despair. And in 1930, when the bank foreclosed on the rectory where Kate and John Mark lived, the Havliceks asked her to come and work in their house three days a week, so that she could earn a little money in a respectable way. Kate adored them. She went on keeping house for them even after John Mark was hired at the factory, because they were getting old and it was nice to have a little extra money coming in.

The work was not hard. She cleaned their house, bought their groceries, cooked a bit, and generally oversaw the running of the household. The Havliceks had a laundress who came in on Kate's day off and a gardener for the heavier chores. Ben had a pension from the Army and was part owner of a dry goods store, so the Depression had not changed life much in their home.

"How's Marie's boy doing?" Betty asked.

"Oh, better. He's talking more, anyway. Growing like a weed. *Pani Havlicková*, I have just got to buy a bed for him as soon as I can find one and put him up in the attic with the boys. I'm tired of not having any privacy at night." Kate looked over at Betty and the two women nodded at each other. Betty could always understand her when she talked.

"Too close for comfort, honey, that's right," Betty said. "I thought you wanted to buy an icebox next."

"Well . . ." Kate hesitated. "I think I need to get the bed first. There's still time before the hot weather comes."

Betty nodded and gave her a little private smile. "Ben, do we have a bed we can give them for Marie's boy?"

"No, *Bétuska*, dear," Ben shouted. "We gave away the extra bed a long time ago. Remember?"

Betty was not upset at the idea that she might have forgotten that a bed had been given away. She stirred her tea and thought for a while.

"Well, do we have anything left up in the attic? Why don't you go up there this afternoon and look around, now that it's not so cold. Can you get up there by yourself?" The attic in their house did not have stairs and could only be reached by a ladder.

"I'll take a look later on," Kate said. "After lunch."

Kate helped Ben settle down with the polish and the shoes to be shined, and left the two of them together while she tidied the house and organized the laundry. She went out for groceries and then made lunch. The Havliceks usually took a nap in the afternoon, and Kate could bake or mend or sometimes even read a magazine before she fixed their evening meal and went back home.

This afternoon she baked a pie, using a jar of cherries she had canned for them last summer. Hardly any fruit could be found in the markets at this time of year, and the cherries would be a nice change from all the cakes she had been baking. When the pie was in the oven she pulled out the ladder and climbed up into the attic. Not much was up there anymore, except for a few trunks full of outdated clothes and Ben's old army uniform with all its medals still attached, hanging under a dust cover against the side of the wall.

Kate brought down the uniform, thinking that Ben might like to look at it. She put the ladder away, checked the pie, and went out to the front room. Ben was snoring gently in his favorite chair, and Betty was sound asleep in the bedroom. Kate went back to the kitchen and sat at the table, looking out the window and thinking.

It was nice of them to want to help Marie's son. There had been a time when no one wanted to help Marie or speak about her son at all. Marie had been a sweet little sister and a beautiful girl, but by the time she was seventeen years old, she had already been swept up into the storm of trouble that would wash her life away.

Kate was eighteen and Marie was seventeen in 1919, when the Great War had ended and Prohibition had not yet begun. The world outside their apartment bustled with energy and the promise of better times ahead. Kate and Marie walked to school together in the mornings, and when they came home in the afternoons they lingered in front of the shop windows, looking at clothes and shoes, but Josefina was a strict parent so they did not linger long. After chores and dinner the girls sat in the kitchen and sewed. When Martin came home, they retreated to their tiny bedroom and sat by their window watching horse-drawn carriages and cars go by, and the occasional courting couple walk past in the evening light.

Kate was considered the smarter of the two sisters, and she was attractive, but she walked too briskly and looked at people too sharply to be anyone's darling. Marie, though, was truly beautiful, and she had a tender manner about her that made people stop and look, even on the sidewalks or in the market. By the time Marie was fifteen, men were trying to talk to her, and Kate kept a sharp eye on her sister when the two of them were out by themselves.

Martin and Josefina were united on one thing — keeping their daughters eligible for marriage. Martin did not allow his daughters to go out in the evening for any kind of activity. Other Czech girls from good families joined social clubs that met in the evenings to sing traditional songs and give concerts, or paint colorful china plates and Christmas ornaments. One time Kate pointed out to her parents that she and Marie were qualified to join the clubs — they were both girls of good character, and their father was considered a fine hardworking man by the rest of community. Martin turned red with anger at the idea of his daughters going out in the evening, and no one brought up the subject again.

That all changed in May of 1919. The *Mojovy Venecek*, or May Wreath Dance, was held every year on May first in the Sokol Health Club's gymnasium, and girls decorated the gym with spring flowers after school and then dressed up in their best traditional clothes for the *Besada* folk dance that night.

"*Matko*, the Svobodas asked me to come help them decorate for *Mojovy Venecek* after school today," Marie said to Josefina at breakfast that day, referring to their neighbors who lived in the apartment above them.

"You're not going," Josefina had snapped at first. "You don't go out after school. You come straight home."

But Marie begged and whined, and finally Josefina gave permission, as long as Kate went with her and they were home by supper so that Martin wouldn't know.

The afternoon was fun. Kate and Marie envied the other girls who left the hall planning to return after dinner for music and dancing. The sisters hurried home, fearful of arriving later than their father and getting in trouble. Supper was a cheerless meal as they sat and thought about the excitement they were missing and the unfairness of life with Martin and Josefina for parents.

When Martin came home and they went to their bedroom, Marie changed into her embroidered Sunday clothes.

"What are you doing?" Kate hissed. Any words louder than a whisper could be overheard by their parents in the next room.

Marie threw a determined look at Kate. "I'm going to the dance," she whispered. "I'm going to climb out the window and come back later. It's not fair that we can't go."

"Are you crazy?" Kate whispered back. "Don't you dare! They'll find out! Someone will tell them you were there even if they don't see you leave!"

Marie twisted up her shining hair and pinned it smoothly in place. "I'm going," she said, and let her whisper get just a bit louder. "And if you try to stop me I'll make noise."

"You can't do this!" Kate said as forcefully as she could while still whispering. "You're going to get us all in trouble!" She tried to stand between her sister and the window, and the two girls pushed and glared at each other while trying to not make any noise. Marie finally picked up her sister's favorite china ornament and made as if to fling it against the wall.

"If you throw that and they hear, they'll come in and you'll be the one in trouble!" Kate gritted out. Marie only held the ornament higher. "You *idiot*," Kate complained. "You're going to ruin your life and mine too. If they come in, I'm telling."

Marie smiled in satisfaction. "Just don't lock the window and everything will be fine," she said to Kate, and then struggled out the window and hurried down the street.

Kate spent that night in agony, too angry to sleep and too worried about her sister to do anything else. She lay awake in the darkness for what seemed like ages, so tense that her head hurt and her back ached, until long after midnight when her little sister finally came back to the window and slipped inside. Marie undressed and lay down beside her in the dark. She smelled of smoke and beer, and some other sharp scent that Kate didn't know.

"Don't you ever do that again, you stupid ninny," Kate whispered.

Marie rolled over and threw the blanket back. "I had the most wonderful time," she whispered back. "I danced all night, and I met someone. He drove me home in his car."

"You *what?*" Kate was shocked.

"I met a wonderful man," Marie said, "and I'm going back next Friday to see him again. He loves me and he's going to marry me."

"Marie . . ." Kate began, but her sister cut her off.

"I'm sick of living here," Marie said. The room was lit by moonlight, and Kate could see the intensity of her sister's expression. "I found someone who loves me and I'm going to leave. I don't care if Mom and Dad find out right now."

"Who is this guy?" Kate asked after a moment.

"Randall Mott," Marie said, and hugged herself.

Kate shivered with fear. A Czech boy could be counted on to marry Marie if things got serious, but who was this person?

"What kind of name is that?" she asked sharply. "Where's he from?"

"He's from Chicago. He works for the railroad, he's thirty-one, and he looks like a dream," Marie whispered. "He lives over on the northeast side. Every girl there wanted to dance with him, but after we met, he only danced with me. This is the best night of my life, ever."

"Marie . . ." Kate tried again.

"Don't try to tell me," Marie whispered fiercely. "You want to leave as bad as I do. If you met someone who loved you like Randall loves me, you'd leave too. You should have come tonight. Then you'd understand."

Kate heaved a frustrated sigh. "Marie, men don't fall in love like that in one night. You're acting like a baby! Some guy from Chicago, and you believe him? How do you even know that's his name? You're going to get into so much trouble . . ." her voice trailed off as she pictured what could happen to her little sister, far away in the hands of some unprincipled older man.

Marie reached over to stroke Kate's hair back from her face and smiled her most winsome smile. "Kate, don't worry. I'm so happy," she said, and then rolled onto her back and stretched her arms up joyfully in the moonlight. "Be happy for me. It's going to be all right. Maybe you can come and live with me after I'm married and get my own place."

Kate stared at her, feeling her heart quake with the knowledge that her sister's world had changed forever. She tried her worst threat. "Marie, this isn't going to work out, and you're going to end up in trouble instead of in a house. I'll tell Mother if you go back again."

"It's too late for me now," Marie said bluntly. "So there's no point trying to stop me." She gave Kate a long look in the pale white light before she rolled over and fell asleep.

Marie went out the next Saturday night and then the Sunday night after that, even though there was no dance at the community hall that evening. She crawled out the window almost every night that week and came back home just before daylight with stories of how Randall Mott took her to bars and clubs, bought elegant drinks and dinners and danced with her long into the night. Marie was in heaven, but Kate was in agony, for her sister and for herself as well, because word would eventually get around that Marie Vesely had been with a man.

A month went by, and Marie kept going out, and still Martin and Josefina didn't know. But one morning Marie was sick to her stomach. She was sick the next morning as well, and Kate knew that her sister's time had run out.

Josefina finally noticed that Marie had morning sickness. She heard Marie throwing up in the bathroom and looked across the kitchen at Kate with an unreadable expression on her face. She said nothing, though, and Kate wondered if perhaps her mother was too afraid to speak about it. If Marie, unmarried, was discovered to be with child, Martin would throw her out. She would be outcast from decent Czech society and her family would be shamed as well. So Josefina, Kate, and Marie spent their last month together in despair, not looking at each other, barely speaking, and hoping that somehow the worst would not happen.

"Isn't he going to marry you?" Kate finally whispered to her sister as they lay in bed one night.

Marie was silent for so long that Kate thought she must be asleep, but she finally rolled over and looked at her. Her eyes were blotched and swollen. "Oh, Kate," she said, choking on her tears, "he's already married." Marie turned back over and sobbed into her pillow. Kate just lay there for a long time, looking up at the moonlit ceiling, stroking her sister's shaking shoulders and wondering when her father would find out.

They didn't have to wait long. Martin came home right away on the day when the gossip caught up with him. He flung open the door to the apartment and headed straight for Marie as she sat at the kitchen table with her mother and sister. Kate screamed with fright at the expression on his face, and Marie just sat, white with terror, until her father grabbed her by her hair and flung her to the floor. Josefina began to weep, then fled to her bedroom and locked the door behind her. Martin pulled Marie up and slapped her hard across her face, bringing a stream of blood from the side of her mouth. Then he took aim and slapped her again with the full strength of his work-hardened arm.

"Stop it! Stop it!" Kate finally cried out, catching at her father's arm. He wrenched free of her grasp and hit her on the side of her head so hard that she lost her balance and fell.

Martin turned back and cornered Marie as she tried to run from the kitchen. He raged and shouted in the old language, and grabbed her by the hair again and beat her until she sank to the floor, arms over her face, still trying to get away. Then he kicked her in the stomach with enough force to throw her halfway across the room. He stood red-faced and panting as she retched out her dinner and covered her blood-smeared face with her hands.

Kate sat up and tried to get to her feet, but Martin turned and strode toward her and she fell back with fear. Her father stood, breathing hard, face almost purple with anger as he looked around. Then he grabbed Marie by the arm and threw her into the front room.

"Get OUT!" he roared, and Marie began to sob hysterically. "Get out of my house, you whore! Now!" He pulled her up off the floor where she had fallen and flung her against the door. "So, you're smart, young lady, eh? Got a friend, eh? Well, go live with him! Let him feed you! *Potvora! Jdi do pekla!* You filthy, worthless whore!" And Marie had stumbled through the door and down the street.

A loud *pop* from the oven made Kate jump. She was still sitting in the Havliceks' kitchen, waiting for her pie to finish baking. She got up to check it, but her hands shook as she opened the oven door and tears blurred her eyes when she looked to see if the pie was done.

"*Kateřina?* Are you in here?" Betty walked slowly into the kitchen with her short, uncertain steps.

"Oh . . . hello." Kate's voice trembled. "I'm baking a cherry pie for tonight," she said, and brushed her hand across her eyes.

Betty came closer so that she could see Kate's face. "What did you say? Why, you're crying. What's the matter, dear?"

Kate ducked her head and swallowed. There was no point in trying to hide the tears. Betty knew the whole story anyway.

"I was thinking about Marie," she finally said. "I guess talking about Joe got me started. I was remembering the day when Father threw her out," and then her voice broke and she started crying in earnest. "*Oh, pani Havlickova*," she sobbed. "I should have gone with her. I should have."

Betty patted her back and then put a handkerchief in her hand. "There, there, dear. No sense fretting yourself about what's past. It doesn't do any good. There's not a soul on earth who doesn't look back and wish they'd done things different."

Kate wiped her face and tried to catch her breath. "But Marie died . . . because I didn't go with her."

"She didn't die right then. She could have come back and lived with you after you married John," Betty pointed out. "I remember how you two talked about trying to find her. Besides," she added, "If you had gone with her, maybe you wouldn't have met that nice young man of yours." She sat back and nodded, her head trembling a little bit from the effort of talking so much.

Kate looked out the window again, thinking about what Betty said. Marie had come back to the apartment the next day, while Martin was working and Kate was at the market. Josefina had let her in long enough to pack some clothes, but she was angry with Marie and afraid of Martin, so she would not let her daughter stay long. Marie came back again that night, tapping at the bedroom window, and after Kate let her in they hugged and cried together in the dark.

"Are you all right? Where did you go? I'll come with you," Kate had whispered.

"I'm all right. I'm staying with a friend," Marie had whispered back.

"Who?" Kate asked, amazed that any of her friends' families would allow a girl in Marie's kind of trouble to stay under their roof.

"One of Randall's friends," Marie said. "You can't come."

"Oh, Marie, what's going to happen to you?" Kate whispered.

"He has a little apartment over the Blue Moon bar, up on First Avenue," Marie said. "You can come and visit me sometime. He's a really nice guy, better than Randall. I'm not going to come back here ever again. I hate it here and I'm leaving, now that I said goodbye to you."

Kate pulled back and looked at her sister, wondering how she could sound so confident. Marie's face was bruised and swollen from the beating the day before, but there was still a proud tilt to her head.

"That's so far away . . . who is he?" was the only thing that Kate could think of to ask.

"His name is Jim and he's a bartender," Marie said. "He's waiting for me outside. I have to go now. I just want to say goodbye, and I love you." Suddenly her young voice broke, and she flung her arms around Kate and kissed her on the cheek. "I have to leave right now or he'll get mad." She struggled out the window one last time, waved, and ran off. Kate leaned out to look after her and saw Marie slip into a waiting car and sit next to the driver. Then the car went down the street and disappeared into the night.

Kate blinked and came back from her memories once more. Betty was still sitting at the table, waiting for her to go on.

"I still wish that I had done more," Kate finally said. "I feel like I . . . just let her go."

"Honey, you can't do a thing about that now. There's no sense in breaking your heart over and over about it," Betty said. "You did your best and that's all a person can do. Now, let me tell you what I came in here for."

She fumbled in her dress pocket and pulled out a worn leather coin purse. "I have some pin money here that I haven't used for a month, and I want you to buy a bed for Marie's boy with it." Betty took out a five-dollar bill and set it down on the table.

Kate felt tears flood her eyes again. "*Pani Havlicková*, I can't take your spending money," she protested.

"Sure you can," Betty said, and tucked her hands into her lap like a little girl playing a game. She smiled at Kate and her old face crinkled into kindly lines. "I might be old but I still like to do a little something for people. That boy's had a hard life and I'd like to buy him a bed."

Kate could no longer hold back her tears, and she leaned over to give Betty a hug. She could feel the older woman's frail arms around her, too shaky to do more than just touch her lightly with unsteady fingers. But then both of them caught the scent of burning crust, and the hug was cut short in order to save the cherry pie.

Kate still felt teary even after she got back on the streetcar and went to the hardware store. Betty's gift would be enough to pay for a bed frame, a mattress, and a pillow. After that, Kate was so distracted that she walked straight past the meat market and was almost home before she remembered that she had planned to buy a chicken for dinner.

She stopped just as she was crossing a street and wondered what to do. *Stupid, stupid me!* she thought. Was there time to go back? She turned around for a moment, but the store was probably closed by now, and in any case, it was late and she was tired. She finally turned back and kept on walking toward home.

They had potatoes and leftover bacon grease at home. She could make fried potatoes. Kate wondered if John Mark would be upset and yell at her for serving such a skimpy supper.

Where had that thought come from? He never got upset with her about food, and he hardly ever yelled at anyone. *My father was the one who would complain about dinner not being good enough,* she thought. *I'm just imagining things. John Mark isn't like that, thank God.*

When she stepped through her front door, she found John Mark's shoes and socks scattered across the front room floor along with his shirt and jacket. His Bible lay open on one of the rocking chairs, next to an empty coffee cup and a dirty plate. Books, papers, and a pencil lay under the rocker. She could hear boys talking in the kitchen.

Kate made an exasperated little noise, gathered up his belongings, and put them away in their bedroom. It seemed as if she had done nothing but clean up after other people all day long. She picked up the coffee cup and plate and headed for the kitchen, where the boys were gathered around the table looking at the newspaper.

"Mom! Guess what!" Johnny said as soon as he saw her. "*The Count of Monte Cristo's* showing at the Paramount Theater!" All of them turned to look at her, brimming with excitement. "Dad says we can all go!"

"Even me! Even me!" Stephen sang out at the top of his voice, jumping up and down.

Kate looked at them. Johnny and Joe were leaning over the newspaper, looking up at her to see what she would say. John Mark was barefoot and in his sleeveless undershirt, grinning like a happy little boy himself. She suddenly felt more tired than ever, and wondered how they could possibly expect her to be excited about seeing a movie when there was still a supper to cook and a house to clean. Her mother's words from the morning came back to her for a moment . . ." *fool-headed minister.*"

"That might be nice for all of you, but I've got work to do before I can spend time wool-gathering about a movie," she said sharply. Peeled potatoes were sitting in a pot, covered with water, waiting to be cooked, and she bent down to light the stove. The ashes from morning were still piled in the grate. "If you all have so much time to think about the movies, then why hasn't somebody taken out the ashes? Do I have to do everything myself?" She pulled out the iron coal scuttle and started shoveling ashes into it.

The kitchen was silent. Kate glanced over and met John Mark's look, then turned back to the stove.

"You boys go on out and turn on the radio," she heard him say. "You can do your homework after supper." Joe and Johnny made a hasty exit.

"I want to stay here with you, Daddy," Stephen protested. "I want to look at the movie pictures."

Out of the corner of her eye, Kate watched John Mark give Stephen a hug and a kiss. "Take them with you," he said. "Go on now." Stephen left, trailing newspaper sections on the floor behind him. John Mark got up and came over to her. Kate tensed up, waiting for the fight to start.

"Here, let me do that," he said, pulling the coal shovel out of her hand. "What's the matter?"

Kate's throat hurt at the thought that he still loved her even after she had just lost her temper and ruined everyone's happy moment.

But she only said, "Nothing. I'm just tired."

John Mark was quiet for a moment while he shoveled out the ashes for her. Then he said, "I talked to Karel about building a bed frame today,"

"Oh, that's why I'm late. I found a bed. But if you and Karel can make a frame, then we won't have to pay for that part. Betty wanted to do something for Joe and she gave me some money for a bed." Kate leaned against the cold stove and put her hands to her cheeks, trying to calm down. "I tried to say no, but it made her so happy . . ." She sighed again. "We were talking about Marie."

John Mark looked up at her from where he was putting wood into the grate.

"And I forgot to buy the chicken," Kate said, and suddenly she felt as if she could do nothing right. "So I guess we'll just have potatoes tonight. And toast. I'm sorry." She pressed her hands to her forehead and then looked back at John Mark. Her eyes hurt from all the crying. "I'm sorry I yelled. I even burned the pie this afternoon. I can't do anything right today."

"Karel gave me some eggs when I was over there. We can make scrambled eggs." John Mark looked up at her again. "Don't you want to go to the movie tomorrow? We could go and just eat hot dogs at the snack stand. Then you wouldn't have to cook supper."

Kate shook her head. Didn't he understand? She was not upset about cooking. She was upset because some days it was so hard to get everything done, and even then she made mistakes no matter how much she tried. And on top of that, everybody else made more work for her and just thought about things like movies instead of trying to help. She shook her head again. She didn't think she could explain it.

"I don't think Joe and Johnny can make a meal off one hotdog each. We better eat something here first," she finally said.

John Mark stood up, grinning so happily that Kate had to smile in spite of her weary eyes. He pulled her into a hug.

"Good," he said, and gave her a kiss. "Now, send all those boys back in here, and I'll show them how to make scrambled eggs."

Kate rolled her eyes. "God help us all."

Before dinner, Kate apologized to the boys for losing her temper, which brought her a hug from Johnny and a long, puzzled look from Joe. Stephen was solemn at the idea of his mom saying she was sorry.

"I'm sorry too," he told her. "Can I still go to the movie?" They all laughed, but even after the dishes were cleared away Kate still felt haunted by the gloom that had followed her all day. When John Mark and Joe stayed in the kitchen after supper to do homework together, she sat down with them and pulled out her Bible.

She paged through Psalms for a while, looking for relief. She found Psalm 23:

The Lord is my shepherd; I shall not want.
He maketh me to lie down in green pastures:
he leadeth me beside the still waters.
He restoreth my soul . . . .

And later came Psalm 25:

Unto thee, O Lord, do I lift up my soul.
O my God, I trust in thee:
let me not be ashamed,
let not mine enemies triumph over me . . . .

Kate read the psalm and then sat and watched Joe and John Mark work on a math problem. *I have a pretty good life. Sometimes it seems like my own thoughts are my worst enemies.* She had a wonderful husband, by anyone's standards. *Except my mother's.* She smiled to herself and went back to reading.

Show me thy ways, O Lord; teach me thy paths.
Lead me in thy truth, and teach me:

for thou art the God of my salvation; on thee do I wait all the day. . .
Remember not the sins of my youth, nor my transgressions:
according to thy mercy remember thou me, for thy goodness' sake, O Lord.

She turned a few more pages and lingered over Psalm 37.

Delight thyself also in the Lord: and he shall give thee the desires of thine heart . . .

After Marie left home for a new life with her boyfriend, Kate had felt a restless urge to follow her. Martin and Josefina seemed like fools to her now, people that she no longer even wanted to talk to, let alone live with. Kate stayed in her room by herself most of the time. Sometimes she read or sewed, but often she sat at the window and stared down the street, hoping to see Marie coming back, or wondering what was out there that she could find if she went looking.

She planned to get married as soon as possible. She was finished with school now, and there was no reason to go out of the apartment at all, unless she ran some errand for Josefina. Young women did not work at outside jobs like young men did, and Martin kept complete control of the family because he held the money. She was trapped. Marriage was the solution. There was only one problem — she didn't know any boy that she liked enough to marry.

Sometimes Kate studied her face in the mirror late at night, wondering if there might be anyone who would want to marry her. Her nose was not as straight as Marie's and her lips did not have the perfect angelic shape that her sister's did. She practiced smiling at herself in the mirror. She wondered what would happen if she just packed up and left. But she had no place to go, so she stayed, and waited for something to happen.

Life changed for all of them that summer because of what Marie had done. Josefina quit going to church because of the embarrassment. People criticized her for letting her daughter run wild, and said that she was a bad mother. Kate's friends avoided her. Martin stayed out at night until the bars closed. When Kate's neighbors from upstairs invited her to church with them one Sunday, she went with them out of sheer boredom.

She never forgot the sermon she heard that day. The minister preached from the first chapter of Ephesians, reading the lines "*Let all bitterness, and wrath, and anger, and clamour, and evil speaking, be put away from you, with all malice: And be ye kind one to another, tenderhearted, forgiving one another, even as God for*

Christ's sake hath forgiven you. Be ye therefore followers of God, as dear children; And walk in love . . ."

The idea that God loved her, that He was tenderhearted and kind to people, hit her like a thunderclap that morning. How had she never realized it before? *This is how I want to live, she decided that day. I want to learn about God, and I want to be like Him. I don't want to be like my mother or my father, or even like Marie, although I love her so much. I want to be better than that . . . I want to be a better kind of person who will be kind to others and inspire people to be better, instead of causing so much pain.*

Kate lingered after the service and met the Havliceks, and spent time visiting with her neighbors upstairs that week instead of staying alone in her bedroom every night. She went back to church the next Sunday, and again the week after that. Josefina and Martin grumbled a bit, but Kate was always polite to them, so her parents, wrapped up in their own unhappiness, left her alone.

Ironically, the summer that was so miserable for Josefina and Martin became the happiest time of Kate's life. Instead of feeling trapped, she felt free. She learned how to read the Bible and pray, and she committed herself to following God in a more heartfelt way than she had as a child when her mother had taken her to church. Furthermore, she slowly became aware that the assistant pastor — a tall, thin young man named John Starosta — had an interest in her.

When he invited her to lunch at his brother Vincent's house after church one Sunday, she looked him over and wondered if she might like to marry him. He was a little too thin for her taste, but he had a way of making her laugh, and a sincere respect for others, especially women and children, that made her feel safe when she was with him. Kate accepted the invitation, and when she met Vincent's wife, Amalia, she liked her right away. During lunch the two brothers cracked jokes and the two women laughed and teased them. She fell in love with John that day, and she decided that if he proposed, she would say yes. Then she decided that she would do everything possible to encourage him along.

By this time, Martin Vesely was too deep in his drinking and his own personal misery to care much about his daughter's courtship. He still would not allow Kate to go out at night. But John came to visit with her parents in the evenings and talked politics with Martin. He ignored the old man's drunken behavior and asked if he could take Kate to lunch after church on Sundays. He drove her home in his brother's car afterwards, with Vincent and Amalia always along as chaperones. As soon as John could properly do so, he asked Martin for her hand, and they were married at eight o'clock in the morning on a glorious October day. John asked Vincent to be his best man, and since Kate could not find Marie, she asked Amalia to be her matron of honor.

Married life was fun. Kate now had her own home to manage and an ardent young man to share her bed. John believed in praying together every day, and her faith in God grew along with her love for her husband. He didn't make much money, and he had told her that he probably never would, but Kate didn't care. There was nothing that could compare to the joy of feeling close to God and the sweetness of feeling loved.

Kate finally closed her Bible and put it back in the kitchen drawer. She kept her stack of family photos right beside it, and on impulse she pulled them out and went back to the table with them. There was one of John Mark, dressed in his best suit, that she loved to look at. He had filled out very nicely after they married, she thought with a little private grin. Marriage had been good for him too.

Joe looked up from his homework. John Mark had left the kitchen. "Aunt Kate?" Joe asked softly. She looked at him. "I'm sorry I didn't clean out the ashes."

Kate didn't know whether to smile or start crying again. "Oh, honey," she said, and reached over to take his hand. She could feel the puckered scar along the inside of his fingers. "I shouldn't have yelled like that." She arched a brow at him. "Even the best of us makes mistake, huh?" She smiled, trying to get him to see that she was poking a little fun at herself. He looked uncertain, so she patted his hand and said, "That's a joke."

He smiled then, and her heart warmed toward him. She motioned to him to scoot his chair a little closer to hers. "Look, here's a picture of your grandma and grandpa when they came over from the old country."

Joe leaned over to look at the photo. Martin and Josefina stood stiffly in front of a little wooden house, looking young and nervous.

"Do you remember anything about your grandpa?" Kate asked curiously.

Joe took his time answering. "Me and mom went to visit him once, when I was little," he finally said. "I just remember that he sat in the corner, looking mad."

Kate nodded. "That's pretty much how I remember him too. He was a miserable old man. I hate to say it, but that's the truth. And our last name is Vesely. Imagine that." When Joe looked up, not understanding, Kate explained, "*Vesely* means 'happy' in Czech."

"Oh," Joe said. He looked at the next photo. "Who's that?"

"That is your grandma, believe it or not," Kate said. The photo was of a young, pretty Josefina, dressed in traditional Czech clothes and smiling. "I think this must have been at some festival, back when I was a little girl. I remember her wearing that dress."

"Gosh," Joe said. "She sure looks different."

"Your grandma's maiden name was Dvorák, and Amalia's maiden name was Dvorák, too," Kate told him. "You know — Vincent's wife, Amalia, Anton's mother," she reminded him. "Amalia and I used to joke that maybe we were related, just like John and Vincent are related."

Joe thought that one over. "So then Anton and I would be related," he said after a while.

"Well, we never did figure it out, but it's possible. Amalia named Anton after Antonín Dvorák, the famous composer. Your mother named you after her parents. Joseph Martin."

"Huh," Joe said. "I never thought of that."

"That's what she did," Kate said. She turned to the next picture. It was of Marie. "Look, here she is. She was sixteen then."

Joe bent to study it. Marie's sweet smile and lovely face shone up at them from the old-fashioned oval cardboard frame. Kate felt her eyes fill with tears one more time.

"She was so beautiful," she said. Joe nodded, not taking his eyes off the picture. Kate looked at him as he gazed at it. "You take after her. In a . . . a manly way, of course," she quickly stammered when Joe flushed at her comment. "You know what? I'll give you this picture. I'll just keep it safe for you until you get out with a home of your own, and then I'll go through all these photos and give you the best ones of your mom. How about that?"

Joe swallowed. "Oh, thanks," he finally said. "Really, thanks. That's so nice of you." He slowly turned over more photos, lingering over the ones of people that he recognized. There was one of Kate and John Mark on their wedding day. There were photos of Johnny and Stephen when they were little.

Then there was another one of his mother, holding a little boy and standing next to a man. Joe blinked and caught his breath.

"Is that . . . is that my dad?" He stared hungrily at the man in the photo.

Kate bit her lip. *Oh, no.* She hated to say it, but she had to tell the truth. "No, honey. I'm sorry. I never saw your dad. He left before you were born." *That's just one of Marie's friends,* she almost added, but then she stopped. Joe would know that.

Joe kept on looking at the photo, as if by sheer force of will he could turn back the years and bring to life the moment when he was a little boy in his mother's arms, standing next to a man who might have been his father.

"She looks happy," he finally said, but in his own voice was a deep sadness that made Kate's throat turn hot with grief.

"Yes, she does," Kate said. "I love her very much. I still do, even though she's gone."

Joe did not say anything to that, but looked at the picture for a long time. After a while, he sorted through the rest of the photos. There were no more of Marie, though, and when he was done he handed them back to Kate in a neat stack.

"Thanks," he said.

She smiled at him. "Remember, some of these are yours now. I'm just keeping them for you." They both got up from the table, and she impulsively put her arm around his waist and gave him a hug. He had grown taller than she was, although he was still a little thin.

"I'm so glad you're living here with us now." She looked him in the eye and held him in the hug a little longer than usual, and gave him an extra squeeze like John Mark did to her sometimes, so Joe would know she meant what she said.

He raised his arm to her waist and gave her a shy squeeze in return. "Me too," he said, his own eyes wet with tears, and then he left the kitchen.

Kate packed John Mark's lunch box for work, and then sat down with the stack of photos again. She sifted slowly through them, stopping when she found one of herself and Amalia. Someone, probably John Mark or Vincent, had taken a picture of them as they were walking down the sidewalk in front of the stores along the Avenue. They were in their best dresses, their hats tilted at a stylish angle, and they were laughing at whoever was holding the camera. Kate had one hand tucked through Amalia's arm and held a shopping bag with the other.

Oh, Amalia, sister of my heart, why did you have to leave us? Kate gazed down at the photo, caught between grief and laughter as she remembered the fun that she and her sister-in-law had shared. Why did Marie and Amalia both have to die so young? *You always think that you'll have lots of time with a person, and then sometimes it turns out that you don't.*

Kate got up and put the photos away. She walked through the front room where her boys were gathered on the floor, listening to the radio. She looked at them and smiled, but she didn't linger there. She opened the bedroom door and went in to find her husband.

He was putting on his shirt, getting ready for work. The little lamp gave off only a soft golden glow and left half the room in shadow. She closed the door and came over to put her arms around him, pushing in close and getting in the way of his hands. He looked down at her with a question in his eyes.

"I just want you to know I love you," Kate whispered. "I love you, John." She put her face up for a kiss, and they stayed there for a while, making the most of the time they had together.

Six: April / *Baseball*

Boys, you will have to watch your physical condition and your mode of living if you want to be champions," Coach Kovar declared as he paced in front of the bench where Joe, Rudy, and Johnny sat along with the rest of the Packers, which was the name of the Sinclair meat-packing plant baseball team. "It just gripes my soul when some goof gets into trouble and misses a practice. Life is like baseball. What you get out of it is what you put into it. Do everything with integrity, on and off the field. I expect you to act like gentlemen wherever you go. Remember who you represent." The Packers were part of the Manufacturers and Jobbers city league, and the workers from the factories came to the games and cheered for their teams. Kovar reached the end of the bench and turned back to walk the other direction, hands clasped behind his back. All the boys' heads followed, eyes glued to him as he talked. "Develop your faculty of observation . . ."

"What's he saying?" Joe whispered to Rudy.

"Shut up!" Rudy hissed back.

"And don't get in a lather about the umpire. Keep on playing and stay in control of yourself and your ball. Don't get it into your head that the umpire is your worst enemy." Johnny stared wide-eyed at the coach as if memorizing every word of the speech.

"The uniforms came in," the coach said, and smiled as the boys broke out into a cheer. "I'll bring 'em next practice. Nice work tonight, team. Mind your own potatoes until next time."

Joe, who played third base, and Rudy, the team's catcher, said their goodbyes and strolled off the practice field with Johnny straggling behind them. Their cleated shoes all clicked in rhythm on the pavement as they walked along, and Joe luxuriated in the glorious sound of real baseball player's shoes on his feet and the way he felt tired but happy after a good practice. The April evening was cool and moist. A sliver of moon and a few stars lit the sky between puffs of misty pink clouds.

"Geez, I don't want to play catcher. I want to play first base like I did last year," Rudy griped. Wence had been catcher last year, but this year he was working every night after school and didn't sign up for the team. "Batters get hit with a ball, everybody feels bad for them and they get to walk. Catchers get hit with a ball, they don't get zip." He sighed. "Lou Gehrig's manager doesn't let him get banged up all the time like that."

"Yeah, but you get a lot of action," Joe said. Baseball always put him in a good mood. He could hit pitches, run bases, dive for falling balls, and fire off long-distance throws all night long. Coach Kovar had watched him field balls and immediately put him on third base. Joe felt like a prince on a throne when he played. It was nice to feel noticed for something good.

"I just don't want to louse anything up," Johnny said from behind them. "I don't care where I play." No one knew exactly how Johnny had managed to make the team, because he wasn't really big enough, but he had wormed his way into the tryouts and shown enough hustle to be allowed to stay. He was playing right field and glad to be there.

"I think I could pitch," Joe said. "All I need is a chance." Anton's trumpet-playing friend Bob Stastny was the team's best pitcher because he could throw a curve ball as well as a straight ball, and he had generously given Joe pointers on his pitching and helped him practice. Joe could only throw straight, but his speed was getting better, and he hoped to get called up to pitch sometime. "Bob's helping me on my curve. I'm going to tell Coach that I'm starting to pitch really good."

"Wait and see how you do in a real game," Rudy advised. "It's different from practice. Anyway, there's lots of guys who can pitch."

"I'll win forty-five games all by myself," Joe announced. "Call me Diz." The St. Louis Cardinals' ace pitcher Dizzy Dean had just publicly boasted that he and his brother Daffy would win forty-five games between the two of them during the 1934 season.

Rudy smacked him on the head with his glove. "Half-cocked humdinger." He raised his voice to a high-pitched snicker, imitating the coach's speech. " 'Watch your physical condition and your mode of living.' " He reached back and smacked Johnny, too, for the fun of it. " 'Mind your own potatoes, boys.' "

Johnny grinned at the attention. "See ya," he said, because they were at Rudy's corner.

"See ya," Rudy called back as he headed off. Joe and Johnny walked on, their spikes scratching in the gravel along the side of the road. Joe finally spoke up.

"I gotta get a glove." Johnny had one, but Joe didn't, and it was impossible for them to play a game of catch at home.

"Dad said no more money for baseball stuff," Johnny said immediately. Joe sighed. Johnny could be so bossy, and besides, Joe already knew what his uncle had said. Although the team's sponsors paid for the uniforms, John Mark had to buy the shoes and all the other bits and pieces of gear that the boys needed, and he had declared that he was not spending another nickel on either of them.

"I have to make some money," Joe said.

"How you gonna do that?" Johnny asked.

"Maybe I can find a job at a grocery store," Joe said vaguely. "Wence has one."

Johnny laughed. "He got that 'cause his dad knows the grocery store owner. Anyway, you have to speak Czech to work at a grocery store. Otherwise the farmers don't understand you when they come in."

"Maybe I can get a paper route," Joe said after a while.

"Try again, pal," Johnny scoffed. "Dad knows five men who're trying to get one. He says you have to know someone at the newspaper before you can even get on the list."

Joe thought about what else he could do to buy a glove. Whenever he walked to school or ran errands, he watched the streets for things like empty bottles or tin cans that he could trade in for a little money, but the streets were picked clean during the day by men who had no work and were desperate for cash.

"You can look for pop bottles," Johnny suggested.

Joe didn't reply. The scrap shops paid almost nothing for bottles, and a good leather glove cost two dollars.

"Maybe we could sell rabbits," Johnny said. "That's what Rose does. We could do it together and split whatever we make."

Joe thought about that. Rose always had new shoes or a new hat or some such thing. He had heard her talk about tending her rabbits. She kept them in hutches under a stand of pine trees, next to the garden in Vincent's back yard, just out of the guard dog's reach.

"How's she do that?" he asked.

"People come over and buy 'em for dinner when there's no chickens at the market. Fifty cents for a little one and seventy-five for a big one. A big one can feed a lot of people," Johnny said.

"We could do that," Joe said. "Would she give us two to start with?"

"Not her," Johnny said. "She'll sell 'em to us, though." He thought for a while. "She might lend us a couple and let us pay her back. It would take, I don't know, maybe a month or so? For them to have babies and get big enough to sell?"

Joe didn't answer. A month was way too long, and anyway, it would probably be more like six weeks.

"We can borrow Anton's glove," Johnny suggested. Anton had decided not to play baseball this year, because he was playing tennis after school instead.

"I want my own," Joe said after a while. "Aren't there any rich parts of town over here? Where I lived before, there was a rich part and you could go over there and find a way to make some dough."

"No rich parts around here," Johnny said. "There's a golf course. But it's pretty far away. It's past the oat factory."

"That's good enough," Joe told him. "You can find balls and sell them back. I used to get a quarter a ball, for good ones."

"Wow," Johnny marveled. "Dad says not to go there, though. He says no crossing First Avenue without him."

Joe laughed to himself at the thought of stopping at a street instead of going across it to make some money. He gave Johnny a superior little smile, thinking about how dumb the other boy sounded, but the evening light had faded to darkness, and Johnny didn't see him.

" . . . and Bob was throwing everything at me, curve balls and all kinds of stuff, just like a real game. I was down oh-and-two," Joe told John Mark the next Friday evening at supper, "so I waited it out and hit fouls until he walked me. But next time up, I got him. I hit a fastball on the inside corner and got clear to second."

"Kovar say anything yet about you pitching?" John Mark asked.

"Uh, no, but I'm going to ask him tonight," Joe said. "I heard him say we need another one."

"I want to go!" Stephen whined. "I want to go too." The older boys were eating fast, trying to finish early in order to get to practice on time.

"You can't go. You'll get in the way," Johnny said.

"Oh, let him go with you this one time," Kate said.

"Mom!" Johnny groaned. "Stevie, don't you want to stay home and listen to Uncle Don on the radio tonight?" he wheedled. *Uncle Don* was a children's variety program that came on at 7:30, and Stephen usually listened to it just before he went to bed.

"No," Stephen said.

"It wouldn't be a bad idea for him to go with you, Johnny," John Mark said. "I used to take you with me when I played."

"Dad, that's different," Johnny pleaded. "He's too little. He'll do something to make Mr. Kovar mad."

"I think he should go," Kate said. "The Svobodas are coming over after supper tonight to talk and we'll need the front room, so he can't listen to the radio anyway. He'll have to stay upstairs all by himself."

Johnny moaned. Stephen looked around the table, not smiling yet. He couldn't decide if he was happy because he was going to practice, or upset because his brother didn't want him to come along.

Joe leaned over and mussed his hair. "You promise to be good?" he asked.

"Yes," Stephen promised.

"And if we tell you to sit down and don't get up or get in the way, you promise to do it?"

"Yes," Stephen said again.

"Attaboy," John Mark said approvingly. "You all go out to practice, and when you come back we can listen to *One Man's Family* at 9:30." He lowered his voice to make it sound like the show's opening announcement. " 'This show is dedicated to the mothers and fathers of the younger generation and to their bewildering offspring.' You three are crack examples. All you bewildering goofballs ought to be on radio."

Joe looked at Johnny. Both boys shrugged and got up, taking their dishes to the sink.

"Hold up a minute," John Mark said. "Tomorrow, I want you both to start digging up the garden. Turn over the dirt about six inches deep and get rid of the weeds. Do the first three rows along the grapevines. If we start now it'll be ready to plant in a couple weeks."

"Okay," Johnny sighed after a pause.

Joe glanced over. His uncle was looking at him, waiting for him to say something.

"Okay, Uncle John," he said.

"I'm doing a wedding over on the east side tomorrow and Kate is coming with me," John Mark went on. "You boys work on the garden in the morning and then I want you to take a bag of food over to the Kuceras in the afternoon. Their dad is still sick." The church kept a food pantry to make soup lunches for whoever needed a meal during the week, and John Mark usually sent whatever was left on Saturday to his parishioners who were sick.

"Dad, that's so far," Johnny protested. "Can't Uncle Vincent take it?"

"That's a good idea, live wire, but your uncle's taking us to the wedding," John Mark said with a grin. "The Kuceras don't live that far away."

"Where is it?" Joe asked.

"Clear over by First Avenue," Johnny huffed.

"That's all right, then," Joe said, silencing Johnny's next protest. John Mark looked over, a little surprised.

"We can do it," Joe said, and returned Johnny's frown with a shake of his head and a private smile. "Where's the bag?"

—————

The next day, working on the garden, Johnny had trouble keeping up with Joe. His older cousin marked off the area that they needed to dig up, divided it in half, and then told Johnny to race him to get it done.

"What's the rush?" Johnny finally panted. "We got all day to do this."

Joe gave his spade a hard kick with one foot and turned over a clump of heavy black dirt. "I want to go look for golf balls this afternoon," he said. "We're going that direction, right?"

Johnny jumped on his own spade to drive it into the ground and thought about how to answer that. He was reluctant to say anything like "Right." He didn't like doing something that wasn't his own idea, and furthermore he had promised his father that he would not go that far away from the house by himself.

"I don't think it's a good day to do that," he finally said. "I think it's gonna rain." He figured that if he didn't bring up the issue of breaking his promise, maybe he would find a way around it.

"Who cares if it rains?" Joe asked. "You gonna melt?"

"Nobody'll be playing golf if it rains," Johnny argued.

"That's the best time to go, goofus," Joe shot back as he turned over another spadeful. "That's when they're all in the clubhouse playing cards and looking for something to do."

"Anyway, maybe we can get another glove when Dad gets paid. You can use Anton's until then," Johnny went on.

"Listen, I want a good glove," Joe told him. "A two-dollar one. I can get it myself if I can just get to that golf course. I can make a whole lot more money in one day than mowing lawns all week long."

"Let's go next Saturday so I can ask first," Johnny finally said.

"Stay home if you don't want to go," Joe told him. "We can find more balls if there's two of us, but if you don't go, I'm still going. I might be able to buy the glove before next practice if I get enough balls today." He looked over at Johnny. "Your dad's out of money, and I'm going get some. I don't see what's wrong with that."

Later that afternoon, after delivering the food, Johnny sat down on the curb that ran along First Avenue. Cars rushed past him. His hands were blistered from digging up the garden and his shoulders ached from carrying the food bag to the Kuceras' apartment. Even though Joe had shared the load, it had been a long walk and he was tired. The sky was overcast, and it still looked like rain.

"I dunno," he said again. "I don't think we ought to."

Joe was standing, watching up and down the street for a break in the traffic so he could cross over. "I can't see anything so wrong with walking over there to make some dough," he said. "We're helping out, is what we're doing."

Johnny frowned. "What if Dad finds out?"

"Talk about dumb bohunks," Joe said in frustration, and started counting on his fingers. "Number one, he's not gonna know, unless you tell him. Number two, I need a glove. Number three, no one's making you go. What's wrong with you guys? Anybody's dad ought to be glad his kids go out and make some scratch on the side. He ought to thank us for it, not get us in trouble. Tell him at supper, if you want. Or just go home now. Which way is the golf course anyway?"

"You'll get lost if you go alone," Johnny grumbled.

"I'll ask directions, idiot," Joe snapped. Just then the traffic slowed down and he started off across the street.

"All right! Wait up!" Johnny said, and hurried after him.

"Oh, geez," Johnny breathed an hour later. The two boys were standing in the parking lot at the golf course, looking at cars. "Look at that." The sky-blue car in front of him had a cream-colored leather interior and a shiny chrome greyhound on its hood.

"That's just a Lincoln," Joe told him. "This one's the real beaut. It's a Nash. Ever been in one of these?"

Johnny looked over at the bottle-green coupe next to the Lincoln. It was huge, with white-walled tires and silvery chrome detailing.

"This car has shatterproof glass windows and a back seat so big it's like a double bed," Joe told him. "It has a place to put a champagne bottle. And in the winter it's warmer than a house."

Johnny had never been in any car except for his uncle's black Model A Ford, which his father had told him was a very good car, much better than the Model T's that were hard to start and couldn't go uphill without stalling. Vincent's Model A seemed like an old horse buggy now, compared to these dazzling beauties.

"How'd you ever get to ride in one of these?" he asked.

"My mom went with this one bootlegger guy for a while," Joe said. "They like the Nashes because of the windows."

"Wow," was all Johnny could say. "So, what's it like to ride in it?"

Joe didn't answer right away. Johnny looked over at him. He was staring at the car.

"I said, what's it like to ride in it?" Johnny said, a little louder.

It took a moment for Joe to snap out of whatever daze he was in. "I only rode in it once," he said after a while. "The bootlegger guy didn't like kids. He was a goon, anyway. I hated him."

"What was he like?" Johnny asked. "Did he have a gun?" He looked back at the Nash, picturing a dark-haired man who looked like Clark Gable sitting in the driver's seat.

Joe gave a harsh laugh. "You see this? You ever been hit this hard?" he asked, tapping the scar on the side of his face. "Know what I got this for? For coming inside when I wasn't supposed to. I was ten. He didn't like me to sleep inside with them at night, so I had to sleep on the porch."

"Man, that's tough," Johnny marveled. "Didn't you get cold?"

"Well, yeah, idiot, I got cold. Why'd you think I came inside and got clocked like that?" Joe snapped. "I hated his guts. He'd beat me up and I'd steal his cash and cigarettes to get back at him. That's how I got this," he held up his hand with the burn mark across the palm. "A fire poker," he said to Johnny. "He said that was how he'd cure me from stealing."

Johnny was shocked now. "But didn't your mom make him stop?" he finally stammered out. "Or move out, or something?"

Joe's expression turned so deadly furious that Johnny flinched just from looking at him. "My mom was a drunk," he said. "She never did a thing about it."

Johnny just looked at him. He couldn't think of anything to say.

"You got no idea," Joe told him. "You go to school and eat three meals a day and make a big fuss over all your little problems. You got no idea how I lived." He shook his head and turned away from the beautiful car. "Let's go," he said.

The boys searched through a pond along the side of the golf course's first green and found nine balls in the shallow end where the cattails and lily pads grew. Joe thought that five of them were good enough to try to sell, and he kept the other four "for bargaining," he said.

Both Joe and Johnny were wet and muddy from the pond when they headed for the clubhouse with their collection of balls. "That's okay," Joe told Johnny. "It plays better if you don't look too sharp when you're trying to sell balls. Now, mess up your hair. Roll up your jacket and hide it behind those bushes. We're gonna try and find some old high hat with a snootful of booze, or a daddy who wants to help out some poor kids down on their luck. You just keep quiet, look sad, and don't louse anything up."

The bartender looked up as the two of them entered the clubhouse. "Beat it, kids, right now," he told them. Johnny froze.

"Yessir. I just got some golf balls here, if anybody wants to buy 'em," Joe told him. "We're trying to get a little cash to buy some grub for our mom tonight, sir. We lost our credit at the store." Johnny turned and looked at Joe in astonishment, and then remembered to not louse anything up. He looked back at the bartender and tried to look sad.

In the end, Joe traded the five best balls for a dollar, and then managed to get another fifty cents for the four that were not as good. Just as he had predicted, a group of men were playing cards and ready to give out a little money to a pair of mournful-looking vagrant kids. Both boys said "Thank you very much, sir," and ran out of the clubhouse when the bartender looked sharply at them and said, "Now scram, you two. No more hard luck stories today."

Supper that evening was a quiet meal at first. Stephen was sniffling because Josefina had criticized him for not sweeping the floor properly, and Josefina was frowning because Kate had spoken firmly to her for being so harsh and making Stephen cry. John Mark had already changed from his good suit into his factory clothes and was the only one at the table who seemed happy.

"How'd practice go last night?" he asked, and Joe filled him in about how the team had practiced bunting. Joe already knew how to bunt, so the coach made him cover first base while the other players practiced, and one of the big eighteen-year-olds had charged right down the line at him, knocked him over, and then tried to taunt him into a fight.

"But no way was I gonna fall for that during practice," Joe said. "That kid's just dumb. I wouldn't play him if I was the coach. Can't keep his head in the game."

John Mark was impressed that Joe had been chosen to play third base.

"Put you right in the hot corner, huh? I better come out and see a practice," he said. When he heard that Johnny was playing right field, he winked at him.

"You got to start somewhere. I have to hand it to you, *Jan*. I didn't think you'd make the team. Good job there." He turned back to Joe. "If we can scrounge up two more gloves, we can all play catch and get you guys some practice in the evenings."

"Anton's not using his glove. I bet we can borrow it," Johnny said.

"I think I can get a glove," Joe said after a moment.

"Oh?" John Mark asked, reaching for more bread. "From where?"

"I think I can buy one," Joe said. Johnny was holding his breath and looking down at his plate. "I've been . . . looking for things I can pick up and sell." Joe glanced over at Johnny. "Around here."

John Mark was mopping up gravy with his slice of bread and not paying much attention. "You'll have to be pretty good to find enough stuff around here to do that," he said. "I can probably borrow a glove somewhere." He glanced around the table, then looked at Johnny curiously.

"You're not eating very much. Are you sick? What'd you do all day today?"

Johnny picked up his fork. "Oh, nothing. I'm fine, Dad. Sorry."

" . . . so I wrote my essay on Dizzy Dean, and the teacher gave me an F because she doesn't like him," Joe said as he walked home after school with Anton and Rudy later that week. "And guess why she doesn't like him? Because he says 'ain't' and 'slud into third' and things like that. What about how good he pitches? She doesn't know a thing about him." Joe changed his voice to sound like his teacher's. " 'That Dizzy Dean is a bad example to young people everywhere.' "

"That's baloney," Rudy said.

"She really gave you an F just because she doesn't like Dizzy Dean?" Anton asked.

"Oh, then she said I could go home and rewrite it, about anything except Diz," Joe said. "It just gripes me. I thought it was pretty good. I put in the part where he said, 'There's a lot of people in the United States who say 'isn't,' and they ain't eating.'"

The other two boys laughed. "What'd you expect? She's an English teacher," Anton told him.

The April afternoon was clear and sunny, and they would have good weather for practice that night. Rudy and Joe started talking about the team's batting lineup.

"We could use another hitter," Rudy said. "The coach is still looking for guys. C'mon, D, be on the team. Tennis is a girl's game." All the boys knew that Anton's mother had named him after Antonín Dvořák, and they had called him "Dvořák" and "Door" before finally shortening the nickname down to "D."

Anton, unflustered, bared his teeth in a growl and snapped them shut with a menacing click. "*You* come play *me*," he told Rudy. "Baseball's boring. You stand around forever waiting a turn to play. Now, tennis — you're killing something every fifteen seconds." He ran ahead a few steps and practiced an imaginary serve, jumping up into the air and bringing down his arm in a smashing arc. "The coach uses me to punish the other guys. They call me The Whip." He smacked another pretend stroke, a backhand this time. "There's a city championship this summer and I'm going to be in it."

"Who you gonna play? The girls' team?" Rudy smirked. Tennis was mostly a country-club pastime, played by well-dressed people who lived far over on the east side of the river.

"Talk about dumb games," Anton smirked back. "A batter misses the ball two-thirds of the time, people think he's great. Come over and count how many times *I* miss the ball, bud. Can't you get Wence to play instead?"

"He works every night now," Rudy said. "He doesn't want to play this year."

"What's he doing with all his money?" Joe asked.

Rudy and Anton shut up.

"Geez, guys, swell," Joe complained.

"He's just saving it," Rudy said.

"Huh," Joe said. "Got something to do with Rachel?"

"Keep it under your lid, or I'll knock you silly," Rudy threatened.

Joe grinned. He didn't mind when Rudy teased him anymore. Now that he was playing third base on a city league team, he felt better about everything, even school. Families came out when the weather was nice and watched the teams practice, and people were noticing him, in a good way this time. Coach Kovar was a favorite to watch because of the colorful way he bawled out the boys when they made mistakes. Joe didn't make very many mistakes, though, so when he did, the insults that came his way seemed a little half-hearted, which was as good as a compliment as far as he was concerned. Even his uncle was impressed by the way he could hit and throw.

"Hey, Anton, if you're not going to play, can I borrow your glove? Until I get my own?" he asked.

"Sure," Anton said. "Keep it all season. I won't miss it." Rudy called him a name and shoved him into the street. A car squealed its tires and honked at them as it whizzed past. Anton chased Rudy and pushed him into a tree trunk. Joe grinned again and ran to catch up with them.

The next Saturday, John Mark and Kate went to a funeral, and Joe and Johnny dug up the next section of garden. Joe was ready to head over to the golf course as soon as they were done. He needed another fifty cents to buy a glove, and he figured he could probably find enough balls to make at least that much.

"You coming?" he asked Johnny.

"I dunno," Johnny said. "If I find any, I want to keep the money for myself this time."

"Okay," Joe said. "Fair enough. It'll work out better if we split it, though. Why don't we just buy the glove first, then split anything else we get?"

"All right," Johnny said cautiously, as if he couldn't really decide if that was a better deal for him or not.

Joe looked at Johnny for a moment, feeling a little sorry for him, since he obviously didn't know much about making money. "Some days I'm gonna find more balls, and some days you're gonna find more," he told him. "I used to do this all the time with all different kinds of guys. I think that if we just split everything, right down the middle, it'll work out better."

"What'd you do with all your money?" Johnny asked him.

"Bought food."

Johnny looked at him for a moment. "Didn't your mom do that?" he finally asked.

Joe felt his stomach lurch at the question. Suddenly he wished that he had not said so much about himself to Johnny. Telling anyone about what had happened in his life before he came here seemed like a very unsafe thing to do. It was better not to talk about it at all. He hardened his face and turned away.

"You coming or not?" he snapped.

"What's eating you all of a sudden? Let me go in and tell Mrs. Vesely that we'll be gone for a while," Johnny said sullenly.

The two boys had walked almost to the golf course when Joe looked behind them and stopped. "Oh, no," he groaned.

"What?" Johnny gasped.

"Look," Joe said, and pointed. Farther back down the street, a little boy with blond hair was bobbing along as fast as he could walk, following them.

Johnny let out the breath he had been holding. "That . . . kid!" he finally said in exasperation. "I can't believe it! How on earth did he get across First Avenue without killing himself?"

Joe laughed. "What a pain," he said, but he smiled as he watched Stephen huffing along as fast as he could, trotting towards them with a big grin now that they had stopped and were waiting for him. The little boy waved and broke into a run.

"Stephen, what are you doing? Go back home!" Johnny said as soon as he was close enough to hear.

"I followed you!" Stephen panted. "I thought you were going to Anton's house. Where're you going?"

"None of your business," Johnny said.

"Dad says it's rude to say that, so shut up," Stephen told him. Johnny glared at him, but he was silenced by the reminder of his father and what John Mark would say if he knew that they were so far from home.

"Dad says it's rude to say shut up, too, so you better shut up or I'll tell," he said to Stephen, trying to regain the upper hand in the argument.

Joe hunkered down with his hands on his knees so that he could look Stephen in the eyes. "Look, Stevie, we're going on a really long walk, and you're going to get too tired to keep up, so you shouldn't have followed us," he said. "I think you should go home now. When we come back we'll bring you some sort of a surprise, for being good. Okay?"

Stephen looked from one of them to the other, suspicion in his eyes. "What're you guys doing?"

"We're just walking around looking for stuff," Johnny said firmly.

"Why can't I come too?"

Joe looked at Johnny and shrugged. "He can't get home by himself anyway," he said. "He's too little to cross big streets. He'd probably get lost."

"No! He can't come! He'll tell!" Johnny hissed back at him.

Joe looked down the street and then back towards the golf course, tantalizingly close now. "Maybe you should take him back, then."

Johnny snorted. "Right, and let you make all the money?"

Stephen sucked in his breath. "You're making *money?*"

"No, we're just walking around trying to find stuff," Johnny said quickly. "Look, you sit down and stay right here, and we'll be back in a little bit and take you home."

"Naw, that's not gonna work," Joe protested. "Someone could come along and kidnap him or something."

"Go on," Johnny snorted. "Who'd want to kidnap him?"

"Something could happen," Joe said. "We can't just leave him here." He bent down again. "Stephen, we're going to a park, and when we get there, you have to do exactly what we say. And then you keep this a dead secret, from everybody, or else we'll never take you with us anywhere again, hear?"

Stephen nodded. His eyes were huge with excitement. All three boys headed on towards the golf course again.

"This isn't a good idea," Johnny muttered.

"Like I said, you don't have to come," Joe pointed out.

Johnny just bit his lip, and shook his head.

Johnny let Stephen help him find golf balls, but he made his little brother sit outside the clubhouse and wait while he went inside with Joe to sell them. They came back out with a dollar and a quarter, and agreed to split the money since Joe would have enough from his share to buy the glove. Joe stopped at a bar on the way home and bought penny candy for all of them out of his share. He also bought a pack of cigarettes.

Back outside, he lit up and blew a thin plume of smoke as he walked. He looked suddenly glamorous.

"Let me try that," Johnny said. Joe looked at him and held out the cigarette. Johnny inhaled and choked a bit, trying to smother the cough. Joe took the cigarette away.

"Let me try again," Johnny said when he could talk.

"Nope. Buy your own, if you want some more," Joe told him. "You've got your own money now. Nobody likes a sponger."

Afterwards, Johnny always remembered that moment as kind of frozen in time, the moment when he decided that he would rather spend his money on something other than a pack of cigarettes. He was embarrassed that he had coughed, and mad that Joe wouldn't share, but a slender line of logic inside him won out that day, and he decided not to buy a pack. Years later, he looked back in amazement. It was as though the angel of death had passed him by.

"Now, Stevie, you can't tell anyone where we went," Joe said when they came back to the house. "Not anyone. Promise?"

"Not even Mom?" Stephen asked, a puzzled frown on his face.

"Right. Not even your mom," Joe told him. "Just tell her that we went on a walk, but don't tell her that we went across First Avenue. Otherwise, you'll get us all in trouble, big fella. You don't want that, do you?"

"No," Stephen said.

"Good kiddo," Joe told him. They were at the front of the house now. Joe leaned down and gave Stephen a hug, then picked him up by his overalls and swung him up the porch stairs to the door. Stephen shrieked and giggled with glee, then opened the door and ran inside.

Johnny looked at Joe. "He's going to tell. I don't think we ought to go anymore."

Joe shook his head in disbelief. "You're nuts," he said. "I don't see how it's such a big deal. It's not like we're stealing or anything."

"Yeah, but I don't feel good about not telling Dad," Johnny finally said.

"Tell him, then," Joe said. "Or else don't go. You want me to tell him?"

"No!" Johnny said. "Not yet, anyway."

Joe rolled his eyes. "Make up your mind," he said, and went inside.

"I've got enough money to buy a glove now," Joe told John Mark later that night. Stephen was asleep upstairs, Kate had gone to bed early, and the rest of them had just finished listening to *The Ed Sullivan Show*. His uncle was putting on his jacket because he had to leave for work, and Joe figured that the time was right to let him know about the glove. After living for years with constant trouble from adults, he knew how to pick the right time to say things.

"You're kidding me," John Mark said. "How'd you do that?"

"Oh, I just got lucky, finding stuff to sell," Joe told him.

John Mark paused in the middle of buttoning his jacket. He looked at Joe for a long moment.

"How did you do that?" he finally asked.

"We found stuff and sold it at the scrap store," Johnny said quickly, referring to the neighborhood junk store where people traded in pieces of copper and tin and got a few pennies for the scraps of metal.

"Huh," John Mark said, and looked from one boy to the other. Joe yawned loudly to distract him from whatever he was thinking. Johnny dropped his eyes and stared at the floor.

John Mark looked as if he was going to say something more, but then he looked at the clock.

"I have to leave now or I'll be late, but we'll talk about this again tomorrow," he finally said.

"Okay, Dad. Bye," Johnny said.

John Mark studied him again, then looked back at the clock and sighed.

He picked up his hat. "Be sure and lock up." He glanced at Joe.

"Yes, sir," Joe said. John Mark paused, then said, "Well, good night," and went out the door. Joe locked it behind him, then turned around and glared at Johnny.

"Idiot," he hissed. "What'd you say that for? Now you're in trouble."

"Says you!" Johnny whispered back. "It was all your idea anyway." He got up and headed for the attic.

Joe caught up with him as he climbed the narrow stairs. "Look, I never lied," Joe said. "I can come clean and say that I never actually lied about any-thing."

"You did so lie," Johnny came back at him. "That first night at supper, you lied."

"I don't remember telling any lie," Joe protested. "If I did, it wasn't a whopper like you just told. You shouldn't have said that about the junk store. Your dad's going to check that store and find out that you've never been there, and then you're going to double-cross me and say that it was all my fault and leave me holding the bag."

Johnny pulled off his clothes and flopped onto his bed. Moonlight lit the little room, streaming through the attic window. "Naw," he finally said. "Dad's too busy." Both boys could hear Stephen's sleepy breathing now, soft and clear in the quiet attic. "As long as Stephen doesn't tell, we'll be all right."

Later that week, John Mark pushed himself back from his desk in the church's office and stretched. He was sitting with Frank Chada, the book-keeper, and the two of them were going over the bank statements and recon-ciling the check ledger. Vincent had kept the church's books for years, until the church's board of directors had decided that it would be better to find someone not related to the minister to do that work. They were concerned about keeping proper safeguards on the money taken up each Sunday. John Mark agreed with the principle behind the thinking — any man would be tempted by money, these days — and Frank was a good worker, but he still missed Vincent at times like this. His brother had a steady, reassuring atti-tude about money. Vincent didn't get rattled if the church had a thin week in the collection basket. But Frank tended to worry if the contribution didn't look like it would be enough to cover the bills, and his faithlessness affected John Mark more than he liked to admit.

"You wrote a check here?" Frank was asking. John Mark quit stretching and looked back at the ledger. "What does this say?"

John Mark had to stop and think. "Two dollars and thirty-nine cents. Sorry," he said. "I know I should have been more careful." He rubbed his eyes. "That was for groceries for the lunches this week. We had to buy some extra food to keep up." Instead of putting money in the contribution plate, some parishioners brought in food such as bread or eggs for the lunch kitchen. Cash was hard to get and had to be saved for expenses such as rent, which could not be paid in barter. Food passed in and out of the church every day, but there was not always enough for all those who came looking for a meal. John Mark hated to see people go hungry, so at times he bought groceries to keep the lunch kettles full.

"Well, looks like we're all right for now," Frank said with a sigh of relief. "The water bill isn't due yet. Don't spend more than four dollars until Sunday." He closed the ledger and looked over at John Mark.

"Gotcha. Thanks for doing all this, Frank," John Mark said. He reminded himself to be grateful. Frank was keeping the books for very little pay, mainly because he wanted to help out. Vincent had done it for free, but there was no point in thinking about that now.

"*Rádo se stalo.* Glad to do it." Frank put on his coat and hat. "See you later." He still worked part-time as an accountant for a department store across the river, although his hours had been cut after the stock market crash. He came in to work at the church on his days off.

After he left, John Mark got up and walked out to the kitchen. The lunch workers had washed up and gone home. Immaculately clean pots and ladles sat lined up on the counters, and the late afternoon sun shone through the deserted dining hall. There was still some lukewarm coffee left in the bottom of one of the big urns and John Mark poured it out for himself to drink before he locked up the hall and headed back to the office to work on his sermon.

He had a hard time focusing on it. Through his window he could see the light green leaves of spring on the tree branches, and they reminded him of baseball, which reminded him of Joe's new glove. Joe had not mentioned it again after Saturday night and John Mark had almost forgotten about it.

Sunday was a busy day for him, and then he had to work at the factory on Sunday night and was exhausted all day on Monday. But now the nagging memory of what Joe and Johnny had said about the glove, and the way they had acted, was bothering him.

There was very little chance that the two boys could actually have found enough scrap metal to trade for the amount of money that a glove would cost. They must have either lied outright or kept back some part of the story. John Mark stared out the window and thought about the possibility that Joe had stolen some item from the house and pawned it, or done something else equally bad. That was not too hard to imagine. Joe had probably been a slick little thief when he lived with Marie, just like countless other boys who lived in shacks or shanties and were desperate for food.

But Johnny had chimed right in with the scrap metal story. John Mark hated to think that his son had lied to him. All these years, even before the Crash, he had always believed that the love and trust he had with Kate, and now with his sons, was worth more than the money and other fine things that he did not have. During the nightmare year when his church had fallen apart and he had been evicted from his home, he had comforted himself in his family's unfailing love. He had especially taken pride in Johnny. Little *Jan*, even with all the troubles that they had been through, was growing up to be so smart. A fine young man.

John Mark put his head in his hands. He had tried to help Joe get along with Johnny. Well, now they were getting along, and as a result Joe was teaching his son how to lie. What else was he doing? Showing Johnny how to steal, too? Destroying the whole family, after they had taken him in and fed him and bought clothes for him? A slow rage started burning in his heart.

He had suspected it right from the start. The first day that Joe had come to live under his roof, he had suspected that the boy was going to bring some kind of trouble to his home. He had grown to like Joe, though, and had put away his suspicions about him. He had been foolish. He should have known better.

And he should have followed up with the boys about that piece of business the next day, as he had said he would. He had let himself be distracted by all his work. How could he have done that? Neither boy had said anything about the glove, or even about baseball, since that night. They were up to something, and every day since then he had forgotten about it and let it slip by without getting to the bottom of the story. It made the whole situation worse. If they had already done something wrong, and he hadn't said a word to them about it, then there was nothing to stop them from doing it again. He had to talk to them about it tonight.

He was putting away his books and planning to stop by the scrap metal store on his way home to check up on their story, when someone knocked on the office door.

"*Vistoupit*," he called out.

A hollow-faced man stepped through the door and took off his cap. "Reverend Starosta?"

"Yes, I'm John Starosta," John Mark said, and held out his hand for a shake. "What can I do for you?"

The man looked down and shook his head. "I was hopin' you'd have some food left over from the lunch," he said so indistinctly that John Mark could barely understand him. The man glanced up. "I been out of work for a year and a half and I got six kids." The man kept talking, but for a moment John Mark didn't hear the words. He could visualize the man's ragged wife and children, probably without coats or proper shoes. He had seen so many like them over the past four years. He had kept watch with parents over too many thin, sick children, and seen too many of them die from diseases such as influenza or pneumonia because there was not enough money to buy food and coal and medicine for them all.

"Let's go see what's left over," he said to the man, and he went back to unlock the dining hall door. John Mark couldn't leave for home and eat his own dinner with the thought of those six children going to bed hungry. He himself only had a paying job because he knew someone at the oat factory who had helped him get it. As he started looking through the pantry shelves, he reminded himself to talk to the boys about the glove as soon as he could. He could not afford to forget about that problem for even one more day.

The next Saturday morning, Joe straightened up from turning over a spadeful of dirt and sighed. Even though the day was cool and cloudy, he was working up a sweat. "I dunno. I don't think we ought to go today." He leaned on his spade for a moment, resting. "That last Saturday was a close call. I think your dad's onto us."

"Naw. I don't think so. He never said anything about it," Johnny argued back. He was spading up dirt as fast as he could. "I want to get a bicycle." He looked up at Joe and stopped working, since Joe was taking a break. "You got what you want. Now I want to get something."

Joe glanced back at the house. John Mark was home, but still in bed. "He might wake up and want us to do something," he warned. His uncle had been out late every night that week at the church, and one day he had even gone straight from the church to the factory without coming home to change first. Kate had told him to sleep late that morning.

"Mom's going to the market with the Prazskys and no one will notice if we're gone for a while," Johnny pointed out. "It won't take that long." He went back to his digging, and after a moment Joe did too.

Stephen was running after them before they had even gone around the corner of their own block. "Wait up! Wait up," he begged. Joe and Johnny stopped and turned around.

"You can't come this time. We're going to walk fast and you'll slow us down," Johnny told him. Stephen looked at Joe for sympathy, but Joe shook his head.

"Sorry. You got to stay home today, big fella. We'll bring you a surprise when we come back, okay?"

Stephen looked from one to the other. "That's no fair. I'm telling, if you don't take me."

Johnny groaned. Joe shook his head again. "Now, don't go rat on your friends. That's a bad move. Just stay home this time."

Stephen was stubborn. "I'll help. I'll keep up."

"No," Johnny told him. "Go back. We'll bring you something. Come on, Joe, let's go." The two older boys started walking again.

Stephen followed them anyway, just far enough behind to not be seen.

Later, at the golf course pond, Joe looked around and decided it was time to go home. The day had been a bust. Stephen had followed them again, they had only found two balls, and the sky had darkened. It was going to rain.

"Let's go," he called. Johnny looked up and started walking over from his side of the pond. Stephen was still looking for something in the water, so Joe splashed over to see what he was doing.

"Come on, let's go. Time to go," he said. He felt a drop of rain on his head.

Stephen looked up, fear written all over his face. "I lost my shoe," he said.

"You what? You lost your shoe? You had your shoes on in the water?" Joe could hardly believe how bad this day was turning out. "Why didn't you take your shoes off, you dimwit?" Both the older boys had taken off their shoes and socks before going into the water.

Stephen started crying.

"Oh, great," Joe said. A lost shoe was a disaster. The whole day was turning into a nightmare.

Johnny joined him. "What's the matter?" he asked.

"He lost a shoe," Joe said grimly.

Johnny panicked at the thought of explaining a lost shoe. "Stephen, doggone you! Come on! We gotta find it!" he gasped. "Look around! Where'd you lose it at?" He plunged into the water and frantically started looking through the tangle of reeds and lily pads that grew along the edge of the pond.

Stephen was still crying. "I don't know! I just . . . *lost* it somewhere . . ."

"Well, you better find it!" Johnny snapped. "I told you not to come! Now look what's happened!"

"All right, calm down," Joe ordered. "Stephen, where were you when you found out that it was gone?" He tried to organize them and search the area, but Johnny wouldn't follow directions, and Stephen only cried and wouldn't listen to him. Joe finally gave up and went to the clubhouse to sell the balls while the other boys kept on looking.

He came back out with only twenty cents in his pocket, because the men inside were deep in a poker game and the bartender had taken the balls, given him two dimes, and told him to get out before someone got mad. Outside, the raindrops had turned into a sprinkle. Johnny and Stephen were waiting for him under the cover of the clubhouse's front entryway, wet and miserable. They had not found the shoe.

"Twenty cents," Joe said when Johnny looked over at him. For a while, no one said anything, and the sprinkle turned into rain. A low growl of thunder sounded in the distance.

"We better get going, or we'll really be in trouble," Joe finally said. "Come on."

The walk home was wet and chilly. Stephen couldn't go very fast with only one shoe, so Joe and Johnny traded off carrying him piggy-back, and Joe ended up carrying him most of the time because he was stronger. The rain settled into a steady drizzle and Stephen's nose started to run. Halfway home, Joe stopped at a bar so that Stephen could go inside and warm up for a while. He bought doughnuts for all of them out of their earnings, even though Johnny protested about losing his ten cents.

"Dry it up," Joe said. "Ten cents isn't going to buy you a bike anyway, and I gotta get something to eat." Johnny was quiet after that.

When they were almost home, Johnny finally asked, "What are we going to say about the shoe?"

Joe had been thinking about that. "Stick as close to the truth as possible," he told both boys. "Let's just say that we were over at Riverside Park, by the river, and Stephen fell in and lost his shoe. That's pretty close."

The other two boys thought about that for a while. "That's lying," Stephen finally said.

"It's pretty much what happened, though. It's just easier for everybody this way," Joe told him. "Let's not get in trouble, okay?"

"What if they ask why we were gone so long?" Johnny asked.

Joe shrugged. "We'll just say that we were walking around looking for stuff," he said. "That's not really lying."

"What if they ask about exactly where we went, though?"

"You want to tell them?" Joe asked. Johnny looked away.

"We could say that we went to the scrap shop. You still have five cents," Johnny said. "Or that we were at Anton's."

"Okay. Stephen, you got that?" Joe said. "We went to the river, and you fell in and lost your shoe. And then we went to the scrap shop and Anton's."

"Okay," Stephen said. "I just want to go home."

"Here they come," Kate said to John Mark. The two of them were sitting in the front room, waiting for the boys to get back.

John Mark looked out the window. He felt jumpy and irritable, and a headache pounded right behind his eyes. He had been looking for the boys all day.

"I'm so mad I could just line them up and shoot them," he said.

"John, maybe you better let me handle this, until you calm down," Kate said.

John Mark snorted. "Oh, no." He looked over at her. "I think you better leave the room. And close the door."

When the boys came through the front door, they all smiled and nodded at John Mark, then headed towards the kitchen. Stephen had on only one shoe.

"Wait a minute," John Mark called out. "Come back here." All three of them tensed up as they turned around and came back. John Mark just looked at them for a while, letting them sweat a bit.

"Where've you been all day?" he asked. "Where's Stephen's other shoe?"

No one spoke at first. Then Joe said, "We were down at the park, by the river, and Stephen fell in and lost his shoe."

"We looked all over, but we couldn't find it," Johnny said in a hurry.

John Mark looked from one face to the other. He had already been to the park and he knew that they hadn't been there. "And that took you all day?"

There was a pause. "We looked for stuff and went to the scrap metal shop too," Johnny said.

John Mark looked at him. "Like you did before?" he said with an edge of sarcasm in his voice.

"Uh, yeah," Johnny said. He looked nervous. *You better be nervous,* John Mark thought. *You're about to be skinned alive.*

"Stephen?" he asked. "Is that what happened?"

"Yes, Dad," Stephen said, and John Mark felt his heart turn over in pain when he heard his youngest tell a lie while looking right at him.

He looked back at Joe. "Anything else?"

Joe had flushed red. He looked at John Mark for a moment, then dropped his eyes. "No, sir," he said. He looked back up. "We finished the garden first, though."

"We went to Anton's too," Stephen said brightly. Johnny bit his lip.

John Mark took a breath. "Oh, is that where you were?"

Stephen nodded. Johnny kept perfectly still. Joe stared at the floor, his face expressionless.

John Mark felt his face get hot with anger. He stood up. "I want you to know, you little pack of liars, that I just came from there and Anton said he hadn't seen you all day." Stephen lost his smile. "And the people at the scrap shop don't have any record of *you*" he stabbed his finger at Johnny, "going in there for even a penny's worth of stuff." Johnny turned red.

"I never thought you boys would lie like this to me," John Mark went on. He looked straight at Joe. "Johnny and Stephen, anyway. I don't know about you." Joe looked down. "You better tell me right now where you've been and where you got that money for that glove before I throw you out of here!" By this time, he was shouting. His head throbbed with pain, and he dropped back into his chair, glaring at them.

After a long silence, Johnny said, "I'm sorry, Dad."

"Not as sorry as you're going to be, if you don't answer the question," John Mark said sharply. He got up again, his hands clenching into fists. "I want to know exactly what's been going on here and I want to know *now*." His voice made the walls ring and the boys jumped. "You better start talking and every word better be God's honest truth or I swear I will make every one of you sorry that you were ever born. Where'd you go today and where'd you get that money?"

"We went to the golf course," Joe said after a while. "That's all."

"Is that the truth this time?" John Mark snapped.

Joe looked up at him, miserable. "Yes, sir."

"What were you doing there?"

"Picking up golf balls." Joe said. His face had hardened and he looked angry now, not miserable. "To sell. That's where we got the money."

"The money for the glove that you just had to have this week," John Mark said.

"Uh, yes," Joe said after a moment.

John Mark turned away from him. "Johnny?"

"Yes, Dad," Johnny said. His lips trembled. "That's what we did. That's the truth."

"Stephen?" John Mark's chest hurt again as he looked at him.

Stephen's eyes shifted, and he looked like he was going to start crying.

"Stop crying. Time for you to knock that off," John Mark said. "If you're old enough to lie now, you're old enough to stand there and tell the truth." Out of the corner of his eye, he saw Kate come out of the kitchen and lean against the doorway, watching him.

"Is that what you did today, Stephen?" John Mark repeated. "Or did you go to the park and Anton's house?"

"The golf course," Stephen whispered.

John Mark took a deep breath and tried to calm himself, conscious of Kate's presence. "How long has this been going on?"

"Joe and me went three times. On Saturdays," Johnny said. John Mark looked at him, then at Joe. Johnny still could not meet his eyes, but Joe looked right back at him.

"I just went two times," Stephen said in a small voice. "I followed them."

"You didn't walk with them?" John Mark asked sharply. "How'd you get across First Avenue?"

"By myself," Stephen said.

John Mark looked at the two older boys.

"By yourself," he repeated. "You crossed First Avenue by *yourself*." He looked over at Kate. She looked horrified.

"So. Let me get this straight. For three weeks," John Mark gritted out, "I have been . . . " he stopped, trying to find words, "working day and night, trying to keep food on the table, spending my money on your precious special baseball shoes, and you've been lying to me through your teeth the whole time. Not to mention almost getting Stephen killed."

The boys were looking everywhere but at him. "Look at me," John Mark said.

He sat down and waited for them to obey. Johnny had tears in his eyes. Joe was the last one to look at him.

"You don't even know the worst of it yet," John Mark said. "When you trust someone, you have something special. Best feeling in the world. You don't have that with everybody. I don't have that with everybody. But I have it here. Used to have it."

Tears were sliding down Johnny's face. John Mark went on. "But once you lie and break that trust, it's gone. No matter how much you wish, you can never go back and make it that way again. Never. I will never again be able to trust you like I did before. Whenever you tell me something from now on, it's always going to be in the back of my mind: are they telling the truth? And I'll have to wonder, and go check up, and that special thing is gone now, because you lied."

Stephen was crying now, too, but silently. "Sorry, Dad," he whispered. "I won't lie anymore. I promise. Okay?"

"Me too, Dad," Johnny said urgently. "I'm really sorry and I promise I'll never do it again. Okay?"

John Mark jumped up from the couch. "No! It is not okay!" he thundered. "You boys still don't know what you did! You know what happens next? After a while you think that everyone else is lying, too, and so you don't believe what anybody says to you, and then you start lying all the time and ruin everything." He towered over them, his face hot with rage, staring straight at Joe.

Joe was looking at the floor, but he glanced up and caught the stare. He cleared his throat. "I wanted to go make some money to buy the glove," he said. "I didn't think it was such a big deal." He looked at John Mark. "I told Johnny that he didn't have to come if he didn't want to."

John Mark looked at Johnny, who nodded without looking up.

"And you didn't think to just come talk to me about it?" John Mark said. "You didn't think that you just could have said, 'Gosh, I want to make some money, what about going to the golf course?' and I wouldn't have let you? Or helped you?"

The boys looked up at him.

"But instead you decided it was a better idea to lie, and just put one over on me, and then you made Stephen lie about it, too, in order to save your own skins. Taught him how to lie right along with you." He couldn't help looking right at Joe as he said it. "So now Stephen knows how to lie. I hope you're happy. He could've been killed, crossing First Avenue by himself." The boys looked down again. "You thought it was nothing? Let me tell you, your world's never going to be the same again. All because you thought it was no big deal to lie."

"Dad, I am really, really sorry," Johnny said again.

"You haven't even begun to be sorry," John Mark said harshly. "All three of you, turn around."

He took off his belt, doubled it up, and thrashed their backsides, one at a time. Stephen was so scared that he bawled before the belt even touched him, and John Mark sent him over to Kate before he started on Johnny. Johnny took his whipping better, only gasping a little as the leather hit him. He went upstairs without a word when John Mark was done. Joe was silent clear through the beating and walked away as soon as it was over.

"Come back here," John Mark ordered. "What do you have to say for yourself?"

Joe looked at him, expressionless. "Sorry," he said after a while.

John Mark bit back a harsh reply and pressed his hand to his forehead for a moment, trying to ease the pain there. "Go on," he said wearily. "Leave. Get out of here."

After Joe left the room, John Mark went outside and sat on the porch. A nagging little thought wouldn't leave him alone. He couldn't decide if he should feel better because he had finally caught the boys in their lie, or if he should still be angry at Joe.

So that contrariwise ye ought rather to forgive him, and comfort him, lest perhaps such a one should be swallowed up with overmuch sorrow. . . a verse from Second Corinthians, chapter two, suddenly came to mind.

No, he argued back. *That's not what I should be doing right now. When boys go out and do something wrong, their fathers have to discipline them and bring them back in line. That's exactly what Your Word says to do.*

The nagging thought wouldn't go away, though.

Wherefore I beseech you that ye would confirm your love toward him . . .

John Mark shook his head in frustration. *Lord, You ought to be on my side here. Doggone it, those kids know I love them. Here I am, working at the factory, working for You, trying to take care of . . . everyone . . .* John Mark looked out at the street. He had been caught up in church business, trying to sort out everyone else's problems instead of paying more attention at home. And now, partly because of that, he had even more problems. Maybe he shouldn't have been so harsh with his words. Maybe he should have just thrashed the boys and sent them upstairs without dinner. That thought made his head hurt again. He put his hands up to his temples, trying to rub away the pain.

Someone slammed open the front door and went down the front porch steps. It was Joe, with a half-filled pillowcase hanging from his hand.

"Hey!" John Mark called out. "Where do you think you're going?"

Joe spun around and stiffened up when he saw John Mark.

"I . . . I'm leaving now," he said. "Ah, thanks for everything." He started towards the street.

"Joe," John Mark called. "Stop." Joe took a few more steps before stopping. He kept his face turned away.

John Mark pushed himself to his feet and walked out after him. "Come on. You're not going anywhere." He put his hand on the boy's shoulder.

Joe jerked away. "You want to bet? I'm not sticking around to take this kind of" – his voice broke – "crap anymore."

John Mark sighed and took a step towards him. Joe backed out of reach and yelled, "You want to act like you're so much better than everybody else? Right? You and all this . . . this . . ." he looked like he was going to say something but then changed his mind, "crap about God and love and family. I got news for you! You're just like all the rest. You don't want me around? Fine! Just fine! I'm going!"

John Mark grabbed his arm, but Joe twisted out of his grip and jumped away into the middle of the street. "Now wait a minute," John Mark said, following him. "No need for all this. I didn't mean for you to think I was telling you to leave."

Joe was still glaring at him, but he paused and waited.

"Look," John Mark started. He was painfully aware that he was standing in the middle of the street trying to reason with an angry boy, and that curious neighbors might be watching. "What you did was wrong, but that doesn't mean you have to leave."

Joe's eyes were blazing. "Listen, I'm telling you, and I don't care if you're God's own right hand, I was trying to help you out. Help out! And then you go and do that to me! Let me tell you something," he said fiercely, and took a step forward. "I lied and stole stuff practically every single day of my life. Because I had to! Had to! Every — single — day! Or starve to death! You're in a house, you have money, you have this great life and . . . and . . ." his voice broke again. "Try being me. You just try once and see how it feels. And I'll tell you what else."

Tears were streaming down Joe's face now, and John Mark waited. He was not thinking about the neighbors anymore. Joe raised his hand and pointed his finger, stabbing it in the air a few times before he could get his words out.

"I don't see you throwing Johnny out, and he did the same stuff I did. You just don't want me around because I don't have a dad, and my mom was a drunk, and you don't want me to louse up your nice family. Well, fine. I'm leaving."

"Joe, I'm not throwing you out," John Mark said again, more quietly now, feeling his own throat tighten up with pain. "Listen to me. I'm not trying to make you leave." Joe turned his head away. "Come on, let's go sit down."

"You don't know," Joe said after a while. "You don't know how hard it is. You don't know how hard I try just to fit in around here. All this church stuff, prayer stuff, going to school. Every day I try not to mess up so you won't throw me out. Every day it's so hard. And then I mess up anyway. No matter how hard I try. I'm always the one that gets screwed. Every time."

John Mark reached out and took his arm again, gently this time. Joe made as if to pull away, but only half-heartedly.

"No," John Mark said. "No, that's not it. You've done good here." John Mark closed his eyes for a moment, wishing that he had said this weeks or months earlier, instead of now, when the words sounded so lame.

Joe looked around. He hadn't pulled his arm away. Heartened, John Mark went on. "Come on home now."

At the word "home," Joe looked at right at him. John Mark understood, then, what he had to say. "You belong here with us. This is your place now. Come on."

Joe looked down the street, then back at him. "Look, I didn't mean to lie."

John Mark waited, relieved that the boy was talking.

"I know you work a lot," Joe said. "I see you get tired. I was trying to help out. And now you're never going to trust me again. I'm screwed."

John Mark waited some more.

"I didn't mean for it all to turn out this way," Joe finally said.

"I know," John Mark said. "You made a mistake. I make mistakes too, but I don't have to leave home over them and you don't either. Come on, sit down. I'm tired." He tugged on the boy's sleeve, and Joe followed him to the porch. They both sat down. Joe sniffed hard and wiped at his eyes.

"I know that your mom . . . that you didn't grow up learning about this stuff," John Mark said after a while. "I understand that. But you know better now. You gotta stop lying, Joe. It'll ruin your life. Every time you lie, you . . ." he slowed down, trying to find the right words, ". . . when you lie, you never feel the same way about yourself, or the person that you lied to either. It doesn't even matter if anybody else finds out or not. You didn't feel the same around me after you started lying, right?"

Joe looked away, but he gave what looked like a little nod. John Mark went on.

"You can't go down that road. You're my nephew, you're in my family, so if one person's lying and then another person starts lying, it'll destroy the whole thing. And I will not let that happen here. You get it?"

Joe was silent.

"You know what's right and wrong, and you have to live by it now, just like everybody else. I expect all my family to be honest all the time."

Joe sat still, staring down the street. After a while, he said, "So if I screw up, you're going to throw me out?"

John Mark sighed. "Let's just start over." He looked at Joe until the boy looked back at him. "You can tell if a person's trying, right?" Joe gave a little nod. "If you make a mistake, then come clean and tell me as soon as possible and make it right. If you'll do that much, then I promise that I'll listen to you, and not yell, and we'll just go on, and you keep on living with us, because this is your home now. Fair?"

Joe sat hunched over, arms crossed tight across his chest, chewing on the inside of his lip.

"What do you say?" John Mark asked after a while.

Joe blew out a sharp breath. "Okay," he said, but his voice trembled in the middle of the word. He swallowed hard.

John Mark slapped his back. "Attaboy," he said, for lack of any better word. He thought of something else to say, and punched Joe on the arm to get his attention.

"If you catch me screwing up, you can remind me about our little porch talk and say the same thing to me," he told him.

Joe snorted. "Yeah, right. You'll never admit it if you screw up."

"Oh yeah?" John Mark laughed. "Me, the preacher, I will tell you right now, I will screw up and you will see it. In fact I have screwed up more times than you have, because I'm older and I've had more chances."

Joe stared down the street, chewing on his lip again.

"Look, you can't promise that you'll never make a mistake again," John Mark said. "Neither can I. Right?" Joe finally looked over at him.

"So we could do this, right?"

Joe looked back at the street and shrugged his shoulders. "Okay," he said again, a little more confidently this time.

John Mark was feeling better. " *'Before a word even comes out of my mouth, the Lord already knows about it. He knew everything I was ever going to do before I was even born.'* " He grinned at Joe. "Psalm 139. My own translation. Do you ever think about how God already knows about all the stupid stuff we're still going to do that we haven't even done yet, and He answers our prayers anyway?"

Joe shook his head and sighed. "Do you always have a Bible saying for everything?"

"Yeah, pretty much," John Mark said. They sat together in silence for a while longer, both relieved to feel better.

"Joe."

"Yeah?"

"I want to ask you to help me with something." Joe turned around to look at him. "I know you're a good kid at heart. I see it in you all the time. You kind of take care of people."

Joe's eyes widened.

"Yeah, I mean it. I want to ask you to look out for Johnny and Stephen, when you guys are out by yourselves. You're the oldest boy in the family." John Mark paused to let Joe know that he meant what he was saying. "You know a lot more about some things than they do. Keep an eye on them. Don't let them go running around getting into trouble."

"Sure," Joe said after a while. "I do that anyway."

John Mark blinked and frowned. Was someone not getting something here? Was it him, or Joe? Surely Joe didn't think that what he had done this afternoon was what John Mark meant by looking out for Johnny and Stephen.

"What I'm saying is, help them grow up right and stay out of trouble and not lie," John Mark said, trying to make his meaning clear.

"Well, I don't know if I can do all that, but I'll keep an eye on them," Joe said. "Don't worry, Uncle John. I get it." John Mark looked at him for a while. The boy had calmed down and looked positively happy.

They sat on the steps for a while longer. The sun had finally come out, touching the treetops with a last bit of golden light, and the sounds of Kate making dinner drifted through the front screen door. She was telling Johnny and Stephen to set the table and get the milk from the cellar. John Mark felt a sudden wave of gratitude for his family.

Oh Lord, he prayed, *help me. You know better than anybody how many more times I'm going to make stupid mistakes. Keep us all away from the sins that tear families apart. Help us stick together in love. Help me to be a good dad . . . teach me, humble me, discipline me all You want, but please, help my family. Be with us every day. I'll never figure this out by myself.*

He heard someone turn on the radio inside. A familiar announcement droned through the mild evening air. "This show is dedicated to the parents of the younger generation . . ." *Please take care of us all,* he prayed. *All of Your bewildering offspring.*

Seven: May / *Graduation*

Joe caught the ball in the deep fold of his glove and felt the hard smack of a good catch clear up to his elbow. He stepped back and threw to John Mark, who was playing catch with him and Johnny in the street in front of the house. They were trying to pass the time and ignore their hunger until supper was ready. It was later than usual that evening, because a parishioner had brought over a live duck as a kind of contribution to the church, and Kate had made the three of them slaughter it, pluck it, and clean it out before she started cooking. It was so late that Karel had come over to visit them after finishing his own supper and was sitting on the front porch steps, watching them and smoking his pipe. The long May evening was still light, with a strong breeze from the south. The wind had been coming from the north all day, full of the stink from the corn syrup factory, but it had shifted to the south in the evening, and now they could smell the stench from the meat packing plant instead.

John Mark threw the ball to Johnny, and Johnny threw to Joe. Joe caught the ball with casual ease and then fired it off at John Mark hard and fast, as if he were gunning to put out a runner at first base. John Mark grunted from the impact of the ball in his glove.

"Who you trying to kill?" he called out.

"The other guy!" Joe called back. He worked hard with his throwing arm every night, even when there was no practice. He wanted to be ready for his moment on the mound.

John Mark grinned and threw another easy pitch to Johnny. Johnny threw to Joe again, but this time Joe kept the ball in his mitt and waved the other two out of the street, because a car had turned the corner and was rambling down the road towards them. It was still two blocks away, but Joe liked the grown-up feeling he got whenever he had a chance to tell Johnny what to do. He glanced at John Mark to see if his uncle had noticed that he was watching out for Johnny.

"The car's not that close," Johnny complained. "C'mon, throw it." Joe tossed the ball up in the air and caught it himself a few times, then took pity on Johnny and threw a grounder to him as they stood by the side of the street and waited for the car to pass by.

Instead, it stopped in front of their house, and two men got out and waved at John Mark. He pulled off his glove and walked over to them. Johnny threw the ball to Joe, and the two of them played catch while the men sat on the front porch and talked. After a few minutes John Mark got up, went inside the house, and came back out with mugs in his hands and Stephen right behind him. Joe and Johnny quit playing and walked over to find out what was going on.

The men had a jar of home-brewed beer with them and poured out portions into the glasses. John Mark let Joe and Johnny each have half a glass. He invited Stephen to take a sip of his own, but Stephen only sniffed at the foam and wrinkled his nose. Everybody laughed.

"*Dobrý pivo,*" Karel said, complimenting the beer. "No need for a five-dollar bale of hay tonight." The men laughed again. During Prohibition, a feed store right on the Avenue had sold whiskey by hiding the bottles inside bales of hay and then selling the special bales for five dollars each.

"This stuff's better anyway," John Mark said. Home-brewed beer had never been illegal to drink, and he had made it a point of honor to obey the law and drink only legal brew during the entire Prohibition.

"Where's your boys at tonight?" one of the men asked Karel.

"Working." Karel coughed to hide his pride in the fact that both his sons had part-time jobs after school. "Rudolf works at the feed store and Wenceslaus works for Jelinek's grocery on Third Street."

"Wence's graduating high school this month," John Mark said. Both men congratulated Karel, who coughed again, frowned, and gazed down the street so as not to seem too bigheaded about his eldest son receiving a high school degree.

"*Ano, děkuji,*" he said. "Yes, thank you. Now we need to get him into college. He's going to study law. The work is just beginning," he said, putting on a serious expression and nodding at them. The other two men were silent for a moment, taking in the idea that Karel could afford to send a son to law school.

"Well, whaddaya know," one of them finally said, a little weakly. "Good for you, Prazsky. Always good to have a lawyer in the family these days."

Karel inclined his head and took a long pull on his pipe. "We need lawyers," he said. "All the Czechs want to be farmers, like the old country, but we need some lawyers or we'll end up serfs again." He frowned and nodded again to make his point. The men nodded back and looked away.

John Mark leaned over and ruffled Stephen's hair. "Stevie, these guys here are from *Ochotnicke Druztvo*, the drama society, and they're putting on a play. They need a little boy for a part. What do you think? Want to be in a play?"

Stephen blinked and looked at the two men. "It's not hard," one of them said. "We just need a smart little boy to go onstage a couple times and say some lines. There's some other kids too, so you won't be by yourself."

Stephen looked at Johnny, who shrugged, then back at John Mark, who said, "Sure, you ought to do it. Plays are fun. And I get free tickets, right?" he asked, poking one of the men on the arm. "Because I have to take him to practice and make him learn his lines?"

"He'll only have three lines, and there's a prompter in front of the stage anyway in case he forgets them," the other man said. "Practice is Monday and Friday nights. The little kids only come on Fridays. I'll come over here and get him and you can just pick him up afterwards. Then you're right in time for Friday night dance at the Hall." The drama society staged four plays at the C.S.P.S. Hall every year, on Sunday nights when there was no dancing.

"Say, do you have any parts for these two guys?" John Mark asked with a wink at Johnny. Joe and Johnny choked on their sips of beer.

"No, but if you send them over they can help build the set and paint the backscreen," one of the men said right away. "They good workers?"

"Pretty good," John Mark said. "Stephen's the one you have to watch out for. Don't let him near anything that breaks or spills."

"Dad!" Stephen said in dismay. John Mark pulled him closer and mussed his hair, making him giggle.

"All right, then. Stephen can be in the play, and Joe and Johnny can go with him to practice on Friday nights and help build scenery," he said. Both older boys sighed. They already had baseball practice on Tuesday and Thursday nights. Wednesday night was church night. Now Monday was the only night free during the week.

"Good enough," one of the men said. He looked at Joe. "Say, are you the kid who plays third base for the packing plant?" he asked.

Joe felt his face flush with pleasure. "Yes, sir," he said.

"Looking good out there," the man said. "You think you guys have a chance at the championship?"

Joe flushed again, trying to think of something to say. "Maybe," he finally came up with.

"How do you like old Kovar?" the other man said, and started laughing. Coach Kovar was as much fun to watch as the team, when a game was close and he got excited.

"Oh, he's fine," Joe said cautiously. He did not want any bad reports about himself getting back to the coach.

"I'm on the team, too," Johnny said. "He let me on."

Both men started laughing. "Well, that's good for you, son, but your dad must be broke," one of them said. "Two boys in baseball!"

"Yeah, I'll be in the poorhouse before it's all over," John Mark said. "They're going to nickel-and-dime me to death. Maybe I should make you pay rent for Stephen. How much is he worth for a play?"

"Dad!" Stephen said, and made as if to pull away from his seat beside his father. John Mark pulled him back, mussed his hair again and gave him a hug. Joe watched Stephen rest his head against his father's arm as the men laughed and talked. *It's nice to play third base and have people say I'm looking good, but I'd trade it all to have a father.*

The evening was dark by the time Kate called them inside. She had dumplings and yeast rolls to go with the duck, but nothing else except for a few early spring scallions. The canned vegetables from the summer before were almost gone. Josefina put most of her meat on Joe's plate after he ate his own share.

"*Jíst, Pepík,*" she said. Johnny huffed loudly from his seat, upset at Josefina's display of favoritism. Kate looked hard at her mother.

"*Maso je moc tuhé.* The meat is tough," Josefina said with a sniff. "I don't want it."

Joe was embarrassed. "Here," he said, forking over part of the meat to Johnny's plate and ending the argument.

"I don't know why we're even trying to buy an icebox," John Mark said to Kate. "We never have any food left over to put in it."

"Maybe we should get a telephone first," Johnny said. "Like before." They had a telephone when they lived at the rectory, and Johnny had been allowed to call Anton whenever he wanted.

"Oh, no. Icebox first," Kate said.

"I don't really want a telephone anyway," John Mark said. "It just rings all the time." During the last year in the rectory, after the Crash and before they were evicted, the telephone had rung almost nonstop day and night. Every call seemed to be more bad news about people losing jobs and homes, or needing food, and hoping that John Mark could help. He had been relieved to see the telephone go.

"Do we really have to go to play practice with Stephen? Can't we just stay home on Friday night?" Johnny asked.

John Mark was not sympathetic. "It'll be good for you boys to get out. You'll meet people," he said as he finished up the last of the dumplings. "You work hard, you get noticed, and then someone will ask you to do a little work for them once in a while. That's a lot better than selling golf balls to a bunch of drunks."

Joe kept his eyes on his plate. After John Mark had found out about what they had done at the golf course, he had lectured the boys about how they needed to find some kind of honorable work instead of looking for golf balls.

"You're just putting on a big lie and playing up to a bunch of stupid drunks who couldn't care less about you," he had told them. "Have a little more respect for yourselves, even if you're broke. And I don't like you being so far away from our part of town. There's plenty of work around here, and you won't get into trouble because everybody knows who you are. You can work in the gardens or mow grass. That's honest work that'll help out somebody else and give you some muscles. Those guys at the club need another ball like they need a hole in the head."

Joe had not minded the scolding too much. It wasn't very bad, and anyway, now that the weather had warmed up, he suspected that other people would be out hunting for golf balls. It wouldn't be worth the long walk.

The boys had all promised not to go past First Avenue again. But John Mark wasn't finished.

"One thing I've learned from all this is that I haven't been doing my job as a father. The Bible says that I'm not fit to lead a church if my own kids are running wild. First Timothy, third chapter," he added with a glance at Kate.

"So things are going to change around here," he had continued. "Instead of me just reading to you in the morning, each one of you gets a verse to memorize. Then I want to know exactly what you're doing, where you're going, who you're going to be with. If you've got time to walk clear to Ellis Park Golf Course, you've got time to do plenty of other things instead."

Now, at the end of supper, he pushed his chair back from the table and said, "All right, who's first?" He looked around the table. "Stephen, say your verse. Proverbs 13:20." He had told them that the book of Proverbs was written for young people and that they would study it first.

Stephen sighed. "Proverbs 13:20. Um, he that walketh . . . with wise men shall be wise . . ." he hesitated.

John Mark finally said, "But . . ."

"But . . ." Stephen said, then trailed off again.

" . . . . a companion of fools," John Mark prompted him.

" . . . a companion of fools, um . . . is going to get into trouble?" Stephen offered.

"Close enough," John Mark said. "Johnny?"

"Proverbs 14:15. The simple-minded believe everything anybody tells them, but the prudent man checks around first," Johnny said quickly.

"That's not exactly the King James," John Mark said dryly. "I'll let it pass if you tell me what it means."

"Only idiots believe everything they hear," Johnny said.

"Okay," John Mark nodded. "Joe?"

"Proverbs 18:16," Joe said. He liked the verse he had today and had no problem saying it. *"A man's gift maketh room for him, and bringeth him before great men."* He had written it down on a scrap of paper and kept it in his pocket in order to memorize it. John Mark had told him that everyone had a special talent, and that Joe was at the point in his life where he would start finding out what his was.

"Good, Joe," Kate exclaimed, and John Mark said "Nice job," at the same time. Josefina snorted in disgust at the idea of memorizing Bible verses. She got up from the table and left the room.

"Okay, Dad, come on," Johnny said. "Your turn." John Mark had let the boys talk him into memorizing a verse that morning also, and Kate had picked it out.

"I thought you'd never ask," he said with a grin. "Okay. Proverbs 18:22. *Whoso findeth a wife findeth a good thing, and obtaineth favor from the Lord."* He leaned over and gave Kate a hearty kiss. The boys all groaned.

"Me and my wife are going into the front room and listening to the radio," John Mark told them. "See you when the dishes are done."

The next morning, Joe stepped away from the privy hole in the Prazskys' outhouse and buttoned up his overalls. The Prazskys had the nicest outhouse he had ever used. A little brick pathway led to it from their kitchen door. The path was bordered with roses, and the entrance to the outhouse was shaded and screened by a huge grape arbor that arched overhead and gave enough privacy that whoever used the privy could leave the door open on a hot day. The roses and grapevines were pretty, although nothing could really cover up the smell.

Through the screen of grape leaves he could hear Karel talking to Johnny and Rudy as they dug up the new part of the garden. It was Saturday, and Karel was expanding the garden in Vincent's lot, so John Mark had sent Joe and Johnny over to help. Wence was working at the grocery store. Stephen had stayed home to weed their own garden and go shopping with Kate to help her with the bags. Joe sighed and walked back to where the rest of them were digging into thick-rooted, grassy sod.

"Start from over here this time. Keep the line straight," Karel said. Joe looked around as he worked. Rudy was panting and sweating as he dug up spadefuls of damp black dirt. Johnny was struggling with his spade and had to jump on it to push it far enough into the ground to do any good. Karel moved smoothly, faster than any of them, tossing up huge clumps of dirt as easily as if they were puffs of cotton. He talked while he worked.

"Back in Bohemia, we did this all summer. Me and my brothers. We'd get paid in wheat. That was so we'd take it home to our parents and not waste any pay on ourselves. You boys don't know how good you have it here in America. Work for money and play baseball."

Joe kept on digging. He didn't see how he was getting an especially good deal out of this situation, because John Mark wouldn't let Vincent pay the boys for the work on his garden. Anton was in a special tennis tournament on the east side of the city that day, and Vincent had driven him over and was not at home, but he had promised a special meal for the boys that night as a kind of thanks for their help. Even as hungry as Joe always was, one meal did not seem like enough payment for a day spent working for Karel Prazsky.

"And another thing you boys don't appreciate," Karel said as he moved down his row, flipping gallon-sized clumps of earth out of the way, "is how lucky you are to go to school. Back in Bohemia you couldn't go. You had to know someone to get in. Those *sacramenski Sudentanland Deutsche* didn't want the Czechs to get any education. I could never go. All the colleges, all the good jobs were for the *sacramenski Deutsche*. And Bohemia was the land of schooling before the *Deutsche* came in and took over. Even back in the sixteen-hundreds," at this point he stopped and wagged his finger at the boys, "even back then, the great Czech teacher Jan Komenski said that every single Czech should be educated, even women. You meet a hundred Czechs, ninety-eight of them know how to read. You meet a hundred Slavs, maybe only fifty of them read."

He cleared his throat and spat, and then went on, still jabbing his finger at the boys for emphasis. "*Ano*, that's what made Bohemia great. Schooling. Until those *sacramenski Deutsche* came in and ruined everything. You boys need to be proud of your heritage and get as much school as you can. You should all go to college." He went back to his digging.

The boys had stopped shoveling the instant Karel had halted to wag his finger, and when he returned to his digging they reluctantly began working again. Joe was next to Rudy.

"You going to college?" he whispered to Rudy.

Rudy snorted. "I don't even go to the library," he whispered back.

"Is Wence really going to law school?" Joe asked.

Rudy glanced at his father and didn't reply. Joe looked over to see Karel watching them.

"Mr. Prazsky, who are the saremski Dutch?" he asked quickly.

"That's what my Dad calls the Germans," Rudy said. "Don't say *sacramenski* or you'll get in trouble."

Karel nodded grimly and dug out another ten-pound clump of dirt. "*Ano*, and they're not done making trouble yet. Our President Masaryk's trying to keep that *sacramenski* Hitler out of Bohemia, but that one's trouble for the old country, mark my words. You boys just mark my words! Hitler's trouble for the old country," he repeated, shaking his head. "He wants our factories there. Bohemia has the best farmlands, the best factories, the best workers. Somebody better watch sharp, or he's going to get them. Mark my words."

None of the boys said anything to that, and for a while they all worked in silence, except for the occasional gasp or hiccup from Johnny as he struggled with his spade. A breeze came up from the south, bringing with it the stench from the packing plant.

"Yuck," Joe said, and sneezed. "I hate that smell."

Karel hawked and spat again. "That's money you're smelling," he growled in Joe's direction. "Men work there. Quit griping."

Joe shut up after that. He felt like he was dying of thirst. He stole a look over his shoulder at the outdoor water pump, just outside the Prazsky's kitchen door. Ruzina and Rose were tending the raspberry bushes close to the house, and they were wearing blue denim work pants. Joe could not remember ever seeing women in denim work pants before. The combination of denim and women was oddly fascinating. He felt torn between his desire to look at them and his fear of Karel catching him looking. It was a relief when Karel finally called a halt and told them to go inside for lunch.

The Prazskys' home was the smallest house that Joe had ever seen. It had one room. One side had a kitchen table, a dish cabinet, a water pump and a washstand, and the other side had a couch, a chair, a violin on a music stand, and a bookshelf. Two rag rugs covered the wood floor and a big cast-iron stove decorated with flowered ceramic tiles stood in the middle. The May sun and the hot stove had steamed up the little room, and the boys took their plates of food from Ruzina and went outside to eat. They sat down in the shade, at a safe distance from the guard dog, and tore into the food.

"Where do you all sleep in there?" Joe asked Rudy, between bites. He took a long drink of water from the dipper in the water pail and pushed the pail companionably over to Rudy.

"Upstairs," Rudy said through a mouthful of potatoes. He took his own drink from the dipper and moved the pail along to Johnny.

All three boys sat in silence for a while after they had finished. Joe was inspecting the calluses on his palms, hoping he wouldn't get blisters, when Rudy spoke again.

"My dad's been saving his money all his life so he can send Wence to law school," he said. "That's why we live here. Because he doesn't have to pay rent."

"I thought Wence was going to marry Rachel, soon as he graduates," Johnny whispered.

Rudy shrugged and shook his head. "I dunno what he's going to do," he said. "He wants a real house, with plumbing and electricity. He's sick of living like a peasant in the old country. I'm sick of it too. Don't tell Dad."

Joe was not about to say anything to Karel Prazsky. He glanced back at the little house. It was pretty, with fresh white paint and a window and flowers all around it, but Joe could understand why Wence would want a regular house instead.

"Why'd your dad come over here anyway, if he likes Bohemia so much?" he asked.

"Conscription," Rudy said, and yawned. He lay back in the grass and closed his eyes.

"What's that?" Joe asked when Rudy didn't say anything else.

"Germans picking up guys for the army," Rudy said without opening his eyes. "During the German occupation. Dad says that Germans would go around Bohemia and take the Czech men back with them for the army, and then you'd never see them again. He said he was too big to hide, so he got married and came over here to live with Uncle Vincent."

"Is Vincent really your uncle?" Joe asked.

"Kind of," Rudy said after a while. He sounded like he was trying to fall asleep. "Him and Dad grew up on the same block in Prague. They knew each other when they were little kids."

Joe left him alone after that. He thought about uncles for a while, and whether Vincent was more of a real uncle to him than he was to Rudy. If John Mark had been his father, then Vincent would really be his uncle. But Kate really was his aunt, and John Mark really was his uncle, and Vincent was John Mark's brother, so it seemed that Vincent must really be Joe's uncle too. That was a satisfying thought. That meant that Anton was really his cousin. And Aunt Kate had said that maybe she and Amalia were related. That would make Anton even more his cousin, if it were true.

All three boys were asleep on the grass when Karel's voice came booming at them from the doorway of the tiny house. "Get up," he called. "No time to lay around. You boys want to eat next winter, dig up this garden now."

Karel Prazsky watched Joe and Johnny put away their spades and head back home after the work was done. Little Johnny looked like he was half dead after the long day of spading sod, but Joe was tougher. That one was putting on some muscle, Karel noticed with satisfaction. He had certainly grown taller since showing up on John Starosta's doorstep last November. Now, with a little more work like he had done today, he would fill out that lanky frame.

Karel stood in the yard a while longer, enjoying a smoke and the evening air before he went indoors. Rose was talking to a neighbor who had come over to buy one of her rabbits for supper. Ruzina was with her, but Karel stood and watched anyway, to make sure that people didn't take advantage of his daughter and her little business. Rose wanted to buy fabric for another special dress, and it was always good to stay close by when money was changing hands.

After finishing his pipe and washing up, he went to Vincent's house for supper. Ruzina and Rose were already there in the kitchen, boiling dumplings and heating sauerkraut to go with the generous pork roast that Vincent had bought for the evening meal. Since Amalia's death, Karel had often sent his wife and daughter to cook and clean in Vincent's house as well as do the laundry. It was the least he could do. In Karel's opinion, Vincent had gone a little crazy after the death of his wife. Nothing that anyone else would notice, except perhaps his brother John. But Vincent had been mourning for over a year now, not listening when people talked to him and drifting around the house like a sleepwalker. Karel privately thought that Vincent should be more of a man and put his grief behind him, but until he did, Karel could see to it that Ruzina cooked for him once in a while.

Inside, Vincent's house was full of men in business suits and tennis clothes, standing around with glasses of beer and shouting into each other's faces. Karel soon found out that Anton had won first place for his age group in the tournament. Vincent stood in the front room with his arm around his son's shoulders and a huge grin on his face, and Anton was still in his tennis whites, looking excited and embarrassed at the same time. Karel pushed through the crowd to slap Anton on the back and shake Vincent's hand, and then got himself a glass of beer and sat down beside John Mark.

"Hey, Praz," John Mark said comfortably. Karel had to admit that he liked John Mark in spite of the fact that he was a *sacramenski* minister. Karel had rejected anything to do with church and God a long time ago, when he was a teenage boy in Bohemia and the invading German army had forced his entire village to convert to the Germanic state religion or else forfeit their farms to the government. It had been a relief to come to America and have the freedom to live as he wished. Karel had let everyone in the new country know right away that he was a Freethinker and would not be joining any church. John Mark was the only minister he talked to.

"*Jak se mas?*" Karel said in return. "Is Johnny still awake?"

"No," John Mark laughed. "He went straight to bed after his bath. What did you do today, Karel, try to kill those boys?"

"Ah, a little work won't kill them," Karel said. He looked around the room and saw Joe standing next to Anton. "It'll do that one plenty of good," he went on, nodding at Joe. "Make a man out of him."

"What do you think about Anton winning that tournament?" John Mark asked. Karel nodded and took a swig of beer.

"*Ano.* Good for that one, too," he said with a meaningful look at John Mark.

Karel had always thought that a life spent playing piano was not good for a boy. He had even been glad when Anton had won his fight with his father about playing tennis, although Vincent had complained to Karel many times about his stubborn, fool-headed son who was wasting his incredible talent. Karel glanced over at the piano. It was covered with dust. Amalia would never have let that happen. Karel made a mental note to remind Rose to dust more carefully the next time she came to clean.

Men were pushing into the kitchen now, coming back out with steaming plates full of roast pork and dumplings, but Karel and John Mark waited, to let the guests go first. John Mark told Joe to wait also, until the rush for food died down. The boy looked disappointed, but he took it well enough and drifted over to stand by Anton, who was talking with another young man as the front room emptied out.

"That was our radio circuit that Byrd used when he went to the South Pole last year," the man was saying to Anton. "You want to talk about pressure. Radio conditions are terrible in Antarctica, and the whole world was watching to see if our circuits would hold up. It was perfect. Perfect wireless communication. We maintained successful contact, even when the government stations couldn't do it."

"Did you go too?" Anton asked.

"No, I didn't, but now I wish I had. There were five engineers at the base camp in Little America and twenty-four transmitters in use before it was all over. It was expensive, but when I saw how much publicity the whole thing was kicking up, I'd have paid three times as much. It turned out to be the best thing that ever happened to us. We've got the contract now for all the communications equipment for his next South Pole expedition."

Karel stood up and walked over to hear more of the conversation. Anton saw him coming and introduced him.

"Mr. Collins, this is my uncle, Karel Prazsky," he said. "Uncle Karel, this is Arthur Collins. I play on his factory's tennis team."

Karel shook hands. "What kind of factory?" he asked. This man looked too young to be important.

"Radios, sir." Arthur Collins grinned up at him. "Transmitters. Wireless communication systems."

"You own a factory?" Karel asked again. The man didn't look more than twenty-five.

"Well, you could call it a factory, but it's pretty small," the young man replied. "In fact, until just a little while ago it was in my dad's basement. But we're getting bigger now."

"At least your factory doesn't smell," Anton laughed. "That's where I want to work when I get out of school. Now that I know the boss."

"Take physics and all the math you can get while you're still in," Arthur Collins advised. "There's orders coming in from all over the world. If war breaks out in Europe, everyone is going to want our radios. The sky's the limit." He slapped Anton's back. "Nice work today, ace. So when do you graduate?"

"Next year," Anton said. "My dad wants me to go to college, though."

"That's fine," Collins said. "Stay in touch. Always good to know who's coming along."

Joe spoke up from his place at Anton's side. "Do you have to go to college before you can work on radios?"

The factory owner grinned again. "Well, no, but it helps," he said. "Do you ever take radios apart?"

"No, sir," Joe said.

"Don't start with mine," John Mark called out from where he was sitting. "Not unless you can talk Mr. Collins here into putting it back like it was before."

They all laughed, and the young man put on his hat. "See you next time, Anton. Nice to meet you, Mister, ah, Prashy." Karel glared at him.

Anton and Joe walked the factory owner out to his car. Karel headed for the kitchen. The house was full of east-side American men that he didn't know, all standing around eating and talking, and as he passed through the crowded dining room he could hear one of them telling a dirty joke. He paused and stared at the man until he stammered in mid-sentence, then finally stopped talking altogether.

"My wife and daughter are here," Karel told him. "Watch your mouth."

These east-side Americans are stupid, he thought as the man apologized. *All this money and freedom and they still know nothing. Sappy little idiots. At least we Czechs have decent manners. Once we get a start in this country, people will see how much more advanced we are. More Czechs should be like me, send their sons to college, and then we would all move up faster.* He gave a final warning stare to the joker, then shouldered his way past the rest of the crowd and went to get a plate of food. *Wenceslaus will do well in law school*, he thought. *That will show them.* He glanced around the room, at all the well-dressed men who thought that he and his family were ignorant foreigners, content to work for pennies in stinking factories for the rest of their lives. *He graduates next week*, Karel thought with satisfaction. *The time is almost here.*

⚬〜〜

"Wence! Wenceslaus!" Andrew Jelinek shouted from the front of the little grocery store on Third Street where Wence worked on Saturdays. "Eggs to candle!"

Wence straightened up from his mopping and groaned. Saturdays were long at Jelinek's. He started work early in the morning and usually didn't finish until ten o'clock or later at night. He had started mopping the floor at nine o'clock this evening, hoping to finish up faster than usual and have a little free time for himself before bed, but a farmer had arrived late with a truckload of produce. Now there would be eggs to check and vegetables to weigh so that the farmer could get credit and do his Saturday night shopping. That meant at least another two hours of work before the store closed for the night.

Wence walked up to the front counter and took the box of eggs from the farmer. He groaned again, but to himself this time. At least six dozen eggs. Every egg had to be checked before Jelinek gave the farmer credit for it. This would take a long time, and then the new vegetables would have to be put away, and the floor still had to be mopped and the counters and windows cleaned. He'd be lucky to get out by midnight at this rate. Wence pulled out the wooden candling box, set the egg on the little holder inside it, and lit the candle that stood behind the egg to show if there was a chick forming inside.

The sound of hogs squealing drifted through the front screen door, along with a whiff of manure.

"I'm going up the Avenue to the meat market to sell these hogs, and then I'll come back and shop with you," the farmer said in Czech to the grocer. "There's six dozen good eggs there," he called to Wence. "Careful now."

"Yes sir," Wence called back. He checked one egg, set it aside, and then took a second one out from the box. He checked it and set it aside. Then a third.

Wence hated candling eggs, partly because it was so boring and partly because it was really a kid's job. He had worked at Jelinek's for four years, since he was fourteen, and the work that had seemed so exciting when he first started had become embarrassing to him now. He was too big for this job. The little stool that sat in front of the egg candling box was too short for comfort, and the mopping and stocking that he did on Saturdays could be handled by a smart twelve-year-old. He made two dollars a Saturday, which was not bad pay, and he liked Jelinek, but he felt ashamed to still be working as a grocer's boy, candling eggs at nine o'clock on a Saturday night when most men were home with their wives or out with their girls.

But his girl was going to come and visit him tonight. He felt a rush of pleasure as he thought of her walking up the steps of the store, glancing around inside to see if he was there, and then smiling when their eyes met. Rachel had a special smile just for him, and his insides turned over with a kind of joyful pain when her face lit up because she was glad to see him. The little strands of her glossy brown hair curled so tenderly along her neck . . . her eyelashes were perfect, long and dark, shading her lovely eyes. Wence bit the inside of his lip, thinking of her.

The farmer left after a while and the store quieted down. Wence kept on candling eggs as fast as he could, hoping to hear the store's screen door open and his girl's light footsteps come walking in. Rachel lived with her grandparents, who were straight from the old country and didn't approve of young women going out by themselves without a family member along. They were also strictly religious and didn't like Wence, because Karel was a Freethinker and did not go to church. But Rachel had asked to stay with one of her girl friends this Saturday night, and the friend lived close to the store, so there was a good chance that the two girls could walk over for a secret visit.

"How they coming?" Andrew Jelinek called from the front.

"Pretty good. No bad ones yet," Wence called back.

"How much longer?" Andrew wanted to know.

"I'm almost halfway," Wence said after a moment.

"Good enough," the grocer said absently. He was counting money. "You going anywhere tonight?"

"Ah, just home, I guess," Wence said, and then added, "Rachel might stop in before we close up." He stole a look at Andrew to see what he thought of that.

The grocer looked back at him and shook his head, trying to frown, but he ended up smiling anyway. "You got it bad," he told Wence. "Don't you get that nice girl in trouble or I'll have your hide."

Wence grinned and went back to the candling. "Yes, sir," he said. Andrew liked Rachel and had told Wence more than once that he needed to behave responsibly toward her and not ruin her life. A man could live down a little gossip in this neighborhood, especially if he married the girl in question, but a woman whose reputation was damaged was marked for life. Even spending time alone with a man was enough to blacken a girl's good name. Wence knew Marie's story, and he had vowed that he would never cause Rachel that kind of harm. *I'd cut off my right arm before I hurt you*, he had told her once, and he took pride now in the memory of that moment and the way that she had trusted him ever since.

The only problem was his father. Karel still expected Wence to go to law school, in spite of the fact that Wence had tried to tell him that he didn't want to go. Karel would not hear of any other plan. He had even frowned at the idea of Wence having a sweetheart who might take away his focus from his studies. Karel could be brutal with his sons when there was a question of obedience, and Wence was not yet ready to argue openly with him.

But when Rachel had finally told him that she loved him, a new resolve steeled him to do as he wanted instead of as his father expected. He had lived his entire life in a fixed-up stable, and Rachel had lived hers with her grandparents over their grocery store. He wanted to marry her as soon as possible and live in a home with electricity, indoor plumbing, and a front room that he could be proud of. And they would be married. They would be man and wife, and have the right to be together day and night . . . Wence felt a wave of desire sweep through him, and he closed his eyes. When he opened them again it took a moment to realize that he was still sitting in front of the candling stand, dreaming of Rachel instead of checking the eggs.

He took a deep breath and went back to work. He would graduate from high school on Thursday night. Now all he needed was a real job. The dream was so close now. Perhaps less than a week away.

The screen door opened and the sound of women's footsteps came through the door. He turned to look, and there she was, just as he had imagined, her eyes sweeping across the store and finding him, and her smile lighting up the room.

He rose to meet her. When they stood next to each other they could not hug or kiss, of course, and because of the joy of seeing each other they could barely speak, but his fingers brushed the back of her hand, out of the sight of Andrew or any passers-by on the sidewalk, and he breathed in the scent of her hair and skin. Wence glanced at the grocer, who shook his head and grinned, and then he took Rachel's arm and guided her to a corner where they could stand unseen for a moment, while Rachel's friend stood guard in the aisle.

He took her hand and twined his fingers through hers, feeling a whole new life waiting there in the touch of her palm. He stroked a stray tendril of hair back from her brow. They spoke only a little, because of the fullness of their hearts and the lack of privacy. But Wence could tell that something had made Rachel sad. Her grandparents were harsh with her sometimes. He risked an embrace, pulling her close and feeling the curve of her back beneath her dress and the sweet warm air of her breath as his face came down close to hers. *Only a little while longer.* With a choked sob Rachel turned her face to his chest and clung to him. Something wet touched the skin of his throat, and he thought, *No, not tears, she should never have to cry, not my Rachel.*

"I love you, Wence," he heard her whisper, the words warm against his neck. He could feel the tip of her ear beneath his lips, and he tightened his arms around her, rocking her ever so slightly as they stood in the dim corner of the store.

"I love you too," he whispered back. "It'll be all right."

"Don't ever leave me," she said, and his heart almost burst with love.

"Hush. You hush, now," he breathed into her ear. "I'm here. I'll never leave you." He pressed his lips against her silky hair. Her grandparents might despise him, and his father might disown them, and people might say that the whole world would end tomorrow, but it had not ended yet, because she was here in his arms, and not yet, because he could still feel the tender warmth of her face nestled against his chest, and not yet, not tonight, not ever, because she was his Rachel, and he loved her.

Even after she left, with a last backward glance for him as she walked out through the door, Wence had to bite the inside of his lip and force his hands to stay steady and not tremble as he worked through the last of the eggs. The farmer's truckload of produce was waiting, though, and the hard work calmed him down as he cleaned and sorted vegetables away. He had gone back to mopping the floor when the screen door opened again.

Two men came in, nodded at Jelinek and said hello. "Wence Prazsky here?" one of them asked. Andrew looked surprised, but nodded in Wence's direction. Wence stopped mopping and looked over at them.

"Yeah?" he asked, and set the mop aside, drawing himself up to his full height and crossing his arms, as he had seen his father do. "You want to see me?"

"Oh, hello," one of the men said. "Charlie Krejci, from the packing plant." He reached out his hand.

Wence shook it, puzzled. "John Krall," said the other man.

"Wence Prazksy," Wence said in return, shaking the second man's hand, and feeling a wild hope stirring inside himself. "What can I do for you?" He had heard his father say that before, when he was not sure why someone had come to see him.

"We need another hitter for the ball team, and we need a better catcher, too," the man named Charlie said. "Your brother really ought to play first base, not behind the plate. We were, ah, hoping you'd want to make the team again this year. We could use you."

So here it was. His opportunity for a real job had just materialized, right when he least expected it. Wence had applied for work at every factory in town. The clerks had taken his applications and put them on stacks with what seemed like a hundred others, and no one had offered much hope of employment. But now, a job had come to him, right when he needed it.

He crossed his arms again, set his feet, and drew himself up an inch taller. He took a deep breath. "I work nights," he told them. "But if you've got a day job for me, I'll play." *No point beating around the bush.*

The two men grinned. "Well, as a matter of fact, we do," one of them said. "There's a place opened up in the hog slaughter room. Twenty-five cents an hour. Not bad for a new worker. You want it?"

"Fine with me," Wence said, controlling his excitement. He brushed away the thought that an opening in the slaughter room usually meant that someone had just got hurt, or worse, on the job. "When do you want me to start?"

"You graduate this Thursday, right?" one of the men asked. Wence nodded. "You can start on Friday." Wence nodded again. That was easy enough.

And now he could go and rent the upstairs apartment he had found in a rooming house over on Second Avenue, one that was small but nice enough for Rachel.

"... and we want you to start practicing right now because games start next month," one of the men was saying. Wence snapped back to attention.

"I'll ask Mr. Jelinek if I can get off Tuesday night," he said with a glance at Andrew. He reached out his hand for another shake. "I'm a good worker," he told them in his best imitation of his father's forceful voice. "You won't be sorry."

The men shook hands again, said goodnight, and left the store. Wence and Andrew looked at each other across the quiet room. The two of them both sat down at the same time, Andrew behind the counter and Wence on a wooden crate of onions.

"Well, Wence, good luck," Andrew finally said.

Now that he was actually leaving his job as stock boy, Wence felt a rush of affection for the grocer. Andrew had been a good boss, and the only person, really, who knew about Rachel and understood how important she was to him. He ducked his head.

"Thanks for everything, Mr. Jelinek," he said. "You've helped me a lot."

Andrew coughed a bit and said, a little more lightly, "Now you better find me a replacement, and whoever it is better be a good worker, or I'll come out and tan your hide no matter where you're working."

"I will. Don't worry," Wence said fervently. He knew at least twenty boys who would jump at the chance to work at Jelinek's. "Uh, would you do me a favor and not tell anybody about this?"

Andrew Jelinek looked at him for a moment without replying. "Sure, Wence," he finally answered. "Like I said, good luck." He turned back to his paperwork.

Wence gazed out the window for a while before going back to his mop. The view outside looked just as it had before. The same buildings still sat along the street, the same trees stood in their places. Yet everything had changed, as if the whole world had somehow turned a different color, or as if the season had suddenly changed from winter to spring.

His rush of excitement dwindled away. He would have bills to pay and a wife to support. He wondered how difficult the new job would be, and if he would measure up and be able to keep it. Men told grim stories about work in the slaughter room. Wence sat and stared out through the window for a while, wondering about the new life he had just stepped into, and what his father would say.

Joe and Johnny showed up for practice at Riverside Park on Tuesday evening and looked at each other in wonder when they saw a crowd gathered to watch them play. A black Model T with the gold-painted words *Cedar Rapids Gazette* lettered on its doors was parked by the curb, and dressed-up men holding clipboards and cameras clustered on the field, talking to the coach.

"This can't be all for Wence," Joe said uncertainly. Rudy had told them that Wence was going to play, and Joe was looking forward to a more exciting practice with a better catcher on the team, but that wouldn't explain why the newspapermen had come out.

They walked up to join the rest of the team. "What's going on?" Joe asked.

"Coach got a new pitcher," one of the outfielders said. The boys glanced at Joe to see how he took the news. "This big German guy from the Amanas. Straight from the farm and can't even speak English. He's supposed to be really fast."

"I hear he's got an agent and a contract to play pro," the shortstop said.

"Naw, he doesn't have a contract yet," Bob Stastny put in. "They're just looking at him. I heard he's here to pitch some league games because he's only played out in the country so far."

"Aren't you mad?" Joe asked him. Bob had been their best pitcher until now.

"You kidding?" Bob said. "Now we have a really good pitcher and a good catcher. Oh, Rudy, yeah," he smirked, "sorry, a good first base too." Rudy smacked Bob with his glove in return for the insult and went on watching the newsmen standing around the new player. Some of the men were taking photos.

Joe felt as if he had just taken a slug to the belly. Another pitcher. *Just when I was going to get my big break, this guy shows up.* He scowled at the tall young man in the new Packers uniform who was getting his picture taken.

"This is great. Maybe some scouts'll come out and watch us," Bob said. He took his pitching seriously and hoped for a baseball scholarship from the University of Iowa.

"Well, let's wait and see how this guy pitches first," Joe huffed.

The new player's name was Bill Zuber, and at first he didn't impress anyone. Joe watched him during the warm-up, and Zuber missed an easy fly ball. Then he let a grounder get away from him, right between his feet. A ripple of laughter ran through the crowd and the rest of the team exchanged glances. *This guy isn't so hot,* Joe thought. He began to hope that maybe the new pitcher wouldn't make the team after all.

When it came time for batting practice, Kovar put the new pitcher on the mound to find out how he would throw. Rudy was first in the lineup, Johnny was second and Joe was third. The first pitch went six feet to the right of the plate and sent Wence scrambling to track it down. Laughter ran through the crowd again, louder this time. Zuber's second ball flew high over Rudy's head and Wence didn't even try to catch it, letting it bounce off the backstop before he gloved it and threw it back. The next pitch went far left. Kovar turned his back to the players for a moment, passing his hand over his face as if he didn't want to see any more bad pitches, and Joe grinned with private glee. Rudy stepped out of the batter's box and walked around a bit, shaking his head, before he stepped back in and swung up his bat for another try.

The fourth ball rocketed over the middle of the plate and hit Wence's glove so hard that a puff of dust billowed out of it. Wence fell on his rear in the dirt. Rudy jumped backwards out of the box and didn't even try to swing. The crowd gave a big cheer, and Johnny looked over at Joe, eyes wide.

"Did you see that?" he asked. "You ever hit anything like that?"

Joe didn't answer. He watched the tall pitcher wind up. The ball smashed right over the plate again, and Rudy swung late and missed. Wence had braced himself for the catch this time. The crowd applauded, and most of the team did too, except for Joe and Johnny, because Joe was too amazed, and Johnny was too scared.

"Strike two!" Kovar shouted.

"Hey!" Rudy protested. This was batting practice, not a game, and people didn't call balls and strikes during practice. "I can't even see 'em coming!"

"That's good!" Kovar roared.

Rudy went back to the bench without ever hitting the ball. Johnny was up next, and he took deep breaths and swung his bat around hard in the air, working up his courage before he stepped into the box. Zuber's first pitch went just behind him, causing him to skip forward out of the way. The second ball went over his head and the third glanced off his hip, making the whole team wince in sympathy. The crowd laughed again at all the wild pitches. But the next ball came in so fast and close that Johnny dropped his bat and jumped back. The crowd cheered and Johnny looked around wildly at his teammates, as if asking what he should do. The team called out encouragement and he picked up his bat and got back in the box, waiting for whatever came next.

The fourth pitch came so fast Joe could hardly see the ball. It flashed past Johnny, high and inside, and this time Johnny threw down his bat and yelled, "How'm I s'posed to hit that? I can't even see it!" The crowd roared with delight. Johnny stormed back to the bench and flung himself down next to Rudy.

"That's right! That's right!" Kovar exulted. "We'll scare the pants off 'em when we play!"

The tall pitcher was smiling now. Joe stepped up to the plate and smiled nastily back at him. *Okay, big guy. Come on. You don't scare me.* He thought that the first pitch would be wild like the other first pitches were, but instead it whistled past him right over the plate and made him jump back in surprise.

"Strike one!" Kovar yelled. Joe glared at the coach, then at the pitcher.

He must be getting his rhythm. Joe pulled his cap down tighter, gripped his bat again and watched the next windup. *Here it comes. Put it over the plate. I dare you.*

The pitch went wide, far to the left. So did the next one. Joe elaborately stepped out of the box and walked around, swinging his bat, while Wence chased down the ball. The next ball came fast but dropped and drilled into the dirt only six inches away from his foot. Joe danced out of the way to keep from being hit.

The crowd had turned against the pitcher again. "Go practice hitting the side of your barn!" someone yelled. *"Dumkopf!"* someone else called out. Zuber turned red.

He narrowed his eyes, looked hard at Joe, and started his windup. *Here it comes.* Joe focused on the ball with all his might and swung hard. The ball tipped off his bat and fouled out. *Good. I hit him. I knew I could. Try me again and see what happens, Show-off.*

His team was yelling now, their voices higher and more excited than the sound of the crowd. "Throw that one again! I dare you!" Joe hollered. Zuber glowered at him and yelled something in German. Joe glowered back and banged his bat on the plate. "Right here!" he yelled back, and raised his bat.

The ball blurred through the strike zone faster than anything he had ever seen, and Joe swung late and missed. Wence threw the ball back and Zuber wound up again. Joe dug in hard with his left foot and narrowed his eyes to see better. When the next pitch screamed towards him he swung with everything he had, and finally, finally felt the shock of wood connecting. The ball flew off with a magical *toc*. The crowd cheered as he jogged a magnificent home-run trot around the bases, and he finished off the run by shooting a quick smirk at the tall pitcher when no one else could see.

Only one other player hit Zuber's pitches that evening, and by the end of the practice even Joe had to agree that the Packers were lucky to have him. The team clustered around him for a moment after practice was over, but Zuber only grinned and didn't say much, and his agent quickly bundled him into a car to go back to wherever he came from. The rest of the boys stood around and watched the car drive off.

"Geez, my hand is killing me," Wence complained, shaking out his right arm. "I'm gonna get me a big steak from the beef line to put on it."

"You catch that guy, you better get yourself the whole dang cow," Bob said.

The crowd drifted away and Kovar gave the boys a long lecture about teamwork before dismissing them. As they walked home, Rudy teased Johnny a little bit about throwing down his bat, and Johnny gave Rudy some grief about striking out, but mostly they spoke admiringly about the pitching they had seen that night. Joe walked in silence, wondering if he would ever pitch a ball like Bill Zuber could.

I'm more valuable because I can field a lot better than that crazy German. The whispery rustle of leaves above him seemed to laugh at that thought, but he kept on thinking up reasons why he was the better player, and tried to make himself believe.

Joe groaned when Kate's voice rang up the stairs the next morning. He still hated waking up early. He yawned and stretched, then curled up under his quilt again for a few more minutes of sleep.

Something hit his leg and his eyes flew open. He sat up and found a shoe on his bed. He threw it back, catching Johnny square on his shoulder.

"Ow!" Johnny complained as the shoe clattered to the floor. "Stop it!"

"Stop it yourself," Joe griped back as he swung his feet to the floor. "You started it."

"Stop arguing and get down here now," his aunt called up from the kitchen. "I want all of you out of the bathroom before John Mark comes home."

Joe pulled on school clothes, picked up his shoes and dashed down the stairs, getting into the bathroom ahead of Johnny. He locked the door and started brushing his teeth. In a minute, Johnny was twisting the doorknob and trying to open it, then pounding on the wood and hollering to be let in. Joe put an angelic smile on his face and opened the door.

"Oh, I must have locked it by mistake," he said. "How come you're so late this morning?" Johnny snorted and pushed past him. Stephen was right behind.

"I'm first," Joe told them. "Get in line." He washed and dried as the other two jostled for space at the toilet and fetched clean rags for their own washes. Joe took his time drying his face, elaborately searching his reflection in the mirror for new traces of facial hair. He had a faint hint of blond fuzz coming along on his jawline, but it wasn't enough to justify shaving yet.

"Geez! Get a move on!" Johnny said, pushing him away from the wash basin. Joe moved aside and snapped a towel at him. Stephen was sitting on the toilet. Joe patted the little boy on the head and went into the kitchen.

Kate threw him an exasperated look. "Since you're done, please fill up the woodbin before we start eating."

"Okay," Joe said cheerfully. Getting the best of Johnny always put him in a good mood.

By the time Joe filled the bin, John Mark was home and Kate was serving oatmeal. Food on the table always settled everyone down. Along with the oatmeal there was a plate of *kolaches*, a little stale now because they had been baked on Monday and today was Thursday, but still good enough to eat.

"Pass me your Bible, hon," John Mark said to Kate after a while. He started browsing through Proverbs, looking for verses. Joe watched as he turned the pages, wondering what his uncle would find for him to memorize today, and why he chose the verses that he did.

John Mark found something he liked. "Stephen, here you go," he said. "Proverbs 15:16. *'Better is little with the fear of the Lord, than great treasure and trouble herewith.'*" He quizzed Stephen until he was satisfied with his understanding of the verse, and then turned to Johnny.

"Here's yours. Chapter nineteen, verse one. *'Better is the poor that walketh in his integrity, than he that is perverse in his lips, and is a fool.'"* Johnny sighed. "Tell me what that means, and use golf balls for an example." Johnny managed to express his new understanding that self-respect and honesty were better in the long run than lying to impress other people. John Mark and Kate both nodded after he was done.

Joe waited for his turn. He had come to enjoy the moment when John Mark gave him his full attention. His uncle looked at him now with a little grin. Joe braced himself, hoping that the grin didn't mean that he was going to get an especially long verse.

"Proverbs 31:9," John Mark announced. "*'Open thy mouth, judge righteously, and plead the cause of the poor and needy.'"* He sat back and looked at Joe expectantly.

Joe could not immediately come up with something to say. "Can you read that again?" he finally asked, buying a little time in order to figure out what the verse meant.

" 'Open thy mouth,' that is, speak up," John Mark said, " 'judge righteously, and plead the cause of the poor and needy.' 'Plead the cause' means to speak up for someone."

Joe thought for a while, as much about why his uncle would give him this verse as about what the verse meant. "People who have it good should help out people who're poor," he finally said.

"Yes, and who else?" John Mark went on.

Joe shrugged. "The needy?"

"And who would that be?"

"Someone who needs something," Johnny said smugly.

Joe and John Mark both looked over at him reprovingly.

"People who can't stand up for themselves," Joe said decisively. He would not let Johnny show him up like that at the table.

"Very good," John Mark said, and sat back with his coffee cup. "Now, what are you all doing today? School, and then what?"

Everyone looked around at each other. "Just Wence's graduation party tonight," Kate said.

"Yeah, no practice tonight, because Wence's on the team now, so Coach said we can go to graduation instead," Johnny said.

"Oh, Wence's on the team now?" John Mark asked.

"Catcher," Joe told him.

"Huh," John Mark said. "Well, then, all three of you come home and weed the garden this afternoon. Then you won't have to do it on Saturday and maybe we can go do something fun. Maybe go fishing."

The boys exchanged surprised glances. Kate told them to go get ready to leave, but Joe lingered in the kitchen after Johnny and Stephen went into the front room and started putting on their shoes.

"Uncle John?"

John Mark looked up. "Yes?"

"What are you doing this afternoon? Need any help?"

His uncle grimaced. "I have to go to the morgue today. There's a body I need to identify." He looked meaningfully at Joe. "Not my favorite thing to do."

"Want me to go with you?" Joe asked. "I could keep you company."

John Mark gazed at him for a moment. "Thank you, Joe," he finally said, in a gentler tone that reminded Joe of the way he used to speak to him when he first moved in. "No, I wouldn't want to take you. It's no place for kids."

"It's okay," Joe persisted. "I've seen dead bodies before."

John Mark shook his head, firmly now. "I appreciate the offer, but no. You'll help me more by staying home and making sure the garden gets weeded. Don't let those other two sit around after school."

Joe changed topics in order to keep the conversation going. "Why'd you pick that verse for me?" he asked.

His uncle grinned. "I think that's going to be your special gift. Standing up for the needy."

Joe frowned. "I think my special gift is pitching."

John Mark stood up and ruffled Joe's hair, like he did Stephen's. "Just a hunch," he said. He patted Joe on the shoulder and said, "Go on, now. I'm gonna check that garden when I get home tonight." Joe left the room, ridiculously happy to have talked with his uncle and gotten his hair ruffled, but also glum, because he wanted very much to spend more time with him than that.

Joe had never been to a graduation party before and he was surprised by the number of people who came over to Vincent's house after the ceremony at the high school. More guests arrived than the Prazskys expected, because Wence was so good-natured and friendly to everyone, and also because the entire baseball team showed up. Vincent took photos of the new graduate in his cap and gown, standing with his parents in front of their little home, and then everyone went into Vincent's house for cake.

People milled around and talked. The baseball team gathered in the yard, so that the Prazskys and their invited guests could sit in the front room and toast Wence's future with glasses of Ruzina's homemade wine. Joe stayed outside with the team until people began to leave, and then he went inside to find Anton and Johnny. They were in the kitchen, eating the leftover cake and washing it down with swallows from a fresh bottle of milk, so he joined them and took his own swig from the bottle when Anton passed it to him.

Wence came into the kitchen, still in his black graduate's robe. Anton waved the bottle of milk at him.

"Hey, Wence, get out of that dress before I think you're a girl and kiss you."

Wence glared at him. "I'm thirsty. This thing's hot," he griped, and headed for the water pitcher.

"So take it off," Anton said again. "Want some cake?"

Wence chugged down two tumblers of water and took a breath. "My dad . . ." he took another breath and closed his eyes. "My dad doesn't want me to." He opened his eyes and gave a sudden mirthless laugh that turned into something like a snarl. "He wants me to sit and listen to him tell all his friends that he's sending me to law school." He set down his glass and leaned over the sink, looking like he was going to throw up the water he just drank.

Joe watched Anton put down the milk bottle and get up to close the kitchen door.

"They're almost done in there. It'll be over pretty soon," Anton said.

Wence looked over at Anton, and then he shook his head. There was an expression on his face that Joe could not quite read.

"What?" Anton asked.

Wence shook his head again, and then he said, "I'm starting at the packing plant tomorrow."

Joe blinked. A packing plant job seemed like big news. He wondered why no one was talking about it.

Anton had an unreadable expression now, too. He stared at Wence, and then said, "You didn't tell him."

Wence shook his head again. Now he looked miserable. "I'm going to move out and marry Rachel, and then I guess he'll know that I'm not going to law school."

"Oh," Anton said. Joe and Johnny sat in stunned silence.

Wence suddenly tore at the black fabric of his robe, ripping it as he pulled it over his head, bunched it up and threw it across the kitchen against the wall. He turned around and slammed a fist against the wooden cupboard, rattling the dishes inside. Joe flinched. Anton went over to him.

"Listen, talk to my dad, or something," he said uncertainly. "I'll ask him to help you. Or, I know," he said a little more urgently, "talk to Uncle John. Maybe he can tell your dad for you. When he finds out . . ." Anton stopped talking.

"Wenceslaus!" All the boys could hear the forceful voice booming at Wence from the front room, right through the kitchen door.

Anton looked at Wence as if he felt sorry for him. The door burst open and Karel came in. "Why'd you take off that robe?" he asked. "You need to be proud of it. Proud of it! Next time you're in a robe like that you'll be a lawyer!"

"Dad," Wence started.

"Come back in here," Karel commanded. "Ernie Stejskal wants to talk to you."

"Dad, please don't talk about law school any more," Wence said. Joe froze in horror.

Karel looked at Wence. His happy expression faded away and a suspicious look spread over his face.

"What did you say?"

"Look, Dad," Wence said. He stopped and took a breath. "Just don't talk about law school right now. I, um, have to talk to you about that."

Karel's eyes narrowed. He took a step forward, clenching his fists at his sides.

"What . . . do . . . you . . . mean?" he asked, but this time his voice came out in a menacing growl. Johnny jumped out of his chair and fled into the other room. Joe looked over at Wence. Unbelievably, he was still standing at the sink and looking right back at Karel as if he had seen his father this way before and wasn't afraid of whatever was going to happen next.

"I'm going to work at the packing plant tomorrow," Wence said.

Karel took another step forward and pointed his finger at Wence.

"I forbid it! You will quit that job!" he bellowed. "You are going to law school!"

Vincent walked into the kitchen now, with John Mark right behind him. "Karel, what's this all — " Vincent began to say.

"Shut up!" Karel snapped, rounding on him.

"Dad!" Wence yelled. "I'm taking the job!"

Karel turned back and closed the distance between himself and his son with one long stride and grabbed the front of Wence's shirt. "You are young and stupid," he began in a low hiss, but his voice rose as he continued. "You don't know what's best for your life, but *I* do. You little *fool!*" he thundered, shaking Wence by the collar. "You want to waste your life in that stinking factory? Making someone else rich? After all I have worked for? Saved for? You think I will let this happen? No!" He let go of the shirt and pushed Wence hard in the chest, throwing him off balance and into the table and chairs. Glasses crashed to the floor and Joe heard someone scream.

Wence picked himself up from the table and moved away. His own eyes were narrowed now and his fists were clenched. He looked across the room at Karel, and Joe suddenly realized that the two of them were almost the same height. John Mark moved around the table, trying to get between them.

"I'm taking the job and I'm getting married," Wence said in a tight clear voice. "You can yell at me all you want but . . ."

"*Sacramenski potvora! Potvora syn!*" Karel roared as he charged across the kitchen. Vincent and John Mark both went after him, catching at his arms. Wence easily dodged the intended punch and in a burst of anger pushed all three of them back into the tangle of table and chairs.

"It's over! Over!" Wence shouted. "*Sacramenski* yourself! I'm not going, and you can't make me! I'm sick of you telling me what to do! I don't care if I never see you again!" Karel, red with rage, struggled against Vincent's and John Mark's grip on his arms, finally throwing them off with a wordless shout and turning back to swing a fist at his son. But he was too late. Wence had glanced around the room with something like an apology in his eyes, and run out into the night.

The party broke up after the fight. Karel stomped out of the kitchen and slammed the door. Ruzina charged out after him, shouting in Czech all the way across the back yard. John Mark and Kate helped Vincent clean up the mess, and then took their family home. They walked a little in front of the boys, but Joe could hear them talking.

"I can't believe he'd do that. Lose his temper like that. He'll never live this down," Kate said.

"That's not really important, though," John Mark replied. "I'm more worried about Wence."

"I can't believe that boy either. Of all the bad times to tell Karel that he doesn't want to go. What was he thinking of?"

"Ah, he's just a young man, wants to get married," John Mark said. He reached over and put his arm around Kate's waist for a hug, then took her hand and held it as they walked. "Young and dumb," he went on. "I wish he'd look down the road a ways. A little college wouldn't be so bad. Better for his family, in the long run."

"I don't know. I think it's wrong to make such a big deal about that," Kate said after a while. "What's so bad about not going to college? Wence is a fine young man. He's going to make a decent living and he's marrying a very nice girl. You'd think Karel would be proud of him."

"That's not it," John Mark said. "You don't know about the plant, Kate. That place will take a young man like him and ruin him with work. They'll keep him in jobs that will make him old before his time. And he'll just think that if he's a good enough worker and never complains, they'll promote him someday. Someday when he's so crippled up he can't swing a hog carcass anymore, is when that'll happen."

Kate was quiet for a while, and Joe thought that they were done talking. But his uncle finally spoke again.

"I'll tell you what I'm worried about. Things as they are now, Karel might never talk to him again. Might not ever let him come back home. He's so . . . muleheaded, I really think he might."

They all walked in silence after that. Joe thought about Wence, picturing him going through restaurant garbage for food and sleeping behind buildings, as he and his mother had done. Despite the warm May evening, a cold chill stole down his backbone at the memory. He looked at his aunt and uncle, still holding hands, then at Stephen and Johnny walking beside him.

He had not understood, had not known until that moment, how much he loved living in a family, how deeply comforting it was to have a home where he could always walk in the door and be safe and known and welcome. When he met people now, he could tell them who he was and where he lived. He had a permanent place in the world that was not going to disappear overnight. How had he ever lived without it? How could Wence bear to lose it? The strange cold chill made him shiver again, and he reached out to ruffle Stephen's hair and warm himself with the touch.

Joe spent the next day in a fog. He was tired from the long week of early mornings and late nights, and the painful memory of Karel and Wence's fight turned breakfast into a silent meal. John Mark was late coming home from the factory, and Kate was preoccupied with sorting laundry for her mother to wash. Josefina scolded Stephen about his table manners until Kate spoke sharply to her in Czech and made her stop.

The men from the drama society picked them up after dinner for play practice and Joe and Johnny painted the stage backdrop while the actors practiced their lines. The director kept the actors late and Johnny fell asleep on a bench after the painting was done. Joe sat by the stage and waited, wishing his uncle would hurry and come get them so he could go home to bed. Anton finally walked into the hall and came over to him. None of the adults in the family felt like going out, so he had driven the car over to pick up the boys.

"They're not done yet. We have to wait for Stephen," Joe told him.

Anton sat down next to him, beside the old upright piano that someone had donated to the Hall. He experimentally touched a key, testing the feel of the keyboard, and the director turned and frowned at him. Anton hastily took his hand away.

"Heard from Wence?" he asked Joe.

"No," Joe said. "You think he's going to come back?"

Anton blew dust off the piano keys. "I just thought maybe he'd talk to Uncle John."

"Naw, I don't think he did," Joe said.

He wondered where Wence had slept last night. John Mark had said that the packing plant work was hard. Had he started today?

Anton was quiet and Joe wondered if he was thinking about the same thing. After a while, he asked, "Do you think he should go to law school?"

Anton shrugged. "He doesn't want to be a lawyer."

"Do you want to go to college?" Joe asked.

Anton shrugged again. "I don't know. My dad wants me to. All I know is, I don't want to spend my life in a room killing hogs all day. Or playing piano either." He looked at Joe. "I want to get out and do interesting things. Maybe that new factory. I'm going to take physics next year and see if I like it."

Joe had seen the inside of the school science lab from the hall. He always thought that it looked interesting, with long wooden tables holding Bunsen burners and little glass beakers full of different colored liquids. The boys in the lab wore special protective aprons over their school clothes. They were mostly tall, and looked like seniors.

"Would they let me take it?" he asked.

"You have to take two years of math first," Anton said. "That's what the principal told me. Do you have a year of math yet? Maybe they would let you take physics and your second year of math at the same time."

"I only have half a year," Joe said after a while. "I don't think it's enough."

"Maybe you can come in after class and see what I'm doing, anyway," Anton said. "That way, you can figure out if you want to take it."

Joe slid down a little further on his chair and rested his head against the back of it, picturing himself as Anton's special friend in the science lab. It felt wonderful. "Okay," he said. "I'll do that."

The actors finally finished their practice and both boys stood up, ready to collect Stephen and go.

"Just another minute, please," the director called to them. "We need to put him in costume. It won't take long."

Joe heaved a sigh and sat back down. Anton slid onto the piano bench and touched the keys again, playing chords at first, then wandering into a melody. Joe leaned his head against the side of the piano and listened to the music as it rang through the hall. The melody was exquisitely beautiful, so beautiful that it made him want to cry, because Wence might be out on the streets somewhere without a home tonight, never able to come back. Wence was one of the friendliest people he had ever known, always kind to him even though Joe had never done much for him in return. Joe thought about how Wence had helped him rescue his knife on Christmas Day, and how he had stood up for him around the boys at school. Losing Wence felt like losing a foot, or an arm — like losing some essential part of himself that he had not troubled to think about until it was too late.

Finally the director was satisfied with the costume and sent Stephen over to them. Anton finished playing. Some people clapped, making him smile and look embarrassed. Then they woke up Johnny, and at last it was time to go home.

When Joe got to bed, though, he could not fall asleep. He fussed and turned, trying to get comfortable. He finally went downstairs and quietly sliced a piece of bread for a snack, then decided to sit in the front room and look out the window as he ate it. He was almost finished when he saw Wence walk out of the moonlit street and up the front porch stairs, to tap on John Mark's bedroom window.

Joe opened the front door. "Wence!" he whispered. He almost hugged Wence out of sheer joy at seeing him again, but he held back when he saw the older boy's strained expression.

"Is Uncle John home?" Wence whispered.

"Yeah, it's his night off. We just went to bed," Joe whispered back. He thought about his uncle and his one night off. "Maybe you should talk to him tomorrow?"

Wence shook his head and tapped on the window again. John Mark came out at almost the same moment, wearing his pajama bottoms, and looked at the two of them.

"I just came down for something, and then I saw Wence came over," Joe said. John Mark moved over to stand by Wence and pat him on the back. Wence put down his head and leaned into the pat a little.

"You up?" he finally asked. His voice shook a little as he spoke.

"Yeah," John Mark said. He sat down on the porch stairs and Wence sat beside him. Joe sat down behind them in the shadows and leaned against the door.

"Where'd you sleep last night?" John Mark finally asked.

"Jelinek's back shed," Wence said.

"Did you start at the plant today?" John Mark asked after a pause.

"Yeah," Wence replied, and didn't say anything else.

After a longer pause, John Mark asked, "So, how you doing?"

"I rented an apartment today," Wence said. "Over on Second Avenue." He swallowed. "Uncle John, will you marry us?"

John Mark did not answer right away. "Do you have your marriage license yet?" he asked after a while.

"Uh, no," Wence said.

"That'll take a few days," John Mark said. "That'll give you and me time to talk to your dad." Wence made a sound of dismay. "I'm not saying that what he did was right, but you still need to talk to him first and I'm not going to marry you behind his back."

Wence stared down at his shoes for a long time before he said, "Ah, thanks for doing this. I really want you to marry us. I want to have a good wedding for Rachel, not just go down to the courthouse."

"You sure you're ready for this?" John Mark asked mildly. "Getting married so quick? Kate and I waited a while, you know, for me to get to know her family and do everything right."

Wence raised his head and looked at him.

"Yeah, I'm ready. I've been ready since Christmas. And she's ready too. We've done our waiting and I'm not waiting any more. Her family, my family . . ." he shook his head. "I don't want anything to do with my dad ever again," he went on, his voice rising. "I'm tired of him telling me what to think and what to do every single second of the day. I've had it! I'm sick of it!"

"Shhh," John Mark told him. "You'll wake up the neighbors."

Wence put his head back down.

"I didn't mean for it to happen like that," he finally said.

"Probably should have told him earlier," John Mark said.

Wence's voice started to rise again. "You just can't ever talk to him. Nobody can. I try all the time and he just . . . blows up and gets mad, and it makes me just want to . . ." his voice trailed off.

"Well," John Mark sighed, "yeah. But it would have gone a lot better if you had talked to him. If you want me to marry you then I want you to think about some things first. Working at the plant might not turn out to be the good deal you think it is now. How'd your first day go?"

"Fine," Wence said with a note of defiance in his voice. "I can handle it easy."

"Wouldn't Rachel wait for you, if you get a little more schooling first? Your dad still wants to send you to college. Maybe you could talk him into something besides law school, if you're so set against it," John Mark went on. "So you don't have to work at the plant your whole life?"

Wence sighed. When he spoke again, the tone of defiance was gone.

"Yeah, she'd wait for me, if I told her that's what I want to do. She loves me and she'd wait. But I don't want to. I don't want to go to school anymore. I want my own home and my own family. I want to be married to Rachel and she wants to be married to me. You talk about waiting," he said, earnestly now. "I've never done anything to her, never touched her that way, not even once. And now I finished high school and I want to get married. Why is that so bad? Why does everybody think I'm so wrong?" Wence sighed again and put his head in his hands.

John Mark didn't answer right away. He picked up a stray piece of stick lying on the wooden porch and scratched circles on the step with it.

"It's going to be tough, Wence," he finally said. "No matter how smart you are, no matter how much Rachel loves you, being a husband is tough. There's going to be storms down your road. It doesn't even matter which road you choose. If you don't go to college there's going to be storms, and if you go there's going to be storms anyway."

He scratched some more circles with the stick. "I guess I'm trying to talk you into something that I think is good for you, but in the long run the storms are going to come no matter what you decide. I don't know the future, and you're an adult now and you're going to do what you want anyway." He tossed the stick away.

"In the Bible there's a story about two men who each built a house," he said slowly. "One was a wise man who built his house on rock, and one was a foolish man who built his house on sand. Then a big storm came along, like it always does, and hit both houses. Whose house do you think made it through the storm?"

Wence didn't realize for a while that he was supposed to answer the question. "Ah, the guy who built on the rock?" he finally said, when it was obvious that John Mark would not go on without a response.

"Right," John Mark said. "The house that was built on something stronger than the storm. Do you know what that story means?"

Wence shook his head.

"The house is like your life. The man who built his house on the rock was one who heard God's teaching and decided to live his life according to it," John Mark said plainly. "The man who built his house on the sand heard the teaching too, but he ignored it and didn't care about God. They both heard, they both built, but when the storm came, only the house that was built on something stronger than the storm made it through. The rock isn't college. It isn't even a good job. It's God. God is the only thing bigger than all the hard times that life can throw at you."

Wence was silent.

"Your storm's coming," John Mark said. "That's just the way life is. It doesn't matter if you go to law school or work at the packing plant, there's going to be lots of storms before your life is over. They hit everybody. I watch some people make it through and I see some that don't. The difference is whether they've got a life built on God or not."

"This is what I want, more than anything in the world," Wence finally said. "To get married. To Rachel. I think this is what God would want me to do. I love her."

"I know you love her. I don't doubt that at all," John Mark told him. "If I'm going to marry you, what I want to know is, if you love her so much, how are you going to build your life? Are you going to build it in a way that will get you and her through the hard times when they come?"

They were all quiet for a while, thinking.

"Seek God while you have the chance," John Mark said after a while. "There's another verse I like. It says that in the time of God's favor, He hears you call, and in the day of salvation, He helps you. And then it says that now, right now, is the time of His favor, and now is the day of salvation. Now's your time. You can do what you want. Seek God while you can, Wence. Do it right."

Wence picked up his own twig and twirled it as he spoke. "I want to make a good life for us," he said. "I just want for us to get along, talk, be happy together. Like you guys," he ended up.

John Mark laughed. "Let me tell you, Wence, if it wasn't for us trying to follow God, we wouldn't have a butterfly's chance in a blizzard of having a happy day. I think we'd be in one big long fight the whole time. You should see the stuff that goes wrong around here." He twisted around to see if Joe was still there. "Right?" he asked when he saw him.

Joe nodded.

"If you're absolutely set on getting married, then get your license, let's talk to your dad, and then you and Rachel come over here for dinner," John Mark said. "If this is what you want to do, I'll see if I can help get you started off right."

Wence shook his head at the idea of talking to Karel. "I don't think it's a good idea for me to talk to Dad," he said. "There'd just be another fight."

"Oh, Karel's going to come around. You should've seen what happened over there today," John Mark said.

Joe perked up, wondering what his uncle was talking about.

"Your mom followed him around the place all day, yelling at him about what an idiot he was to lose his temper like that. Then Vincent and I cornered him and told him that he needs to talk to you and not let this turn into some big feud that people gossip about for the next twenty years." John Mark stopped and chuckled. "And then, the funniest thing was, Rose was there listening to everything, and out of the blue she says, 'Dad, I want to go to college, so just let Wence get married and give me the money instead!' Your Mom laughed and your Dad got all red in the face and yelled, 'Don't you go getting ideas, missy,' and Rose just looked right at him, and then she said . . ." John Mark was trying not to laugh too loudly, " . . . she said, 'Dad, the famous Czech teacher Jan Komenski said that all Czechs ought to be educated, even the women.' I thought I was going to bust a gut, trying not to laugh."

Wence had finally laughed when he heard about Rose's little speech. "She ought to go," he said. "She's smart as a whip. Except she'll scare off all the guys if she gets that smart."

"Oh, you haven't heard the end," John Mark continued. "So after she says that about Jan Komenski, she goes on, 'And I'm going to marry a college man, and we're going to buy a car and a big house with electricity, and you and Mom can come live with us when you're old.'"

All three of them laughed. "Well, anyway, I think we can go over there tomorrow and talk about what you're going to do," John Mark said afterward. "And you try to listen to his side. Maybe he'll have an idea that makes sense. If you just stay calm, we'll work something out so you don't go without a family for the rest of your life. Karel loves you, even if he's a little pigheaded."

Wence snorted.

John Mark elbowed him in the ribs. "'Honor thy father and mother,'" he joked. Wence said nothing after that, but Joe was watching his face, and saw him smile.

Eight: June / *The Secret*

"5-7-21-25-23-17-7, 12-23, 12-10-7, 8-7-25-4-7-12, 8-23-25-6-7-12-22. Is that what you got?" Joe asked. He leaned over from his seat on the couch to see what Johnny had written.

"Yeah, that's what I got," Johnny said, and then they hushed in order to hear the rest of the announcement.

"So, mail in your Ovaltine label today, and get your own Radio Orphan Annie's Secret Society decoder so you can decode the secret message and get the Secret Society Members' clue to tomorrow's exciting adventure!" Theme music rose up over the announcer's voice, bringing the show to a close.

The boys exchanged glances as the evening news began. The secret message had been announced three times during the show. The first time they hadn't known that it was coming, and didn't have anything to write with, but by the second announcement they had paper and pencils ready, and by the third time the message came around they had compared notes and could double-check their numbers with the radio.

"Huh." Johnny stared at the numbers. "Maybe we can figure it out."

"Let's just buy some Ovaltine and send in the label," Joe said. They had worked in a neighbor's garden that day and each of them had earned twenty-five cents.

Johnny frowned. He was saving his money for a bicycle. "Naw. I think I can figure it out." Joe shook his head as his cousin started making notes under the numbers, but Johnny ignored him and yelled, "Hey, dad! Come take a look at this!"

John Mark and Kate were sitting at the kitchen table, looking at bills and adding columns of figures. "Not now, son," John Mark called. "When the news comes on."

"It's on now," Johnny called back. When his father did not answer, he jumped up and walked back to the kitchen, carrying his paper with him. Joe watched him push in between his parents and show them the message. John Mark shook his head and promised to look at it later.

Johnny came back to the front room and flopped down on the floor. "They're doing bills." He went back to frowning at the numbers.

Joe stretched out his legs on the couch, careful to not wake Stephen who lay sound asleep at the other end, worn out from weeding the garden and carrying groceries home from the Avenue with his mother. Josefina was sewing in her bedroom. The long June evening was hot and humid, making everyone sweat a little, even though the house's windows were open to the breeze. The shrill whirring of cicadas rose and fell outside, and the air smelled of damp grass and dandelions.

Footsteps suddenly stamped up the front porch stairs, and Anton came in without knocking, letting the screen door bang shut behind him.

"Hey, look at this," Johnny demanded. "See if you can figure out this secret code."

"Hello to you too," Anton threw back at him, and rolled his eyes at Joe. "Hi, Uncle John, Aunt Kate," he called to the kitchen. John Mark called back an absentminded response. Anton looked around the room, scooped up Stephen from the couch, carried him into John Mark and Kate's bedroom, and laid him down on the bed. He came back out and sat down beside Joe.

"What're you guys doing?" he asked. Now that school was out, Anton took the streetcar across the river to the college for tennis practice during the day, and came over to John Mark's house almost every evening after supper.

"Orphan Annie's got a secret code," Joe told him. Anton leaned over to see the paper. "It's a clue to tomorrow's show. You have to mail in an Ovaltine label to get the decoder."

"I think I can figure it out, if you guys will just help me," Johnny said.

"I've got Ovaltine," Anton said. "You can send in my label." He kept on looking at the numbers, though, and took Joe's pencil and started making some notes himself. "Maybe one of these words is 'Ovaltine.' Huh. Nope. What other word . . ."

Joe watched Anton as the other boy worked on the numbers. Anton had walked into his uncle's bedroom as casually as if it had been his own. Joe wondered what it would feel like to be so free and easy, and why he always felt that there were places where he couldn't go and things that he couldn't do, like push in between his aunt and uncle in order to get their attention, or walk into their bedroom. Just the thought of doing either one of those things made him feel sick.

John Mark came in and sat down in the rocker. "Hi, Anton. So what's this secret code? Figured it out yet?"

"Nobody's helping me," Johnny complained.

"I'm helping," Anton protested, poking Johnny with his foot.

"Just send in the label and get the decoder," Joe said. "They probably made it to where you can't figure it out."

"Let me see it, *Jan*," John Mark said. Johnny got up from the floor and leaned on the arm of the rocking chair, holding out the paper for his father to see. John Mark studied the numbers for a while and then handed it back to Johnny.

"*E* is the most commonly used letter in the English language," he said, "and if that's not enough to figure it out, I think you better get the decoder. How do you do that?"

All the boys spoke at once. "Fine, fine. Go ahead," John Mark said after a while, and rubbed his eyes. "Now, either go outside or quiet down. I have a headache and the news is on."

Kate came in and handed around glasses of ice water. She had finally bought her icebox and she had served cold drinks every evening for a week. The icebox was a cabinet made of wood with a block of ice in the top, and the boys were not allowed to open it because warm air made the ice melt faster. John Mark wanted to put the icebox in the cellar, where it would stay cooler and use less ice, but Kate wanted it in her kitchen, where it would be handier for cooking. In the end they had compromised by putting it in the kitchen and telling the boys that they weren't allowed to open it.

"Thank you, Aunt Kate," Anton said as he took his glass. Everybody sipped for a while, cooling off and listening to the news.

"The year's worst dust storm still darkens the sky over much of Nebraska and Kansas today," the newscaster announced. *"The storm has been in full force for two days now and shows no sign of stopping. High noon is as dark as night, and mothers keep wet cloths over their children's faces . . ."*

"Those poor people," Kate murmured.

"The shooting sprees and violent deaths of Bonnie Parker and Clyde Barrow remain our top news item this week," the broadcaster continued. *"New stories about their wild trail of destruction now link Bonnie and Clyde to even more crimes . . ."*

Joe watched his uncle. John Mark had a deep frown on his face that seemed to grow darker with every item of news.

" . . . and because of the increasing number of bank robberies and the deaths of inno- cent bystanders, the United States Department of Justice has offered a $25,000 reward for news leading to the capture or death of notorious gangster and escaped prisoner John

Dillinger. There you go, folks, if you can't find a job, then just find John Dillinger and you can live on Easy Street for the rest of your life." Everybody smiled at the comment, even John Mark.

"Radio Orphan Annie has devised a new secret code that, if deciphered, will allow listeners to predict what will happen during the next day's program," came the next announcement. Joe and Johnny both reached for their pencils in case any clue to the code came up. *"Folks all over America are probably trying to crack the code right now, but the show's sponsors say that the only way to decipher it is to mail in an Ovaltine label and get the official decoder."*

"Dang!" Johnny said. Kate laughed.

"On a more serious note, we have bad news from Wall Street today . . ." Joe was not interested in bad news from Wall Street, and went back to trying to figure out the code as the news about food riots, unemployment, and Nazis droned on.

John Mark finally stirred in his chair. "Let's turn the station," he said. "There's got to be something better to listen to." Joe moved over to the radio and began searching for other programs.

"Did you hear about that new Clark Gable movie?" Anton asked them. "He takes off his shirt and he's not wearing an undershirt. All the guys at the college were talking about it today so we all played tennis without undershirts on."

"Oh, Anton," Kate said. "I hope no one saw you do that."

"That doesn't sound like a good idea," John Mark said. "You'll get your shirt dirty faster if you don't wear an undershirt."

"It's a lot cooler," Anton said. "You can't really tell. Why do people have to wear undershirts anyway?"

John Mark was listening to the different programs that Joe was dialing through. "That's the *Chase and Sanborn Hour.* Go back," he instructed. Joe backed up the dial to the last station he had paused on. Music filled the room. "At least we won't hear any bad news on this program."

"Hey, I saw Wence and Rachel today on the Avenue," Anton said. "They told me to say hi to you guys."

"Do they look any different now they're married?" Johnny asked, only half joking. "Does Wence still have that big dumb smile on his face?"

"Hush," Kate said. "It's wonderful to see them so happy together."

Wence and Rachel had been married a week ago. Karel had finally been persuaded to speak to Wence, after three days of arguments that shifted first between Ruzina and Karel, then between Karel and Vincent, and finally among all three. Karel had lectured Wence for an hour before grudgingly listening to what his son had to say, but in the end the two of them came to an agreement to get along, for the sake of the rest of the family.

John Mark had married the young couple soon afterwards in a small ceremony at Vincent's house. Ruzina and Kate, thrilled to have another woman in the family, decorated the front room with roses and lilies, and served an elegant lunch of ham sandwiches and creamed potatoes afterwards. Rachel's sister and grandparents had attended. Her grandparents, who still disliked Freethinkers, sat through the ceremony with their arms crossed and stubborn scowls on their faces. But any man with a factory job was a good catch for their granddaughter, so they talked and smiled when the vows were over and lunch was served. Rachel wore a borrowed wedding dress and carried a bouquet of flowers from the Prazkys' garden. Wence wore one of John Mark's old suits, and a broad smile that had only grown broader when the men tried to embarrass him with traditional bridegroom's jokes.

"Yeah, he's still got that dumb smile," Anton said to Johnny, then caught Joe's eye and changed the subject. "You guys want to come downtown with me sometime? After practice I go eat lunch with my dad at the café. You could come with me."

"We've got a job tomorrow," Joe told him. "Painting a fence."

"Where at?" Anton asked.

"Oakhill Cemetery," Joe and Johnny said in unison. One of the men in the drama society had asked them if they would paint a fence for ten cents an hour. They had said "yes" right away.

"You going to walk?" Anton asked them. "Want to take my bike?"

Joe and Johnny looked at each other and shrugged. The cemetery was about two miles away.

"I guess we can trade off," Johnny said. "Riding and pedaling."

"Okay," Joe said. He was thinking about Anton's offer to go downtown. "After we get this job done, I'll go to tennis practice with you."

"Sounds good," Anton said, and leaned back to listen to the happy words of *Flying Down to Rio*.

At ten o'clock the next morning, Joe sat back on his heels, rubbed his forearm across his sweaty face, and looked at the fence he was painting. It was a wrought iron fence, with tall, thin rails that each had four sides and seemed to take forever to paint. His leg muscles stung from squatting and his back ached from bending over. He sighed and looked at Johnny, who knelt a few feet away from him on the other side of the fence, a streak of black paint smeared across his forehead.

"Can I have the water?" Joe asked. They had brought a sack lunch and a jar for drinking water. The cemetery had a well with a hand pump, and they had already refilled the jar three times because of the heat. Johnny handed him the jar through the rails and Joe drained it in four long swallows.

"My turn to get more," Johnny said. The pump was a long enough walk from the fence to make a nice rest break for whoever went to refill the water jar.

"Walk a little faster this time," Joe said peevishly. Johnny seemed to take forever when it was his turn to go for water.

"Shut up," Johnny said. "You took a long time too."

"Don't say 'shut up,'" Joe told him. Johnny gave him a kind of frustrated hiss as he picked up the jar and headed for the pump.

Joe kept on painting. It was harder without Johnny on the other side. The boys had experimented with the fence, trying to figure out the least frustrating way to paint it. They had finally settled on working with one of them on each side and sharing the paint bucket as they went down the row. They were already tired. The early-morning bike ride had put them both in a bad mood, because when Joe pedaled with Johnny behind him on the seat they were fine, but when Johnny insisted on taking a turn at pedaling he turned a corner too fast and tipped over the bike. They had landed hard on the cement street curb, and now they had scrapes and bruises as well as aching muscles. Johnny was still embarrassed and Joe was still mad.

But they had started at eight o'clock and if they worked straight through until five, at ten cents an hour, they would each earn almost a dollar if they didn't stop for lunch. Joe looked down the long line of iron fence. It was taking a lot longer to paint than he thought it would. There was no way that they could get it all done in one day. It might make sense to take a lunch break instead and come back the next day to finish, because he didn't think that they could go straight through the day without a break. He said so to Johnny when he came back with the water.

"The sexton man will think we're pikers if we take a lunch break," Johnny argued. The cemetery caretaker had looked irritated when he handed them the can of paint and pointed towards the fence, and Johnny was worried about making a mistake and getting yelled at. Joe shook his head. Johnny didn't know about how to work.

"Workers eat lunch. It's okay," he told him. "We just have to work fast enough that he knows we're not trying to doublecross him on the hours."

They painted in silence for a while. The sky was blue and the sun blazed down. The caretaker moved around the cemetery, watching the men who were mowing grass and digging graves. Towards noon, he brought over another bucket of paint and looked at the rails they had painted so far. Joe and Johnny held their breath during the inspection.

"Think you'll finish today?" he asked.

"I dunno. We'll try," Joe told him.

"I lock up at five," the sexton said. "You'll have to come back tomorrow if you can't finish by then."

"Yes, sir," Joe said. The sexton nodded and turned away.

By noon they were hungry and tired, and when the other workers disappeared for a lunch break they sat down in the shade of the nearest tree to eat the sandwiches and *kolaches* that Kate had packed for them.

"It's so hot," Johnny grumbled, and unbuttoned his shirt.

Joe felt an old shame rise inside him at the idea of taking off his shirt, and looked away. He had not put on an undershirt that day, because of what Anton had said last night. Johnny hadn't worn an undershirt either, and when he pulled off his shirt and threw it down on the grass, Joe could see his back. The skin was smooth and unmarked. Joe's own shirt was sticky with sweat, but he wasn't about to take it off. He had been careful not to let anyone see his back, and as long as the weather had been cold and everyone kept their clothes on, that had not been hard to do.

Johnny stretched out in the silky grass. He closed his eyes. "You figure that sexton guy is eating lunch too?" he asked after a while.

Joe looked around. Cicadas buzzed above them and bees droned among the flowers, but other than that nothing moved in the cemetery. "I think everybody is," he said, and looked back at Johnny, sprawled so casually in the grass, completely at ease even though his shirt was off.

Johnny's breaths grew slower and deeper. Joe wanted to take a nap too, but instead he leaned up against the tree so that he could see if any of the cemetery men came back from lunch. He sat there in the shade and kept watch, but his thoughts were far away.

When Joe was thirteen, his mother met a plumber who asked her to move in with him.

At the time, they were living in the back room of a restaurant where Marie worked, which was fine with Joe. Whenever they lived in a room or with a friend of his mother's, he had to obey rules and go to school. But in the restaurant his mother worked in the kitchen or tended bar until late at night, and then slept on the threadbare little couch in the back room during the day, and so he was free to roam whenever he wanted. Marie couldn't yell at him when they lived in the restaurant, because everyone would hear, and she didn't want people to think that he was any trouble, or even notice that he was there at all. So Joe spent his days and nights as he pleased, going to school when the weather was bad and doing something more fun when it was nice, like visiting a junk shop or stealing food from grocery stores. The restaurant's cook was an old man who shared cigarettes with him, and Joe could always wheedle a bite to eat by washing dishes and cleaning up the kitchen. So Joe liked the restaurant and didn't want to leave. But Marie wanted to live in a place with a bedroom and a bath.

"He's a plumber and he has his own place," she told Joe with a big smile, which made her face look strange, because she frowned most of the time now. "If we move in with him then I can get away from here, and you can go to school because you won't be out all night."

Joe didn't want to stay in at night and go to school every day. "I'm not going," he told her. "I like it here." He hated life with Marie's men friends. He hated the way that they talked to his mother, always ordering her around, and he hated the way they treated him. The last man had beaten him with a belt and then locked him in a closet, because he thought Joe had eaten more than his fair share of food. His mother had been drunk at the time and didn't even know what happened until she came out of her stupor the next morning and heard his yells.

"You can't stay here without me, so you're going," Marie had told him. "It's an apartment. We'll be like a regular family."

Joe doubted that, but in a secret part of his heart that was still soft and tender he held a hope, so unlikely that he would never say it out loud, that someday Marie would meet a man who would love him like a father would. In spite of all the beatings and disappointments of the past, that unlikely hope rose again in his heart as he walked down the street with his mother, wondering about his next home.

"This is my son Joe," Marie said. "He's a real good boy. Joe, this is Mr. Kramer." Joe ducked his head and muttered hello.

Mr. Kramer had a pot belly, a stained shirt, gray hair, and a suspicious expression. He looked at Joe and then at Marie.

"He's tall for his age," she said quickly, and Joe wondered what age his mother had made him out to be. She tended to tell people that he was younger than he really was. "He's just so smart, and he goes to school and works at the restaurant on Saturdays. He's never any trouble," Marie chattered on, smiling and tilting her head at the man.

Joe looked around the room while his mother spun her lies and tried to divert the man's attention. The place was small, only two rooms on the third floor of a house, and the wood floor hadn't been swept in a while. The room they were standing in held a little stove and table. Joe stole a quick glance into the other room. Inside it was a bed.

" . . . I said, put your stuff over there," the man said. He was pointing at a corner of the room. Joe snapped back to attention.

"Yes, sir," he said, and felt himself smiling nervously, trying to please, as he moved over to the corner with his bundle of clothes. Mr. Kramer did not smile back. Joe put his bag down as he was told, and then stood beside it, because there were only two chairs in the room, and he could tell that he wasn't invited to sit in one of them.

His mother fixed a little meal of fried potatoes and they all ate, the two adults at the table and Joe sitting on the floor. The man had a bottle of whiskey and a radio, and he poured drinks for himself and Marie and listened to the radio after the meal. When he was ready to go to bed, he told Joe to sleep out in the hallway, on the little landing where there was a door to a bathroom and stairs that went down to the house's front door. Marie protested, but the man became displeased, and Joe quickly said that he didn't mind sleeping on the landing. It was better than being too close to the bedroom. If his mother sounded like she was having fun in a bedroom it made him uncomfortable, and if it sounded like she was having a fight in a bedroom that was worse. If he was on the landing then he wouldn't hear anything at all, and he might be able to sneak out and go back to visit the restaurant.

The door down at the bottom of the stairs was locked, though, so he couldn't get out. He wrapped himself in his blanket and slept fitfully on the hard landing floor. The next morning, Mr. Kramer woke him up and told him to go to school. Marie quickly wrapped up some leftover potatoes for his lunch, and the man put a heavy hand on his shoulder, steered him down the stairs, and let him out the door.

Out of sheer loneliness, Joe actually did go to school that day, and the next day as well. He hadn't been going much lately, and he had trouble catching up with the rest of his class. But Mr. Kramer got up and went to work every morning, and he made Joe leave for school every morning as well. Sometimes he stayed in school all day, but at other times he slipped away and roamed the alleys, looking for food and something fun to do until he could go back to the apartment where his mother was napping or listening to the radio. When Mr. Kramer came home, they ate. Joe tried running away, but he always became lonely for his mother after a day or two, and he went back to her because at least she would give him a meal and a place to sleep. Whenever he returned after running away, the man ignored him and said nothing about his absence, and Joe was careful to stay quiet in his little space. There was no sense in starting any trouble.

One morning the man asked Marie if he could take Joe to work with him.

"Oh, of course. That's wonderful, isn't it, Joe? Won't that be fun?" Marie said, and smiled brightly. Joe looked at her, wondering how she could be so stupid, trying to act as if the three of them were having anything like fun, but he said nothing, because it seemed wiser to be quiet and act just like Mr. Kramer.

Joe was a little afraid of spending a whole day alone with the man without Marie to smooth things over if something went wrong, but he was also curious about what men did at work all day. And if he was a good helper, the man might like him more. As the day went on Mr. Kramer didn't say much about the way he worked, either for good or bad, but Joe worked hard and felt a little better after a while, because he had found something that he was good at.

Plumbing was fun. They worked in big brick houses with beautiful furnishings and expensive artwork inside. Joe held tools, carried parts, and cleaned up after the jobs. The man took him to work the next day, too, and after a while Joe quit going to school and became the plumber's boy. Sometimes they worked on big jobs with other men, who were usually friendly and joked with Joe as they dug trenches and fitted pipes together. Joe often wondered why, with so many nice men out in the world, his mother couldn't manage to move in with one. No matter how hard he worked, Mr. Kramer did not talk or joke with him like the other men did. In fact, he didn't seem to like Joe any better than he had that first day.

At night they ate dinner and listened to the radio. The man drank a lot of whiskey before he went to bed with Marie, and sometimes he was hung over the next day. Joe watched him constantly and learned how to steal cigarettes from his pack when he wasn't looking, and gulp mouthfuls of whiskey from his bottle when he wasn't in the room. Now that he had to work with him all day and sleep locked up in the stairway all night, he was lonelier than ever, and he felt no remorse about taking the cigarettes and drinking the liquor. In fact, that was the only time he felt good.

On some days the man didn't need Joe's help and told him to go to school intead. Joe had given up on school, though, so he hid in the bushes across the street and then went back up to the apartment when he was sure the man was gone. It was hard for him to roam the streets like he used to. His clothes were too small, his shoes were worn out, and people looked at him with suspicion when he went into the stores. He preferred to spend the day tucked away in the apartment with his mother, snacking on leftovers and listening to the radio. In the morning they listened to the soap operas. After lunch they shared a cigarette stolen from Mr. Kramer's pack, and then napped until it was time to fix supper. Joe knew that his mother drank during the day, but the bottle was hidden someplace where he couldn't find it. If he said anything about it, Marie would cry and babble about how miserable her life was because she got pregnant when she was young. When she became too irrational Joe would leave and go walk the alleyways, looking for food or useful junk, but he always ended up going back. She might be drunk, but she was his mother, and the world was too lonely to live in without anyone at all.

But one day everything changed. Joe went to work with Mr. Kramer on a job with a crew of men, putting new plumbing fixtures into a huge red brick mansion. He was timid at first, carrying toilet parts and toolboxes through the luxurious house, but he became more confident and walked faster as the day went on, and then, while he was carrying an armload of pipes, he tripped and broke a lamp. It was a beautiful lamp, made of colored glass worked into a pattern of roses and lilies, and it fell with a crash that brought the owner of the mansion and all the other workers running to the scene. Mr. Kramer apologized and promised that the company would pay for the lamp, and then he took Joe by the arm and led him outside.

Joe could remember saying that he was sorry and beginning to cry before the door even closed behind them. Mr. Kramer pulled him around behind the big work truck, grabbed a handful of stiff metal bundling wires and hit Joe across his back with them.

The first blow hurt, but the wires had razor-sharp ends that tore his shirt, and the second blow laid lines of burning fire across his skin. Joe fought to get away as the wires hit his back again and the pain flared into searing torment. He kicked and hit, flailing the air with his fists and staggering to his knees with the force of the beating. The other workers gathered around and he could see their jeering faces through a blur of tears as the wires hit his back again and knocked him to the ground in helpless agony.

"Help me!" he screamed. "Somebody please help me!"

Men cursed and roared around him as Kramer whipped his back. "Good for nothin' kid!" someone yelled. "Get him out of here!" With a sudden rush of desperation Joe pulled back up on his feet, kicked with all his might, and felt his shoe connect hard with something. He heard a grunt and felt the grip on his arm loosen, and then he tore free and ran through the blurry circle of men and down the street, gasping and crying, until he couldn't run anymore.

A train whistle suddenly broke the quiet of the day. Joe caught his breath and blinked. He was not running down a street crying anymore. He was sitting under a tree in a cemetery, with a lunch bag and a jar of cold well water beside him, and his cousin lay sleeping on the grass just a few feet away. Joe took another breath and then reached out for the jar of water. His hand trembled as he held it and his teeth rattled on the rim as he drank. He put the jar down and leaned forward with his face in his hands, trying to come back to where he was and what he was doing here.

Two men appeared and walked across the field in front of him, and then Joe remembered why he was here. He was painting a fence, and it was time to get up and go back to work now. He looked over at Johnny, lying there in the grass lost in sleep, his back smooth and untouched. Joe gazed at his peaceful face and thought that a few years ago he must have looked just like Johnny looked now, relaxed and innocent and trusting.

His voice wouldn't work when he tried to call Johnny's name, so he leaned over and shook his arm, gently, because he couldn't bear the thought of hurting him. Johnny yawned and then nestled deeper into the grass, still sleeping. Joe cleared his throat and got his voice back.

"Hey, wake up. Time to get going," he said. Johnny opened his eyes and sat up.

"Okay," he said. Joe watched him grope around for his shirt and put it on, still half asleep. He didn't feel angry at Johnny anymore, but protective of him, as if he wanted to make sure that nobody ever beat Johnny the way that he himself had been beaten.

"I'll do the outside this time," Joe said generously. The inside of the fence had softer grass and whoever painted that side was closer to the pump, but the outside of the fence had sharp weeds mixed with the grass and it was a longer walk around to get water. Joe had made Johnny work on the outside during the morning because he had been mad at him for tipping over the bike.

"Thanks," Johnny said cheerfully. "Want me to get more water while you walk around?"

"Yeah," Joe said. "Thanks."

Joe brushed paint over the iron rails but hardly noticed what he was doing. He was still thinking about the way the plumber had beaten him with the handful of wires. Why hadn't anyone helped him? *I would've*, he thought savagely. *I would've helped, if it had been somebody else. Why didn't anyone help me?* He looked at Johnny, working on the other side of the fence, earnestly trying to keep up with Joe's greater speed. *How could anybody just go and hurt a kid like that?*

Johnny talked to him once in a while, but Joe barely heard him. He couldn't stop thinking about his mother and the plumber and the day he had been whipped so viciously. It seemed as if he hadn't remembered anything about it for a long time, yet now he couldn't get it out of his mind.

On the day the plumber had beaten him, he had run down the road, his shirt torn and bloody, until he lost himself in a maze of unfamiliar streets and big brick houses. A sympathetic streetcar driver finally picked him up and let him ride into town, where he found his way back to his old restaurant. The cook let him into the kitchen and gave him a shirt, and Joe cried himself to sleep that night on the couch in the back room. A few days later, his mother came and found him. She was crying, too, because Kramer had thrown her out.

"Why did you do that?" she had raged at him, loud enough that the whole restaurant could hear. "How could you be so dumb? Where are we going to live now? This is all your fault!" The manager heard her screaming and shoved both of them out through the kitchen door and told them to not come back. They walked the streets that night, Marie in tears and Joe in a silent stupor, until they found some empty park benches and fell asleep there out of sheer exhaustion. A policeman woke them the next morning and sent them on their way. They slept in church pews the next night, in a park again the night after that, and then they drifted to the shantytown near the railroad tracks. They lived there for weeks, then months, scavenging food and sleeping where they could. At first Marie found ways to spend nights with some of the men, and she bought food and liquor with the money they gave her. But after a while even those men didn't want her company at night, especially not with her strange teenage son underfoot. Finally Joe found the rusted-out car for them to sleep in, where at least no one made them get up and leave.

"Joe!" He jumped. Johnny was looking at him with a puzzled expression. "It's your turn," Johnny said, holding out the empty water jar.

Joe swallowed and looked back at the fence rail. "You go on," he said. "It's too far to walk around." Johnny shrugged and started walking to the pump. Joe kept painting, although when he thought about it, he wasn't sure why. Why try? The fence stretched on, hundreds of rails down the edge of the cemetery, and no matter how much he painted, there were always more. Why work so hard if it made no difference? His life was just like painting this fence, he thought, a lot of dreary motion with no end in sight, and all the effort was not nearly worth the pain.

Later on that week Joe felt better because the baseball season started. During the first game he played every inning, went four-for-four at bat, and batted in five runs. Coach Kovar had grunted approvingly at him, and the whole family had been there to watch, even Vincent and Anton and the Prazkys. Some of the factory men had shaken his hand afterwards and Rose had lingered after the game to tell him how happy she was that the Packers won. Bill Zuber had slapped him on the back and said "Good job" in his thick accent. A private glow of happiness warmed him every time he thought about the game.

Joe stood in his grandmother's bedroom that evening as she fitted a shirt to him and pinned fabric to mark the cuffs. "Stand still, *Pepik*," she ordered. "Hold out your arms. Good." After she finished she patted his arm.

"You're getting big," she said approvingly. "Look at that arm." Joe made a muscle for her, and she smacked him lightly on the side of his head.

"*Bouktha*," she told him. "Idiot. I know you steal *kolaches* at night. You don't fool me."

"They're so good, Grandma," Joe told her. Marie had always referred to Josefina as his grandma, and he liked to call her that, instead of Mrs. Vesely. He was embarrassed if she showed too much favoritism toward him in front of other people, but secretly it was nice to have someone looking out for him, making snacks and special clothes like the new white shirt she was sewing for him now. "Bake some more for me, okay?" She smacked him again and turned back to her sewing machine. Joe grinned and went out to the front room where the radio was playing and Johnny was puzzling over the latest secret message.

"Dad, if you're right about the letter E, then I think that the sevens are the E's," he announced. "There's more of them than any other number."

"Did you send off for the decoder?" Kate asked.

"Anton did," Johnny said. "I wish it would hurry up and get here."

"*Kde je Anton dnes vecer?*" John Mark asked from behind the Czech newspaper he was reading.

Joe and Johnny looked at each other. "What?"

"Where is Anton tonight?" John Mark asked again.

"He's doing something with his dad," Joe said. "I'm going to tennis practice with him tomorrow," he added.

John Mark put down the newspaper and looked at him. "Going to take the streetcar?"

"Um, yes. I'll pay for it," Joe said quickly. He kept his voice casual, trying not to show how thrilled he was to go downtown and eat lunch with Anton at the Harmony Café where Vincent worked.

"Johnny, you going?" John Mark asked next.

"Nope. I'm weeding Mr. Havlicek's garden," Johnny said.

John Mark looked back at Joe as if he was thinking about something.

"You got a shirt and tie to wear?"

"Huh?" Joe asked, surprised. He had worn overalls every day since school let out, except for Sundays.

"You go downtown, you have to wear a shirt and tie. You'll end up shaking hands with all Vincent's banker friends at the Harmony." John Mark stood up. "Come here, shake my hand."

Joe put out his hand and shook. His uncle was not impressed. "Like this," John Mark told him. "You look 'em right in the eye and then *shake*," he said, grabbing Joe's hand and shaking hard. "Try again."

Johnny snickered. Joe looked his uncle in the eye and shook hands ferociously.

"That's better," John Mark said. "And put your napkin in your lap when you eat. Don't start eating before anyone else, if you end up at a table with other people. And don't talk with your mouth full." He paused for a moment. "Just watch Anton and do what he does."

"Okay," Joe said. He felt even more excited than before. He slipped back into Josefina's room. "Grandma, can I wear that shirt tomorrow?" he asked in a whisper.

She turned around and scowled at him. "*Samozfiejmû, Pepik.* Of course, dear. Everybody but a *bouktha* knows to wear a shirt downtown. You think I'm stupid? Now go away," she told him, but he could tell that she wasn't mad. She never got mad at him. He gave her a delighted little hug and went back out to listen to the radio. *This is great,* he thought. *Wow. I'll never get to sleep tonight.*

Vincent Starosta woke up early the next morning in the pale dawn, listening for the sound of Anton's breathing. The birds were just starting to sing and he frowned, concentrating, until he could hear quiet breaths in the bedroom next to his. After his wife died, Vincent insisted on keeping both bedroom doors open during the night, claiming that the air in the rooms stayed fresher that way, but really because deep in his heart he feared that Anton might start coughing in the middle of the night and be dead a week later, like Amalia.

There was not much point in getting up this early, but he had always been an early riser and could not go back to sleep. He heard Anton turn over in bed and clear his throat, and listened until the boy's breathing steadied out again into its usual rhythm.

This is ridiculous, he thought. *Get up and do something, you old fool, if you can't get back to sleep.* He rose and went out to the kitchen, pausing and looking in on Anton as he passed his open bedroom door. Everything seemed all right. Vincent made coffee and then sat by the window with his Bible.

He turned to Psalm Thirteen. *"How long wilt thou forget me, O Lord? for ever? How long wilt thou hide thy face from me?"* Vincent was a Christian, like his parents and grandparents before him, but since the death of his wife he seemed to have lost his old strong love for God. He felt detached from his usual routines, as if his heart had grown numb, and defeated, as if he had tried his best to achieve some goal and failed. But he still smiled and worked and put food on the table, because Anton was still alive.

John Mark had told him to be patient and trust that God still had good things in store for him. *"'Wait on the Lord: be of good courage, and he shall strengthen thine heart,'"* his brother would quote from Psalm 27, and Vincent agreed, in theory. The Creator who made him was still the same, and probably had a plan, just like the Bible said. He should be getting over his grief by now. A man didn't just give up on life because a wife died. But it was hard to feel any real hope in the gray mornings, when he was getting grayer every day himself and lonelier every time he thought about how Anton was growing up and would move out of the house someday soon.

Now stop it, he scolded himself. *That's the last thing you need to do – tie him down when he should be going out and making his way in the world.* Vincent went back to his psalm. *"Consider and hear me, O Lord my God: lighten mine eyes, lest I sleep the sleep of death . . . I have trusted in thy mercy . . ."* Vincent looked out the window a long time afterwards, praying, although he didn't know exactly what for. Something had to change. Surely the Lord would not be so cruel as to leave him in this misery for the rest of his life.

" . . . ye have not, because you ask not . . ." Vincent sat up a little as the words from the book of James came to mind. *Well, I'll ask then. I'm asking, God. You say to ask, so I'm asking now. I have to get better. Show me some sign that You hear me,*

that You care, that all these years of faith in You and work for Your people have not just been for nothing. In the name of the Savior, please do something, anything, to help me feel better. He looked out the window again, thinking about his prayer. *I sound like that old complainer Jeremiah,* he thought, and flipped through some pages to look at Jeremiah's words. A section in the third chapter of Lamentations caught his eye, because it was underlined in blue ink. *Amalia must have underlined it. I should read it, if she liked it so much.* Vincent read and reread the passage and then closed the book, thinking over the verses and letting them echo in his heart: *"I remember my affliction and my wandering, the bitterness and the gall. I well remember them, and my soul is downcast within me. Yet this I call to mind, and therefore I have hope: Because of the Lord's great love we are not consumed, for his compassions never fail. They are new every morning; great is your faithfulness . . . I say to myself, 'The Lord is my portion; therefore I will wait for him.' "* Vincent thought of Amalia. She was with the Lord now; her time of waiting was finished. *Well, for some reason I'm still here. May as well make the best of it.* He put away his Bible and thought about what he had to do that day.

When the morning brightened Vincent went to the kitchen and started breakfast. Anton was playing a lot of tennis every day now, so he needed more to eat in the morning than just a bowl of oatmeal or a piece of toast. Vincent cracked eggs into a bowl for scrambling and sliced up some leftover ham. His son would get a good breakfast and then a midday meal at the restaurant. If they were too tired to cook supper, then they could just make sandwiches, or maybe Ruzina would bring over a plate of whatever she had cooked for her family.

He heard a rustling in the bedroom, and then Anton came in, still in pajama bottoms and rubbing his bare arms to wake himself up.

"Morning," he yawned.

"You got up?" Vincent asked in mock amazement. "On your own? Will wonders never cease?"

Anton sighed and headed for the coffee. He was used to his father's teasing. "Joe's coming with me today, so I have to leave early," he said as he poured himself a cup. He yawned again.

"Look at you, yawning and drinking coffee. You stay up too late," Vincent scolded. "You should go to bed at a decent hour." He dished up the eggs and ham while Anton set out bread and butter.

Anton grinned as he sat down and tackled his breakfast. Karel and one of his friends had come over to play cards the night before, and Vincent and

Anton both had stayed up late playing pinochle with them. "C'mon, Dad. You had fun." His eyes were very blue in the morning light and his hair was still tousled from sleep. Vincent looked him over and shook his head.

"Anton, that hair . . . son, you need a haircut. You look like an Italian opera singer. No wonder those girls at the restaurant won't leave you alone." Anton grinned again, a little self-consciously this time, but he had a mouthful of eggs and ham and couldn't answer right away.

Vincent couldn't resist teasing him some more. "But you've got a good idea there, taking Joe along with you. Give those girls someone new to moon over. Get you off the hook for a while." Anton rolled his eyes, and Vincent laughed and let him eat in peace.

His happy mood faded as he dressed for work. Gas and parking fees were too expensive for him to drive his car every day, so he usually took the streetcar. The ride was depressing because he went past six banks, all closed because of the Crash. The Citizens' Savings Bank on 16th Avenue was still open because the Czech bankers had made only cautious loans during the nineteen-twenties while other banks had recklessly overextended themselves, but even that building held bad memories for him. The head teller there, a personal friend of Vincent's, had shot himself two years ago when the bank examiner showed up one morning to audit the books. The United States Bank's windows were boarded over. The spacious Cedar Rapids Savings Bank, where Vincent himself had worked, was locked up now. Even the large National Bank was closed, except for the Harmony Café, which was still open for business on the bank's first floor and served lunch to the remaining downtown merchants and their wealthy clients.

It had been humiliating for Vincent to go to work at the Harmony, waiting on the same people that he himself had once done business with. The first time that his former banking acquaintances left a tip for him, he felt more like throwing the money out the door after them than picking it up and putting it in his apron pocket. But he had a wife and son to support, and he needed to be reasonable, so in the end he had swallowed his pride and kept the tip.

As the Depression tightened its grip on the city and more men lost their jobs, Vincent saw other men reduced to circumstances like his own, or worse, and eventually he came to appreciate the job he had and the way it kept him in touch with the banking community. The few banks downtown that remained in business had problems with delinquent loans and bankruptcies.

Vincent talked with bankers every day and kept up with the local news. Because he was a waiter, he got a free plate of the restaurant's lunch special every day, and when the cooks met Anton, they liked him so much that they started giving him free lunches, too. All in all, it was not a bad situation, but Vincent still missed his old position with the bank and dressed just as carefully to wait tables as he did when he had been head teller at Cedar Rapids Savings.

He carried plates and poured drinks for customers. Well-to-do couples, the women beautifully dressed like Amalia had always been, sat and chatted in intimate voices over their lunches. Later on his regular group of bankers came in and pulled tables together so they could sit down and hash out whatever problems had come across their desks that day. As two o'clock grew near, Vincent cleared plates, poured after-lunch cups of coffee, and began to watch the front door for Anton and Joe.

One of the bankers signaled for more coffee and Vincent walked over to refill his cup. "I'm sick and tired of having to be the one to clean up all these bad loans," the man was telling the group. "They never should have been made in the first place. It's not just the economy. It's the way those idiots made loans ten years ago. If I had the money I could start a bank right now and do a better job."

Vincent laughed. "Sure you could, Van." He had known Van Schaffer from Merchants Bank for years. "You can get the old Savings Bank building for a song right now too, fixtures and all. Dust everything off, open the doors, and you're a bank."

"It could be done," Orrie Becker put in. "Start off as a payer agent for a couple of these closed banks, keep everything conservative, and it's a guarantee. I'd put up money to do it."

"You really want to put up money, Becker?" someone else said. "I will if you will."

"How much you got?" Becker asked back, and men traded numbers for a while and began to get excited.

"I just want to say," Vincent said as he circled the table and refilled more coffee cups, "if you fellas really do this, I want you to come back and get me out of this lunch job. I'd rather be head teller again." That drew some laughs, and then some thoughtful looks.

"You know what, we'll hire you and then you can hire the rest of the tellers," Becker said. "Who's the landlord for the Savings Bank?"

Vincent drew in his breath to answer but didn't get a chance to speak, because just then Schaffer said, "Hey, here's your boy," and Anton and Joe walked in. *They really do look like they're related,* Vincent thought. Joe was not quite as tall as Anton, but they both looked tanned and handsome in their white shirts and dark ties, and some of the customers watched them as they made their way to the back of the restaurant.

"Hello there, Anton," Schaffer said, putting out his hand. "Who's this young man with you today?"

"My nephew, Joe Vesely," Vincent said. "Joe, this is Mr. Schaffer from Merchants Bank." Joe shook hands courageously and Vincent hid a grin at the velocity of his shake. John Mark must have coached him. The boy did all right, though, as he said hello and made conversation about tennis and baseball. *Regular little gentleman,* Vincent thought. *Too bad he's got that scar along the side of his face. It makes you wonder where he's been.*

After the handshakes, the boys went to a table in back, and Anton slipped into the kitchen to say hello to the cook. When he came back out and sat down, a trio of high-school girls in colorful dresses and matching hair ribbons sauntered over to say hello. Vincent kept an eye on them as he finished up his tables. Anton talked and laughed with the ease of a veteran, but Joe was reserved. *I'd be bashful, too, Joe,* Vincent chuckled to himself. *Those girls sure are pretty.* The boy had just worked up enough nerve to smile and say something when the two free lunch plates appeared in the kitchen pass-through window, and Vincent delivered them to the table.

"Well, girls, how are we today?" he asked. "Doing your bit to help out the economy?" All three of them came from wealthy families and shopped for things like hats and gloves and hosiery at the downtown clothing stores. The girls giggled and took the cue to leave, saying goodbye and looking back over their shoulders as they drifted away.

Vincent looked at Anton. Anton looked at Joe, who rolled his eyes and shook his head.

"You got the life. That's all I can say," Joe said, and they laughed.

Vincent tried to sound serious. "Just remember these words of wisdom, boys: you're from the wrong side of the river and you're not in their country club. They'll never marry either one of you. Never forget I told you that."

"I don't care, Uncle Vincent," Joe said.

"That's okay," Anton said at the same time.

"I won't forget that you told *me* that," Vincent said. "I'll remind you for the rest of your lives. Eat up now before the cook changes his mind and makes me pay."

After lunch, Joe gave a last glance around the beautiful restaurant and said one more heartfelt thank you to Vincent before he followed Anton out the door. He had eaten in nice restaurants before, with his mother and her bootleg friends, but in those days he had always been the unwelcome boy, pushed back into a corner and ignored. Now, he grinned with delight as he remembered shaking all the bankers' hands and joking with the girls, just like anyone else would have done. In the restaurant's mirror he had seen a reflection of someone standing next to Anton, and the person in the mirror had looked so grown up that at first he hadn't even realized that he was looking at himself. This had to be the best day of his life.

That morning, they had taken the streetcar over the river and up First Avenue to the college. The morning sun sparkled on the downtown buildings and people smiled and nodded at him as he sat on the streetcar bench with Anton. The walk through the college campus made him feel timid at first, but when they came to the field house and Anton changed clothes to play, Joe relaxed and started to have fun, especially when the tennis coach yelled at Anton just like his own coach yelled at him.

Now, after lunch, the two of them boarded the streetcar again. They could have walked home from the restaurant, but it was a long walk, and Anton's legs were tired and Joe's shoes had pinched his feet all day, so they had decided to spend their nickels for the ride instead.

"That lunch was great," Joe said as they sat together on the streetcar bench and rode slowly through the downtown streets. "Your dad sure is nice."

"Uh-huh," Anton said. He leaned his head against the window frame. Joe looked at him and saw that his eyes were closed.

"You going to sleep?" he asked.

"Just tell me when it's time to get off," Anton said, and yawned. "That coach wore me out today."

Joe sat for awhile with nothing to do, then slipped a pack of cigarettes out of his pocket. He had not been able to smoke much lately. First he had been broke and then he had been busy, but after the cemetery job he splurged and bought a pack. He had brought it with him today, thinking that he would look more grown up with a cigarette in his hand, but some inner warning had held him back from smoking around the tennis team or Anton's father. Now he finally lit up and blew a stream of smoke into the air, coughing slightly. It had been a while.

Anton opened an eye and looked around, then opened both when he saw Joe smoking. "Geez, Joe, get rid of that. Smoking ruins your wind, don't you know that?" he said irritably. Joe paused, torn between smoking and friendship.

"Naw," he protested.

"My coach'd throw me off the team if I smoked," Anton said. "Kovar's a dumb bohemie or he'd throw you off too."

"Hey!" Joe protested.

"Hey yourself. I'm a bohemie but I'm not dumb." Anton didn't seem to care if Joe liked him or not when it came to cigarettes. Joe, glowering, finally flipped the butt into the street. Anton stretched out his legs, closed his eyes and leaned against the window again.

The streetcar stopped at a red light, and when Joe looked out at the people on the sidewalk, he suddenly stiffened with shock because he saw Kramer.

It was him. The man stood there, not ten feet away, staring him right in the face. Joe felt his stomach lurch and his fingers tingle in fear. *Get out of here!* He jumped up into the aisle, looking for a place to run, but then the streetcar lurched forward again and instead of running he sat back down in his seat, doubled over with his head down, out of sight from the man outside. His heart beat so hard that it hurt his chest, and he shuddered until his teeth clicked. He clenched his jaw and wrapped his arms around his middle, eyes shut tight, still stunned by the sight of that face.

Someone was calling his name. A hand touched his back, and he jumped as if he had been hit. A weird swirl of colored dots was all he could see at first when he opened his eyes, but he blinked the swirls away and saw Anton looking at him and saying something.

Joe stared back, hearing nothing but the sound of his own heartbeat pounding in his ears. Anton kept looking at him and talking to him, and after a while he could hear the words.

"Joe? You okay?" Joe blinked and trembled. He was on a streetcar. Anton was looking at him. What was going on? He looked out the window in fear and for a moment he saw the man again, but no, he was not there. He turned around and looked behind him to see if Kramer was somehow in the streetcar, standing in the aisle, ready to finish the beating he had started so long ago.

But there was no Kramer there either, just a few people looking at him with puzzled expressions. He felt a hand on his shoulder and jumped again, flailing out with his fist and almost hitting Anton in the face.

"Geez," Anton said, hands up in defense, "what's the matter?"

Joe put his head back down into his hands, trying to push back the memory of Kramer's beating and the terror he had felt when he saw the man's face again. It was no use. He could not keep it in.

"I saw someone," he choked out. "I saw this man . . ." The words roiled in the pit of his stomach and rose in his throat like bile. He felt his lunch come back up, and he wanted to retch it out along with the nausea he felt inside, but he clamped his jaw shut instead, fighting for control. A rush of sweat drenched his face.

Anton pulled out a handkerchief and pushed it into his hand. He watched Joe for a moment, then asked, "Who'd you see?"

Joe could not hold back any longer. "This . . . this man who beat me up. I saw him." He glanced out the window again, dreading to see who might be there looking back. But the sidewalk was empty.

"Where?" Anton was looking outside now too. "Are you sure? Who're you talking about?"

Joe wiped at the sweat on his face. His voice shook when he answered. "He was my mom's . . . he was a guy my mom knew. I used to help him on his jobs. I broke a lamp . . ."

He could not stop talking. He whispered the whole awful story to Anton in bits and pieces, and as he told it he felt hot with rage one moment and then sick with remembered shame the next. He even forgot where he was and jumped when Anton reached up to pull the cord to ring the street-car bell so they could get off at their corner.

He stopped talking then, and they stepped off the streetcar and started walking home. Joe had calmed down as he told the story, but when Anton said nothing and only walked silently alongside him, he began to worry again. Anton probably despised him now and regretted taking him downtown for the day. If the family found out about the story they would all think less of him, a boy with a such an embarrassing past.

"Look, you can't tell anyone about this," Joe said.

Anton was quiet for a while. "I think you ought to tell Uncle John, at least," he finally said. "Somebody should do something."

Joe laughed harshly. "Do what? Go find this guy and tell him he shouldn't have beat up a kid? Kids get beat up every day." He kicked a rock savagely out of his way.

"Not our family," Anton replied.

"Yeah, well, I didn't grow up here," Joe said bitterly. He stared down the street, angry and heartsick. Why did his mother stay away all those years, when she could have come back and lived with her family? Why couldn't he have grown up here, safe, with his aunt and uncle and grandma? Why did he have to be the one all scarred and ruined now? And the worst part was that even if Anton was his friend, even if the girls did like him and he became a baseball star and all his dreams came true, even then, the scars would never go away. Neither would the memories. Joe raised a hand to the line of scar on his face, wishing bitterly that it would disappear and take his wrecked life along with it.

They came to the corner where they would split up to go their separate ways, and Joe realized that he was still holding Anton's handkerchief. Anton *would* have a handkerchief, he thought resentfully. Anton pretty much had everything.

"Here, take your perfect handkerchief back," he heard himself say. "Must be nice, being Mr. Perfect and rich and playing tennis and everything all day long."

Anton stopped and looked at him, unbelief written all over his face. "What?"

Joe stared back, horrified at what he had just said. He was incurably bad, and the badness went deeper than just the scars on his skin. It was everything about him — the way he thought, the person he was — that was bad.

"Sorry," he said. He twisted the handkerchief between his hands, trying to think of something to say before he gave it back.

"I'm so messed up," he finally said.

Anton looked at him a while longer, then started walking towards Joe's house instead of his own. "Ah, it's okay," he said.

Joe walked beside him, feeling more and more miserable every step of the way. "Look, I'm sorry," he said desperately. "Please don't tell anyone. I don't know why I said that. Here," he went on, handing over the handkerchief. "I'm just dumb."

"Idiot," Anton said, and gave him a little shove. "I don't think you're dumb. I just want to go beat up that guy. Uh, sorry it was such a bad day."

"No, it was a good day," Joe said, close to tears. "It was the best day of my life."

They reached the house, and Anton stopped walking. "Well, I guess that's all right then," he said awkwardly. "Take it easy, bud. Tell everyone I said hi." He raised his hand in goodbye and started across the street toward his own home. Joe stood there on the empty sidewalk and watched him go.

Joe went upstairs and changed out of his good clothes, then flopped down on his bed and wished he could just lie there forever and never talk to anyone again. He couldn't decide if he felt sick, or sad, or both, but he knew that he didn't want to go downstairs and have to answer questions about his trip downtown. After a while he heard someone knock on the front door downstairs, and then he heard Wence and Rachel come in. They had come over for dinner – the third time in a month – but he stayed up in the attic, not wanting to go downstairs even when he heard Wence and Johnny go out to the back yard for a quick game of catch.

Kate finally called him down for the meal. Wence had brought over two bottles of root beer, and Kate let him open the icebox and chip off some ice so they could all have cold drinks. John Mark and Wence joked and teased each other so much during supper that everyone laughed until they held their sides. Even Rachel made a joke. Joe did his best to fit in, but for once in his life he didn't feel hungry, and the jokes couldn't reach far enough through his misery to make him want to laugh. Afterward he said that he was tired and went into his grandmother's room where it was quiet and cool. He lay down on her bed and listened to the rest of the family talk, turning his face to the pillow once in a while to blot the tears that kept coming to his eyes.

John Mark and Kate sat in the kitchen with Wence and Rachel for a long time, reading sections from the Bible and talking. Johnny and Stephen listened to "The Orphan Annie Show" and then left for Anton's house right after it was over. Josefina sat in the front room, rocking peacefully in the cool of the evening. The conversation in the kitchen finally quieted to a low murmur, then stopped altogether after Wence and Rachel said their goodbyes.

Joe could hear Kate start on the dishes, and then John Mark walked over to the bedroom and called his name.

"Joe? You awake?"

Joe heard him, but stubbornly kept his head turned away and acted as if he were asleep. After a pause, John Mark went on to the front room.

"Let's see if Walter Winchell's on," Joe heard him say to Josefina. The radio station changed, and after a few commercials Winchell's famous voice crackled through the air. "Good evening, Mr. and Mrs. North and South America and all the ships at sea . . . let's go to press!" Joe buried his face in the pillow to soak up a new stream of tears that somehow burst out again at the sound of a cheerful voice.

Evidently John Mark changed his mind about the radio program, too, because he kept moving the dial, searching for something else. He stopped at a news program, listened for a moment to the talk about bank robberies and factory closings, then turned to a station playing hymns. Sweet, solemn music filled the air, and after a while Joe's tears dried up as he listened.

My God and I go in the field together
We walk and talk as good friends should and do
We clasp our hands, our voices ring with laughter
My God and I walk through the meadow's hue

He heard Kate finish her work in the kitchen, turn out the light and walk into the front room.

"Is Joe asleep?" he heard her ask.

"I think so," John Mark replied. "He seemed a little down tonight."

"Ah, *vsechno hroznû*," Josefina said.

"*Co je, Matko?*" Kate said after a moment. "What do you mean, everything is terrible?"

"*Ano,*" Josefina said. "All life is sad. All."

There was only silence after that, and then Joe heard his uncle sigh.

"John, it's not that bad," Kate said. "We just ate dinner and the boys are all healthy. Look at Wence and Rachel, how good they're doing."

After another pause, John Mark said, "Kate . . . we don't have even one dollar in the church account today. The factory laid off some guys yesterday and people say more's getting laid off tomorrow."

Joe heard a rustling noise in the front room, as if someone were moving around, and he listened for what his aunt would say, but no one spoke for a while. A new song started to play.

Love lifted me, love lifted me
When nothing else could help, love lifted me

"Look, John, even if everything goes wrong and there's no money and you get laid off, we'll still be all right," he heard Kate finally say. "God hasn't gone away. Even if we lose a house again, we have the most important things. We'll still be happy." She laughed. "We'll just move in with Vincent like we did before."

All my heart to Him I give, Ever to Him I'll cling
In His blessed presence live, Ever His praises sing.
Love, so mighty and so true, Merits my soul's best songs
Faithful, loving service too, To Him belongs.

Love lifted me . . .

"*Kateřina,*" John Mark said tenderly in the beautiful old-country language. "*Miluji tě.*"
"I love you too," Kate said. Joe listened as intently as he could, but they did not say anything else, and all he heard was the music.

When nothing else could help, love lifted me.

Joe buried his face in the pillow, aching for someone to love him like his uncle and aunt loved each other. He squeezed his crossed arms against his stomach and curled up into a ball of misery. Why had his life gone so wrong? *Where are You, God?* he pleaded silently. *Where were you when I needed help? Why didn't You help me, all those years, all that time? Are You just not going to help me anymore, because I've been so bad? What am I going to do, if even You don't love me?*
The song ended and another one began.

Precious Lord, take my hand
Lead me on, help me stand
When I am tired, I am weak, I am worn . . .

As the song played on Joe wept again, wiping his eyes on the pillow and smothering his sobs against the sheets. Finally it ended. After a while his tears ended as well, and he lay back on the bed, worn out from all the emotion.

Life seemed clear now, as if the whole invisible structure of the world was laid out in a pattern for him to see. Love was the hidden secret, the thing that was not seen and could not be bought in stores or from bootleggers. It was the precious strand that bound people together, guarded their hearts from evil thoughts and connected them to everything good. If only he had love, life would be worth the pain.

Uncle John and Aunt Kate love each other, he thought. They have it. Who do I love like that? Who loves me like that? He reached up to touch the scar on his cheek and thought about the hateful words he had said to Anton that afternoon. *Who will ever love me, the way I am?* He stared out the window, feeling unutterably sad.

Footsteps suddenly thumped up the porch steps and the front door banged open. "Mom! Dad! The decoder came!" Johnny's voice rang out. "Where's Joe?"

Joe was rolling over to get up when Stephen ran in, jumped on the bed and bounced. "Joe! Joe!" he yelled. "The decoder came!"

Someone else, bigger than Stephen, tugged on his arm and pulled him into the darkened kitchen. It turned out to be Johnny. "Let's get all the messages and decode them," he said. "Come on. I'll get the papers." Johnny raced up the attic stairs and then the kitchen light suddenly flipped on. Anton stood there, grinning and holding something in his hand. He gave it to Joe.

Joe blinked in the light and looked at what he was holding. It was round, flat, made of metal, and the letters of the alphabet were stamped around the outside rim. He looked closer. A ring of numbers, one through twenty-six, sat just inside the circle of letters. Each number corresponded to a letter. It was the code to all the messages.

He stood there blinking at it until Anton slapped him on the back and said, "It finally came, huh?" He pulled Joe over to a chair and pushed him down in it, then pulled up another chair beside him. "Pretty neat, huh?"

"Yeah," Joe agreed. He turned the decoder over in his hands, amazed that it had finally arrived. He had begun to think that their household had been missed and that they would not get a decoder after all.

"Here's a pencil," Stephen said. He pushed up in between them, standing close to Joe so he could see. "Johnny! Hurry up!" he yelled, right in Joe's ear.

"Ow!" Joe said, and pushed him away, then pulled him back and hugged him. "Just not in my ear, kiddo, okay?"

Johnny came down the stairs, papers in hand. He spread them out on the table and the boys leaned over them together, matching letters to numbers.

"Do this one first," Johnny said. He had dated every message and had them in order. "It's the first one. Five is W. Seven is E . . . hey, look, I was right! I said that the sevens were E's! Remember?"

"Yeah," Joe said. "21 is L. 25 is C. That first word's *welcome*."

"The second one's *to*," Anton said. "The third one's *the*. Then there's *S, E, C*, then four . . . that's *R* . . . Secret! 'Welcome to the Secret Society!' There you go!"

Johnny whooped. "This is great. Let's do the next one. No, let's do tonight's and then we'll have the clue for tomorrow." They all bent over the papers for a while, decoding messages.

"Let me see," Joe heard his uncle say. John Mark was on the other side of the table, craning his head to look at the decoder. "That is really something."

"You got that for free?" Kate asked. She was leaning over them, watching them work. "Want some ice water?"

"Ah, okay, thanks, Aunt Kate," Anton said absently after a while. "Here, Joe, you do this stack and I'll do these."

"Can I do one?" Stephen asked. He was still squeezed in between Joe and Anton.

"You can help me," Joe said. "Here." He pulled the boy into his lap and gave him another hug. It felt good to hold someone who loved him. Joe felt one more sob rise in his throat, but he firmly swallowed it down, and the painful knot that had gripped his heart all evening finally loosened and went away.

I'm going to find love, he thought with sudden resolve. *It's like a decoder. You think that you're never going to have it, and then you do, and then everything makes sense. I'm going to find God, I'm going to be a person who's worth loving, and I'm going to look for real love and find it if it's the last thing I do.*

Nine: July / *The Storm*

J oe stood with Johnny and Anton outside the church's big front door after Sunday service, talking about what was going to happen on the next *Orphan Annie* show. Anton had brought the decoder and the other boys were inspecting it, passing it around to take a closer look. Church members nodded and said hello or goodbye as they walked by. Joe replied politely and, if the person was a man, shook hands. His uncle had told him that he was old enough now to help out with the service by greeting people before and after church instead of running around on the grass and playing with the younger children, like Stephen still did. Johnny overheard the conversation and he didn't play on the grass anymore, either.

"You fellows going to the dance this afternoon?" one parishioner asked. On Sunday afternoons, dances were sometimes held outdoors on the Avenue, at a shady little space next to the feed store where there was a gazebo for the band and a wooden dance floor under the trees.

"Not today," Anton said. "We're going to the play." Stephen's play opened that night, and John Mark had asked an assistant pastor to conduct the evening service for him so they could all go.

"It'll be cooler inside the Hall than on the Avenue," the man's wife said to him. "Maybe we should go there instead of the dance."

"Let's eat first and talk later," the man replied. "I'm starving. Tell your dad I said that he preached a good sermon today," he said as they left for home.

The service had run a little longer than usual that morning. When John Mark preached a sermon he sharpened up his voice and flung out his long arms to make his points, and now that the summer mornings were warm and humid he would even take off his suit jacket at times and preach in his shirtsleeves. The congregation liked those moments, and people would call out "Amen" or some other encouragement, and then a little back-and-forth conversation would develop between the preacher and the listeners. When Joe first attended church with the Starostas he had been surprised by all the activity, but at least the sermons weren't boring, and he even enjoyed them after a while. Sometimes his uncle looked right at him while he talked, or told some funny story about the family's life at home. Kate told Joe that he had to get used to being talked about in a sermon, because that was part of life in a preacher's family.

So church service was not too bad and was even kind of fun in its own way. Joe had learned to blend in. But he still could not feel the kind of heartfelt devotion his uncle preached, even after deciding to seek God that evening when Anton brought over the decoder. He was not sure that God was entirely good, or deserving of his worship. His own life, so far, did not seem to make a good case for either idea.

The service had run late because Wence and Rachel had been baptized. After the sermon they joined John Mark in front of the church, told about how they had come to their new faith, and prayed for their future life in Christ. John Mark baptized Wence first, and then Wence baptized his wife. Everyone stood up, sang a hymn, and then applauded. Now a little knot of people still lingered inside the church getting to know the new couple.

Outside on the entryway, the hot July sun was high overhead, and the boys were hungry for lunch. Joe's stomach growled as he stood and watched the last few people leave. He brightened up as Ben and Betty Havlicek walked slowly out of church, because those two had talked for a long time with Wence and Rachel after the baptism, and if they were coming out, that meant that everyone else would not be far behind.

Ben Havlicek stopped right in front of them. He leaned on his cane with one hand and rummaged in his pants pocket with the other. *"Dobrý den,"* he greeted them. Joe knew enough Czech now to say *"Dobrý jitro, pana Havlicek, jak se máte?"* in return.

"Děkuji, velmi dobrý." Ben Havlicek blinked at him in the sunlight for a moment, then patted at his suit jacket and looked into his inside pocket. He was very old, and his hands shook as he adjusted his clothing and searched his different pockets. "Now, I was going to bring something for you boys. Where is it?" He slowly handed his cane to his wife and started going through yet another pocket. Joe and Johnny waited silently, and Joe's stomach growled again.

"Here you are. What do you boys think of these?" Ben asked as he fished out some paper cards. He carefully sorted out two of them, holding them with difficulty in his arthritic hands. He handed one card to Johnny and one to Joe.

Johnny sucked in his breath. Joe was amazed. Ben Havlicek had just given each of them a beautifully colored 1911 Turkey Red Cabinet baseball card. One featured Ty Cobb and the other one pictured Shoeless Joe Jackson.

"Gosh, *pana* Havlicek," Johnny said, when he could speak. "These are . . . awfully nice."

The old man smiled, and his face turned into a web of deep wrinkles. "Well, that's right. I'm giving them to you," he said, trembling a little bit with the effort of standing and talking for so long, "because I don't really do much with them anymore, and I thought you boys would like them. Joseph, you get Ty Cobb," he added, giving Joe a sharp look to see if he was paying attention and would value the gift. "John Carl, you can have Shoeless Joe."

Both boys were speechless, not sure if they should keep the proffered treasures. "Mr. Havlicek, are you sure?" Johnny finally asked, forgetting to speak Czech in his surprise.

"*Ano, ano.* Take them. Someone may as well enjoy them. They just sit in a box at my house so I want you to have them," the old man said. His white-haired wife smiled and nodded.

"Thanks," Joe said, still hardly believing his good fortune.

"*Mockrát děkuji*," Johnny said enthusiastically.

"*Rádo se stalo*. Take good care of them now," Ben said. "Joseph, you'll be a fine pitcher someday. All you need to do," he stopped and caught his breath for a moment, "is practice." He raised his hand and shook his finger. " 'If at first you don't succeed, try, try again.' Ever heard that before?" Joe hastily nodded. "Practice, practice, practice, and you'll do fine. Remember that now."

"Yes, sir. Thank you again, Mister, I mean, *pana* Havlicek," Joe said.

"You're welcome. Remember, Joseph, practice. It works every time." Ben took his cane back from his wife and started moving away toward his car. Joe finally tore his eyes away from Ty Cobb and ran after them to open the car door for Betty.

"Really, Mr. Havlicek, thanks," he said again. "I'll take really good care of it." He walked back to the church, studying the card and almost tripping when he got to the stairs that led up to the door.

The last lingerers were finally walking out. Vincent came for Anton and the two of them left for home. Someone inside the church was talking with John Mark, and Joe recognized the voice and looked sharply at the speaker. It was the sexton from the Oakhill Cemetery, and John Mark was leading him over to where Joe and Johnny stood.

"Boys, I think you might have another job," his uncle said. "Mr. Schulte here wants to talk to you."

The sexton looked them over and seemed dissatisfied.

"I was hoping to get them big Prazsky boys," he said to John Mark.

Joe and Johnny looked from one man to the other, wondering what was going on.

"The Syrian cemetery by Oakhill needs someone to dig a grave tomorrow," John Mark explained. "Think you can do it?"

Joe and Johnny looked at each other now. "Sure," Joe said with a shrug. "Sir," he added hastily when John Mark looked at him.

"We've been digging up dirt all summer long," Johnny added.

"How much do they pay?" John Mark asked.

Mr. Schulte looked the boys up and down as if he had never seen them before. "Fifteen dollars," he finally said. "They want someone polite, a good worker who doesn't cuss."

Joe and Johnny both spoke at once, telling the man what good workers they were and how polite they would be while digging the grave. John Mark looked slightly stunned at the idea of getting paid fifteen dollars for what might be half a day's work.

"Well," he said, silencing the boys, "if they can't do it, I'll come over myself and finish it. How's that?"

For some reason Mr. Schulte seemed unhappy about the idea of John Mark digging a grave. *Why's he being so picky?* Joe wondered.

"That don't seem right, a minister digging a grave," the cemetery caretaker finally said.

Some people are just strange, Joe thought. *I want that job.* John Mark looked like he wanted to laugh and quote a Bible verse about work. Joe cut in before his uncle could do either one.

"Sir, we can do it," he said firmly. "Do we bring our own shovels?" He had dug up enough gardens by now to know which questions to ask.

"He's got shovels there," the man said. "It's sandy ground. Not like Oakhill."

"What time should we be there, Mr. Schulte?" Johnny asked in the most polite voice he had ever mustered up in his entire life

Mr. Schulte finally seemed to decide that the two boys could handle the job. "Early," he said. "Go to the office at St. George's cemetery and ask for Samuel Abraham. He'll show you what to do."

Joe and Johnny got up with the birds the next morning. Kate scrambled eggs for their breakfast and packed a lunch, and they set off before the sun rose. They were waiting at the cemetery's locked wrought-iron gate when the caretaker came to open up.

Both boys had worn their caps and took them off when he arrived. "Hello, sir," Joe said. "Mr. Schulte sent us here to dig the grave. We're supposed to talk to Mr. Abraham."

The caretaker wore a suit and did not look like he would be doing outdoor work that day. He looked them over for a moment before speaking. "I am Mr. Abraham," he said. "Are you sure that you know how to dig a grave?"

"Oh, yes, sir," Joe replied. "We've been digging up dirt for people all summer long."

Mr. Abraham smiled at that statement. "All right then," he said. "Follow me, please."

This cemetery was smaller than Oakhill, and there were no other workmen around. The sexton took them to a tool shed and outfitted them with shovels, buckets, and a rope. Then he led them out among the graves, picking his way around the granite and marble tombstones, until he came to a coffin-sized rectangle marked out in the grass.

"The grave must be six feet deep," he told them. "Pile the dirt here. This rope is six feet long. When it can extend six feet down on all sides, come and get me, and I will check your work. There is a pump over there" — he pointed — "for water. The soil is sandy, so be careful." He stopped and looked at them.

"Yes sir," Joe said. "Thank you."

The man gave his brief smile again and walked back to his office. Joe and Johnny looked at each other, then down at the coffin-shaped patch of ground. Joe set the lunch bag in the shade of the nearest tree and Johnny stabbed his shovel into the dirt a few times to test the feel of the soil.

"I don't think it'll be too bad, after we get going," he said when Joe came back. The two boys went to work, shoveling fast at first while the morning was cool, and then more slowly as the sun got hotter. They had brought their own clean pail for drinking water, and as the day went on they started pouring water over their heads and shoulders to stay cool. Soon they were streaked with dirt and sweat.

When they were about halfway down the grave they stopped to eat, although they could tell it was not noon yet because the twelve o'clock factory whistles had not sounded and the St. Wenceslaus church bells had not rung the noontime Angelus. They ate quickly and went back to digging, more cautiously now because the sandy dirt walls inside the grave sometimes trickled loose crumbles of dirt into the hole if they shoveled out a lump of earth too fast.

They talked while they worked. The Packers' first game of the city league championship was scheduled for six o'clock that evening at Daniels Park, and they discussed Bill Zuber's pitching and their chances of winning the game. Then they talked about Stephen's performance at the play the night before. Everyone — their own family, Vincent and Anton, Wence and Rachel, and the Prazskys — had gone to see Stephen on stage. Karel had glowered at Wence and made a point of not sitting next to him, but Wence had stayed calm, and in the end it had been a fun evening.

"Can you believe how good Stevie did that little dance?" Johnny asked Joe. "He's gonna have a big head about it for a year." They both laughed. The play's director liked Stephen so much that he had written in a song and dance for him to do, and Stephen had walked right up to the front of the stage and performed as if he had been waiting his whole life long to sing and dance in front of a crowd. Unfortunately, he tripped and fell when he turned around to walk off, which spoiled the overall effect, but the audience laughed so hard and clapped so long that it hadn't totally ruined the scene. Stephen looked embarrassed at first, but the play's prompter yelled at him to smile and bow, which he managed to do, and he ended up being the star of the show.

"Yeah. He'll probably want to be in another play right away," Joe said. "Watch out." He swung a spadeful of dirt over Johnny's head and up to the grass. "We better start using the buckets to get the dirt out."

"Hey, what do you think about the bike?" Johnny asked after a while. "You still like the West Wind better than the Blackhawk?"

Joe grunted. "I don't think you're going to get a new bike. I think you're going to get somebody else's old bike. If you're lucky." Johnny had been cutting out bicycle advertisements from the newspapers, trying to decide what kind of bike he wanted to buy. The problem was that most of them cost fifty dollars, and John Mark had emphatically said that he would not contribute any money to such an expensive purchase for a twelve-year-old.

"Listen," Johnny said. "I saw this ad. For the new Blackhawk. It's forty-one dollars now at Sears." He flung another shovelful of sandy dirt up to the outside ledge. "And," he said meaningfully, "you can put down five dollars, get the bike and take it home, and then pay five dollars a month until you pay it off." He paused to jump on his shovel and dig. They had measured the sides of the dirt walls with the rope, and they were almost six feet deep in the grave now, so the fifteen dollars seemed very near. "See, then I'd have a new bike." He glanced around at Joe to see what he thought.

"Huh." Joe was impressed. "But what if someone steals it before you're done and then you still have to pay all that money?"

"You'd have to – " Johnny started, and then one whole side of the grave came down in a crash of dirt and sand.

Joe saw the sand begin to fall and jumped, dropping his shovel and grabbing for Johnny, but he seemed to be moving in slow motion and could not get across the space faster than the dirt came down. His shovel disappeared and the sand flooded up around his legs and to his waist before he even got a hand on his cousin, who had been caught by the dirtfall while he was leaning down over his shovel and was now nearly covered by it.

"Help!" Joe yelled. Dirt was still moving, angling up inside the walls of the narrow grave and filling the air with thick brownish dust. "Somebody help!" He thought with despair of the man in the office, too far away to hear his cry. *Oh, God, make it stop! he prayed frantically. Make it stop! Just make it stop, and I'll do whatever You want for the rest of my life!*

He hauled at Johnny's arm and pulled his face out of the dirt just as the slide of earth slowed to a trickle and then finally stopped. They both froze in place, barely breathing, terrified of what might happen if they moved and the rest of the wall collapsed.

The wall held, though, and after a while Joe experimentally moved a leg. Nothing happened. He moved the other leg, pulling out his foot and placing it cautiously on top of the loose earth. The wall still held. He carefully eased out of the dirt and stood up. Johnny held out his hand, and Joe grabbed it and pulled him up out of the loosely piled earth. For a moment they stood there and looked at each other, and then they leaped for the grassy ledge and the safe world above. They stumbled to the shelter of the tree and flung themselves to the ground. Johnny coughed and spat dirt out of his mouth.

"Oh," he choked out after a while. "Oh, my God. I was so scared."

"Me too," Joe said truthfully. They lay in silence for a few minutes, glad to be alive.

After a while Joe raised his head. "Is there any water?" he asked unsteadily.

Johnny looked in the bucket. "Here." He pushed it over.

Joe gulped water and lay back down, thinking about the sandslide.

One man built his house on a rock and the other one built a house on sand, he remembered his uncle saying to Wence. *Then a big storm came along, like it always does, and hit both houses. Who do you think made it through the storm?* Joe shivered as he pictured the dirt burying them both in the grave. *Your storm's coming . . .*

Oh, that was scary, he thought, and remembered his desperate prayer in the grave. *Did God make it stop?* He wondered about that for a while. *God, was that You?* He lay in the cool shade of the tree and gazed at the peaceful cemetery, each gravestone marking some person who was dead now and under the ground, while he and Johnny were still up here, on top of the sweet green grass, alive. *Dear God,* he prayed, *Thank you. Thank you for being here and helping me. I swear I'll never doubt You again and I'll be better for You in the future. Maybe you hear lots of people say that, but I mean it. Amen.*

He finally decided that if God really was there with them, they might be able to finish the job. He sat up, got his feet underneath him, and walked back to the open grave.

From up above, the fallen dirt did not look as frightening as it had when they were down inside the pit. Joe looked up at the sun, then back down into the hole. He stomped on the ground at the edge of the grave, testing it to see if it would hold. It held. He looked around at Johnny.

"Come on," he said.

Johnny just looked at him.

"I think it'll be okay, and it's fifteen dollars," Joe said. "Come on. I'll get inside with a dirt bucket, and you stay up here and take it and dump out the dirt."

Johnny got up. "Let me go get more water first," he said. "I'm thirsty."

Joe nodded and sat down at the edge of the grave, testing the wall again, not confident enough to go down into the hole until Johnny came back. The loose earth came out easily when he started dredging it up in the bucket. After a while Johnny joined him. They worked cautiously, careful to not disturb the grave's walls.

They hauled buckets of dirt right through the noon church bells and the noisy factory whistles that signaled the beginning and end of lunchtime.

Finally they worked their way down far enough to find their buried shovels.

"I think we better have just one of us in here at a time," Johnny said when the grave started getting deep again.

Joe agreed. They traded off after that, one of them in the hole shoveling dirt into the bucket, and the other hauling it out and dumping it on the growing pile beside the grave. Finally each side measured six feet from top to bottom. Johnny handed up his shovel one last time to Joe, then gripped the rope and scrambled out, with Joe pulling him from above. They stood on the edge for a moment, panting, and looked back down into the grave, hoping that it would not cave in again. When it didn't, they went to the pump, splashed water over their faces and arms to clean up, and went to find Mr. Abraham and collect their fifteen dollars.

Stephen had sleepily opened his eyes when he heard Joe and Johnny get up early that morning. The attic bedroom was only dimly lit by the early summer dawn, and he wondered for a confused moment why they were getting up so early, and if he was supposed to get up too. Then he remembered they were going to the cemetery and he was staying home, so he closed his eyes, curled up under his quilt and slept until his mother called.

During breakfast he spooned sugar onto his oatmeal and snuck a glance at his grandmother. She sat hunched over her coffee cup, frowning, so that the corners of her mouth turned down and all the wrinkles creased up on her forehead. She caught him looking at her and scowled even harder.

She looked scary when she frowned at him like that. Stephen quailed under her glare and wished that his brothers were there with him to distract her attention.

He thought of Joe as his brother now. It was too much trouble to talk about a brother and a cousin, so he just lumped the two together and called them both his brothers whenever he talked or thought about them. He had always thought of Joe as his brother anyway, because they looked so much alike, and after the long winter when they all slept together on the front room floor, Joe seemed even more like a brother than before.

The best thing about having brothers was that when they were around, his grandmother didn't pick on him as much as she did when he was all by himself. When his mother walked into the kitchen carrying a pile of dirty clothes in her arms, he saw with alarm that she was dressed in one of her good dresses, a red one with white flowers, which meant that she was going out to the Havliceks' for the day.

"Mommy, can you stay home today?" he asked.

"Not today. Mr. Havlicek isn't feeling well and I need to get over there and make sure they're all set for the week," his mother replied. She set the clothes down on the table and began sorting them.

Stephen chewed on the inside of his lip and stole another glance at his grandmother. She was still frowning.

"Can I go with you?" he tried.

His mother looked at him and smiled. He smiled back as nicely as he could. She laughed.

"No, honey. It's Monday and I need you to help *Matka* with the laundry," she said. "And after that I want you to weed the beans. Come here and look," she said, walking over to the window. "I want you to pull all those weeds right there on that row."

Stephen obediently got up and looked out to see the weeds she was pointing at, but he didn't like her answer. "Mommy, please? I want to go with you," he tried again. He could see Mrs. Vesely looking at him and scowling. "I can weed tomorrow when you're home."

His mother looked at him and then sat down in a chair so that they were face to face. Stephen could tell right away that she was going to say no.

"Stephen, you can't. Mr. Havlicek's not feeling well. Even if I wanted to take you, your grandmother needs the help here, with the laundry. You need to be a big boy today and do your part. Everybody has to help out and this is your job."

"If Mr. Havlicek's sick, I could weed their garden today and weed ours tomorrow," Stephen tried one more time.

His mother looked at him sharply. "Stephen, what did I just say?" she asked.

Stephen sighed. His mother stood up and went back to sorting laundry.

"Co se déje s Havlicek? Je to vázn?" his grandmother asked after a while. "What's wrong with Havlicek? Something bad?"

"I don't know. He just doesn't seem like himself," Kate replied. Stephen went back to eating his oatmeal and snuck another sidelong glance at his grandmother. She was still watching him and scowling. He gave her a little smile and looked away. It was going to be a long day.

After digging the grave, Joe and Johnny were so tired they each spent a nickel to ride the streetcar home. The driver and the other passengers frowned at them because of their mud-covered clothes. They slipped silently into the last seat in back.

"We're gonna have to take a bath before we go to Daniels Park," Joe whispered. Coach Kovar had given the team a ferocious lecture about arriving on time and looking sharp for the first game of the city championship. Johnny nodded, then closed his eyes and rested his head on the back of the seat.

Joe looked out the window as the streetcar rolled past shops and houses. The little wooden buildings, gilded with sunshine and peeling white paint, looked spectacularly beautiful to him now, after the shock of that frightful moment in the collapsing grave. He closed his eyes and rested his cheek against the window. *We didn't die. Everything's okay.* He almost fell asleep, feeling as if he were floating in a little cloud of joy just because he was alive and sitting in a streetcar, going home to supper, and playing baseball that evening. *I promised God I'd do better,* he thought just as he was slipping away into slumber. The thought made him wake up and open his eyes. *God, I'll figure out that part later.* He yawned and closed his eyes again. *I think I'll pray for the game tonight.* He fell asleep in the middle of his prayer and didn't wake up until the streetcar driver hollered at him to sit up and watch for the corner where they had to get off.

They trudged the last few blocks in silence, carrying the empty lunch bag and water pail, dragging their feet a little and staying in the shade of the giant elm trees lining the streets. When they finally came in sight of their house, Joe heard a strange sound, like a kitten mewing. He looked at Johnny.

"What is that?"

"I dunno," Johnny sighed. "Maybe it's a cat somewhere." He started up the porch stairs.

"Somebody help! Please, help me!" floated a scared little cry from out of the air above them. "Help! Please!"

Joe and Johnny jumped and looked around.

"I can't get down!" came the little mewing cry again.

"Stephen?" Joe called experimentally. "Is that you?"

The mewing sound started again, clearer now.

"I'm on the *roof*," came the voice. "I'm stuck."

Joe sighed. This was too much trouble for one day. He looked up but could not see anyone.

"Where are you?" he shouted.

"Over here," came the voice.

Joe and Johnny circled the house until they found Stephen, high on the shady side of the roof, clinging to the peak with one hand and wiping away tears with the other.

"Oh, geez," Johnny groaned.

"What are you doing up there?" Joe called.

"Just get me down!" Stephen wailed.

"How'd you get up there?" Joe called again.

Stephen sniffled. "Through the window," he called after a moment.

"The attic window?" Johnny yelled. Joe shook his head in exasperation. The attic window was on the other side of the roof, which meant that Stephen must have climbed out and then crawled clear over the roof's peak to get to the side where he was now.

"Maybe he can slide off and we catch him?" Johnny asked Joe. "I could go up there and help him."

"Maybe," Joe said doubtfully. The house was not large, but the roof had a steep angle, and the ground below the spot where Stephen clung was not level and grassy, but instead slanted sharply down a hill that was littered with rocks and lumps of concrete left over from pouring the house's foundation. It was a bad place to stand and try to catch someone. If Stephen came sliding down fast he could knock over whoever was below. If two people came down together it would be impossible to guarantee catching anybody.

Stephen slipped a little on the steep slant of the roof and started crying again.

"Don't move!" Joe called. "Go see if Uncle John's home," he told Johnny.

"Boys? What's the matter?" Kate's voice asked from behind them. She was walking over to them from the street, grocery bags in her arms, still in her red flowered dress from her day at the Havliceks.'

Both boys pointed up. Kate gasped and dropped the groceries when she saw Stephen clinging to the peak of the roof .

"John Carl! Go get your father right now!" she cried, stepping up to the side of the house and holding out her arms. "Stephen, don't move! Joe, run next door and get a ladder!"

Johnny disappeared into the house. Joe lingered, not wanting to leave his aunt to catch Stephen by himself if he should fall. Kate balanced awkwardly on the rocky hill, her eyes glued to Stephen and her arms out, braced to catch him if he fell.

"Aunt Kate, I don't think you can catch him by yourself," he said hesitantly.

"Joseph Martin, I brought that child into the world and I will catch him if he falls," she snapped at him. "Now go get that ladder like I told you. Mr. Moracek has one in his garage."

Johnny came running back with Josefina hobbling behind him. "Dad's not here. He's at the church," he shouted.

"*Naspéch! Co mozna njdríve!*" Josefina complained. Joe watched his aunt set her lips in the straight line that meant she was angry.

He stepped a little closer to her. "Johnny, go get Mr. Moracek's ladder," he said. "I'll stay here and help catch him if he falls." Johnny ran to the neighbor's house and pounded on the front door, then raced around to the back when no one opened it. They could hear him knocking at the back door and calling out the neighbor's name. After a while he reappeared.

"No one's home and the garage's locked," he told them.

Kate took a deep breath. "Get Karel," she commanded. "If he's not home then go into Vincent's house and call your father at the church." Vincent kept a house key hidden close to his back door and all the boys knew where it was.

"You go," Joe told Johnny. "I'll stay here." Johnny tore down the street.

Joe looked at Stephen and then back at Kate. Stephen had lost his grip on the roof's peak and slid even farther down the side of the roof. He was crying, his face turned down against the roof tiles. Kate stood on tiptoe on the side of the hill, her eyes fixed on Stephen and her arms still stretched out in case he came sliding down.

Let's get this over with so I can clean up and go to the game, Joe thought.

"Aunt Kate," he said, "I'm going up there. I think I can pull him over to the other side and get him back in through the window. That's how he got out."

Kate looked at him, biting her lip. Finally she nodded. Joe ran inside and glanced at the clock as he dashed through the front room.

Doggone that kid! When I get him down I'm gonna kill him! He hustled up the attic stairs and headed for the window, then cautiously climbed through and scrambled onto the roof. *Why'd he go up there anyway?*

Joe started crawling up the slope of the roof. His hands and shoes slid a little with every movement, because the roof was old, made of flat tiles called shake, and it was slippery. The angle of the roof seemed much steeper now that he was actually on it than it did from down below. *How did Stephen ever get up here?* he wondered as he climbed.

Finally he reached the top and looked over the peak. Stephen still clung to the tiles on the other side, a little farther down the roof. Joe leaned over and held out his hand.

"What're you doing up here?" he asked crossly.

Stephen looked up at him, tears and dirt smudged on his cheeks. "Mrs. Vesely made me stay in the attic," he sniffed.

"Well, so what?" Joe retorted. Now that he was on the top of the house and looking down, the rocky ground below looked dangerously far away.

"It was too hot, so I climbed out the window and came over here," Stephen explained.

Joe looked at him and shook his head in disbelief. The attic became stiflingly hot during the summer days, and usually no one stayed in it for very long until it cooled off again at night. Surely Josefina had not sent Stephen up there and expected him to stay.

"You must have done something bad," he said. "What'd you get into this time?"

"Nothing! Nothing!" Stephen started to cry again. "I was being good! I was just listening to the radio and she said," he gulped, "she said I was no good and lazy and she made me turn off the radio and go upstairs." He gulped again. "It was so hot," he pleaded. "I was too hot."

"Boys! Quit talking and get down from there right now!" Kate called.

Joe sighed and wondered why his grandmother was so kind to him but so spiteful to Stephen. He leaned down farther and stretched out his hand.

"Here. Grab," he said. Stephen made a swipe at his hand and missed. He slipped down the roof another six inches and looked up at Joe with panic in his eyes.

"It's more slippery on this side," he quavered. "I can't climb up."

"Don't worry," Joe said, making his voice quiet and soothing. "I'll get you. Just hold still." He swung a leg over the peak so he could lean out even farther. The shake tiles on the shady side of the house were slick with moss that grew in each little crack, and his hand slipped on it at first as he braced himself against the slant of the roof with one hand and reached for Stephen with the other. Stephen grabbed wildly for his hand, missed again, and started to slide.

Kate screamed. Joe lunged for Stephen and latched on to him just as he began to pick up speed. He felt a flash of fear streak through him when Stephen's sudden weight jerked him over the peak and down the other side. He scrabbled desperately on the slick tiles with his free hand and both his feet, doing everything he could to break their slide down the steep slope. But he could not stop. The best he could do was hang onto Stephen, slow his momentum as they slid down the roof, and drop him into Kate's waiting arms before he himself hurtled off the edge and crashed down to the ground below.

Johnny and Karel drove up to the house just in time to see Joe fall off the roof. Johnny was not afraid at first when he saw Joe hit the ground, because he was certain that his cousin, who seemed so competent in every situation, would just roll over and get back up on his feet right away. But when Joe didn't move, he felt a flicker of worry, and then when his mother put Stephen down and knelt by Joe, gently turning his head and calling his name, his heart suddenly clenched up with fear. He jumped out of the car and ran over to kneel beside Kate and get a better look.

Joe looked strange, as if he was dead, and blood was darkening his hair and trickling down his neck. One side of his face was scratched and scraped by the rocks where he had fallen, and blood was oozing from the scratches. His left arm was flung out in an awkward position. Johnny felt queasy when he saw it.

"That arm's broke," he heard Karel say. "Run over to the Moraceks' and call Dr. Smrha."

Johnny tried to speak and had to clear his throat first before any words would come out. "I just went over there. They aren't home."

Karel frowned. "Well, who lives next door to them? Go find someone with a phone and call Smrha. Now!" With an effort Johnny pulled his eyes away from Joe's still face and ran down the block to find someone who had a telephone.

"Call your father too!" Kate called after him.

"Okay!" he hollered back.

He finally found a neighbor with a phone and figured out how to call a doctor. By the time he got back, a little group of people had gathered around Joe, who was still lying on the side of the hill. The people all looked serious, as if they were at a funeral, and he began to fear that his cousin had died. But then he saw Joe move a little bit, and he suddenly had to blink back tears of relief.

Johnny slipped inside the circle of people and knelt beside his mother, who was holding a wet rag to Joe's forehead and blotting up the blood that was welling from his cuts and scratches. His face still looked strange and his eyes were closed, but his mother was talking as if he could hear her.

"Just stay still," she said. "Don't try to move. Can you hear me?" Johnny almost cried for joy when he saw Joe nod his head ever so slightly.

"How is he, Mom?" he asked urgently. "Is he going to be okay?"

"Yes, of course," Kate said in a soothing voice that did not convince Johnny that everything was all right. "Is the doctor coming?"

"Yeah," he told her. "He said he'd be here right away."

Karel was talking to Josefina in Czech, and Johnny could make out enough words to understand that he was telling her to get her bed ready for Joe to lie on and to heat some water. Johnny kept his eyes on Joe the entire time, worried that he might try to move or cry out, but his cousin did not even twitch while people moved and talked around him.

One of the neighbors offered Karel a brown glass bottle with a medicine label on it.

"Here's some hoboko," he said. "You oughta get some into him now, before the doctor comes to set that arm."

"That stuff's straight liquor!" Kate protested.

"Well, ma'am, that's probably right, but setting that arm is going to hurt and this might help," the neighbor pointed out. "I'd want some, if it was me."

Kate and Karel looked at each other. Karel shrugged and took the bottle, then got down beside Joe and raised his head.

"Here, drink some of this. You'll feel better," he said. Joe's eyes flickered open. Karel helped him take a drink. Joe gasped and sputtered after he swallowed.

"Oh," he whispered, "that's awful."

"Now let's get you inside," Karel said. "Stand up." He slipped an arm under Joe's back and raised him up. With Karel on one side of him and Kate on the other, Joe took a few wavering steps, but then his legs collapsed and he slipped back to the ground.

"We could make a stretcher," one of the neighbors suggested, but Karel waved him off, gathered Joe into his arms, and carried him through the crowd into the house.

All the people followed inside, curious about what would happen when the doctor came. Karel laid Joe on Josefina's bed, and Johnny wormed his way into the bedroom and stood in a corner. When Kate went out to the kitchen to check on the hot water and towels, Karel tried to give Joe another drink from the bottle, and Johnny watched anxiously as Joe shook his head and refused it.

"Drink it, boy," Karel commanded. "They're going to set your arm and you're going to need it. Now drink." He coaxed Joe into taking two more big swallows before Kate came back.

"Let's get his shirt off and clean him up before the doctor gets here," she said.

That brought a reaction from Joe. He opened his eyes and looked around the room in panic. "No," he protested and grabbed at the front of his shirt with his good hand. "Please, Aunt Kate, no. Leave my shirt on," he pleaded.

"Joseph, be quiet and don't get yourself all worked up. We'll have to take it off anyway when the doctor gets here," Kate said.

"No, no. Please, Aunt Kate, don't make me take my shirt off!" Joe said, with a note of desperation in his voice that had not been there before. Kate and Karel looked at each other in confusion.

"Well, now, maybe we'll do it later, then," Kate finally said. She looked around the room and saw Johnny in the corner. "Johnny, you need to leave the room."

"I won't get in the way," Johnny objected.

"John Carl!" his mother snapped. Karel gave him a long, disapproving stare.

"Sorry," Johnny said, and turned to leave. As he closed the door behind him he heard his mother say, "Maybe you ought to give him another drink of that hoboko, Karel."

John Mark arrived just then, and Johnny felt an intense wave of relief wash over him as his father came through the front door. He walked through the room, tall and calm in the middle of the gossipy crowd. Johnny almost expected his father to simply wave an arm and make all the bad things go away. John Mark did not do that, but his steady manner made everyone quiet down, and he walked straight over to Johnny and put his hand on his shoulder. Johnny almost burst with pride, because his father was so wonderful and wanted to talk to him first, before he talked to anyone else.

"What's happening, *Jan?*" John Mark asked.

"Mom and Uncle Karel are in there with Joe," Johnny told him. "The doctor's on his way and there's hot water and towels in the kitchen."

"Good," his father said, then glanced around. "Any of you have some hoboko we can use?"

"They've got it in there already," a neighbor said with a nod to the bedroom door. John Mark thanked him and went inside.

The doctor came a few minutes later. Johnny watched in awe as the crowd parted for him when he came up the porch steps and into the room, neatly dressed in a suit and carrying his big black bag. He looked tired and hot.

"So, where's the boy who fell off the roof?" he asked, and the crowd pointed toward the bedroom door. Johnny moved out of the way as the man headed straight for him.

The doctor paused with his hand on the doorknob. "You live here?" he asked.

Johnny nodded.

"I need a big basin of hot water," he said, "and lots of towels and rags. Not right now. I'll tell you when."

"Yes, sir," Johnny stammered.

The doctor went into the bedroom and closed the door. Johnny went to the kitchen to make sure the water was heating, and then he pulled out more towels and rags from the laundry stacked on the kitchen table. He organized everything as best he could and then went to stand by the bedroom door again.

At first, all he could hear was the low murmur of adult voices, but then he heard a sharp "Ow!" from Joe and the doctor saying, "Oh, that doesn't hurt. Here, give him a rag to bite on." Then there was silence, until a sharp scream rang out and a sudden rush of voices followed. There was another cry of pain, muffled this time, and then silence again.

Johnny jumped at both cries and felt his heart beat faster as he heard each one. His mother came out of the bedroom, closed the door behind her, and went to the kitchen. He hurried in behind her. Stephen and Josefina were sitting at the table, looking guilty.

"How is he, Mom?" Johnny asked.

Kate's face looked strained. "The doctor says it ought to mend fine. He's going to put the cast on now." She looked first at Josefina, then at Stephen. "What made you think you could go out on the roof?"

Stephen looked at Josefina. Josefina scowled.

"*Ach, on je pitomec*, stupid boy," she said. "I put him upstairs and he goes on the roof. *Pitomec*."

Kate looked from her mother to Stephen.

"What did you do?" she asked.

Stephen looked at his grandmother and then back at Kate, as if deciding how much to say. "Mommy, I was being good," he said steadily. "I helped with the wash and weeded just like you said." His voice started to quiver. "Cross my heart on the Bible, I was just listening to the radio," he threw a defiant look at Josefina, "and she said that I was bad and lazy, and she made me go upstairs."

"*Matko*, is that what happened?" Kate demanded.

Josefina turned red and started shouting in Czech. Kate put her hands on her hips and shouted back in the same language. The words flew too fast for Johnny to understand, but he could tell that his mother was winning the argument. Josefina finally stopped talking and sat at the table in silence, a sullen expression on her face.

Karel appeared in the kitchen doorway. "Can we get some hot water in here?"

Kate stopped her lecture, gave Josefina a long stare, and then looked at Johnny. "Go get the big pot. There's a hurt boy in there who has to get a cast put on," she added with a final glare at her mother. Johnny helped take the hot water and towels to the bedroom, and he managed to stay inside the room this time to see what was happing.

Joe lay on the bed, eyes closed, shirt off, and overalls turned down at the waist. He was still dirty, although Johnny could see that someone had tried to wash off the worst of the grime. Blood and tears streaked his face. The doctor sat beside him on a chair, one hand on the inside of his wrist and the other probing lightly at his arm, while John Mark leaned over the other side of the bed, cleaning Joe's face with a blood-stained towel.

"*Jan,* run and get me a clean rag and a bowl of ice water," he said, and Johnny went back to the kitchen again.

"Dad told me to get a bowl of ice water," he said defensively to Josefina when she frowned at him for opening the icebox. "And a rag." Stephen jumped up to fetch a bowl and rag for him. Johnny got what he needed and went back to the bedroom, giving them both a glare of his own as he left.

Joe's eyes were slightly open when Johnny came in the room, but he didn't seem to be looking at anything. The doctor had spread out towels on the bed and was busy soaking long strips of cloth in a plaster mixture and wrapping them around the broken arm. The plaster smelled funny and made a mess all over the towels. Johnny watched in fascination as the doctor finished up his work, wiped off his hands on yet another towel, and took a small bottle of pills out of his bag.

"Here's some aspirin. After he wakes up, give him two of these every four hours, but no more than eight in one day. Go buy more if you run out. Got that?" he said. John Mark and Kate both nodded. "He has to stay in bed until the cast sets. Keep that arm still so the plaster doesn't move. After it's dry, he can get up and walk around if he wants to. He probably won't want to do much for a couple days, though. That arm's going to hurt. The head, too." John Mark and Kate nodded again.

The doctor looked around the room and saw the hoboko bottle. He frowned. "You gave him that?" he asked. "How much?" Kate and Karel looked uncomfortably at each other.

"Oh, two swallows is all," Kate said.

Karel coughed. "Ah, four," he corrected her. "Maybe five."

The doctor guffawed. "He's going to be sick as a dog! I tell people, and I tell people, and no one listens. That stuff's no better than rotgut liquor. It'll make him feel worse than the arm will. I am telling you right now, never use that stuff again. You want to help someone, give 'em aspirin. Either that or a knock on the head. At least that won't give 'em a hangover." He suddenly looked straight at Johnny and said, "You hear me? Never buy that stuff.

Never take it either."

"No sir," Johnny promised. "I won't."

"Good," the doctor huffed. "Maybe there's hope for the next generation. This one's got their brains addled from drinking all that Prohibition hooch. Well, that's it for me," he finished, packing away his bag and closing it with a snap. "Two dollars."

John Mark had cleaned up Joe's face and then wrung out the rag with ice water and laid it over his forehead. At the doctor's words, he stood up and pulled out his wallet.

"Will you take one dollar now and one next week?" he asked. "I get paid on Friday."

The doctor nodded, but Karel growled, "I got a dollar," and pulled out his own wallet. At that moment, Joe stirred and groaned. Everyone stopped and looked at him, but his eyes were closed now, and he did not move again.

"Better keep a lot of towels around for when he wakes up," the doctor said. "Or maybe a bowl. Like I said, he's going to be sick as a dog. Hoboko." He shook his head in disgust, and Kate and Karel looked away, embarrassed. "Call me if you need anything."

"Thanks for coming over," John Mark said, rising and extending his hand. "We really appreciate it." The adults left the room, but Johnny lingered behind and tiptoed up to the bed.

"Hey, Joe," he said softly. He thought he saw a little crease form between Joe's eyebrows, as if the other boy could hear him. "Hey, Joe, it's me, Johnny. How you feeling?"

Joe sighed and then, to Johnny's delight, opened his eyes. He looked groggily at Johnny for a moment before closing his eyes again.

"That's okay," Johnny told him. "You probably ought to go to sleep. I just want to tell you Stephen's all right."

Joe seemed to nod just a bit, as if he understood, and after that his face smoothed out and his head fell to the side a little, and Johnny could tell that he had gone to sleep.

Joe woke up in a haze of pain. Because of the constant throbbing in his arm and head, he tried hard to not wake up at all, and hide in the comforting darkness of sleep instead of coming back to full awareness. But finally his stomach hurt so badly he had to roll over and retch, and that made him open his eyes. His uncle was there, holding a towel for him to throw up in, and then wiping his face and chest with a cold damp rag after he finished the painful heaving. The second time he woke up, he was terribly thirsty and had a piercing headache. His uncle was still there, and helped him drink some water.

Joe threw up a gush of bitter greenish bile right after he drank, and he couldn't stop a few tears from leaking out of his eyes when the pain in his arm and head blazed up again as he moved. His uncle slipped a soft pillow behind his head and brought another glass of water to his lips.

"Just take a little sip and rinse out," John Mark said. "Spit in the towel. Here." Joe rinsed and spat, then eased back onto the pillow and closed his eyes.

"Head hurt?" his uncle asked sympathetically. Joe did not want to nod, but he tried to say something. His voice wouldn't work.

"As soon as you can keep some water down, there's medicine for you," John Mark said. Joe started to retch again when he thought of the hoboko bottle, but he had nothing more in his stomach to throw up, and finally he settled down.

"No more. It makes me sick," he croaked. He had to push to make his voice loud enough to hear.

His uncle was saying something but Joe didn't listen to the words. He was in his grandmother's bed. What had happened?

He looked at his uncle. "What happened?" he whispered.

"You fell off the roof," John Mark said. He took a rag from a bowl of water, wrung it out, and laid it over Joe's forehead. The cool cloth felt wonderful. "Stephen was on the roof and you helped him get down. Remember?"

Joe tried to think. His left arm was in a heavy cast and ached with pain, and he could not find any position where it felt comfortable. Something else was making him feel uncomfortable, too.

"I, ah, have to go," he finally said.

"Can you get up?" his uncle asked. "You can go in a jar if you want to."

Joe felt his face turn red at the thought of relieving himself into a jar. For an answer he tried to sit up, but he couldn't get off the pillow by himself, and when John Mark helped him to stand he suddenly got so dizzy that he was afraid he would throw up again. He clenched his jaw hard and clung to his uncle until the dizziness passed, then held onto his arm as he walked unsteadily to the bathroom. Each step made his arm hurt. John Mark positioned him in front of the toilet and then kept a grip on his good arm to make sure he didn't fall over as he stood there.

It wasn't until he finished and was making his way back to bed that he realized that he was wearing pajama bottoms but no shirt. He stopped walking, right in the middle of the kitchen.

Who put pajamas on me? Now that he had gone to the bathroom and was moving around, his head seemed a little clearer. His arm still hurt so badly that he could tell something must be wrong with it.

"What's the matter?" his uncle asked.

"Is my arm broke?"

John Mark sighed. "Yes," he said. "It is. But the doctor set it and it should heal up okay. I've got some aspirin you can take for the pain."

Joe's head started pounding again.

"Did I miss the game?" he asked next. *No. I can't have missed the game.*

"Yes, you did," his uncle said. "I'm sorry."

"Oh, no," Joe whispered. "No. It can't be broke."

"Come on," John Mark said. "Let's get you back to bed."

"No," Joe said again. *No. Not that. Anything but a broken arm.* "Why?" he asked, his voice cracking as he spoke. "Why now?" He started shaking his head, agonizing over the unfairness of breaking his arm right when he was playing so well and was going to be in a championship series. John Mark almost carried him back to the bed and sat him down.

"My arm's broke. I'll never be a pitcher now," Joe anguished.

"Nonsense," his uncle told him. "It's only your left arm. It's not your pitching arm. You'll be right as rain and playing again before you know it. You oughta be glad you didn't break your neck." He ducked his head, trying to get on Joe's eye level and smile at him. "Now, that would end a baseball career for sure."

Joe thought about it. "Are you sure it's broke? Do you think maybe it'll get better by next week?" He thought some more. "I missed the game," he said again. "Did we win?"

"Yeah, but it was close, and Wence said that Kovar was fit to be tied the whole time, hollering about how he needed you on third base and where the . . . where were you," John Mark said. "Packers won, though. Zuber pitched."

"Did anybody tell Coach I broke my arm?" Joe asked, alarmed.

"I told him. He came over after the game, ready to wring your neck, until he heard about what happened," his uncle said. "Here, lie down. Try to drink a little. Just a sip." Joe obediently lay down and took a sip of water. John Mark put the cold rag over his forehead again.

Joe closed his eyes, but between the pain in his arm and the agony he felt over not being able to play ball, he could not go back to sleep. *Why can't I have one good thing happen in my life? Just one thing? Why am I always the one who has something bad happen to me? Why?*

After a while he opened his eyes again and looked around. His uncle was still there, watching him.

"What is it?" John Mark asked.

Joe felt a lump of despair grow in his heart. "How come this happened?" he finally asked. "How come bad things always happen to me?"

John Mark was quiet for a while. He finally pulled his chair around so that Joe could see him better.

"You know God made the world," he said. Joe nodded and felt the lump rising into his throat. He did believe that. Why, then, did God not help him? Would he never be good enough, no matter how hard he tried? Did God just not love him?

"And you know that the world isn't perfect. There's good and bad both. Right?" his uncle continued.

Joe nodded. There was no sense denying that.

"God says over and over again in the Bible that He is good and He loves us. So why would He let bad things happen?"

Joe impatiently pulled the cloth off his forehead with his good hand. He was feeling frustrated now. "That's what I'm asking," he said with an edge in his voice. He had to resist the urge to add a curse word to the end of his sentence.

"Do you know anybody who's had it easy their whole life long?" John Mark asked him. "What're they like?"

Joe thought. He could not think of anyone who had a life that was truly easy.

"Anton," he offered.

John Mark sat back and thought. "Well, Anton lost his mother, and between you and me, his dad isn't easy to live with," he said. "Even Vincent would agree with me on that. So, I think that counts as a hard time. Do you know anyone who has never, ever had anything very bad happen to them? Someone who just grew up, never had to work or worry about anything? If you knew somebody like that, what would they be like?"

Joe heaved a sigh. "Kinda dumb, I guess." He thought briefly of some of the children he had seen in the wealthy homes where he had worked. At the time, he had envied them intensely.

"That's right," his uncle said. "It's funny, but the hard things, the ones that hurt the most, are the things that make people grow up. I see it all the time. Something goes wrong, you're hurt, you're discouraged, or whatever, but you work your way through it, and it changes you, and then you become better. Smarter, more understanding of people. The way I see it, the good times are great, but they don't make people better. I even think that having too much of good things makes some people worse off in the long run." He stopped and looked away, and Joe thought about all the things people must have told him about themselves, because he was a minister.

After a moment John Mark went on. "So, I think God lets bad things happen because He sees the person that He wants you to become, and He makes life a combination of good things and bad things to help you grow to be that person."

Joe thought about that. He could not see how breaking an arm at this point in his life would do any good for him. The terrible whipping he got from the plumber had not done much to make him a better person either. He had seen children get sick and people die for what seemed like no good reason.

"Naw," he finally said.

His uncle looked at him for a while. "You're thinking that some things don't work out for the best, as you see it."

Joe nodded.

"There's no question that there's evil in this world," John Mark said after a while. "You look around . . ." he stopped and sighed. "You see hard times everywhere. I don't understand it. But I do believe that we have to go through hard times in order to learn how to really love other people, and love God, and appreciate God's love for us. If we didn't go through problems we'd be like spoiled children our whole lives long. The best people I know are mostly the same ones who've had the hardest times."

He stopped and looked at Joe thoughtfully for a while, then spoke again.

"So God might have something special planned for you, and He's using all these things in your life to mold you into the best person you can be."

Joe sighed. His head hurt and it was hard to think. He looked around his grandmother's bedroom. The sky was dark outside, and her little lamp lit the room with golden light. The window curtains stirred in the breeze and crickets were singing in the damp night air. He suddenly wondered why his uncle was home.

"How come you're not at work?"

John Mark gave a short laugh that didn't sound funny. "The factory cut my hours." He gave the short laugh again. "Good thing I'm having this talk with you right now. I oughta write it down and read it to myself."

Joe was struck with a sudden fear that they would be turned out of the house and have to live in a shanty camp. "Are we going to have to move out?"

"I don't think so. We should be able to make it until the new harvest comes in. End of August, maybe. The hours'll come back then. No buying any extra stuff for a while, though."

Joe looked at his uncle and thought some more about hard times changing people for the better.

"What about my mom?" he finally asked. "What about Mr. Kramer? Bad things didn't make them better."

John Mark looked confused. "Who's Mr. Kramer?"

Joe was too worn out to feel embarrassed. "He's the jerk that beat me up so bad," he said with all the energy he had left. "Didn't you see?"

"Oh," his uncle said. "Oh." He took a deep breath. "Well, not everybody tries to get better. You have to try. Some people just get . . . I don't know . . . taken over by hard times. They get worse."

"Well, what about them?" Joe asked.

His uncle took his time in answering. "There's lots of stuff I don't have an answer for," he said after a while. "I'd like to find the guy who did that to you and send him straight to hell myself." He exchanged a meaningful glance with Joe.

"But I'm not God, as you well know, and nobody put me in charge of figuring out punishments and rewards. The Bible does say that God will be a righteous judge for everyone. I figure, I'll do the best I can in this life, and trust that God means what He says. And He sees everyone's heart, so maybe He has a different measuring stick than you or me." He laughed. "For better or for worse," he joked, with another meaningful little glance.

"But," he went on, "the Bible also says that God loves us and goes through the hard times with us. He never leaves us to fight the battle alone, even when we're right in the middle of our own worst sins. He commanded us to be like Him and love others, whether we think they're sinners or not, and leave the rest up to Him."

Joe tried to picture himself talking to Kramer as if he were a decent person.

"That's too hard," he said.

"Nobody said it was easy," John Mark replied. "Not Jesus himself. If it was easy, everybody'd be a Christian. You know, for the good things, like how you can pray and God hears you, forgives your sins and you go to heaven and all that."

Joe had no heart to argue any more. All he could think of was the despairing conviction, deep in his heart, that he had made too many mistakes to ever become the wonderful person that God might have intended him to be.

"I'm so messed up," he finally said. "Everything I do turns out wrong."

"Oh, no," his uncle said. He sounded surprised. "You're good at lots of stuff. Johnny thinks you're the greatest thing since talking movies."

Joe snorted.

"Yeah, well, he doesn't know everything."

"Now, don't go thinking that way," John Mark said earnestly. "Look at all the hard times you've gone through and how much you've changed. That's more important than . . . than . . being in the movies or running for president. That's the most important thing in the world. No one's perfect. What counts is that you're coming through."

Joe looked away, blinking hard. John Mark handed him a rag and continued.

"I have to keep on thinking about this too, like everyone else. Sometimes I feel like I just make so many doggone mistakes, day after day. I have to kind of give myself a little pep talk and pray for help."

Joe dabbed at his face, blinked some more and looked back at his uncle.

"Hey, I've got a verse for you." Joe couldn't help smiling, even though it made his bruised face hurt. John Mark grinned back and went on. "*He who began a good work in you will carry it on to completion until the day of Christ Jesus.*'

Philippians chapter one. Look, God doesn't make mistakes. He chose you to come here and live with us and learn about Him, and He's going to finish what He started. You just keep following Him, and He'll help you out and take care of you and make sure your life turns out right."

Joe had to blot his eyes again and wipe his nose. John Mark waited until he was done.

"I think that God looked down on you with favor, because He knew that you would try, and He put you here with us. He gave you a special time to get better. Now, look how good you've done with what He gave you. You could've just turned into another nasty kid, but here you are, helping the family, going to school, working, watching out for Stephen and Johnny and Kate when I'm not around. I love having you here, like if you were my own son."

Joe gazed at his uncle, scanning his face to see if he truly meant what he had just said. John Mark held his gaze for a while, letting the force of his words linger between them, and then he leaned forward.

"I really mean it," he said, and very carefully, so as to not disturb the broken arm, he leaned over and embraced him, and let Joe blot his tears on his shirt collar while he gently patted his scarred back. "I love you."

The next time Joe woke up, it was his aunt who was sitting in the chair by the bed. She brought him a glass of water and made him swallow two pills that dissolved in his mouth and left a bitter taste. It was the first time he had ever swallowed a pill, and after the horrible way he felt after drinking the hoboko he was a little afraid of what might happen, but the pain did seem to lessen and after a while he went back to sleep.

Sometime later he realized that his grandmother was in the room, fussing over him and adjusting the sheets so that he was neither too hot nor too cold. She brought him two more pills and a glass of iced root beer to drink. He lay awake for a while, watching her as she moved around the room, folding towels and sorting through her collection of thread and fabric. His head didn't feel as bad as it had before, but his face was swollen and his left arm still pained him, so Josefina put a cold cloth over his forehead and slipped a soft little pillow under his arm, positioning it so it did not hurt as much. He finally got up and walked to the bathroom by himself, traveling slowly across the kitchen floor. He tried to wash, using only his good hand, and when he looked at his face in the mirror he saw that besides being swollen, it was covered with cuts and bruises, and he had two black eyes. *I look like Frankenstein,* he thought. *Good thing no one's around to see me.*

He wondered what day it was. The house was silent, except for Josefina rustling around in the kitchen. Joe climbed back into bed, pulled the little pillow under his cast, and gazed out the window at the trees' leafy branches swaying in the light summer breeze.

He was almost asleep when he heard the front door bang open and Stephen's quick light footsteps patter across the wooden floor. Joe opened his eyes in time to see him peek around the door. The little boy grinned.

"I brought you something," he whispered. He was smudged with dirt and his bare feet were muddy. Joe did not want to sit up again, but he managed to smile, and Stephen climbed up on the bed beside him and pulled something out of his pocket.

"Look," he said. Cupped in the grubby palm of his hand was a tiny fish, hardly two inches long. "A baby fish!"

Joe tried to focus his eyes and see what kind of fish it was. He had to blink and move his head a little before he could see it clearly.

"Hey, I think it's a tadpole," he said after studying it for a while. "If you keep it in a bowl, you can watch it grow legs and turn into a frog, and then one day it'll jump out of the bowl and hop away."

"Wow," Stephen marveled. "I'll go get a bowl and put it in here so you can see it. You can have it," he said earnestly. Joe smiled at him again, although he felt too weary to say any more.

"*Odstranit člen určitý dno! Tebe ar nečistý!*" Both boys jumped as Josefina shouted at them from the doorway, and Joe winced at the sudden pain that shot through his arm. "Get off the bed! You're all dirty! *Tebe ar deska s bláto!*" Stephen looked regretfully at Joe and scrambled off the bed.

"*Vysléknout se z ālen urāity komnata.* Get out," Josefina snapped. "*Tebe ar jeden bolovy chelapec,*" she said under her breath as Stephen slipped past her and into the kitchen.

Joe had closed his eyes in pain when Stephen jumped off the mattress. He opened them as Josefina stepped to the bed and brushed dirt off it. "*Deska s bláto,*" she grumbled. "So dirty. Bad boy."

Joe closed his eyes again. How could his grandmother be so nice to him and so mean to Stephen? He thought about how tired he felt, and how much effort it would take to speak to her about it. Then he thought about Stephen, enduring her jabs and insults every day.

"Grandma?" he said, without opening his eyes. "Grandma?"

"*Ano?*" she asked. He heard her come closer to the bed, and then felt her hand on his forehead. He opened his eyes.

"*Co se déje?*" she asked. "What is it, *Pepik?*"

He hesitated. She looked at him and waited.

"Grandma, what did you just say to Stephen? Did you say he was bad?" Joe finally asked.

Josefina frowned.

"I want you to stop saying those mean things to him," Joe said. "It's not right. He's not bad, Grandma. I love him." His arm throbbed with pain and he felt his eyes start to close. He forced them open again. *What is it I'm trying to do?* he wondered. *Oh, yes.* He made an effort to focus on Josefina's face.

"You're so nice to me. I love you, Grandma. Please be good to Stevie. I feel bad when you yell at him. He's just a little boy," he managed to say. "Be nice to him like you are to me. Promise."

She frowned again. Joe lifted his head a little from the pillow.

"He tries to be good. He's just little. Please be nice to him or he'll hate you, and then he'll . . . he'll . . . " Joe was losing his concentration. "Grandma, I have to forgive my mom, and not hate Mr. Kramer . . ." *she wouldn't know about him,* he thought, and sighed. He was too tired to explain. *She knows what I mean, though.* "If I can do that, you can be nice to Stevie."

Josefina looked at him silently, as if she were thinking about what to say. Joe could feel his eyes closing again. He gathered his strength to speak one more time.

"You have to say it. Promise," he said, "or I . . . or I . . . I won't make shirts with you anymore," he finished. *That's so dumb,* he thought right after he said it. *Why would I say that? I hope she promises.*

He could not see Josefina clearly, and his head fell back down on the pillow. He made an effort and opened his eyes. She was still standing by the side of the bed, looking at him and doing something with her face so that her wrinkles deepened. He couldn't tell if she was frowning or smiling.

"*Dobrá, dobrá, Pepik. Já budit nadůji,*" he heard her say. "All right. I promise."

Joe fell asleep then, until the sound of people talking woke him up. He could see that the sunlight had changed from afternoon to evening, and he could smell onions frying. His stomach suddenly rumbled with hunger. He sat up and looked around the room to see if any clothes were within reach.

Johnny looked in the door. "Joe's up!" he shouted over his shoulder. He looked back at Joe. "Geez, your face looks awful."

"So does yours," Joe said as rudely as he could. "Go get me a shirt so I can get up and eat."

Johnny made a face and left the doorway. Stephen came in next, carrying a bowl. He showed Joe that the little fish was inside it and set it on the table next to the bed. Then he looked at Joe.

"I'm sorry I went on the roof," he said.

Joe felt all the disappointment of his missed baseball games rush back over him. He tried to frown, but that made his face hurt, and then he felt worse. Now that Josefina wasn't going to yell at Stephen any more, he felt a need to do it himself.

"Doggone it, you gotta start thinking before you do that kind of stupid stuff. You knew you shouldn't have gone out there." Stephen hung his head. Somehow that irritated Joe even more.

"Looking sad isn't going to make my arm get better. Someone could have died. And now I can't play. From now on . . ." he paused and fumed, trying to think of what he could possibly say. "From now on, if something's stupid, just don't do it. Just don't. You hear me?"

Stephen nodded. "Uh huh. I won't." Joe glared, not believing him. Johnny came back in with a shirt, and Kate came in behind him.

"Joe! You're up!" She laid her hand on his forehead and scanned his face. "How're you feeling? Better?" Joe nodded and held out his hand for the shirt. "Do you want to eat in here or do you want to eat in the kitchen?"

"In the kitchen," Joe said, and then stopped and looked in dismay at his shirt. How could he put it on with just one hand? His aunt briskly took it from him and held out the left sleeve so he could try to angle his broken arm through it. He winced as he moved the heavy cast. It wouldn't fit through the sleeve.

"John Carl, go get one of your father's old shirts," Kate ordered. Soon Joe, dressed in a combination of pajama bottoms and ragged work shirt, was sitting at the table and wondering how he would cut up his food. Fortunately his aunt had cooked liver with onions and dumplings, which didn't require much work to eat.

Halfway through the meal, John Mark tried to make a sling for him out of a dishtowel so that his broken arm wouldn't shift around so much and hurt him every time he moved. Josefina shook her head at his uncle's clumsy attempt at a sling, and went to her room for a bigger piece of cloth. The whole family stopped eating and fussed over the making of the sling, except for Joe, who finished his first helping of liver and dumplings and started on his second while they argued about it.

Johnny and Stephen washed dishes after dinner. Joe went to the front room, and had just turned on the radio and settled on the couch, trying to ignore the pain in his arm, when a car pulled up in front of the house. Someone walked up the porch steps and knocked at the screen door.

"*Is neko doma?*" called a voice. John Mark came out from the kitchen.

"*Vitáme vás,*" he said. "Who's this here with you?" Joe sucked in his breath and sat up as his coach walked into the room. He tried to pull his shirt farther down around his pajamas and tuck his bare feet under the couch. Johnny looked out from the kitchen for a moment, saw the coach, and disappeared again.

"*Dobrý vecer, Starosta,*" Kovar replied. He turned and motioned toward the door. "This young man is Bill Zuber. He's pitching for us this season."

Oh, no, Joe thought, as the lanky German boy followed Kovar into the house. *Not him. He's the last person on earth I want to see now, when I'm wearing pajamas and looking like Frankenstein.*

"Hello, Bill," John Mark said, and put out his hand. "Congratulations on your game the other night." Joe felt a stab of envy at the sight of the other boy standing there, healthy and free from pain, smiling at the mention of his win.

Joe sat stiffly, trapped on the couch, as John Mark shook hands and asked the guests to sit down. Kovar took a rocking chair and Zuber sat on the couch beside Joe. The men talked about baseball for a while and Kovar asked Joe about his arm.

"So, you broke it," he said, shaking his head, after he heard the story. "Got your face banged up, too. I oughta smack you silly, pulling a dumb stunt like that."

"Hey," John Mark interrupted, "let me tell you, there aren't many people who would have gone up on that roof like he did. There's things more important than a game." A flush of red showed in his face.

Kovar's face turned red, too, and he drew in a breath to say something in return, but Kate walked in just then with glasses of iced lemonade. She passed around the drinks and then handed two aspirin to Joe.

"Time for you to take your medicine," she said with a big smile, and the men looked at him and grinned. Joe wished with all his heart that he could just sink into the couch and disappear.

The two older men finally left Joe alone and started discussing John Dillinger's death, which was the most interesting item in the news that week. Bill Zuber drank his lemonade and looked around the room. He caught Joe's glance and smiled.

"You like aspirin?" he asked with his strong German accent. "I took aspirin when I broke my leg."

Zuber looked friendly, sitting there and waiting for his reply. Joe felt a little better.

"Uh, yeah," he said. "It's the first time I ever took a pill."

"It helps, *ja?*" Zuber asked.

"Yeah, a little," Joe said. He couldn't help asking, "You broke a leg?"

"My leg, three years old. This," he tapped his collarbone, "eight years old. This arm," he went on, raising his left arm, "eleven years old and twelve years old."

Joe forgot his embarrassment. "You broke that arm two times?"

"*Ja*," Zuber said. "Jumping off the barn. The worst, this leg, very bad," he pointed to his left leg and shook his head, "ah, thirteen years old. Bad luck. The arm hurts, huh?" he asked sympathetically.

Joe looked at him in amazement. "You broke all those bones?"

"*Ja*," the other boy replied. "*Sehr schlecht.* Terrible. I hope never again."

"So, it didn't stop you from playing baseball and pitching?" Joe asked.

Bill Zuber laughed. "Where I live, Amana, no baseball until some years ago. *Verboten.* Forbidden," he explained. "People say, how do you say, it is wasteful. Bad for boys. So I not play. Broken bone," he shrugged, "so what? I play now."

"Huh," Joe said. He thought about that for a while. "Huh," he said again.

The evening light was fading from the sky, and John Mark paused in his conversation and turned on the lamp in order to light the room. Bill watched him closely and then gazed at the lamp with a curious expression.

"Very good, *ja?*" he said to Joe, and nodded at the lamp.

"You mean the lamp?" Joe asked incredulously.

"*Ja*," Bill said, and nodded at the lamp again. "In my home, no ... ah ..." he shook his head in frustration, trying to find words.

"Lamps?" Joe offered.

Bill shook his head. "*Elektrizitat*," he said.

"Electricity?"

"*Ja*, Electricity. *Danke*."

Joe just looked at him. "Wow," he finally said. He shifted his cast in the sling, trying to find a more comfortable position, and winced.

The older boy turned away from the lamp to look back at him. "You are very good ball player," he said generously. "You hit, run, field the ball. You field better than me." He nodded to emphasize his point, and Joe felt his face grow hot. He had just been thinking that same thing.

"Joe," John Mark called. Joe looked at his uncle, who pointed toward the coach to indicate that Joe should listen to what he had to say.

"I am sorry to lose you, Joseph. Very sorry," Kovar said. "I was hoping to groom you for pitching next season. You've got a good arm and you're accurate. You oughta work on a curve ball. Ask Robert Stastny to help you."

Joe didn't know whether to feel overjoyed because Kovar wanted him to pitch, or miserable because he couldn't do anything about it until his arm healed. "Thank you," he finally managed to say. "I will," he added, a little more enthusiastically.

"What about working out with Bill here? Are you going to school in town next fall?" John Mark asked. "You've got quite a fastball, young man. Pretty scary stuff."

Bill grinned at the mention of his fast and wild pitching. "Thank you, sir. Ah, no, I will not school here," he replied, and glanced at Kovar.

The coach cleared his throat with an air of importance. "Bill has just signed a contract with the Cleveland Indians," he announced. "He's going to play minor league ball with the Fargo-Moorhead Twins. So he'll be leaving us after this season." He shook his head dramatically. "I can't keep him here. Wouldn't want to hold him back, of course."

Everyone noisily congratulated Zuber at the same time, even Johnny, who had joined them in the front room after he was sure that Kovar was not going to yell at him for missing the game. The young pitcher smiled and thanked them. Joe was awed. *He broke all those bones and he's still going to play for the Indians.* "That's great," he said after the others had finished. "Good luck."

"Now, we'll all get free tickets when we come out to see you play, right?" John Mark said with a wink.

Bill looked confused. John Mark laughed. "Don't worry about it," he said. "We'll come and see you anyway."

"I have a big family, sir," the young German explained. "I do not know about the tickets."

John Mark was still laughing. "That's okay. We'll spring for the tickets ourselves," he told him. Bill looked even more puzzled.

"Hey, that's what I want to talk to you about," Kovar interrupted. "After city leagues are over, I want to take the boys down to St. Louis to see the Cards play. What do you think? Want to go?"

Joe and Johnny were speechless. They looked at John Mark.

"Maybe. My hours got cut at the factory, so I've got some free days now. But we're short on money," he said slowly. The boys sighed.

"We could help pay," Joe said with a glance at Johnny.

Johnny brightened up. "Yeah. With our cemetery money."

"I don't think it'll cost that much," Kovar said. "I've got a friend, Gene Burgess, who's got a gas station right on Grand Avenue by the ball park. Dizzy Dean fills up there all the time. We drive down, see the game, Burgess gives us a tank of gas to get back. We take sandwiches and blankets and sleep on the side of the road."

John Mark looked interested. "Let's take a look at it. I don't want to go without Joe," he added. "We'll have to wait until he can travel."

"Oh, sure," Kovar agreed. "We oughta go before school starts back up, though."

The men went on to talk about other things. Johnny came over and sat down on the couch and asked Zuber questions about professional baseball contracts. Joe listened to them talk and wondered how long it would be before his arm didn't hurt anymore. He eased the cast in the sling again, then gingerly touched the scrapes on his face. The swelling seemed to be going down. *It shouldn't take too long.* He looked around the room full of people talking. He had a family, he was friends with a professional baseball player, and his coach wanted him to pitch next year.

This is the best time of my life. He looked at John Mark, who was cracking jokes with Kovar, and wondered where he would have been without his uncle. *I wouldn't be living this good, for sure. I oughta tell him thank you.*

Kovar and Zuber finally got up to leave, and John Mark and Joe walked outside to see them off. The night fell quiet after they drove away. Crickets sang in the damp night air and a silver-blue sky still glowed above the elms.

John Mark yawned. "Nice out," he said, and sat down on the porch steps. Joe sat beside him and watched fireflies flicker over the lawn.

"Ah, Uncle John, I just want to say thank you," he finally said. "For everything."

John Mark patted him on the back. Joe yelped. "Sorry," John Mark apologized.

"It's okay. I really mean it, thank you," Joe said again.

"*Rádo de stalo*," John Mark said. "I'm just glad you're still alive."

It was hard to go on. "Ah, there's something else I want to tell you."

"Uh huh?"

"I decided I'm going to live God's way." Joe paused, testing how it felt to say the words out loud. It felt a little awkward, but he was committed now, so he went on. "That day in the grave . . . God's the one who kept me alive. Know what I mean?" He glanced at John Mark, who nodded. The words started coming more easily. "So I figure He deserves it, for me to learn about Him and live His way and show respect for what He wants me to do. And I want that kind of life, that clean kind of life." Joe paused again. There was another reason. "Besides, that's what you do, and it's . . .it's so good . . ." to Joe's horror, his throat tightened up in a sob. He swallowed hard and pushed on. "So good to live here. . . " The sob came out anyway and he had to wipe hot tears off his face. He felt John Mark put an arm around him, carefully this time, and he closed his eyes and leaned against his uncle.

"Well, amen," John Mark said. Joe heard, more than saw, his smile. "God is so good to us, isn't He? Look how He blesses, even in the middle of trouble." Joe nodded agreement against his uncle's shoulder. "Let's have a prayer and start your new life." He took a deep breath. "Dear Father in heaven . . ."

Afterward, Joe raised his head and looked around. The world seemed different for a moment, then suddenly very right and natural. Some painful weight was gone. He felt calm, secure in a deep understanding that he had come through a time of pain to reach this moment, and now it was here. He was suddenly happy, sitting with his uncle who loved him, listening to the crickets sing their hearts out under the stars. He was who he was, Joe Vesely, and it was good.

Ten: August / *Joseph Vesely*

Joe was baptized, cast and all, on a bright August Sunday morning. The cast melted into a mess of soggy plaster afterward and had to be replaced, but the doctor laughed when he heard about it and put on a new one for only the cost of materials. Joe paid for it out of his cemetery money and had a good time telling the story.

He sat on the porch one morning a few days later, watching Stephen and two other boys play in the street. The tall elms shaded the street and yard, but the house was already so hot that he had come outside to cool off. Kate was at the Havliceks', Johnny had gone to the Avenue, and Josefina was standing at the fence in the back yard, gossiping with the neighbor women who gathered to hang out wet laundry and keep up with the news.

Joe's arm itched under the cast, and he scratched at it with a long stick. The arm didn't hurt much anymore, but the cast was hot and heavy and his skin prickled with sweat underneath it. He sat and scratched, watching Stephen and thinking about how long it would be before he could do anything fun again.

He perked up when a horse-drawn cart with a worn canvas cover came around the corner. "Joe! The ice man!" Stephen yelled, and the little boys ran to the cart and tagged along behind it, hoping to get ice chips when the driver stopped to make a delivery.

Joe walked out and waved at the driver to pull up to their house, then went to the back yard to fetch Josefina. When he returned, the ice man had stopped the cart and was standing at the back of the wagon, tossing ice chips to the boys.

"*Jedna, prosím, pana Loupar,*" Josefina told him. One, please. The driver carried a twenty-five-pound block of ice into the house with his big clamp and placed it in the top section of the icebox, and Josefina gave him a coin. Joe followed the driver back to the street to get an ice chip himself before the cart pulled away.

Josefina came out to the porch. "Go sit down. Rest the arm," she ordered, as she had told him every day since he had fallen off the roof. Joe sighed and went inside. His grandmother's constant attention had been nice while he was in pain, but now that he felt better, her fussing made him irritable. He turned on the radio and scanned the stations. All the programs during the day were soap opera stories about romance and housekeeping, so he turned it off and wondered what else to do.

A loud honk and a chorus of yells from the boys outside made him jump up. A pickup truck with Karel Prazsky in the driver's seat pulled up in front of the house. Joe walked out to say hello.

"*Dobrý den*, Mr. Prazsky," he called. His Czech was getting better and Karel grinned at him.

"*Tvůj náruci citépe lépe, Chec chlapce?*" he called back. When Joe blinked and didn't reply, he translated, "How's the arm, Czech boy?"

"Better," Joe replied. "Is this your new truck?" Anton had told him that Karel bought a truck with part of the money he had saved for Wence's law school.

"*Ano*," Karel said, and stood with his arms crossed, looking at it, while Joe admired the vehicle. It was an old Model T and would be hard to start, but the truck's bed was deep and roomy and had wooden railings along the sides. The little boys all climbed into it and begged for a ride.

"Get in," Karel said to Joe. "We'll go around the block." Joe sat up front in the passenger seat while the boys in back held onto the railings and jumped up and down.

Karel glanced at Joe's clean new cast and smirked. "So, you found God, eh? Right here on 16th Avenue? Was He lost?"

"Nope," Joe said. He was not afraid of someone like Karel Prasky, who was really not a bad person. "He was right here all along." He grinned at Karel, daring him to argue about it. *Nobody can really argue against God. After a while they just die and God's still there.* Karel shook his head, still not convinced, but the two of them chuckled companionably together as the truck rolled along the shady streets and the little boys in back screamed with joy.

Another truck rambled toward them, and the two drivers waved at each other and stopped in the middle of the road to talk. The conversation was in Czech and Joe paid no attention to it until Karel turned around and started talking in English.

"Frank Mahalicek here wants to drive some kids out to his brother's farm to pick tomatoes. You get a sandwich and five cents an hour. Want to go?"

"Sure," Joe said. "Johnny's at the Avenue but he'll go too."

Karel talked to the other man again, then said goodbye and started back to the house. "Frank's going to the Avenue to find more kids. He'll pick up John Carl," he told Joe. "Ask your *babička* if you can go."

Josefina scowled when she heard the news, but she said he could go if he kept his sling on, and gave him a clean pail and dipper to use for drinking water.

The other man came back with Johnny and Bob Stastny in the back of his truck. Stephen's friends came back with permission to go, and finally they all climbed into the back of Frank Mahalicek's truck and drove to Karel's house so they could pick up Rudy.

A new kind of stench hovered around the little home. Joe made a face and tried not to breathe.

"What stinks?" he asked. "Did something die?"

Johnny and Bob started laughing. "Hey, Mr. Prazsky, Joe likes the smell of your sauerkraut!" Bob yelled. "He wants to know if it's ready so he can eat some!"

"Shut *up*," Joe hissed, and reached over to punch him with his good arm. He glanced at Karel to see if he was mad, but the big man was laughing too.

"Two more days," he called back. "Unless he wants some right now. Hungry today, *Chec chlapce?*"

"Not that hungry," Joe said, and shoved Bob again when the other boy wouldn't stop laughing.

Johnny ran over to Vincent's and came back with Anton, who was at home because there was no tennis practice in August. Anton vaulted over the side of the truck bed and sat down next to Joe.

"Hey, my dad got a bank job," he said. "Van Schaffer and Orrie Becker hired him to work at the new bank they just opened. Today's his first day. Isn't that great?"

"Someone opened a bank?" Frank Mahalicek asked. "Are they nuts?"

"They're calling it Guaranty Bank," Karel said. "Ed Pochobradsky says he thinks they'll make it. I heard about it yesterday at the Little Bohemia."

"Well, don't go looking for me to put my money in any durn bank," Mahalicek frowned. "I don't care what old Pokie says. He's wrong sometimes just like everybody else."

"Dad says it's a solid bank," Anton said. "He's head teller again, right in the same building where he was before the Crash." He lowered his voice, leaned toward Joe, and said under his breath, "Van and Orrie are having him to dinner tonight. They're trying to fix him up with some lady friend of theirs."

"You know her?" Joe whispered back.

Anton shrugged. "I met her. She's okay, I guess." He made a face and Joe made one back at him.

Rose, dressed in white slacks and a navy-blue-and white striped shirt styled to look like a sailor's, came out of the house along with Rudy.

"Wait a minute! I want to go too!" she called.

"Naw, Rosie, you take too long to change clothes and we'll be here all day," Mahalicek yelled back. He was a neighbor of the Prazskys' and he grinned at Rose while he teased her. She held up her hand and called back, "One minute! Just one minute!" and ran inside. The boys started chanting, "Fifty-nine! Fifty-eight! Fifty-seven!" until Karel made them stop.

Rose came out, wearing her denim work pants and an old shirt with faded pink flowers, and clambered into the truck. Karel decided to ride out with them as well, to keep Frank company and see how the farm was doing. The truck started up with a lurch that made everyone yell and sit down, and they drove out of town on Sixth Street into rolling green farmland rich with corn fields spreading out under the hazy sky.

They passed a race track with a wooden fence around it and a sign in front that read "Welcome to Hawkeye Downs," and then the truck turned into a farmyard. They all jumped out and looked around at the tidy white house and the huge red barn with a brick grain silo on one side. A lush corn field stretched to the horizon on one side of the barn. On the other side, hogs were dozing under a tree in a pasture, and in between those two fields was the largest vegetable garden Joe had ever seen. It looked as big as a ball park, and every row of plants was loaded with red tomatoes and ripe green vegetables.

"See if you can pick the beans. They're next to the track," Rudy whispered. "I was here last year and you can look over the fence at the race cars. Dad!" he yelled. "Hey, I'll pick beans!"

"Mr. Mahalicek'll decide who he wants where," Karel replied. A farmer dressed in overalls and a battered straw hat came out of the barn.

"*Dobrý den*," he called. The men stood and talked for a few minutes before they turned and looked at the group of children and teens. The farmer frowned when he saw Joe's sling.

"Now, what good are ya going ta do out here? Ya can't work with a broke arm," he groused.

Joe grinned. "Sure I can. If you've got a bag I can put over my shoulder I'll outwork everybody here," he said. "Sir," he added.

"Huh." The farmer looked sharply at him, then turned to the little boys. "You there, go with the missus." The farmer's wife had come out of the house and the younger boys followed her over to a pile of buckets and baskets by the barn. "I want them picking the squash and the cukes, 'cause they won't try to eat 'em," he said to Karel. "You"—he pointed to the taller boys—"do beans and tomaters. I don't want any tomaters broke and I don't want any of 'em et neither. Fill up these here bushel baskets. You"—he pointed at Rose— "take the berry holder and pick raspberries. Don't bruise 'em, don't eat' em, and get a apron from Mom so you don't muck up your clothes. I ring the bell fer lunch."

Everyone nodded and headed out. "You there, with the sling!" the farmer called. Joe stopped and turned back. "Come here. I got a shoulder bag for you." Joe followed the farmer inside the barn and was handed a dusty canvas bag to sling over one shoulder.

"Use that when you pick and then put your haul in a bushel basket when it's full up. Don't bruise the tomaters when you switch 'em over." The farmer watched while Joe awkwardly settled the bag over his shoulder. "Now, son, the rules are if you don't work you don't get paid, broke arm or no."

"That's fine," Joe said. "I can work. It doesn't hurt anymore."

"What'd ya do, fall out of a tree?" the farmer asked.

"Off a roof," Joe told him. "My little brother was stuck on the roof and I was getting him down."

The farmer shook his head and laughed. Joe laughed too. "I heard about that. Dumb kid," the farmer said. "The little one, I mean." He looked Joe up and down. "So you're the big hero now, huh? What's your name?"

"Joseph Vesely, sir," Joe told him.

"Vesely, huh. That means happy, ya know," the farmer said. Joe nodded and grinned. "I guess you look happy enough," the farmer said after looking at him for another moment. "Well, don't just stand around."

Joe headed out where Rudy, Anton, and Bob were already picking tomatoes on the far side of the garden. They picked quickly while they were in the section close to the farm house, then more slowly after they worked their way over to the race track fence. Whenever they heard a car come around the track, they straightened up to watch as it roared past them in a cloud of dust. Rudy, who had gone to the races with his father, identified the cars as they flew past.

"That's a Chrysler! There's a DeChesneau!" he called as they craned their necks to see over the fence. "Hey, I think this next one's a Model B!"

The farmer yelled at them whenever they stopped picking, but the boys worked out the timing of exactly how long they could stand and watch before his shout came across the garden at them, and after that the field was quiet except for the roars of cars sweeping past and the drone of an occasional bee. The sky was cloudless, gleaming with heat and dust. Joe trudged back and forth in the soft black earth of the huge garden, hauling bagfuls of tomatoes and beans to the bushel baskets stacked by the side of the field. The morning seemed to go on forever. His arm started aching long before the lunch bell finally clanged.

They all trailed back to the house and sat in a ragged circle under a shade tree. The farmer's wife handed out bread and lunchmeat for sandwiches and the farmer let them eat the tomatoes and cucumbers that were too damaged to sell. Bob filled up the water pail from the pump in the barnyard and started it around the circle. There was no sign of Karel or Frank Mahalicek.

"Where'd your dad go?" Joe asked Rudy.

"Oh, probably back into town for a beer," Rudy said. "He says that's how he gets his jobs, drinking beer with people." He rolled his eyes.

"Well, he must be doing okay if he can buy a truck," Joe said.

"Here," Rose said to Joe, and handed him the dipper. She placed the water bucket on the grass right in front of him so that he wouldn't have to drag it over one-handed.

"Thanks," Joe said. He looked at her after he finished his drink. *She's so cute when she wears those denim work pants.* Rose smiled at him and he grinned back at her.

After a while the farmer sent them back to work. Joe picked and carried, stooped and stood, walked and sweated as the sun traveled across the sky. Every once in a while he looked around for Johnny and Stephen, checking on them as they traveled up and down the long green rows of overloaded cucumbers and squash. Finally, late in the afternoon, the pickup truck roared back down the road and swung into the farmyard.

At the sight of the truck everyone stopped picking and brought in their last loads of produce. They clustered around the pump, taking turns drinking water out of their cupped hands and rinsing dust off their sunburned arms and faces. The farmer handed out quarters, and when he came to Joe he flipped the coin in the air to him. Joe caught it and grinned.

"You're Happy Joe today, all right," the farmer said.

"Hap-py Jo-oe," the boys snickered.

Joe grinned again. "I'm just happy to get out of my grandma's bedroom. This quarter's gravy."

"Give it back then," the farmer said, and everybody laughed. Johnny filled the water pail for the drive back and they climbed wearily into the truck. The pickup roared to life and started home. The breeze felt wonderfully cool after the long day in the sun, and Bob and Anton started talking about school.

"The coach at Iowa City came out to see me pitch and he said he'd give me a scholarship if my senior year turns out good and I have decent grades," Bob said. He had pitched well during the city championship games, even though the Packers had lost the last series.

"I'm taking calculus and physics," Anton said. "I'm going to work at that new radio factory when I graduate."

"I'm taking football and lunch," Rudy said. "Geez, D, give it a break already. You're gonna make me look bad."

"I'm gonna be a doctor," Johnny announced. "What do you have to take for that?"

"Shut up," Rudy groaned.

"What are you taking?" Rose asked Joe. "I don't get to pick classes until I get to high school." She sat crowded into a corner of the truck bed, with her knees pulled up and her arms wrapped around her legs. Her face was tanned from the sun, and her eyes looked very blue.

She really is cute, Joe thought again, and sat up a little straighter. "I'm taking second year math, and I'm going in the physics lab with Anton after class to see what they're doing, and then I'm going to take it next year." *That sounds pretty smart,* he decided.

Rose looked impressed. "I like science," she said. "I think I'll take physics too. It sounds like fun."

"Uh, I don't know if girls take physics," Joe objected. He had never once seen a girl in the science lab.

"Oh, yeah? Marie Curie?" Rose retorted. "You know, radium? X-rays? Don't you ever read the paper?"

"So?" Joe snapped back, hoping to get out of the moment without letting her know that he had no idea what she was talking about.

"*So*, Marie Curie discovered radium and invented X-rays and got a Nobel Prize for physics," Rose retorted. "*So*, she was a woman and she took physics. *So*, I can take it if I want to."

"Geez," Joe said under his breath. "Sorry I asked."

"Joe broke his arm that week so he didn't hear about it," Anton said.

"Oh," Rose said. She looked back at Joe. "Well, anyway, some girls take physics." She smiled at him and Joe's irritation dissolved away.

"Just be sure and take two math classes first," he said in the most authoritative voice he could manage. He saw Stephen nodding off and reached out with his good arm to pull him over so the little boy could lean against him when he finally went to sleep. Joe pulled too hard, fell over on his left side, and winced from the sudden pain.

"Oh! Do you want some aspirin?" Rose asked. "I brought some for you." She pulled out a tiny pillbox from a pocket of her work pants. "Here."

Joe dithered a bit about the significance of taking two aspirin from a girl who had just won an argument with him, but his arm hurt and he decided that accepting them would be all right, under the circumstances. He took the pills and washed them down with a swallow from the dipper.

"Thanks," he said, and gingerly felt at his arm. It ached from the long day of work. "It's pretty sore," he admitted. She smiled again. Her pink flowered shirt collar lay softly against her tanned skin and her eyes were very blue in the evening sun.

The truck bounced over a rut in the road and everybody yelled as they flew up and came back down hard. The water pail flew up too, and when it came down it sloshed water all over them.

I'm happy, Joe thought as he laughed along with everybody else. He marveled at the thought. *It's going to be a good year.*

Epilogue

Old Ben Havlicek passed away in his sleep later that month, a week before school began and a few days after the boys came back from their trip to watch the Cardinals play. Betty called Vincent's house for help, and Vincent walked over to John Mark's house with the sad news. All the adults went to help Betty except for Josefina, who stayed home and laundered shirts for the funeral.

The day of the service was bright and clear. Kate wore her black dress, John Mark wore his suit, and the boys wore their white shirts. Josefina had tailored an old suit jacket for Joe to wear, and she even stitched up a little bow tie for Stephen.

A long line of cars drove to the graveside service at the old Czech cemetery. Kate rode with Betty in the Havlicek family car, and John Mark and Vincent rode together in Vincent's car with all four of their boys crammed into the back seat. During the ride to the cemetery Stephen sat on Joe's lap and alternated between looking down at his tie to admire it, and trying to take it off because of the heat. Joe kept pushing Stephen's hand down and whispering to him to leave it alone, until John Mark spoke up and told Stephen that he had to leave the tie on until after *Taps*.

"What's that?" Stephen asked, momentarily distracted.

"It's a song they play on a bugle," Johnny told him. "It's a military funeral."

As they rode along, Joe thought about the slim leather wallet he now carried in his back pocket, the only thing besides the cast that he had purchased with his summer money. He kept his savings hidden away in his bed, but after all his years of hardship he liked to have a dime or two with him whenever he left the house, in case he needed something. Unlike Johnny, he did not plan to spend his earnings on anything as expensive as a bicycle. He didn't want to sink his money into something that could be stolen. He had the whittling knife that Josefina had given him, the Ty Cobb baseball card, the wallet, and some money of his own. That was plenty for now.

By the time they arrived, Betty and Kate were already seated in the front row under the canvas awning next to the grave. People talked quietly as they walked across the grass and found places to sit. The casket, draped in an

American flag, gleamed in the sun, and twelve gray-haired veterans in old-fashioned Army dress uniforms stood alongside it. John Mark directed the boys to sit with Vincent and Anton, and then he walked up to the front of the crowd. The veterans came to attention with a flourish.

John Mark began the service with a prayer and then spoke of Ben Havlicek's life and family. Joe stared at the distant trees while he listened, thinking about how the old man had given him the baseball card not very long ago. *Did he know he was going to die?* he wondered. *Can people feel it, sometimes?* Anton stirred in the chair beside him. Joe glanced at him and thought about how both their mothers had died young. *I wonder if Anton's mom had a funeral like this one.* The thought of a funeral with family and friends around was comforting somehow, and even his vague memory of Marie's little service felt good.

"The gospel of Matthew, chapter twenty-four, warns us that none of us knows how long our life will be," John Mark was saying. "For any of us, the end could come sooner than we think. Just like that." He snapped his fingers. "One thing about Ben was that he found something to enjoy every day of his life. He had problems like everybody else, but he would come up with something good to talk about, some little joke or story to cheer people up. He was a good man to know during these bad times." Betty and Kate were nodding, dabbing handkerchiefs to their eyes.

"Ben helped a lot of people," John Mark continued, and heads nodded and a few "amen's" followed his statement. Joe nodded, too, remembering the baseball card. "He was kind and generous, a good husband and father. Ben was like a father to a lot of us, in fact," he said, and heads nodded again throughout the group. "He was the one," John Mark's voice faltered and he looked at Kate to steady himself, "ah, he was the one who told me I should keep on preaching even when the church went bankrupt. I'd go over and sit on his front porch, mainly because I didn't have the money to go anywhere else," his voice was stronger now, "and he'd read Bible verses to me, reminding me that God hadn't gone away and I could still depend on Him. He said I shouldn't walk away from my church just because everybody lost their jobs. And their houses, and their shirts," he added with a little grin, and a little murmur of good humor washed over the listeners.

"Ben knew about going through hard times and coming back out of them. One of the things I remember best about him was the way he would talk to people about what they could do in the future. He was always encouraging someone to keep on going, no matter what kind of trouble they had."

John Mark paused. "I think," he said slowly, "that Ben could do that for people, day in and day out for all those years, because he had a tremendous faith in God. He read his Bible and prayed every day, no matter what else was going on. His favorite psalm was about a man who felt defeated when he looked around at all his troubles and all the things he wanted but didn't have, until he looked at God and . . . saw things differently. I want to read a few verses from it."

He opened his Bible and cleared his throat. "Psalm Seventy-three:

" '. . . So foolish was I, and ignorant: I was as a beast before thee.
Nevertheless I am continually with thee: thou hast holden me by my right hand.
Thou shalt guide me with thy counsel, and afterward receive me to glory.
Whom have I in heaven but thee? and there is none upon earth that I desire beside thee.
My flesh and my heart faileth: but God is the strength of my heart, and my portion for ever.'

"Today," John Mark said, "Benjamin Havlicek has seen what this psalm promises. After all his troubles in this lifetime, God has received him into glory."

Betty and Kate were both quietly weeping. John Mark glanced at them.

"May the memory of our good friend Benjamin inspire us to do our best in the days ahead."

He closed his Bible, looked out at the crowd, and ended with a prayer.

Afterward the captain of the military honor guard gave a short speech about Ben's service to his country, and the soldiers folded the flag into a triangle and presented it to Betty. The captain called out commands and the soldiers reformed their line and raised their rifles, then shot three ceremonial volleys into the air. Everybody jumped as the rifle shots shattered the quiet. After the last echoes from the rifles faded away, a soldier raised his bugle.

Day is done
Gone the sun

From the lakes, from the hills, from the sky
All is well
Safely rest
God is nigh

Joe watched a flock of birds circle the sky as the silvery notes of the bugle rose and fell. He had not known Ben Havlicek very well. *Too bad I didn't know all this about him before,* he thought. *I would've talked to him more.* He looked over at Vincent and Anton sitting beside him, then at John Mark, standing by the casket and waiting respectfully for the honor guard to finish their ceremony. *But I've got some people now.*

When the funeral was over people began talking with more energy than they had before. Stephen wriggled out of his bow tie, gave it to Joe, and ran off to join the other boys playing under the trees. Johnny drifted over to join them. Joe, dressed in his new suit jacket, felt too grown up to play, so at first he stood with Vincent and Anton, and when they left to fetch the car he joined John Mark.

The captain, resplendent in his navy blue dress uniform with gold trim and white gloves, came up and shook John Mark's hand. "Fine service, Starosta," he said. "Always the evangelist, aren't you?"

"*Preach the word, in season and out of season,*" John Mark quoted with a grin. "Got to do my job. Say, I want you to meet someone." He reached around to pull Joe forward. "This is my new son, Joseph. Joe, this is Mr. Oujiri."

"Nice to meet you, sir," Joe said as he shook hands.

Years later, Joe still remembered that moment clearly, because his eyes were almost level with his uncle's when they looked at each other and smiled, and he realized how much he had grown. He lingered and talked with his uncle until Kate walked up, with Stephen and Johnny close behind. Almost all the people were gone now. John Mark went over to his wife and took her hand.

"Time to go," he said. "We did our best here today." They all walked across the grass together, going home.

Here is an excerpt from the sequel to Found on 16th Avenue, *in which Joe Vesely and a mysterious young woman from his past are swept together into danger and love during World War II.*

My Portion Forever

Karen Roth

My Portion Forever

Karen Roth

Cedar Rapids, Iowa
November, 1933

When the clock finally reached seven-thirty Sana hung up her headscarf and left for school. In spite of her prayer to die, nothing happened along the way, so she went to class as usual, pushing through the chattering rush of boys and girls in the hallway. The girls usually ignored her, because she was a foreign girl who "knew about men," and the boys sometimes harassed her, trailing her in the hallway or pressing up against her in a crowd, for exactly the same reason. Sana had developed a cold look and a standoffish manner to protect herself from all of them.

Ahead of her, two girls with styled hair sang a song from the radio and danced a jitterbug step as they sauntered down the hall. Tall American boys grinned and hooted back. Sana followed behind, stealing glances at all the young men who would graduate and marry soon, and envying the girls who could talk to them so freely.

If her parents were still alive, she would be living in a pink three-story stucco house in Constantine, with a cook, a gardener, and three maids. She would still be attending private school during the day and playing piano or reading at night with her parents in their plush red-and-gold front parlor. She would still be looking forward to a comfortable life with a suitably wealthy husband.

Sana could still remember the evening when she was twelve and the after-dinner parlor talk had turned to her future. "Don't worry, *cherie*. I'll find you a wonderful man," her mother had promised. "You'll have a husband who is educated and can afford a good home. Quite apart from wanting to see you happy, we don't want to spend holidays with a son-in-law who's an idiot and a cheapskate, do we?"

"That's right," her father had teased her. "I'll inspect all the applicants before you even see them. I'll make sure they have all their teeth and lots of money in the bank. That's all you care about, right?"

"Daddy!" Sana had protested. "I want a handsome husband who can drive a car like you!" They all laughed, and the next day while she was at school, her parents went for a drive in the high mountain passes outside the city, and did not come back alive.

Now, four years later in an American high school, her last precious hours of freedom were flying past. Even the rush through the crowded halls, which she used to dread, seemed like wonderful fun compared to the life that waited for her back at the store. Sana lingered in the classroom after her last class of the day, putting off the moment when she would have to walk home.

"All right, Sana, you can clean off the blackboard for me and put those books back on the shelf by the window now. Are you going to water my plants today?" Zula Hruska, the senior math teacher and Sana's favorite person in the world, smiled at her. Sana usually stayed after math class to do little chores and talk for a while before she left school. Today she had sorted six stacks of homework assignments into alphabetical order and sharpened all the pencils, while golden afternoon sunshine poured through the classroom's open windows and glistened on the wooden desks and chairs. The bright green potted plants glowed on the windowsills.

"Here's your test back. This should cheer you up," the teacher said. Sana walked over and took the paper from her. The large red "A" at the top of it lightened her heart for only a moment, though, and she sighed before turning to clean the blackboard.

"Now what on earth is wrong with you?" Sana glanced around to see Mrs. Hruska watching her. "A pretty girl like you with all your life in front of you, and you haven't smiled all day. What's the matter? Did you fill out those citizenship papers like I told you to?" Sana dropped her eyes and didn't respond. "Don't sulk at me," the teacher went on. "Come over here and tell me what's wrong."

Sana walked back and dropped into a chair close to the teacher's big desk, still holding the eraser and rag she used to clean the board. "I, ah, can't fill them out yet, Mrs. Hruska. I've only been here four years and the rules say I have to be here for five."

"Oh. Well, time will take care of that, right? So that's not really a problem. What else is wrong?"

Sana felt tears brim up. "Oh . . . I hate to bother you, Mrs. Hruska." She folded and then refolded the rag she was holding.

"Just tell me, honey," her teacher said.

"Oh . . . I'm . . . sad that school's going to be over," Sana said, and suddenly her tears spilled over. She wiped her eyes with her shirt sleeve and tried to regain her poise. "I'll miss you so much."

Mrs. Hruska came over to sit beside her and put an arm around her. The friendly touch brought another rush of tears and Sana finally put her head down on the older woman's shoulder and sobbed. Zula Hruska knew the story about her parents and let her cry for a while before patting her back and offering a hankie.

"All right. Here, let's see about all this. You can come and visit me any time you want after school is over. Now, what's the matter with you? Are you just down in the dumps today, or is something really wrong?"

"I won't be able to go anywhere anymore," Sana choked out. "My uncle will make me stay at the store all the time. And no one will marry me so I'm going to be there *forever*." The thought of dusting cans of vegetables and sweeping the floor of the grocery store every day for the rest of her life brought a new flood of tears, and she buried her face in the handkerchief. "I miss my mother," she whispered when she could speak again. "Mrs. Hruska, I miss my mother so much."

Zula Hruska was dabbing at her own eyes now. "I'm so sorry, dear. I'm so sorry about your parents." She paused, as if wondering what to say.

"Why on earth do you think that nobody will marry you?" she finally asked. "You're a beautiful girl. The boys must be nuts about you."

Sana shook her head and started crying again. Hadn't Mrs. Hruska heard about her? If not, then she must be the last person in town who didn't know. "My uncles . . . when I lived in their house. . . they . . ." she choked out. She could not bring herself to say the actual words. "That's why my aunts over there sent me away." She lifted her face and gazed at her teacher as if sheer willpower could make the other woman understand. "And my uncle tells everybody."

"Ohhh. Oh. I see," Zula said. She tightened her arm around Sana's shoulders. "Hmm."

"I just want to die," Sana said after a while.

"Oh, no you don't. You're far too smart a girl to go wasting all your life dying young," Zula said briskly. "If you can't get married right now then you ought to do something until you're ready, or until you meet the right man. Oh, you'll meet one," she went on, ignoring Sana's shake of the head. "Don't think this hasn't happened before. Someone's going to fall in love with you.

Until then you ought to think about doing something. You could be a teacher or a nurse. Make a little money of your own. Why, when Marie Curie was your age . . ." Zula launched into a story about how the famous scientist had moved away from her home town, attended a university, met the love of her life, and went on to discover radium and develop the world's first X-ray machine.

Sana dried her tears as she listened, and began to wonder if she had said too much by telling the story of her shameful past to her favorite teacher.

"That's wonderful about Marie Curie, Mrs. Hruska, but my aunt and uncle would never let me." She made a polite little movement, asking to be released. Her teacher studied her face for a moment, then let her go.

"Well, I just want you to think about it," she said. "You never know these days where life is going to take you."

"Thank you very much for trying to help me," Sana said. "You are so kind to me, ma'am."

"You and your darling little accent," Mrs. Hruska said. "I should think that every boy who meets you falls in love. Don't worry, honey. Your story's not over yet. Just smile a little more and see what happens."

"Maybe, ma'am. Thank you again." Sana doubted that smiling at men would solve her problem. It usually brought her more trouble, not less.

After meticulously cleaning every streak of chalk off the blackboard and saying goodbye, she left for home. Once out in the sunlight she could not stay gloomy for long. New-leafed trees and spring flowers shone in the sun, and a woman tending rose bushes in her front yard smiled at Sana as she walked past. Violets had come and gone already, but irises and wild roses were blooming, and as she crossed a street she caught sight of a brilliant purple lilac tree in full flower halfway down an alley. She impulsively turned toward it, picking her way across the rutted road to breathe in the rich sweet scent.

She was almost to the tree when footsteps sounded behind her. A hand gripped her shoulder and a male voice said "Whatcha doing here?" in a tone that made her skin crawl even before she turned and saw three boys standing between her and the street.

"Don't touch me," she snapped, shrugging off the hand, but her voice cracked from nervousness and the nearest boy caught her arm and pulled her back. She recognized him now, from school. He wore a ragged cap, an uneven fuzz of reddish beard, and a grin. *They won't do anything. They're just try-*

ing to scare me, Sana thought, but her heart pounded in fear as she jerked away again. The other boys came closer, grinning.

"Get away from me," she said in her haughtiest voice. The grins only got bigger. She was stiff with fear now. *Oh, God, help me!* If she screamed for help and people saw her in a back alley with a group of boys, that would be bad enough, but if the boys tried to . . .

"So, doll, you looking for someone?" The boy grabbed both her arms. "Come here often?" He jerked her forward, pulling her up against himself. Sana panicked when she felt his hand slip behind her waist.

"Stop it! Get away from me!" she cried out. "Let me go!" She shoved and wrestled with all her strength, but he kept her pinned against him and pushed his face toward hers. She could hear the other boys laughing.

Rage flamed up inside her. *Not again. Not again. I will die before I suffer that again.* Sana drew in her breath and lunged forward, biting at the leering face so close to hers. Her teeth sank into the flesh of a lip and she clamped down with all her might. She felt his hot saliva against her mouth, and then the rusty taste of his blood.

Someone was shouting. The boy pulled his face away and yelled in pain. Sana wrenched her arm away and then someone charged between her and her tormentor and pushed the boy to the ground with one strong shove. She was free. Sana floundered for her balance, backed away in a hurry, then stopped to wipe blood off her lips with the back of her hand.

The new person, a boy taller than the others, stood there between her and the group, still shouting in some language that Sana did not understand. But her attackers looked embarrassed and started backing away. The boy with a bloody lip got up off the ground, and the new person switched to English.

"Aren't you just a bunch of heroes, ganging up on one little girl you catch in an alley. You lily-livered punk snots, you oughta all be horsewhipped and sent home to your mommies. You!" He took a quick step toward the leader and shoved him again on the chest, throwing him back against the other two. "Get outta here, you . . ." he switched back into the language he had spoken before and yelled again, pointing toward the street. The boys turned and fled.

Sana stood still, watching him as he turned back to her. She recognized him now. He was a student from her class in school, a Czech boy who had never spoken to her before. He was tall, with blond hair and shoulders strongly built, and blue eyes intense with anger. He looked back at her, and the anger went away.

"I, ah . . . are you all right?" he asked.

Sana nodded. Every muscle in her body was trembling

"You were really brave," he said, and grinned. "Bit him, huh?"

Sana closed her eyes for a moment, sick at the memory of the boy's mouth on her own. She couldn't speak.

"You sure you're okay?" He frowned slightly and said, "You know who I am, right? Joe Vesely? I'm in your math class." He crossed over to her and patted her on the back like a child who needed comforting. She could smell a scent like grass and wind when he stood close to her. "Don't worry. Here, show me the way you go home. I better walk you in case those guys come back." He took her elbow, prompting her to move.

Sana would have stepped away from his hand, but her legs were trembling and she was afraid that she might fall. She let him walk her to the end of the alley before she took her arm away and turned to face him.

"Thank you," she said, and then, trying to pull her world back into order, offered him her hand. "I'm Sana Toledo. My uncle is Abraham Tabcharani."

Was it her imagination, or did he hold her hand a second longer than he should have? He stood still for a moment, gripping her hand, and then suddenly dropped it, stepped back, took a breath, and said, "Oh. Ah, Tabcharani's Grocery?"

"Yes!" she said and realized that she was nodding and smiling. *Stop it*, she told herself. Her heart was still racing painfully and she put her hand to her chest, trying to slow its beat.

"Here," said Joe Vesely, taking her arm again. "You're still upset."

Sana jumped uncontrollably at his touch and unexpectedly started to cry. Her heart hammered at her ribs again and she turned her face away, embarrassed by her tears.

"I'm sorry," she heard him say. "I didn't mean to scare you."

She shook her head, still crying. All she could think of was reaching the safety of her uncle's store. "Thank you. You are so kind," she forced herself to say. "I want to go home now." A sob rose in her throat and she backed away. "I can go by myself. Thank you."

"Wait a minute," he said, looking confused. "Don't you want me to walk you home?"

Sana could barely see him through her tears. *He's the kindest man I ever met. Yes, please walk me home* . . . but she shook her head and whispered *no*, before she turned away.

Joe Vesely walked homeward in a daze, his hand tingling with the memory of her touch. *I'm Sana Toledo.* She was so pretty. How was it that he had never really noticed her before? Her dark, brilliant eyes under finely arched brows . . . . . . the curve of her cheek, the heartbeat in the hollow of her throat, her skin the color of palest honey . . . those eyes had filled with tears and she had seemed to fold up into herself like a flower at night when he reached for her arm the second time. The girl must have been scared to death. He should have walked her home. But he would see her again tomorrow.

Arriving home, Joe jumped the three stairs up the porch in one long-legged leap and smelled onions frying as he opened the door. He glimpsed his grandmother standing at the stove in the kitchen before something trapped both his legs and brought him crashing down on the hard wood front room floor.

The "something" turned out to be ten-year-old Stephen, his cousin who acted exactly like a bothersome little brother. Stephen pounced on him now, trying to climb on his back and pin him down.

"Ow!" Joe rolled to his feet, grabbed Stephen by the ankles, held him upside down and shook him.

"Put me down!" Stephen hollered, trying to kick free. There was not much furniture in the front room – only a threadbare couch and two rocking chairs – but the room was small and the boys managed to hit every piece as they scuffled across it. Joe dragged the smaller boy clear across the floor by his heels before giving him his wish and dropping him with a thump.

"You're a long way from whipping me, kid," Joe told Stephen. "Try that on Johnny when he comes home." His other cousin, Stephen's brother Johnny, was sixteen and would be home from school soon. Stephen stuck out his tongue, then went back to the door to lay in wait for the other boy.

Joe walked on into the kitchen. "*Dobrý den, Bubi,*" he said to his grandmother. "What's to eat?"

Josefina Vesely stirred the onions in her frying pan and frowned. "*Bouktha,*" she groused at him in Czech. "Idiot. You raise the dead with all your noise."

Joe grinned and leaned down to kiss his grandmother's wrinkled cheek. "*Promiňte,* sorry, Grandma." He looked around the kitchen for the plate of food she always had ready for him after school.

"*Sedût*, sit down," she told him. "Here." Josefina handed him a plate with a peanut-butter sandwich and leftover fried potatoes. Joe gave her another kiss before he sat down to eat. She shook her head and waved him away before turning back to the onions.

"Is Uncle John up yet?" Joe asked between bites. He had lived in this little house with his cousins, grandmother, aunt, and uncle for four years, since he was fourteen.

"I'm up now. Some herd of elephants must've come through the house." Joe's uncle, John Mark Starosta, came through the doorway and sat down at the table. He yawned and rubbed his eyes.

"Sorry," Joe said through a mouthful of potatoes. "Tough shift last night?" He looked his uncle over. John Mark pastored a church during the day and worked a factory job at night, because his congregation was too poor to support a minister, and he was almost always tired. His uncle started to say something, then stopped and yawned again instead, and watched Joe wolf down food.

"You know," John Mark finally said, "we're going to eat supper in half an hour."

Joe forked up another mouthful. "And I am so happy about that," he said with a straight face. His uncle could take a joke. "Hey, Uncle John, listen to this." He told his uncle about the girl in the alley. "I was going to walk her home," he finished up, "but she just said no, and left. How do you figure that?"

John Mark looked at him thoughtfully. Joe waited. His uncle always seemed to know more about people than most men did, and Joe had noticed that whenever the talk turned to women, John Mark chose his words carefully.

"Huh. Abe Tabcharani's girl?" he asked after a while. "Real pretty?"

"Yeah," Joe said.

"Huh," John Mark said again, and was quiet for a little longer. "Well, I figure you came out good on that one, son. One against three, and you ran 'em all off? I would've let you walk me home, if I was a pretty girl."

Joe grinned, absurdly happy that his uncle noticed his victory. "Ah, they were a bunch of dumb kids. I just yelled and they ran away. Picking on a girl like that."

John Mark laughed, and Joe suddenly noticed the little lines around his eyes and mouth, etched more deeply than he remembered. *He's getting older*, he thought with alarm. *I hope he doesn't die soon.* "You gotta quit working so hard, Uncle John," he said. "Make the factory give you a desk job. Look at you, all worn out. You've even got gray hair now. Look. Right here." He leaned over and tousled John Mark's graying brown hair, still unruly from sleep.

His uncle kept on laughing. "I wouldn't have all these gray hairs if you boys didn't eat me out of house and home. I gotta hang onto this job." He turned suddenly serious.

"Listen. Don't tell anyone about that girl in the alley."

"Why?" Joe asked.

"It'd embarrass her," John Mark said. "Get her talked about."

Joe looked at his uncle for a while. "What else do you know about her?"

" 'Treat the elder women as mothers, and the younger as sisters, in all purity,' John Mark quoted. "First Timothy, five-one. That girl doesn't want people talking loose about her and neither do I. She's had a hard life." He gave Joe a meaningful look. "Just like you."